CLOUDS OVER MARIDAAN

Rhodar Book One

HERBERT GROSSHANS

CLOUDS OVER MARIDAAN
Copyright © 2018 by Herbert Grosshans

ISBN: 978-1-68046-596-9

Melange Books, LLC
White Bear Lake, MN 55110
www.melange-books.com

Published in the United States of America.

Cover Design by Caroline Andrus

Author's Note

The first books I read when I was just a boy were stories about knights, giants, dwarfs, sorcerers, witches, and gods. The old legends fascinated me. As a teenager, I was introduced to science fiction and later to fantasy. I read all the Conan books and other Sword and Sorcery books written by writers like Lin Carter, Michael Moorcock, Roger Zelazny, and, of course, Edgar Rice Burroughs. I have most of those books in my library. Sometimes I wish, I could find the time to read them all over again, but now I spend my free time spinning my own tales about muscular heroes and powerful, evil sorcerers. And let's not forget the beautiful maidens that need rescuing.

Many years ago, I created Rhodar, the Barbarian for a short story titled "Pythese." You can read about him in my anthology *Tapestry of Dreams*.

Rhodar does not exist in our universe. He lives in a different universe, in another dimension.

His world is similar to ours in many ways, yet also vastly different. In Rhodar's universe, we'll meet witches and warlocks, evil sorcerers and conjurers, because there magic works. He may seem familiar and not much different from most other heroes, but he is Rhodar. And that makes him different. He has his own personality, his own past. He is not above killing or stealing, like most heroes, but he lives by his own code of honor and ethics. He would never commit cold-blooded murder, nor would he take from a helpless creature, but then again—he is not above taking another man's woman, if she is willing. Or taking from a thief who has already cheated another victim.

Rhodar is a barbarian, a savage, but in his own way as civilized as any of us. Rhodar is who we secretly would like to be.

Relax and enter his world for a few hours. Follow him on his adventures and dream about heroic deeds.

Enjoy.
Herbert Grosshans

Prologue

SEAL AND RUMOS, the two night suns, illuminated the grisly scene below.

The riders burst upon the small camp from out of nowhere. One of them killed the old man who stood guard with one vicious thrust of his lance. The others spread out, plunging their lances into the dark shapes on the hard ground.

Men and women, lost in their dreams, died without knowing their murderers. A few woke—too late. Death came mercilessly on swift, dark wings even to those.

When it was done, the riders slid off their mounts, stalked through camp on long, stiff legs, overturning cooking pots and scattering bales of cloth and garments from the low wagons. Some walked among the slain bodies, turning them over to look into the dead faces.

They searched for something or someone. One of them, who appeared to be their leader, spoke words in a harsh, hissing language. He was taller and broader than the others, his face hidden inside the hood of his cloak. Only his eyes glowed in the darkness of his cowl.

Lifting those eyes to the sky, he uttered a shrill, piercing cry. Moments later from close by came an answer. A large shadow separated from the branches of a tall tree and glided silently toward the caller.

The light of the night suns reflected momentarily on outstretched talons and a long, wicked beak, as the creature settled on the shoulder of its master, folding black wings like a cloak around its feathered body.

"Obviously, Saleen isn't among the slain," the hooded man said aloud to one of his companions. "She may not even have been here. It seems we had the wrong information."

The riders mounted their steeds and disappeared as silently as they had come, leaving their bloody deeds behind.

A sob and then a loud cry came from one of the low shrubs surrounding the clearing. Two figures emerged, one small, the other one taller. The pale light revealed a white, oval face, framed by long, blond hair—a girl by all appearances. She hurried after the small figure that ran toward one of the still shapes on the ground.

"Come back, Kalo," she called, her voice quavering and breaking as she saw the bloodstained earth.

"They killed my Momma," cried the little boy. He cradled the lifeless head of a woman in his arms.

The girl reached him and gently pulled him away. As the dead woman's head lolled to the side, blood oozed from her open mouth. The girl screamed, grabbed the boy, and ran blindly into the protection of the trees.

———

AT DAWN, the first scavengers moved in, tearing and ripping the welcome meat from bones, growling and snapping at each other with bared teeth, not willing to share the bounty even with their own kind. When an intruder dared to disturb them at their meal, they lifted their heads, snarling angrily.

Tall, with wide, massive shoulders, his muscular arms and bare upper chest were bronzed by long exposure to the sun. Two steely blue eyes narrowed as they took in the gruesome scene. A short kilt fashioned from the striped skin of a lion-wolf covered his lean hips.

He rode a large, muscular horse with a glistening black coat.

"Looks like we've stumbled onto something unpleasant, Nightwalker," the big man rumbled. He reached for the battle-axe slung across his back, hefting it easily.

When the tall warrior advanced, the carrion-eaters bared their long sharp fangs, but slunk away, their thick tails between their legs. One, bolder than the others, tried to take a stand and died screaming as the double-bladed weapon split its skull.

Turning his broad back to the watching animals, the man bent to examine one of the dead. "Pretty," he murmured as he peered into the face of a young woman. A thick crust of dried blood hid a deep wound caused by the murderous thrust of a lance between her full breasts. "Much too young to have died so horribly." His eyes glimmered with a cold fire and the muscles of his jaws stood out rigidly.

As he bent over another of the still bodies, his sharp ears detected the sound of someone approaching. Straightening, he turned to look at the trail spilling into the clearing from the other side.

A lone rider burst out of the forest. He was young, with a scowling face, short but broad and muscular. Padded leather armor protected his deep chest; his thighs were bare and the boots he wore reached over his knees.

In his right hand, he carried a short, curved sword. A long bow and a quiver filled with arrows were slung across his back.

His steed reared on its hind-legs when he brought it to an abrupt halt, clawing the air with cloven hoofs.

The two men looked at each other, but before either of them could react, a score of men broke from among the trees. Small and agile, they were clad in green garments. They carried short bows, arrows nocked and aimed at the tall warrior.

"Admiring your work?" said the horseman.

The tall warrior chuckled without humor. "Surely you don't think I, one man, killed all these people? Besides, they've been dead for hours."

"Enough time for your accomplices to get away."

"Let us use him for target-practice, Lord Carn," said one of the green-clad men.

The young lord shook his head. "No, he must be punished in the proper way. Shackle him but don't harm him." He turned to the others. "See if she's among the dead."

While most of the small men searched the bodies, three of them cautiously approached the tall warrior. He watched them come closer, his battle-axe half raised, but then he shrugged, dropped the axe and held out his arms.

The young lord, who had been watching him with curious eyes, spit into the dust. "Somehow I didn't expect you to give up so easily. But it doesn't surprise me. You're not only a murderer but also a coward. Do you have a name or do you prefer to be executed nameless?"

The warrior stood rigid for a moment; his eyes narrowed slightly, but then he relaxed and smiled. "Better a live coward than a dead fool. I am Rhodar."

"Rhodar," Carn mused. "Your mode of dress tells me you're an outlander. Where do you come from?"

"From the Western Plains. Beyond the mountains."

"A barbarian." The young lord nodded. "I guessed that much. Where are your companions?"

"I told you I travel alone. This is not my work. I do not murder help-less women and children."

"So you say, but the evidence is against you," Carn said coldly. "Enough of this babble." He turned away, sheathing his curved sword. "Did you find her?" he asked the nearest of the green-clad men.

They shook their heads. "No, she's not among the slain," said one of them.

"There might be a chance then she's still alive. Search the grounds," Carn commanded. "Perhaps she fled into the forest."

They searched the surrounding area but didn't find anyone. Suddenly one of the men came back. "My Lord, I think I have found something. There are two sets of tracks leading into the swamps. One was made by small feet, a child's feet, and the other one could be those of a girl or young woman."

"Could be?" Carn said sharply. "I thought the Quinx were expert woodsmen?"

"The person who made those tracks was of light stature and wore soft leather boots, the kind most slave girls commonly wear when going outside. That is all I can tell you, my Lord. She was running, obviously in a great panic."

Carn nodded, seemingly satisfied. "We'll follow those tracks."

"There is something else, my Lord," added the woodsman. "The tracks of many horses—leading south. The tracks are all over the camp, as you can see for yourself. Single-hoofed animals, the same breed the prisoner is riding."

4

"Proof that he is guilty. I wonder why he lingered on."

"Maybe he wanted to have some fun with the dead women?" suggested one of the woodsmen. "I've heard ugly stories about these barbarians."

Rhodar glared at the man. "Only a so-called civilized man would get ideas like that. We honor our dead, especially the women."

"How? By each male member of your tribe giving them one last ride?" The man laughed.

The huge muscles on the barbarian's arms corded as his hands became fists, but after a tense moment he relaxed. He even managed a grin. "It would become quite tedious to lead a horse around with a dead body tied to its back. No, we have a different ceremony."

The other one looked at the big man, a puzzled expression on his elfin face. Suddenly he laughed again. "You have a strange sense of humor, Barbarian; also, a temper but very well under control. I like that."

"Who cares what you like!" thundered Carn. "Stop fraternizing with the prisoner and let's get moving. You,"—he pointed at one of the woodsmen—"take four men, round up the pack-animals, load the dead onto the wagons, and take them back to the city. Tie the prisoner behind one of the wagons. He looks strong, he can walk. Don't forget his axe. I'd like to add it to my collection."

The woodsman bowed. "Yes, my Lord." He bent to pick up the big battle-axe but managed to get only the handle off the ground. Straining unsuccessfully, he called another one to give him a hand. Both tried without success. The shiny double-bladed head stayed on the ground.

"What manner of weapon is this?" cursed one of the men, straightening. "I've seen the barbarian carry it in one hand, apparently without strain."

Rhodar, who had been watching, laughed. "Singar is a special weapon. No man but its rightful owner will ever wield it."

"An enchanted blade," Carn said. "How is it you possess such a weapon?"

"My father gave it to me, but the magic will fade soon. It must be renewed by the sorcerer who once, a long time ago, put the spell on it. That is the reason I travel through your Kingdom—to find Arguss, the Sorcerer, so I can become the true master of Singar."

"How can you wield this weapon if you are not its true master?"

"Singar was given freely to me by my father. If I don't use the axe too often, the spell will last until I have found Arguss. Another reason I would not waste its power by indiscriminately murdering innocent people."

Carn stared at Rhodar, a brooding expression on his dark face. "Maybe you are not what you seem. Maybe you are a magician in disguise. Perhaps you are this sorcerer Arguss, come to visit your evil colleague Kastabaan."

Rhodar laughed again. "If I were a magician I wouldn't stand here now waiting for you to shackle me."

"Easy for you to prevent with one of your spells," murmured the young lord. He looked into the sky. "Oh, if only Saleen were here. No spell could touch me. Why did she have to escape? I always treated her fairly."

"Who is Saleen?" Rhodar said.

"Saleen?" Carn gave him a long stare. "She's a girl. A special girl with a special gift. Kastabaan wants her dead, but I need her alive. She's our only protection against his evil." His hand chopped down. "Enough!" he roared angrily. "I don't know why I converse with you. Pick up the axe and put it on one of the wagons. Don't try to use any of your magic tricks. My men will be watching you. Even a sorcerer can die by a well-placed arrow."

Rhodar did as ordered. They tied a strong rope around his wrists and fastened the other end to a wagon. When that was done, Carn gathered most of his men together and rode off, his men following single file.

Five stayed behind to take care of the wagons and the prisoner.

Chapter One

THE LITTLE BOY stumbled over a protruding tree root and fell to the damp forest floor. When the girl pulled on his arm, he refused to get up. "Please, Saleen, I must rest. My legs won't move anymore."

"We can't rest, Kalo. We must get to safety first." She stared at the narrow trail ahead, and then back the way they had come, a haunted look in her green eyes. She was tired. Keeping that protective spell around her and the boy to save them from being discovered by the marauders was taking its toll.

"Where is safety, Saleen?" His fingers dug into her hand as a sob escaped his lips. "Why did they kill my Momma, Saleen? My Momma always kept me safe."

Saleen sank down beside him and held him close. A flood of tears burst from her eyes. "I don't know, Kalo," she sobbed, rocking him in her arms. "I'll keep you safe from now on. I'll keep you safe, I promise."

The screech from an animal close-by made them both jump to their feet. They stumbled on, down the narrow, sometimes nearly overgrown trail.

When they stopped again, Kalo sank to his knees, his breath rattling in his throat. "Where are we, Saleen?" he cried. "You promised we'd be there soon."

Leaning against a tree, the girl looked down at the boy. "We will be, Kalo," she said. "We will be."

Staring into the dark forest, he shook his head. "I think we are lost," he said gravely. His eyes were large when he looked at her. "Are we lost?"

Saleen stayed silent. She reached down to pat his head.

His face held a serious expression. "It's alright," he said, trying to sound brave. "I'm not really scared. My uncle will come and look for us. He'll get us out of here, you'll see."

———

CARN SLID FROM HIS STEED, bent to examine the barely visible footprints. Then he looked across the moor and stared into the thick rolling fog.

"If they went into there, they are surely lost, my Lord," said one of the woodsmen.

Glaring at him, Carn smashed one fist into his open palm. "No, they will be found! Saleen, Saleen," he called in a thunderous voice. He listened into the eerie silence, straining his ears, but the dense fog swallowed his words and not even an echo answered his call.

One of the small, green-clad men came back. "I think I found their trail again. It seems they're wandering aimlessly in and out of the swamp, but I believe they finally went into the forest."

"They can't be that far away, unless..." Carn didn't finish the sentence. He mounted his steed. "Come," he called to the others. "We have a trail to follow."

The cloven-hoofed animal let out a defiant scream when Carn mounted its scaly back and dug his boots into the animal's soft flanks. "Easy, Desert-runner," he said soothingly and clucked his tongue. He knew the Sekua did not like the dense forest they were about to enter.

He followed the two men who focused their whole attention on the trail searching for tracks. Even though he had spoken scornfully to them, he knew that once they found a trail they would not lose it.

The Quinx were forest dwellers and closer to nature than denizens of the cities. They understood the language of the plants and animals.

He had sheathed his sword but stayed vigilant. There wasn't much chance they would encounter hostile marauders on the narrow trail, but being unaware of one's surroundings could prove fatal. The forest was not without dangers.

He hoped to find the girl alive and unharmed. Her special powers protected him and the castle from Kastabaan's spells. He didn't want to think of the possibility she might be dead. His thoughts drifted to the tall barbarian who called himself Rhodar. Should he believe his claim he was searching for the sorcerer who put a magic spell on his battle axe? There was no doubt the weapon was enchanted.

He had never seen such a weapon before and it intrigued him, as much as the barbarian. He could use a man like him, but could he trust a barbarian? The man had seemed arrogant with no respect for nobility.

A flock of silver-grouse burst from the dense bush to his right with the sudden noisy rush of fluttering wings, startling him momentarily. His hand reached for the hilt of his curved sword, but he left it sheathed.

They path they followed spilled into a small knoll. The scouts stopped to survey the area.

One of them walked over to a fallen tree to examine it closely. "They rested here, my Lord," he said. "We are on the right trail."

"Did you have any doubts?" Carn felt irritated.

Desert-runner hissed loudly, sensing its master's uneasiness.

The rest of his warriors milled behind him, watching him with their colorless eyes. He had hired their services for only a few days; and knew they were anxious to get back to their villages hidden deep in the forest. The Quinx despised civilization almost as much as the giants that lived in the mountains.

"We never had any doubts," the scout by the fallen tree said, his voice not betraying any emotion. "They went that way."

Carn's gaze followed his pointing arm. The narrow trail he spotted was barely visible and he wondered why Saleen would choose that one when there were two wider, more accessible ones to choose from.

There was no question in his mind that one set of the footprints belonged to Saleen, because she had not been among the dead. The small footprints were those of a young child. He pressed his teeth together until his jaws began to hurt. He had seen the lifeless body of Lady Arneena, whose grandfather was Lord Galasan, who was also the grandfather of Lady Gwenlin, King Ordar's wife.

Lady Arneena was the wife of Kaloss, the shipbuilder. They had only one son—Kalo.

If anything happened to him, there would be hell to pay. He swore he would hunt down the ones responsible for the senseless slaughter of those travelers in the caravan and bring them to justice.

———

RHODAR WATCHED the young lord and his group of green-clad men disappear among the trees of the forest. Then he turned his attention to the five who had begun to carry out the grisly task of loading the bloody corpses onto the wagons.

He had no intentions to stay a prisoner for long. Checking the rope they had tied around his wrists, he suppressed a chuckle. The Quinx might be expert woodsmen, but, apparently, they weren't experts when it came to tying knots.

Using his teeth, he managed to loosen it enough to free himself. His axe lay on the wagon he had been tied to. Grabbing it, he sprinted toward the nearby forest. Before his captors realized he was free, he was hidden by the trees.

Emitting a series of low sounds, he called Nightwalker. Moments later, the black-coated horse came crashing through the shrubbery. Rhodar swung himself onto its broad back and galloped away as fast as the trees would allow. He had made a note of the trail Lord Carn and his men took and he made certain not to use the same one.

Breaking out of the trees, he found his path blocked by a swamp. Tendrils of thick smoke reached out of the moor, beckoning him to follow the siren call of the hidden dwellers.

He knew of the dangers lurking in the moor's darkness and of the strange, magical creatures that waited for the unwary intruder. Nightwalker snorted softly and shook its long head as if to warn him.

He stroked the animal's neck. "Don't worry, my friend, we will not take this path."

Skirting the edge of the swamp, Rhodar followed a narrow trail that took him back into the forest. Stopping, he pulled out a roll from one of the saddle bags and smoothed it out. It was an old map and probably not very accurate.

According to the map, there was a small city about a day's ride to the south by the ocean. Unfortunately, the mapmaker had not recorded the swamp. Neither did the map show any roads or trails.

It didn't matter. He was in no great hurry. When he found a trail that led in the southerly direction, he took it.

———

SALEEN REALIZED with a sinking feeling that they were lost. She had no idea where the path they had followed was leading. Twice they emerged by the swamp and twice she chose the wrong path and now she had no way of backtracking.

Kalo stumbled beside her; his small fingers held her hand in a tight grip. He acted brave, but she knew he was scared—as scared as she was.

"I'm hungry and so tired, Saleen," he complained. "When can we rest?"

"When we find a safe place," she said.

"That's what you've been saying, but where is a safe place?"

"We'll know when we find it." She tried to sound reassuring, even though she felt like sitting down and crying. She was afraid of the night. The forest was not safe at night.

The path became wider and ended suddenly. Before them lay a cleared area and it was evident the clearing was not natural.

"There is a cabin," Kalo said, pointing excitedly.

Saleen looked in the direction he pointed and saw it, too. With walls built from trees and a roof covered with branches and grass it looked like a natural part of the forest.

"Have we found safety?" Kalo said, his small voice hopeful.

"Perhaps, but we have to be careful," she cautioned.

Gingerly and with apprehension they walked on. They had closed the distance to the cabin about halfway when the door opened and a stooped figure waddled into the open, squinting against the light.

Saleen stopped walking, warily eyeing the old woman. She was ugly and clearly not human. Her nose was a short trunk and her eyes big and slightly bulging. Large, flapping ears stuck out on either side of her narrow head. While her leathery skin was black, her straggly hair was as white as the bright clouds in the sky. Two long teeth grew from her wide, protruding lower jaw.

Even though she was short, her gross body made her appear larger. Her breasts were like two misshapen lumps on her naked chest. She wore a skirt fashioned from some furry animal, but it was filthy with caked mud and other disgusting substances. Her wide mouth opened into a huge grin when she saw Saleen and Kalo.

"Two human children," she croaked loudly.

Coming closer, she studied Saleen with her bulging yellow eyes. "Perhaps only one child," she observed. "You look like a fully-grown woman."

"I'm not," Saleen protested. "I'm just a girl." She shuddered and took a step backward, suddenly afraid. She had never seen a Hogee before, but she had heard stories, none of them encouraging. "We don't taste very good," she said, hastily.

The Hogee woman cackled. "We don't eat human flesh, but my sons will be excited to have their way with a human female. They are young and eager to mate."

"I told you I'm not a fully-grown woman," Saleen protested. "Besides, I'm still a virgin."

The old woman clapped her clawed hands in delight. "A virgin? Wonderful. So are my sons. I cannot wait to watch as they become men and make a real woman out of you."

Saleen grabbed Kalo's hand and pulled him with her as she ran back toward the forest. Looking for the path they had come from, she couldn't locate it and lost precious moments. When she finally made up her mind it was too late.

Two grotesque looking shapes emerged from the forest. They were taller than the woman and just as fat, but males, judging by the large appendix between their hairy thighs.

"Stop them," the old hag cried.

Both males lumbered toward Saleen and the boy, cutting off their retreat into the protection of the forest. As fat as they were, they were surprisingly agile and quick. One of them caught Saleen, while the other one grabbed Kalo.

"A human woman," rumbled the one who held Saleen, his wide mouth showing large, yellow teeth in a grin.

She struggled in his grip, beating his hairy chest with her fists, but he threw her down and lay on top of her, pinning her to the ground with his heavy body.

"She's a virgin," panted the old woman who had reached them. "Take her now."

Pushing up her leather skirt, the male exposed her lower body.

Saleen screamed and tried to get free, but it was useless. Her captor smashed his large fist against the side of her head.

Darkness descended upon her like a welcoming blanket, but it lasted only for a little while.

———

"THAT SOUNDED LIKE A SCREAM," Rhodar said aloud and stopped to listen, but everything seemed quiet, except for the droning of a Barkeater in one of the nearby trees.

"I could have sworn I heard a scream," he murmured. "Am I beginning to hear voices?" He urged Nightwalker to walk faster. Straining his eyes, he seemed to see a lighter shade in the path and knew there must be a glade ahead.

The moment he and the large horse broke out of the path into the clearing, he saw the unmoving body of a woman lying on the ground while a fat shape lay between her spread legs; clearly a male Hogee. Beside them, stood another Hogee male. He had one huge hand clasped around the neck of a little human boy.

He and the female crouching on the other side of the couple on the ground stomped their huge feet and made hooting and grunting sounds.

Rhodar didn't have to guess what was happening. Jumping from his horse, he grabbed his battle-axe. They never saw him coming. Too late they realized there was an intruder among them.

He laid the side of the heavy blade against the thick skull of the male Hogee. The hairy creature stumbled sideways; his hand released the little boy and reached for the long knife hanging from a shoulder strap. Rhodar hit him again, dropping him to the soft forest floor where he lay still.

The old female screeched and attacked Rhodar with outstretched talons. He rammed the blunt end of the axe handle into her fat belly. Then he kicked her in the leathery face with one heavy boot. She fell backward and joined the male who lay lifeless in the high grass.

The male on top of the woman seemed oblivious to his surroundings. Rhodar grabbed him by his long, coarse hair, pulled him up and gave him a kick to send him sprawling. Lying on his back, he stared at Rhodar with his yellow, protruding eyes. When he tried to pull his knife, Rhodar lifted his axe.

"I will split your ugly skull before you can draw it out of its sheath," he growled.

"I give up," the Hogee rasped. "Don't kill me."

"I should kill you for what you did," Rhodar said, menacingly.

The Hogee got onto his knees and crawled away, like a huge, hairy swamp-crab.

Rhodar bent over the woman on the ground, realizing she was just a girl. She had her eyes closed. At first, he thought she was dead, but then he saw her eyelids flutter and he knew she was alive. "You are safe now," he said softly, but she didn't seem to hear him.

She opened her eyes and screamed.

Chapter Two

WHEN CARN BURST into the glade, he saw the tall barbarian standing over Saleen, his battle-axe in his brawny hand. Letting out an angry combat-cry, he drew his curved sword and slid from his steed.

The barbarian turned around as Carn charged him. Grabbing the handle of his axe with his other hand, he lifted it into the air in front of him to ward off Carn's descending weapon. Lashing out with one foot, he kicked Carn in the chest hard enough to make the air whoosh from his lungs with a suppressed cry and sent him sprawling.

"Don't make me kill you," the barbarian growled. "I have no quarrel with you."

As Carn fell backward, he spotted the unmoving body of a male Hogee and realized he may have misread the situation. Rising to his feet, he sheathed his weapon and spread both arms in a gesture of good will. "Perhaps I was wrong about you," he said grudgingly.

"Whatever you assumed happened here you certainly assumed wrong," the barbarian said, lowering his axe. "This is the second time," he added with a thin smile.

"You must admit, both times I found you in a compromising position." He turned when he heard a child's sob beside him and found a small shape rushing up to him, throwing thin arms around his leg.

"Kalo," he said, relieved to see the little boy alive and, apparently, unharmed. Voices behind him made him look toward the forest. The Quinx men had finally caught up with him.

"Everything alright here, Lord Carn?" Lukor, the leader of the group, inquired, his eyes fixed on the barbarian.

"Everything is fine." Carn bent over Saleen, who still lay on the ground, her leather skirt pushed up past her hips, exposing her naked lower body. Her eyes were wide open and she appeared to be in shock. He offered his hand. "You are safe now, Saleen."

She let out a sudden loud sob and pushed down her skirt. Ignoring his outstretched hand, she rose unsteadily to her feet.

"What happened here?" Carn demanded, even though he knew the answer.

She stared at him. "I want them dead," she said without emotion.

One of the creatures on the ground stirred. Carn noticed that it was an old female. He hadn't seen her before and now he realized that there were two Hogee lying in the grass.

He had no love for their race. The Hogee were ugly, vicious creatures and a great nuisance. Most of them lived at the foothills of the mountains to the south, but sometimes a few of them built their homes in the deep forest, preying on hunters and humans foraging for herbs and fungi. From time to time, they invaded human settlements, capturing young women and children. They used them to satisfy their depraved desires. When they tired of them, they killed and ate them.

He shuddered when he thought that Saleen and Kalo had barely escaped that terrible fate. In a fit of anger, he stalked over to the female, drew his sword and, with one swift stroke, he severed her ugly head from her gross body. Then he kicked the male.

Opening his protruding eyes, the Hogee stared at him for a moment, hatred clear in his yellow eyes. A low growl escaped from his wide mouth and his clawed hand shot out to grab Carn's leg.

Stepping back quickly and out of the Hogee's reach, he watched the squat creature rise. The Hogee stood on trunk-like legs; the long toes on his huge, bare feet dug into the soft ground as if getting ready to attack or run.

Carn gave him one last look, turned, and stalked away. "Use him for target practice," he called to the Quinx, who had their arrows already trained on the grotesque creature.

With a chilling howl, the Hogee took off, his speed belying his fat, ungainly body.

The first arrow hit him in the arm, the second in the thigh and the third one buried itself deep in his hip.

Carn knew that the Quinx were playing with the Hogee; either arrow could have pierced the wide back with deadly accuracy. However, they had no intentions letting him escape. Before he reached the trees, he stumbled and fell, his body riddled with arrows. At least two had hit vital organs.

Carn didn't bother checking if the vile creature was dead. If he wasn't, he would bleed to death, anyway; fodder for the carrion eaters that were never far away. "Why didn't you kill them, Barbarian?" he said to the stranger.

The big man shrugged his massive shoulders. "I do not kill for sport."

Carn pointed at the decapitated female. "You don't believe they deserved to die?"

"The males perhaps, but not the female."

Carn shook his head in disbelief. "I am surprised to hear you talk that way. Didn't you tell me you come from beyond the mountains, from the Western Plains?"

"I did."

"Isn't that area populated mostly by barbarian tribes?"

The big man laughed. "The word Barbarian is a matter of interpretation. Just because we don't live in stinking cities does not make us any less civilized than city-dwellers. Life is a precious gift from the gods. We do not waste it unnecessarily."

"I've heard different stories, Barbarian," Carn said scornfully.

"Stories!" The barbarian snorted. "That's all they are—stories."

Carn turned to look at the girl. She stood there with a fierce expression on her pretty face and her eyes blazed with green fire. "There was another one," she told him.

"We will hunt him down," Carn promised.

"No." She looked toward the forest. "When he was inside me, I marked him with a curse. He will pay and die a horrible, slow death for what he did to me." Her eyes searched for the little boy. She gave him a brave smile and held out a hand. "Come, Kalo. We have found safety."

Kalo pointed a small finger at the barbarian. "He saved us, Saleen."

The girl gave the big man a grateful look. "Thank you. What's your name?"

"I am Rhodar."

———

SINCE IT WAS ALREADY late afternoon, Lord Carn decided to stay for the night and start moving back to his castle in the morning.

It didn't matter to Rhodar. One more day added to his quest didn't make any difference. He'd accompany Carn to his castle, because the young lord promised Rhodar a reward for saving the girl's and the boy's life.

He sat by himself, leaning against the trunk of a tree, watching the log cabin burn. The structure had already collapsed and the flames were dying down. Now only the heavy timbers burned. They'd probably burn all night.

The green-clad men had dragged the two corpses deeper into the forest and he could hear the snarling of the carrion-eaters as they ripped away the flesh from the bones. Even though Rhodar didn't approve the killing of the old Hogee woman, it was probably best. She would have been alone, without the protection of her sons and the comfort of her home.

His thoughts drifted to the girl, Saleen. She had been raped—brutally raped by the Hogee males and there was a good chance it would leave her scarred for life—maybe. Rape was an accepted practice in many tribes. He knew of one tribe in the mountains beyond the Western Plains where the females banded together and forced the males to have sex with them after feeding them herbal extractions to give them more stamina. It was their way of life and nobody questioned it.

Mortals created moral standards and ethics, not the gods. The gods did not interfere in the affairs of the mortals, because they didn't care.

His keen hearing picked up the footsteps of someone walking in the tall grass. When he looked, he saw a slim figure approaching him —Saleen.

The girl gave him a shy smile. "Do you mind if I sit with you?"

"What man could refuse the company of a young, pretty girl?" Rhodar smiled.

She sat down across from him, carefully folding her legs under her skirt. "I don't feel pretty right now," she said, bitterness coloring her soft voice. "Those animals took something away from me that can never be replaced—my innocence. Not only did they take it from me, they also stole it from the one it really belonged to, the man who will be my life-mate someday. Who would want to marry me now? I have been damaged beyond repair."

"You're alive," he said.

"Yes that I am—thanks to you. I'm grateful for that."

Rhodar studied her casually. She was pretty with a slim body and graceful movements. When she brushed her hair out of her face with a quick gesture, he noticed the slightly pointed ears.

"My father is Quinx," she said, answering his unspoken question.

He nodded. "And your mother?"

"She was a witch."

"Was?"

Her long lashes covered the green fire of her eyes. "She's dead."

It was obvious she didn't want to talk about it and he didn't pursue it. "What are you to Lord Carn?" he said instead.

She opened her eyes and looked him squarely in the face. "I'm his slave."

"His lover?"

Her laugh mocked him. "I was told barbarians are keen observers. This morning I was still a virgin."

"You could still be his lover."

"I am his slave," she said again. "A slave has few choices."

"He said you have a gift. He also said that the sorcerer Kastabaan wants you dead. Why?"

"You ask too many questions, Barbarian." Her tone seemed scornful, but her eyes teased him.

"Just curious." He chuckled good-humoredly. "Must be my barbarian upbringing."

"Too much curiosity can be deadly."

"As can be too little. Tell me about the boy. Why is he so important to Lord Carn?"

"Kalo? Lord Carn couldn't care less about him, but Kalo's mother, Lady Arneena, was second cousin to Lady Gwenlin, King Ordar's wife."

"Kalo's mother is dead, I assume?"

Saleen nodded somberly. "She was murdered in her sleep this morning, along with all the others in the caravan. Only Kalo and I escaped. That's how we ended up here."

"Did you see the men who murdered those people?"

"I did. It was still dark, but Seal and Rumos were shining bright and I could see them clearly—the minions of Kastabaan. I didn't see their leader, but he must be a powerful sorcerer, because he commanded a mountain hawk." A sudden sob escaped her lips. "It is my fault they are dead. Those men were looking for me."

"How do you know that?"

"I heard my name spoken."

"Will you tell me now why Kastabaan wants you dead?"

"I am the only one who can protect Lord Carn and his castle from Kastabaan's sorcery." With a look of desperation, she leaned suddenly forward. "Can you help me escape?"

It came unexpected. "You want to escape Lord Carn?"

"Yes."

"Is that why you joined the caravan?"

She nodded.

Rhodar shook his head. "I don't know if I'm the one who can help you. Where would you go?"

"Anywhere. I just want to be free of this responsibility and free to choose what I do and where I go."

"You said your father was a Quinx. Can you not join his people and disappear in the forest somewhere?"

"My father's people reject me," she said bitterly. "I'm not one of them. I'm a Halfling and my mother was a witch. They fear me."

He smiled. "You don't look so fearsome to me."

"Looks can be deceiving."

For an insane moment, he saw the ferocious face of a Treewolf. He blinked and then the vision was gone. "You are a 'Wer'," he said.

There was sudden fear in her eyes. "How can you know?"

"I saw."

"You are truly a barbarian. Still close to the elements. Magic has touched you also."

"My battle-axe. It carries a spell."

20

"I sensed it." Her eyes begged him. "Nobody knows my secret. It is my grandfather's legacy."

"He was one of the Wer-people, I guess."

"A True-blood, but my grandmother was a witch, also a True-blood." Her chuckle was not cheerful. "The line ended with my mother. I am something else—an abnormality, an abomination."

Rhodar sat silent. He couldn't give her a glib comment, because he didn't have one. He grew up in the open spaces of the Western Plains. His people did not live in permanent settlements. They followed the great herds that roamed the Plains. Sometimes they might spend years in one area, but at other times they moved with the living tides, never staying long in one place. The Plains-people were simple people with simple laws and customs handed down from generation to generation.

He was not a man of many words; neither was he a smooth talker schooled in the art of deception and lies. His education came from the Earth and the Sky. The grass and trees spoke to him. The Elders taught the young the knowledge they learned from their Elders.

"You are suddenly so quiet," the girl interrupted his brooding. "Are you horrified by what you have learned about me?"

"No." Feeling awkward, he took her slim hand into his. "You are what the gods decided to make you and only you can deal with that. I do not condemn you. I wish I could help you, but I cannot. I am a wanderer with a mission. I need to find the sorcerer Arguss. That is my priority. After that—I'll see. There is no room for a young girl in my plans or destiny."

"I would not be a burden, I promise." Her green eyes searched his face. "How do you know what your destiny is, Rhodar? Perhaps I'm your destiny."

He released her hand. "Perhaps you are, but I let the gods decide. I worry I could not always protect you. My life is filled with violence. It seems to follow me wherever I go."

She touched his cheek with soft fingers. "I could be grateful in many ways." Her full lips trembled slightly when she spoke.

He removed her hand with a rough gesture. "I'm surprised to hear you say that after what you've been through. Besides, I may be a barbarian, but I do not lie with young girls."

"Forgive me, Rhodar. I spoke hastily and without thinking, but it is from desperation. Deep in my heart I feel that you are a man of honor and I can trust you."

He searched for the right words to say. "The gods in their incredible wisdom will lead you on a path that is best for you."

She smiled. "The gods sent you to save me. It seems our paths have already crossed and merged once. They may merge again."

Chapter Three

THEY BROKE camp early the next morning. Rhodar searched in his saddlebags and found a few strips of dried meat. He chewed on a piece while he followed Carn on the narrow trail. The little boy, Kalo, sat in front of Carn.

Rhodar felt Saleen's soft, warm body as she pressed herself against him from behind. Her slim arms were wrapped around his chest to keep from falling off. She had slept beside him during the night, seemingly trusting a complete stranger more than her master.

With the intuitive feelings of a primitive man, Rhodar sensed the disapproval of Carn and knew he had to tread carefully not to antagonize the young lord. Carn seemed to possess a temper he did not always hide with success. It wouldn't take much to send him into a fit of rage. Rhodar had no desire to create any hostile feelings toward him from the man. Neither did he have any desire to get into a position where he had to kill men with whom he had no quarrel.

The Quinx trotted on silent feet behind him. The small, green-clad men were denizens of the forest and familiar with the dangers that prowled among the tall trees and thick shrubs. They could survive where a more civilized man would perish.

The forest did not frighten Rhodar, but he felt uneasy and restless, like a trapped animal within the confines of the trees—a swamp-tiger held captive inside a cage barred by thick iron rods with no escape. His world was the wide-open savannah of the great Western Plains with a sky so high you could see the stars at night, whereas the sky inside the forest was hidden by the thick umbrellas of the trees. You never knew what lurked in their dark interior.

He breathed easier when they left the darkness of the thick forest and traveled down a well-used trail, with only the occasional clump of trees on each side. The terrain changed slowly. For a little while they traveled along the shores of a lake. He saw the gray sails of boats that carried fishermen trying their luck in catching their share of edible creatures living in the water. Even the lakes were not without dangers. Some of them harbored scaly giants that could easily rip the small boats apart with their toothy maws. The hapless fishermen would make a quick meal for these forever hungry monsters.

When they were surrounded by fields of tall-growing golden stalks, he knew they were close to a city.

"How long until we get there?" he said to the girl.

"Not long," she answered.

"What is the name of this city?"

"Falconview."

"A strange name for a city," Rhodar muttered.

"It is named after Castle Falconclaw."

"I see. Is that where Lord Carn lives?"

"Yes." She sounded sullen. She obviously was not overly excited to get there. "He is not the Master of Falconclaw."

"Who is the Master?"

"Lady Gardina, Lord Carn's mother."

"Hm." Rhodar pursed his lips. "I am a bit surprised to hear that. Who is she? Is she somebody important?"

Saleen gave a small laugh. "Everybody knows who Lady Gardina is. She is King Ordar's sister. Do you think that is important?"

Rhodar grinned, even though he knew she couldn't see his face. "Important enough. I'll better be nice to her."

"If you think of bedding her, forget it," Saleen said, almost scornfully. "She has a lover already and I would not encourage you to tangle with him. He is bigger than you and a soldier. Just for your information, he is Kalo's uncle."

24

"That is good to know." Rhodar chuckled. "Thank you for the warning, but be assured, I do not bed every woman I meet."

"I've heard different stories about you outlanders."

He laughed, amused. "They tell many tall tales about us and not all are true, but we don't dispel them. They lend us a certain mystery and give us an edge when we need it." He turned his head a little to look at her. "But don't tell anyone I said that. It must remain our secret."

She gave him a gentle slap on the shoulder. "Now you are teasing me. Besides, who would I tell? I don't have many friends who would be interested. Actually, I don't have any friends."

"Surely there are a few young people like you living in the castle."

"Yes, there are, but most of them shun me. I think they are afraid of me."

"Why?"

"They tell stories about me." Her laughter sounded like a sob. "You see, you and I have much in common."

He didn't answer.

Carn reigned in his steed and waited for Rhodar to bring his horse abreast of Carn's scaly beast. "This is my city," Carn said, his outstretched arm pointing proudly at the huge settlement down in the valley. "This is where I am Lord and Master."

When Rhodar lifted his eyes to look past the city, he saw the towers and spires of a castle silhouetted against the blue sky.

Falconclaw.

"We will ride through the city and deliver Kalo to his father and give him the terrible news about Lady Arneena."

Rhodar shrugged. It didn't matter to him.

The young lord gave Rhodar a scowling look. "It seems Saleen has taken a liking to you. I must remind you she has not matured into a woman yet."

"Why are you concerned?" Carn's remark irritated Rhodar. "Are you her custodian?"

Carn's eyes flashed angrily. "If you must know, Saleen belongs to me. I'm her master."

"You're saying she is a slave?"

"I gave her shelter and raised her after her mother died and her father rejected her. She owes me her gratitude."

"To the point of being a slave?" Rhodar gave Carn a cold look. "Nobody should be owned by anyone."

"We are all owned and controlled by someone," Carn said, a bitter note in his voice. "None of us is really free." He made an impatient motion with his hand. "I don't need to explain myself to you." Making a clucking sound with his tongue, he gave his mount free reigns. "Let's go, Desert-runner. I want to get out of this heat and with more comforting company."

"If my company gives you discomfort perhaps our ways should part here," Rhodar suggested.

"I promised you a reward," Carn grumbled, looking back at him over his shoulder. "I always keep my promise."

Rhodar kept his distance behind Carn, not wanting to antagonize him even more. He became aware of Saleen's rapid heartbeat against his back as she pressed her body tightly against his.

The girl had kept silent during his and Carn's discussion, but now she spoke softly into his ear, "Now do you understand why I want to flee?"

"I'm beginning to understand, but perhaps his gruffness only hides his genuine affection for you."

"You don't know him the way I do. He has no affection for anyone but himself. I am afraid of him. It is only a matter of time before he decides to take me into his bed, even though it will be against my will." Her fingers dug almost painfully into his chest. "You must help me, Rhodar. Please."

"I will give it some thought, but I promise nothing." He cursed inwardly. He did not need to burden himself with a stubborn girl who would be nothing but a nuisance.

The aroma of food and a host of other odors made him aware of his hunger. He hadn't had a decent meal for days now, living off dried fruits and smoked meat with only water to wash it down. A tankard of ale would be welcome right now.

Looking around, he realized they had entered the city. Most of the houses on either side of the dirt-trampled street were in need of repair. The sidings could use a generous coat of paint and the roofs new shingles to keep out the rain. Too many windows were nailed shut with weathered boards. Smoke trailed from crumbling chimneys.

Rhodar saw debris and refuse littering the street and the yards and it appeared to him the people who lived here didn't care much about their environment. The smell of decay lay heavy in the air.

The men and women sitting on their porches watched with scowling faces and obvious resentment in their brooding eyes as the two riders passed them. Rhodar had the strange feeling that only the presence of the Quinx kept them from throwing rocks at them.

"Why do I sense so much hostility in these people?" he said to Saleen.

"Because they have no love for Lord Carn. They live in poverty with no opportunity to ever escape that. This part of the city is populated by the old and the sick and the crippled. On top of that, it is ruled by criminals who take advantage of them."

"That is one of the problems with families drifting apart and too many strangers living so close together in such a small area with no opportunity to hunt or take care of their needs," Rhodar mused. "In the tribes of my people, families stay together and the young ones take care of their Elders and the ones who are not capable of fending for themselves, but even the old ones can still contribute to the whole in some way." He chuckled. "And you call us barbarians?"

A commotion ahead of them made Rhodar look past Carn. An old woman in tattered clothes stood in the center of the street, holding out a clay cup. "Can you spare a few coins for a poor woman, my Lord?"

Carn slowed down his steed. "Out of my way, you old she-goat." He spoke with a harsh voice.

"My husband and my son died serving you. I have nobody to take care of me. Surely, you won't miss a few wretched coins?" She gave him a hopeful look, but Rhodar read the aversion in her expression and voice. This woman certainly had no admiration for the young lord.

"Be gone or I'll trample your miserable body into the dust, old witch." Carn cursed loudly. He dug his heels into his mount's flanks to make it move faster.

The old woman didn't move and stood in a defiant stance, her bright, watery eyes glaring, not trying to hide the hatred she felt. Before Carn could run her down, a man wearing a dirty, torn robe grabbed her arm and yanked her to safety.

"I curse you. May your castle be overrun by a plague of vicious rodents," the old woman screeched, one skeletal arm pointing at Carn.

"One of these days I'm going to set fire to this vile part of my city and burn it to the ground, including the revolting vermin occupying it. I have better use for it." Carn spoke vehemently and loud enough for Rhodar to hear.

"He surely doesn't mean it... or does he?" Rhodar commented with a quiet voice.

Saleen gave a small chuckle. "He means it. He'd have no qualms sending a troupe of soldiers and doing exactly that."

"Wouldn't there be a few other Lords, possibly even the King, who'd object to that?"

"I can't think of any. After all, these people are considered parasites, living off crime and begging. They contribute nothing to the coffers of any Lord or the King's. As far as the Lords are concerned, they are only a huge burden and a nuisance, like the rodents that infest this area. Besides, Lord Carn is King Ordar's nephew. His only nephew. He can do nothing wrong in the King's eyes."

They came upon a bridge spanning a narrow river. Two heavily armed guards stood in front of a gate that offered access to the bridge. When they saw Carn, they saluted and opened the gate to let them onto the bridge.

On the other side of the river the larger houses looked well maintained. Shrubs and trees grew in the yards. Some had flowerbeds and even gardens. The people sitting in their yards wore clean attire and waved at Carn as he rode by. Not enthusiastically, but they displayed more positive attitudes.

"I assume these people actually love Lord Carn," Rhodar commented.

"Nobody loves Lord Carn." Saleen laughed quietly. "Not even his mother. Many of the people living here have someone working in the castle. They depend on Lord Carn's good will. To be the cause of his displeasure could easily earn them a trip across the bridge to the other side with no return."

Rhodar chuckled. "I'd better remember that."

The road became wider and the houses bigger with flower gardens and trimmed shrubs. He didn't see any rubbish in plain sight anywhere.

"This must be where the affluent people live," he said.

"Yes, the rich and powerful. The predators that live off the blood of the downtrodden, the serfs, the ones who do all the work." She spoke in a lighthearted tone but he detected sarcasm in her voice.

"I'm surprised to hear you say that. You seem to live in relative comfort in the castle."

"Yes, I lack for nothing except what I want most—my freedom." This time the bitterness in her voice was unmistakable.

"Perhaps the gods will be kind and make your desire a reality."

She sighed and pressed her cheek against his bare back. "Perhaps they have already answered my silent tears," she said softly.

He didn't comment, not wanting to dash her hopes. They had been through this before.

He heard the shrill cry of the seabirds and the sound of the surf before his sensitive nose detected the smell of fish and other unidentifiable odors, signaling the nearness of the harbor and the fish market. Remembering Carn telling him that they were going to deliver the little boy to his father, he wondered if Kalo's father lived in this area.

They left the main road and turned into a side road. It didn't take long before Rhodar saw the glittering surface of the ocean. Carn headed for one of the huge warehouses that had been erected along the waterfront.

There were a number of ships moored against the wharf, but one particular ship caught Rhodar's interest. It wasn't finished. He saw men pulling on ropes, trying to erect the mainmast.

Saleen, with her uncanny ability to know what he was thinking, spoke. "Kalo's father is a shipbuilder. That is one of the ships he is currently building."

"He must be very rich," Rhodar said.

"That he is, otherwise Lady Arneena would never have married him. Don't forget, he isn't a Lord and Lady Arneena is..." she paused and swallowed, "...was highborn."

When they reached the warehouse near the ship under construction, Carn slid off his steed. He lifted the boy down and set him onto the ground. "I hope your father is in his office," he said to the boy and held out his hand. "Come, let's go and see him."

Rhodar also dismounted. He looked up at Saleen who still sat on the horse. "Do you want to come?"

She shook her head. "No."

He shrugged and followed Carn and the boy through the door into the building. A short, corpulent man with a strong face and calculating eyes rose from his place behind a massive desk. "Lord Carn," he said. "You brought my son. Where did you find him?"

"We found him wandering through the forest, Kaloss," Carn said. "I'm afraid I have unpleasant news."

"Is it about my wife? Is she safe?"

"I wish I could tell you so, but your wife is dead." Carn said without trying to make the news softer, more humane.

"Dead?" Kaloss stared at Carn. "How?"

"About a day's ride south of here; near the Ridgeland Moor. She was murdered during the night along with everyone in the caravan. I am curious; why did Lady Arneena travel dressed like a peasant and without any guards to protect her?"

"She was on her way to Dragona visiting an old friend and she didn't want to draw attention to her person." Kaloss heaved a deep sigh. "She never told me the name of the friend. All she told me was that she owed this friend a debt from long ago. I didn't question her, but when I asked her not to go, she said that I am too involved in my business and it would do us good if we were apart for a while." His gaze dropped from Carn to the boy. "I am grateful to you for bringing back my son." He opened his arms. "Come to your father, Kalo."

Kalo let go of Carn's hand and walked toward his father. He stopped midway and looked back, pointing at Rhodar. "He rescued me and Saleen from the Hogee. He is a great warrior."

Kaloss fixed his eyes on Rhodar. "You are a barbarian from the Western Plains. I can tell by your mode of dress. What is your name?"

"I'm known as Rhodar."

"From what clan?"

"The Serpent Clan."

The man bowed slightly. "I guessed as much. There is no mistaking the tooth of the Giant Stone Serpent fastened to the gold chain you carry around your neck. It means you fought one of those ferocious reptiles and were the victor. I thank you, Rhodar, for saving my son. Kalo is all I have left now."

At that moment, a door in the back of the office opened and a woman entered. Dressed in a silky gown that was belted around her thin waist, it was plain that she wasn't a commoner. "Any news about…?" She stopped when she realized Kaloss wasn't alone. Rhodar didn't miss her lifting her eyebrows when she saw Kalo. Then her eyes fell on the young lord. "Lord Carn, forgive me, I didn't recognize you immediately. What brings you to this part of the city?"

Rhodar with his animal instincts sensed her uneasiness and wondered about the reason.

"I'm afraid you have the advantage, my Lady. I don't recognize you."

She gave a strained laugh. "That's probably because I'm not in the habit of visiting your castle, my Lord. My name is Lironi and I'm the widow of Mordas. You may have heard of him. He was a fur-trader."

"The one who was bludgeoned to death by a group of hunters because he cheated them?" Carn seemed amused.

She lowered her eyelids, hiding her green eyes. "You have heard of him. It seems my husband was not an honorable man."

"I had no idea he had such a beautiful wife." Carn chuckled. "It's a shame you never came to one of our festivities at the castle. Perhaps that can be remedied."

Her green eyes gave him a look from under lowered lashes. "I was never invited."

"Consider yourself invited." Carn turned his attention back to Kaloss. "Is this woman your friend?"

"We are acquaintances." Kaloss seemed reluctant.

Carn's gaze lingered on the decanter on the desk and the two glasses filled with red liquid. "Close enough to share a glass of wine," he observed.

"We have business dealings."

"I guess it's none of my concern." Carn's expression was one of distaste when he turned his attention back to the woman. "To answer your earlier question, I'm here to tell Kaloss about his wife's murder. He can give you more details should you be interested." He looked at Kalo, who stood uncertain, his eyes flickering back and forth between his father and the woman. "What about the boy? Is there room for him in your life since your days seem to be filled with so much business? I must ensure he is taken care of."

"I must admit having him here without my wife poses a bit of a problem. As you said—my business takes much of my time."

Carn nodded. "I will take him with me to the castle. He can stay there until his uncle comes to visit my mother. Lord Galoor is fond of his nephew."

Kaloss looked at the woman, who gave him a barely noticeable nod. "I'm in your debt, my Lord. That solution is acceptable to me and is probably in Kalo's best interest. He loves his uncle." He grimaced. "Sometimes I think more than me, his father."

"Perhaps if you'd spend more time with him, he might love you as much." Carn was obviously displeased and made no secret about it. He took Kalo's hand and pulled him with him. The boy didn't struggle.

Chapter Four

THERE WAS no easy way to reach Castle Demon's Eye. Located on top of a mountain, it was surrounded by dense forests and steep cliffs. The only road winding its way up the steep slope was rigged with protective spells that would lead unwary travelers to roads with no end or deadly traps. Not that anyone ever wanted to visit the castle, unless they had a death wish or were ignorant of the dangers—or lost.

If by some unexplainable and nearly impossible luck they should survive the many hazards and arrive at the gate of the castle, they still were not guaranteed a friendly welcome. Should they somehow gain entry there was a good chance they might never leave—not alive anyway. Kastabaan, the Sorcerer, was not an amiable man. He wasn't a man in the normal sense. He was a shapeshifter and could change into anything or anyone. Above all, he was the epitome of evil.

His coal-black eyes glowed with red fire inside the hood of his cape as he glared at his apprentice Korallas. "You're lucky she was not among the dead, you imbecile. I gave specific instructions not to harm her and bring her to me. Are you sure Lady Arneena was among the slain?"

Korallas gave his master a cold look. "I'm sure. I killed her myself."

"At least you did that right. And the boy?"

"No sign of him, either. Is it possible you had the wrong information? Perhaps Saleen and the boy were not part of the caravan."

"That would be the only logical conclusion. Did you search the surrounding forest? They could have been hiding in there."

"I did. Even my Hawk did not detect them."

"She might have created a detection spell. Remember, her mother was a powerful witch. She may possess powers we don't know about."

Korallas nodded. "That is possible. What do you suggest we do now?"

Kastabaan threw back the cowl, exposing his bald head. His sunken eyes had lost their glow and Korallas relaxed, even though he did not fear his master's wrath. Kastabaan was growing old and needed him to do his dirty work. Korallas knew few upcoming sorcerers were his equal. Someday he'd be the master of Castle Demon's Eye, but he still had a few things to learn from Kastabaan, even though the old sorcerer sometimes treated him with contempt.

"I will pay Castle Falconclaw a visit, and I want you to accompany me. Perhaps she has returned there. If not, we may gain some useful information about her whereabouts."

Kastabaan walked over to the window and stared into the mist that rose up from the valley below. "I love these early mornings just before the sun comes up. The air is crisp and fresh and you never know what mysterious creatures hide in the mist. I love these surprises and challenges." He laughed softly. "It never ceases to amaze me how many humans are so foolish and believe they can visit me and expect a warm welcome or even make a deal with me. How did they ever come up with the idea that I make their wishes come true?"

"Maybe it's your friendly nature," Korallas suggested and smirked.

"It must be." Kastabaan turned away from the window. He regarded Korallas silently for a moment with his black eyes. The light behind him made his head appear like a skull. Not for the first time Korallas wondered if the man he looked at showed him his true identity. "I've been working on a new creation. If you're interested you can come and see it, even though I'm not quite done yet. Perhaps you have some suggestions."

Korallas followed his master down the stairs into the tunnels and caverns under the castle. Some of them were natural and some had been constructed. The smell of decay and growing fungus became stronger as they climbed deeper into the bowels of the mountain. Korallas had never been fond of spending time in these tunnels. He preferred hunting the wild forest animals and breathing outdoor air, but his greatest thrill was hunting human prey.

Kastabaan stopped in front of an iron gate that barred the entrance into one of the smaller caverns and used a large key to open the rusty lock. The gate swung open on screeching hinges. Korallas breathed through his open mouth as the stench that could only come from a reptilian creature assaulted his nose.

Kastabaan deposited the glow-crystal he carried into a small bowl fastened to one wall. The old sorcerer pointed into a corner of the cavern. Korallas strained his eyes to see where he pointed and saw sudden movement. Then a large shape separated from the rough wall and moved toward them. He heard the scraping of scales against the stone and the clanking of a chain.

A hideous face that may once have been human but now was covered with warts and hard scales emerged. The elongated bald head sat on a sinuous neck swaying on a squat body supported by four trunk-like legs. The long tail ended in a ball covered with spines. At first, he though the creature was wearing a cape until he realized it wasn't a cape but wings sprouting from the bony shoulders.

Opening its mouth, the creature hissed loudly, revealing a row of sharp teeth. Two canines grew from the upper jaw. Then it spoke. "Did you come to free me finally from my bonds, Kastabaan?"

Korallas was taken aback by the melodious voice rolling across those repulsive lips. The creature's protruding eyes fixed on Korallas.

"Or perhaps you have brought my executioner to release me from this miserable existence. Why are you torturing me like this, Kastabaan?"

"You brought this on yourself, Cordaras. You wanted wings. I gave you wings." Kastabaan laughed hollowly. Even Korallas shuddered when he heard the evil sound.

"I did not ask you to make me into a revolting beast and neither did I ask for visible wings. I wanted the ability to fly, that's all. You betrayed me. I brought you a dozen young children. What did you do with them?"

Kastabaan shrugged. "Magic is not always reliable. Sometimes things go wrong. It happens. Those children you brought me are not of your concern."

"I'm hungry. When will you feed me again?"

"What do you think you've been eating, you fool?" Kastabaan chuckled. "Everything has its price." He turned to Korallas. "You're looking at one of King Ordar's favorite knights, but he was not happy with his standing and wanted more. He wanted to bed the King's oldest daughter, who is just coming of age."

"I've seen her," Korallas mused. "She is a pretty little thing. Full of fire. I wouldn't mind having a go at her myself."

"Forget her. She's a child. I have other plans for you, much grander plans. We'll discuss it later."

"I can't wait to hear about your plans," Korallas said, not sure if he would like what Kastabaan planned. He had his own plans and they didn't always coincide with his master's.

They walked back the way they had come. "Speaking of plans," Korallas said. "What do you have in mind for that poor creature you created?"

"I will take away his voice and give him the voice of a beast. He will keep his capability to think, but he won't be able to communicate. Then I will set him free. He will be a man inside but a beast on the outside."

"You must have had a different reason for making him a prisoner?"

"Of course. From him I learned everything I need to know about the King's palace. When I visit with the King, I won't be floundering around in the dark trying to find my way. I know the names of all the important lords and some of the politics. Besides, it was fun to experiment a little with him."

Korallas chuckled. "I must admit, you have a wonderful imagination. Too bad your talents will die with you some day."

"They won't. Saleen will bear me a son who will inherit my abilities and hers. He will be the most powerful sorcerer that ever lived." Kastabaan spoke with conviction. There appeared to be no doubt in his mind he would succeed in capturing the young witch and making her his bride.

Korallas wasn't going to voice his doubts. It wouldn't do any good anyway. Let the old sorcerer live in his dream world while he plotted his own ambitious schemes. Yes, he was ambitious. There was no room for Kastabaan in the world Korallas envisioned for himself. The sooner the old sorcerer departed the world of the living the better.

"When do you want to leave for Castle Falconclaw?" he asked.

"I will let you know. I still have a few things to prepare. Tonight, we will discuss my plan."

————

KALOSS WAITED until Lord Carn and the Barbarian closed the door to his office behind them before he turned to Lironi. "Do you think he suspects?"

The woman came close and put a finger against his lips. "Would it matter? He has no proof. It seems our plans are working out and that is good news. With your wife out of the picture, you are free to pay me more attention. No more secret meetings." She put her hand behind his head and pulled his face close to hers. Then she kissed him.

He returned her kiss, but then he pushed her away. "We still need to be careful. I can't afford for people to become suspicious."

"I don't know why you worry. She was the one who cheated on you with that knight she was going to visit. You said yourself you and she had nothing in common anymore."

"We didn't. Although we still slept in one bed, she showed no interest any longer in becoming intimate with me. We haven't joined bodies for many seasons. That is not what bothers me, though; I worry about Kalo."

She laughed and shook her hair out of her face. "I don't see why. Have you looked at him lately? It is more and more evident that he isn't your son."

"It may sound strange to you, but I do love him. I raised him."

"You barely spent time with him." She came close again and stroked his chest. "We've been waiting for this day. It took much secret planning to make this happen. I had my husband killed for you, and I arranged for your wife to be taken care of. Be happy and let's celebrate. Tonight, I will share your bed without having to worry that your wife might surprise us. You can have me any way you like."

"And I shall." He grinned. "I am happy even though I may not show it right now. I appreciate what you've done and am grateful."

Her hair had fallen back into her face. It was one of the things that excited him the most—her bright green eyes shining through the veil of her blond locks as she regarded him with unbridled desire. She did things to him his wife had never done when they were still intimate. She was wild and uncontrolled as they satisfied their lust for each other. He was well aware that she kept him in sexual bondage but it didn't matter. She gave him what he needed and he had no regrets.

"You can show me how grateful you are tonight," she whispered with a purring voice. "Now, let's take care of that jug of wine."

They had barely emptied their glasses when the door opened again and two men in the black uniform of the Enforcers entered.

That was not a good sign. The guild of the Enforcers represented the law everywhere and nobody ever resisted them. Even kings and lords were not exempt from obeying their law.

The Enforcers walked in with their arrogant swagger and looked around without paying any attention to Kaloss and Lironi.

"Can I be of assistant?" Kaloss finally said.

One of them gave him a sharp look. "Are you Kaloss, the shipbuilder?"

Kaloss nodded. "Yes, I am."

"We are investigating the murder of Lady Arneena, your wife."

"I was informed only a short while ago of her murder. How did you find out so fast?" Kaloss looked at the Enforcer with apprehension.

"That is not of your concern. We have our sources. Why did you allow Lady Arneena to travel without the protection of her guards?" The Enforcer inquired sharply.

Kaloss gave a harsh laugh. "I was only her husband not her guardian. Lady Arneena had her own mind. It was not my place to tell her what to do. I could not stop her even if I wanted to."

"Is there a reason you wanted her to go?"

"I never said I wanted her to go." Kaloss took a deep breath, trying to stay calm. He needed to tread carefully. They had a way of drawing information out of a man by twisting words and sentences and they were trained to read posture and expressions.

"But you implied you didn't want to stop her."

"Perhaps it was a poor choice of words. Let me rephrase that by saying I knew it wouldn't do any good to stop her from going."

"Why did she leave?" It was the other Enforcer who spoke.

"She wanted to visit an old friend."

"The caravan was on its way to Dragona. Who was this friend in Dragona?"

"She never told me his name."

"It was a man she visited? A lover perhaps?"

"How should I know?" Kaloss tried hard not to shout. "I didn't even know it was a man. She told me nothing."

"But you said 'his'. Why did you say that if you didn't know who she was going to visit?"

"Again, just a poor choice of words." His hands turned into fists as he pressed them against his sides. "I just lost the woman I loved and my mind is not thinking straight, so why are you torturing me with all these questions?"

"We have been watching you for some time now and have noticed this woman…" the Enforcer pointed at Lironi, "…visiting you on a regular basis. And here you are drinking wine with her shortly after your wife has been murdered."

"A coincidence, I assure you."

"We find it strange that you would be friends with a woman whom we suspect of murdering her husband. Perhaps you are more than just friends."

"If you are suggesting we are lovers, you are wrong. We are good friends, but right now we are discussing a business deal."

The Enforcer's lips turned into a tight smile. It was obvious he didn't believe it. "A business deal. What kind of business deal?"

"Lironi is thinking of repairing her small ship for her fur-trading business. We were discussing the possibility I might build a new ship for her." He forced himself to smile. "After all, I am a shipbuilder."

"Apparently, you are." The Enforcer nodded and turned to his companion. "They were discussing a business deal," he said.

His companion seemed to study Lironi. "Why did you murder your husband?" His question came almost unexpected.

Lironi drew herself erect and gave the Enforcer an icy stare. "Your accusation is without foundation. I had no reason to murder my husband. It was done by men who are still walking around free. Instead of harassing me, you should be out there trying to find the real murderers."

"Don't worry; we will catch the ones who are guilty of the murder of Mordas. It may take a while but eventually we will be successful. We have ears and eyes everywhere and there are certain rumors floating around.

Be assured, everyone involved in his murder will be caught and punished."

"I can't wait for that day to come," Lironi said.

If the Enforcers caught her sarcasm they didn't react to it. Kaloss heaved a sigh of relief when they left. He didn't need the Enforcers snooping around in his business and private life. They were like tracking hounds. Once they caught their quarry's scent they stayed on the trail until the end.

Lironi seemed to read his thoughts. "They don't know anything. They are only fishing."

"How do they know about my wife already?"

"Probably from Lord Carn. He is obligated by law to report incidents like that to the Enforcers, mostly to divert suspicion from him." She pressed herself against him and he felt the heat of her body through the thin material of her gown. Her breasts lay soft against his chest and his body reacted to her nearness. She laughed throatily and moved her hand to his crotch. "Tonight," she whispered, "but for now be patient, my Love, and don't worry so much."

Chapter Five

CASTLE FALCONCLAW WAS LARGER than Rhodar had expected. Perched on top of a sheer cliff that rose twenty men-heights above the ocean on one side, it was framed by a wide river on the other side; the only easy access into the castle was the road from the city. However, the end of the road was blocked by a thick, wooden gate that boosted no less than ten burly warriors guarding it against any unwanted visitors.

"Castle Falconclaw is secure from attack by Lord Carn's enemies," Saleen said behind him with her uncanny ability to guess what he was thinking.

Rhodar chuckled. "Lord Carn has enemies?"

"Many," Saleen said. "However, Lord Carn isn't worried. The vertical cliff on the ocean side is too smooth to supply any intruder with hand and footholds, making it nearly impossible to climb, unless the intruder has suckers on the end of its extremities. The river is wild and turbulent at this location. Only suicidal fools would try to swim across it. Should they somehow succeed and reach the other shore without being smashed into the numerous rocks jutting out of the water, they would be stopped by a high wall constructed from huge boulders and topped with sharp crystals that would inflict serious wounds."

"A winged enemy could attack from the air," Rhodar suggested.

"There are guards with bows in the towers. No winged creature would reach the ground alive." Saleen sounded quite confident.

"Has anyone ever tried to invade the castle?"

"Not that I can remember. If it happened it was before my time."

"What about this sorcerer Kastabaan? Why is Lord Carn so afraid of him?"

"It isn't only Lord Carn who's afraid. Everyone is. Kastabaan is the evil nemesis of our Kingdom. A dark cloud hangs above Maridaan because of him. People, mainly children, disappear in the night never to be seen again."

"It seems Lord Carn is well protected behind these walls."

"No walls can keep Kastabaan away. He is a shapeshifter and can appear as anyone. It would not be difficult for him to enter Castle Falconclaw in disguise. Nobody would recognize him, not even me." She chuckled. "You could be Kastabaan for all I know."

"I can assure you I'm not. If I were and wanted to kill Lord Carn, I had plenty of opportunity. I'm curious, what can you do to protect the castle?"

"I can weave a protective spell around Castle Falconclaw not even Kastabaan can break."

"You have that much power?"

"I have." She spoke with a low, almost sad voice.

"You don't sound happy."

"I never asked for this power. I just want to live a normal life."

"The gods do not ask what we want, and they don't care if we are happy. We are their pawns, and they move us around as they please. The only thing we can hope for is to not arouse their anger and too much of their interest."

"How can we avoid that?"

Rhodar shrugged and chuckled softly. "Only the gods know the answer to that."

They had reached the gate and stopped behind Carn. The young lord spoke to the guard who scrutinized Rhodar. The guard nodded and turned to the two muscular men operating the gate and gave them an order. The gate swung open slowly as they worked the wheel that operated the heavy gate.

Carn turned and looked at Rhodar. "Welcome to Castle Falconclaw, Barbarian from the Great Plains."

Rhodar nodded. "Thank you for inviting me into your home, Lord Carn. I'm looking forward to meeting Lady Gardina, your mother. I understand she rules the castle."

A momentary frown clouded Carn's face as he glanced at Saleen. "You understand correctly. Even though many people assume I'm the Master of Castle Falconclaw, in reality it is my mother who controls most of the castle's business."

"I guess it could be worse," Rhodar said with a little smile.

"What could be worse than that?" Carn seemed annoyed.

"It could be a spouse or worse—a mistress who is controlling your life."

"I don't have either. Having a mother who sticks her nose into my affairs is enough." Carn actually managed a smile but it seemed forced. He turned away and clucked to signal his mount to move on.

"You should watch your tongue, Rhodar," Saleen whispered into his ear. "Lord Carn doesn't like to be mocked, especially not when it comes to his mother."

"Are you saying he has no sense of humor?"

"His sense of humor may differ from yours. He is a lord and grew up in different surroundings from yours. What you find humorous may offend him."

"I'll remember that." Rhodar laughed. "The Scorpion-spider finds it funny when a Sprite struggles in its web, while the little Sprite is filled with terror trying to gain its freedom. I understand your meaning."

"I hope you do. I wouldn't like to see your head separated from your handsome body."

"I wouldn't worry about that," Rhodar growled. "As long as I can swing my trusted axe Singar, it will be the heads of my enemies that will roll."

Behind them, the hinges of the massive gate screamed in defiance as the guards closed it.

"It is obvious Lord Carn is afraid of something," Rhodar observed. "My people do not hide behind thick walls. We live in the open, and we are afraid of nothing. We are the Serpent Clan and are protected by the

Stone Serpent. Our enemies fear us," he said proudly as he watched the group of Quinx trod past them.

The iron shoes of his horse clacked loudly on the cobblestones paving the courtyard. Buildings on either side of the courtyard provided residences of the castle staff and the stables for the riding animals. Beyond the courtyard, colorful flowerbeds and trimmed shrubs dotted an expanse of manicured green grass. A wide flagstone-covered path led to the castle.

"It must take many citizens and a lot of kaales to take care of this property," Rhodar commented.

"It does. The castle employs many people, but not all are paid. Many citizens of Falconview feel honored to donate their services to make Castle Falconclaw as beautiful as it is."

"Are you talking about free citizens or slaves?"

Saleen stayed silent for a moment. When she answered, she spoke with a low voice, "Nobody is ever wholly free. In many ways, we are all slaves."

"I am no slave to any master," Rhodar said, proudly. "I expect to get rewarded for my services."

"What kind of payment do you expect for rescuing me and bringing me here on your horse?"

"I expect no payment from you or anyone. Rescuing you was done out of my sense of justice and sympathy for a helpless girl who was in trouble and needed help. It was my decision, freely made." He chuckled. "I do make exceptions, especially when a pretty wench is involved."

"You think I'm a pretty wench? That doesn't sound very flattering."

"Just a choice of words. I meant no offense."

She slapped him gently on the arm. "I wish you would see me as a wench and not as some little girl, a child. I am no child. I may not be tall and have the face of a young girl, but my body is that of a grown woman. My breasts are full and firm and…"

"Stop this foolish talk," he interrupted her, harsher than he intended. "Did the Hogee kick you in the head before they violated your body?"

"You are an uncouth barbarian after all," she said with a small sob. "If you must know, yes, they hit me in the head and then they took my innocence. What is done is done. I refuse to let what they did to me break my spirit. I'm a woman now. Every male will look at me from now on with desire in their eyes and assume I'm available. Lord Carn is aware of it and I'd rather share your bed than his."

They had arrived in front of the castle. Saleen slid off the horse as soon as it stopped walking and stalked away without looking back.

Rhodar gazed after her, shaking his head. There surely was a hot fire burning inside the body of that little wench. It'd be a challenge to quench those flames.

A couple of stable boys came running to take care of their mounts. Nightwalker snorted when one of them grabbed the reigns. Rhodar patted the horse's neck. "It's alright, Nightwalker. Let them pamper you." He looked at the boy. "Talk to him in a calm manner and he'll behave. He's not used to being handled by strangers." He took a small coin from the pouch on his belt and handed it to the boy. "Make sure he gets fed and watered."

The stable boy took the coin eagerly and pocketed it. "Thank you, my Lord."

Rhodar laughed. "I'm no lord. My name is Rhodar. What do they call you?"

"I am Aarin." He grinned. "That's the name my parents gave me, but you don't want to know what some people call me." His eyes locked on the head of the battle-axe slung across Rhodar's back. "You must be a mighty warrior if you can wield a weapon like that."

It was Rhodar's turn to grin. "I'm not so sure about the mighty warrior, but I've had my share of battles that required the use of Singar."

"Singar," Aarin repeated. "I've heard of warriors giving their weapon a name." A look of admiration came into his dark eyes. "I wish I were a warrior."

"It's not as glorious as it sounds," Rhodar said with a chuckle. "I'd rather be a lord." His attention was diverted by Carn calling him.

"Rhodar, my mother doesn't like waiting."

"I must go," Rhodar said to Aarin. "Take good care of Nightwalker."

"You can count on me." The stable boy pulled on the horse's reins and Nightwalker followed him without making a fuss.

Rhodar watched for a short moment and then he turned to accompany Carn into the castle. Kalo, the little boy, walked beside Carn like a lost little sheep, but his face carried a brave expression. He was still young and would survive this.

Two warriors with drawn swords stood on either side of the entrance.

They saluted Carn by lifting one balled fist, but they eyed Rhodar with open curiosity.

Rhodar gave them a wide grin. "I've been invited."

The guards stayed silent, but he knew they were staring after him, probably wondering why Lord Carn would invite a barbarian as his guest.

The room they entered was fairly large. A few men and women sat at one long massive table, eating from wooden plates. It was obvious to Rhodar this was the castle staff. A fire burned in a big fireplace at the back of the room, warming the damp interior of the castle, but Rhodar found the air uncomfortably sticky and warm. Oil lamps on the walls lit the room with their flickering flames and added to the warmth. Much of the light was swallowed by the dark, rough stones of the walls. The odor of burning oil and the smoke from the fireplace lay heavy in the air. Rhodar took shallow breaths and hoped he wouldn't have to cough. He was used to the fresh air of the open grasslands. Even in the tents his people lived in the air was of better quality.

Carn stopped beside the table. "Arina," he called.

One of the older women looked up. "Yes, my Lord?"

"Come and take Kalo from me. You have looked after him before and he knows you."

The old woman got up and came closer. Carn bent and patted the little boy on the head. "You will stay with Arina for a little while until we can find someone to take care of you on a permanent basis."

The boy nodded. "What about my uncle?"

"I will inform him of your arrival." He gave Kalo a little slap on the shoulder and turned to leave.

Rhodar gave the boy an encouraging smile and then followed Carn.

They walked down a long corridor, passing a few rooms on either side. Cooking odors from one of them and the hot air escaping into the corridor told him it was the kitchen or one of the kitchens. Surely there were more in a huge complex like this one. Turning into another corridor, they stopped in front of a wide door.

The only guard standing on one side saluted. "Welcome back, Lord Carn. Lady Gardina is already waiting for your safe return. I hope your search was successful."

"It turned out well in the end," Carn responded. He turned to

Rhodar. "I must ask you to leave your weapons outside this room. My mother does not approve of weapons in her chambers."

Rhodar shrugged and pulled his axe out of its sheath. He put it onto the floor and then he removed the belt that held his two knives. "Anything else?"

"That will do," Carn said and gave the guard a nod.

Opening the door, the guard moved to one side to let Carn and Rhodar pass.

Expecting a small room, Rhodar was surprised by the size of it. It was obvious this was the private chamber of Lady Gardina. A wide bed in the center of the room drew his attention. The headboard displayed ornate carvings of naked men and women and the bed was covered with thick, fluffy pillows. Comfortable chairs and one couch for two people filled one corner. The walls were decorated with paintings of nude people frolicking in fields of colorful flowers and bathing in pools of water.

A woman wearing a long, flowing gown stood by one of the windows. She turned when she heard the creaking hinges of the opening door. She was not young anymore, but time had not erased her beauty.

Her full lips curved into a smile when she saw Carn. Then her eyes moved to look at Rhodar and her delicate eyebrows lifted in apparent surprise. "You are bringing a visitor, Carn," she said. "A barbarian judging by his appearance."

"This is Rhodar from the Western Plains," Carn explained. "He was instrumental in saving Saleen. I promised him a reward."

"So Saleen is safe?"

Carn nodded. "She is." He hesitated. "There is one thing, though. She has been violated by a Hogee. She isn't a virgin anymore."

"That is unfortunate." Lady Gardina closed her eyes for a moment. "What will you do now?"

"I'm not sure. According to folklore, she may not be of much use to me any longer. There is a good chance she has only limited powers now and won't be able to protect me from Kastabaan's spells. He is a powerful sorcerer."

Lady Gardina walked over to one of the chairs and sat down. "Come and sit for a while. I want to hear more about what you found, and I also want to learn more from your new friend. I am interested in the places he comes from."

Rhodar and Carn crossed the room to join her. The sounds of their footsteps were swallowed by the thick carpet covering the floor. It almost felt like grass under Rhodar's feet.

"Sit in that chair," she told Rhodar and smiled. "It is lighter near the window and I want to see your face clearly. My old eyes are not what they used to be." She took a small bell from a round table beside her chair and rang it.

Moments later, a curtain in the wall behind her parted and a girl rushed into the room. "Yes, my Lady?"

"Bring us a jug of wine and some biscuits, Kiiri," Lady Gardina instructed her. "And don't forget to bring three cups."

"Right away, my Lady." The girl threw an inquisitive glance at Rhodar before she rushed out again.

She came back within moments, carrying a silver tray and the ordered things. Depositing the tray on the table beside Lady Gardina, she filled three cups with red wine and handed one cup to Lady Gardina. She brought one to Carn and another one to Rhodar.

Her dark eyes looked at Rhodar with curious interest. "Would you be interested in a biscuit, my Lord?" She spoke with a little tremble in her voice.

"Of course, he is," the older woman said. "And he isn't a lord. He's a barbarian. Can't you see that?"

"Forgive me, my Lady." Kiiri threw another glance at Rhodar. "He could still be a lord."

Lady Gardina chuckled. "I doubt that. If you think you can seduce him, forget it. Your legs will stay closed tonight as far as he is concerned. Now leave us. I can serve those biscuits myself."

"Yes, my Lady." She walked slowly back to the curtained door, her hips swinging seductively. Before she parted the curtain, she turned and looked back at Rhodar, giving him a little smile. Then she was gone.

The older woman shook her head. "That girl does not know how to keep her legs closed. I'm surprised she doesn't have a stable full of children already. It is time she finds a suitable husband." She turned her attention back to Carn. "Now, tell me how your day went, my son."

Chapter Six

ONLY SEAL, one of the two night suns, hung like a shiny orb in the sky. Rumos, the second one, was hidden behind a bank of dark clouds. Not a good sign. Rhodar did not believe most of the myths old women dared only to whisper, but neither did he dismiss them. It never hurt to be cautious.

He took a small coin from his purse, put it to his lips and threw it out of the window. Then he closed the curtain to keep out the draft and the small flying creatures of the night. It had been a long day and he was tired. Looking at the bed in the corner, he wondered if it was as comfortable as it appeared. It might even be too soft, since he was used to sleeping on the hard ground or, if he was lucky, on a bed of straw.

He put out the only oil lamp and in the near darkness he lay down on the bed. Even though he knew there should be safety within the castle walls, his senses remained alert as he listened to the different sounds coming from outside.

The night was never silent. In the distance, a loud howl answered the challenging call of a night-hunter. Rhodar tensed for a moment until he realized where he was. He heard the fluttering whisper of wings outside the window, but he finally relaxed and fell asleep.

When he woke and opened his eyes, he saw a frame of light around the curtain that covered the window. He felt rested and slid from the bed.

Looking around, he discovered a bowl and a pitcher with water. Filling the bowl, he splashed a little water into his face and then he looked for a chamber pot. Even though he grew up in the open grasslands, he was not ignorant of civilized ways, having spent time in many towns and small cities during his travels.

Somebody knocked on his door.

"Come in," he called.

It was the girl Kiiri who came into the room. "Lady Gardina invites you to have breakfast with her." She let her eyes roam over his body, not hiding her interest. "Don't you have anything else to wear besides your kilt?"

"I'm afraid not," he said with a little grin. "Unless going naked is considered proper."

Her face colored a little. "Lady Gardina may not appreciate that, but I might. You have a little time before you have to meet her. Enough time for…" She smiled. "You know…"

Before he could answer, she grabbed the hem of her thin robe and pulled it over her head, revealing her nude body.

Surprised by her action, he stared at her young, well-formed figure.

"You don't like what you see?" she said coyly, striking a pose that pushed out her breasts.

Two long strides took him to her and he put his hand into the small of her back, pulling her close. Their lips met and she kissed him hungrily and with great passion. His hand moved lower and with both hands he grabbed her full buttocks and pulled her against him.

She giggled and pushed him away. "Take off that kilt," she said. "I want to see what you're hiding under there."

"*You* do it," he said with a chuckle.

With deft fingers, she undid his belt and pushed down his kilt. Gasping, she reached for him. "As I hoped," she breathed. "Everything about you is big. I want to feel that inside me."

"Not here." He lifted her and carried her to the bed. They tumbled onto it and he moved between her opening thighs.

"No need to be gentle, Barbarian," she whispered, her breath coming in great gasps. Then she writhed under him with the fierceness of a swamp-beast, raking his back with her fingers as passion consumed her hot body.

He was in no hurry and took his time, determent to enjoy every moment. She was agile and supple and, it was obvious to him, not innocent in the ways of lovemaking.

After a time, she spoke in a breathless voice. "I think we should end this before Lady Gardina gets impatient. Besides, you are wearing me out."

He chuckled, "I remember you saying we had plenty of time."

"I didn't expect you to last this long." She gasped again and lay trembling. "You are a tireless beast," she said after she quieted down. "But now you must stop."

"I'm not done."

"I'll give you enough time until you are."

He shuddered in her tight embrace and then with a deep sigh he left her and turned onto his back where he lay breathing hard.

She moved partially on top of him and looked into his eyes, smiling. "Are you finally satisfied?"

Her long hair caressed his face, and he closed his eyes, relishing the feeling of her warm, soft breasts on his chest. It had been awhile since he enjoyed the intimacy of a woman.

"I am," he said. "Are you?"

She bent over him and kissed him on the lips. "You did not disappoint me, but now I really must go." Slipping from the bed, she went and picked up her discarded robe.

He watched her as she put on her robe, admiring her slim but curvy figure. "You are beautiful," he said.

"Spare me the compliments. We better hurry or I will get reprimanded for being tardy."

Laughing good-humoredly, he got up and put on his kilt. "Lead the way, wench."

"My name is Kiiri," she said and walked toward the door.

Lady Gardina was already sitting at the end of a large table. Near her sat a big man who watched with narrow eyes as Rhodar came into the room. There were others at the table. Rhodar recognized only Carn. Beside the young lord sat a young woman. He noticed the similarity between her and Lady Gardina.

"You are late," Lady Gardina said with a chiding voice, looking at Kiiri.

Before the girl could make an excuse, Rhodar spoke. "It is my fault, my Lady. I was quite tired from my journey and last night was the first time I got a good night's rest. I'm afraid I wasn't ready to get out of my comfortable bed when Kiiri came in to wake me."

"I'm not going to ask how the girl woke you, Outlander, because I'm not sure I want to know. I am happy to hear you found your bed comfortable." Her gaze rested on Kiiri. "Just make certain you put clean sheets on his bed for tonight."

The girl bowed. "As you wish, my Lady. Is there anything else?"

"Yes, go and tell the cooks to serve the food. We are ready."

Lady Gardina sighed as she watched Kiiri rush out of the room. "If she weren't Latalia's daughter I would have sent her away a long time ago. Besides, I have a soft spot for her in my heart—only the gods know why. Perhaps because she reminds me a little of myself when I was young."

"I hope you don't mean you were as unrestrained as she," the big man beside her said in a surprisingly deep voice.

"I'm talking about her rebellious nature," Lady Gardina said. Then she turned her attention back to Rhodar. "Come, come. Take a seat." She pointed at one of the chairs. "There—sit beside my daughter Ronewa."

The young woman nodded to him and gave him a friendly smile when he took his place beside her.

Before he sat down, he took her hand and lifted it to his lips. "You must be Lord Carn's sister."

"Half-sister. My brother's father, Lord Caran, was killed in a hunting accident. My father was Lord Raxan."

"Was?"

She sighed. "He died of a mysterious disease when I was still a child. I never really knew him. Enough of me, tell me about yourself."

"He is a barbarian from the Western Plains—an outlander," Carn said from the other side of the table. "It should be obvious from his mode of dress." There was a disapproving tone in his voice. "You should have asked Kiiri for a piece of garment that covers your upper body."

"He looks just fine to me." Ronewa threw her brother a challenging look.

"Perhaps for tonight Kiiri can find him something suitable to wear," Lady Gardina said. "I will tolerate him this morning. After all, he is a barbarian. It seems he has some civilized manners after all. I noticed him kissing your hand, Ronewa."

The big man beside Lady Gardina cleared his throat. "How about introducing me to the outlander."

Lady Gardina patted his hand. "I guess we should. This is Lord Galoor, my consort. He also is Kalo's uncle."

"I've been told you saved my young nephew from the clutches of a family of Hogee. I am in your debt. The boy means a lot to me. Now that my sister is dead, he is the closest and only relative I have. What is your name again?"

"I am Rhodar."

"Rhodar," Lord Galoor repeated with a sudden far-away look in his face. "In my youth, I knew a man like you. His name was Rhor. He saved my life and we became friends for a short time. You remind me of him."

"Did he carry a battle-axe?" Rhodar inquired, curious.

"He did. It was an enchanted weapon and only he could wield it."

"That was my father. He told me stories about a friend he made during his travels, but he never mentioned your name."

Lord Galoor laughed. "I was young and with dreams of grandeur. We were both in a foreign land and I did not want anyone to know that my grandfather was Lord Galasan. Everyone knew and in many ways feared my grandfather. I won't go into details about that. I called myself Nandarin."

"I recall that name." Rhodar chuckled. "Those were some wild stories he told."

"I'd be interested in hearing some of them," Lady Gardina said.

"Those stories happened a long time ago in another Kingdom and are best forgotten." Lord Galoor gave Rhodar a warning look. "It would please me if you'd accompany me on a hunt. I hope you will accept my invitation."

Rhodar inclined his head. "Gladly. I am looking forward to some action."

"Typical males. Always in need of action." Lady Gardina picked up her cup and took a sip. "Let's drink this tirka-brew before it gets cold. I'd hate to have a good batch of those rare leaves go to waste." Turning to Kiiri, she said sternly, "Next time make sure the biscuits are warm when you serve them."

"They were hot when they came out of the oven, my Lady."

"That may be so, but they are cold now."

"Do you want me to take them back?"

Lady Gardina made an impatient gesture with her hand. "It is too late for that. We'll eat them the way they are now."

"I don't mind if they are cold," Lord Galoor said.

"Nothing surprises me." Her eyes searched Rhodar. "I suppose you and your people eat raw meat in the morning. Have you ever eaten biscuits and drank tirka-brew?"

"This might be of interest to you, Lady Gardina, but tirka-leaves are not rare where I come from. The young girls go out every morning to collect them, and—no, we don't eat raw meat, not in the morning or any other time. We do have fire, you know." He gave her an engaging grin.

Ronewa clapped her hands beside him and let out a delighted laugh. Then she put one hand casually on his upper arm. "It is refreshing to sit beside a man with a sense of humor."

"I saw no humor in that." Carn took a bite out of biscuit and made a face. "Mother is right. These biscuits are cold and tasteless."

"Just quit your complaining. What will our guest think?" Rowena took a biscuit, touched it with her tongue and then, with a wicked smile, she put it against Rhodar's lips. "Tell me if this isn't the sweetest biscuit you ever tasted."

He played along and allowed her to push the biscuit into his mouth. She did it slowly and before she pulled her finger out again she let it linger for a moment. He did not miss the meaning of that gesture. If anyone else noticed, they didn't comment.

"You can have more if you want," she said with a low voice and a sidelong glance.

"The offer is tempting, but sometimes it is wise to curb one's appetite." He emptied his cup. "Perhaps I could have another cup of tirka-brew. For some reason, I'm quite thirsty this morning."

Kiiri came rushing and refilled his cup. "I hope it is warm enough, my Lord."

"He is a barbarian not a lord. Why does everyone think he is some kind of highborn?" Lady Gardina sounded annoyed.

"Perhaps he is highborn," Ronewa suggested. "Has anyone bothered to ask him about that?"

"Why don't you? You are sitting beside him." Carn seemed amused by his sister's remark.

"You don't have to ask me." Rhodar gave Carn a challenging look. "We don't have lords and kings and princes or other fancy titles. My father is the Chief of our tribe and the High Chief of all the tribes that belong to the Serpent Clan."

"How many tribes are in the Serpent Clan?"

Rhodar didn't see any harm in telling them. "Over a hundred."

Carn laughed. "You mean you can count to a hundred?"

"Don't be stupid," Ronewa chided him. "As you can see, his father rules over a large number of people, which makes him equal to a king. Since Rhodar is his son he deserves to be called Prince Rhodar. He will probably be the next High Chief."

"I can never claim that title," Rhodar said. "Not in my tribe. I'm the youngest of three sons. It is my oldest brother Rhardon who will hold that position someday. I will always be just Rhodar in my tribe."

"I'll bet you are the strongest of them," Ronewa purred, touching his arm again. "I mean—with those muscles you can be nothing else."

"Now look who is stupid." Carn laughed. "Just because his body looks like that of a skinned swamp giant doesn't make him as strong as one."

"Enough of this foolish talk." Lady Gardina banged the handle of her knife against the table top. "Rhodar is our guest and we will treat him with the same respect we give any other visitor, lord or otherwise. I apologize if anyone offended you, Rhodar. You'll have to excuse me now. I have to prepare for tomorrow night's dinner party. I hope you can make it." She got up and walked away, followed by Lord Galoor.

Ronewa also got up from her seat. "It looks like it is just you and I, Prince Rhodar." Ronewa smiled wickedly. "You can be my consort for today. I've been dying to get out of the castle for a while but never had a reason to do that. Today I have one and I will show you our city."

"Don't fall for my sister's charms," Carn warned. "She is not the wonderful person she pretends to be. There is always an ulterior reason for the things she does and things usually turn out fatal for the person she does them to. She changes lovers like she changes her clothes, which is often."

"Don't listen to my brother. He is jealous of all the friends I have while he has none. It just so happens that most of my friends are men and I love to entertain them. That doesn't make me an evil person. Let me prove to you that I am the nicest woman you have ever had the pleasure to know." She came close to him and looked him in the eyes. "You won't regret keeping me company for a little while."

Rhodar registered the deep color of her violet eyes. He hadn't noticed it before. He also noted her extreme beauty. Spending time with her would not be a chore. "It will be my pleasure."

"Good."

Rhodar didn't miss the triumphant look she gave her brother. Neither did he miss Carn's displeased expression. It wouldn't be wise to have him as an enemy. "Perhaps you and I can join Lord Galoor on the hunt he is planning," he said to Carn.

"Lord Galoor and I are not exactly friends. We don't share the same interests. The only thing we have in common is my mother."

"Why don't you admit you don't like Lord Galoor," Ronewa said scornfully. "You would rather see her lonely than happy." She grabbed Rhodar's arm. "Come, let's go."

With a shrug, Rhodar followed her out of the room. They walked down a short corridor and then through a door into another corridor with a solid wooden door at the end. A thick iron bar prevented it from being opened. Just as they reached the door, a guard stepped out of an alcove.

"Open the door," Ronewa ordered him.

Without a word, the guard removed the iron bar and pulled on the handle of the door. It swung open with creaking hinges. Bright light flooded the corridor for a moment as Ronewa and Rhodar stepped through the opening. Behind them, the doors swung closed again.

"Why are we sneaking out of the castle?" Rhodar asked, looking around. They stood in a small open area surrounded by tall, massive trees. Smooth flagstones covered the ground where they stood. He could see a narrow trail among the trees.

Ronewa laughed softly. "I don't want anyone following us. My mother has her spies everywhere and she doesn't need to know where I go and what I do every moment of the day."

"Where are we going that you have to keep it a secret?"

"Don't ask too many questions. You'll see." She headed for the trail. "Don't worry; I'm not going to bite you. I'm quite harmless, no matter what my brother says."

"I don't worry about you, but I may be concerned with the people I'll be meeting. It wouldn't be the first time a beautiful woman tried to lead me into a trap."

"No trap, I promise." She walked briskly down the trail. It didn't take long before they emerged in what was clearly a garden. Flowers grew in abundance on each side of the path that wound its way through the flowerbeds. A few trees provided shade from the burning sun. The two wooden benches under the trees were empty.

The loud honking of a flock of large, white birds swimming in a pond drew his attention. Ronewa saw him looking. "Swails," she explained. "There are not many of these beautiful birds left. Apparently, their meat is a delicacy. I've never eaten one. Anyone caught harming one of them is severely flogged. My brother will see to that."

"Lord Carn enjoys hurting people, doesn't he?" Rhodar said it casually, not overly troubled with her possible reaction to his remark. It was plain to him that there wasn't much love lost between Ronewa and Carn.

"It seems you see right through him. You are correct. He revels in other people's pain. He is easily provoked and has a cruel streak."

"How about you? After all, you are his sister."

"Half-sister. Remember, we have different fathers. I'm not at all like him." She glanced at him. "I'm not certain he likes you. Be careful dealing with him. Just some friendly advice."

"I can take care of myself." Rhodar grinned wolfishly.

"I don't doubt that. Be careful nevertheless."

They left the garden path and walked across sandy open space. It seemed they were headed for one of the stables he'd seen the day before when they arrived at the castle. He was correct. One of the doors in the back opened and a young man came running. Rhodar recognized him. It was the stable boy Aarin.

"Lady Ronewa," he greeted them in a breathless voice. "Are you going into the city?"

"Yes, I am. Bring the carriage around but be discreet, as usual."

With a quick look at Rhodar, Aarin turned and ran back to the stable. A few moments later, he came around the corner sitting in the front of a small carriage drawn by a horse. Rhodar was surprised to see that it wasn't one of the Sekua, but he guessed the reason. The Sekua were not gentle animals; better suited for riding than pulling a carriage.

Ronewa pulled back the curtain and climbed into the carriage. Rhodar joined her and took the seat across from her. It was dark inside because curtains covered the small windows. The carriage began moving and he wondered where Ronewa was taking him. He didn't think she meant him any harm, but his animal instincts protested against sitting inside a dark carriage without being able to see the outside. He regretted not taking at least his knife. He felt naked without any weapons.

The carriage rumbled across cobblestones and Rhodar was grateful for the cushion that saved his buttocks and back. The rattling suddenly stopped and he knew they traveled on a dirt road, again wondering about their destination.

Then the carriage came to a halt.

"It seems we have arrived." Ronewa opened the curtain and jumped from the carriage. Before Rhodar followed her, he looked around. They had stopped in front of a tavern. By the appearance of the houses on each side of the road and the rundown look of the tavern he knew they were not in the best part of Falconview.

"Be back to pick us up at the usual time," she told Aarin.

The stable boy nodded and gave Rhodar a small sign with his hand.

Ronewa laughed merrily. "He doesn't need any magic spells for protection. I will take good care of him, don't worry."

Aarin smiled thinly, but Rhodar didn't miss the worried look on his youthful face. He watched the carriage pull away and head back the way they had come.

Ronewa pulled on his arm. "Come. This place may not look like much from the outside, but it offers great pleasures for people with unusual tastes. I promise you will enjoy yourself."

He followed her with misgivings. To enter a place like this without his weapons was a foolish thing.

Chapter Seven

THE INSIDE of the tavern lay in semidarkness. It took Rhodar a moment for his eyes to adjust. Surprised by the large number of patrons sitting at the tables at this time of day, he saw mostly scantily dressed women. Not all of them young. A few men loitered near the bar. Even they wore not much. At least he wouldn't stand out in his outfit.

Ronewa steered him toward one of the tables. It was occupied by three young women. They looked up when Ronewa approached and gave her a big smile. "We haven't seen you for some time," one of them remarked.

"Too many duties to fulfill," she said and chose one of the empty chairs.

"Who is your consort?" The woman looked Rhodar up and down, an appreciative smile on her painted lips.

"This is Rhodar from the Western Plains," Ronewa responded.

"A barbarian." The woman chuckled. "I've heard stories about them. Perhaps I should take him into my bed. I don't remember the last time I shared it with a man."

"I have other plans for you. Let a woman who enjoys a man's company more than you have him." Ronewa grabbed the woman's head and placed a lingering kiss on her lips.

"That tasted nice," the woman said when they broke apart. "You are right. I may not enjoy him as much as I do you. Let's go and play."

"Don't forget about us," one of the other two women said.

All four women rose from their chairs and left the table. Ronewa turned around and threw a small leather purse onto the table. "Entertain yourself," she called. "There is enough in there to buy any woman or man in this place."

He watched them heading for one of the doors in the back. "By the tail of the Great Serpent," he muttered under his breath. "This isn't turning out the way I expected. I thought she was attracted to me, but she prefers women to men."

"Hello stranger," said a voice beside him. "Looking for company?"

He looked up and into a pair of dark-rimmed eyes. At first, he thought it was an ugly woman until he realized it was a man. "Don't even think of sitting down," he growled, giving the man a piercing look.

The man sat down anyway, pulling his painted lips into a mock-smile. "Is that any way to treat someone who could give you an afternoon of great pleasure?"

"The only pleasure you can give me is if you leave before my fist connects with that ugly face of yours."

"Perhaps you prefer young boys?"

Rhodar bent forward. "Where I come from a man who lies with another man soon loses that desire to the quick stroke of a sharp knife."

"How barbaric." The man seemed genuinely horrified and hastily rose from the chair. "I can see you're not much fun."

Rhodar rose and walked to the bar. "A tankard of ale," he told the bartender and threw a couple of coins onto the counter.

Without looking at Rhodar, the bartender filled a giant mug with the dark, foaming liquid and pushed it toward him. He took a long swig. Putting the half-empty mug back onto the counter, he sighed. "Better than the finest wine," he said to no one in particular.

He turned when he sensed someone beside him and realized it was a woman who gave him a hopeful smile.

"Any chance you'll share some of that with me?" She was not as young as the three with Ronewa, but pretty enough to arouse his interest.

"Why not. More ale," he ordered and fished two more coins out of Ronewa's purse.

"I am Regani," she said. "What do they call you?"

He emptied his mug and studied her. "My name is not important. I'm not interested in spending time with a man or a woman. I'm going to drink until my money is gone."

"That would be a shame." The woman put her hand on his thigh and squeezed. "You will not regret spending time with me. I can give you much pleasure, because I prefer a man's company to that of a woman." Her hand moved under his kilt. Finding what she was looking for, she curled her fingers around his manhood. He reacted to the warm touch of her hand.

"Not here," he said hoarsely.

She laughed and took another sip from her mug. Then she pressed her body against his and rose onto her toes. Planting a kiss on his lips, she spoke in a whisper. "I don't live far from here. Let's go to my place."

He finished another mug and let her pull him out of the tavern, feeling relaxed and aroused. The house she lived in was nearby. It was small and shabby, but Rhodar didn't care.

"We are alone," she said and pushed open the door.

The air in the room they entered smelled stale, laced with cooking odors. There was an old sofa and a couple of chairs. He could see the kitchen through a door; a small wooden table stood in one corner.

She didn't give him much time to look around. Breathing hard, she lifted his kilt and touched him again. "Hurry," she moaned. "I can't wait much longer." Then she pulled her dress over her head and threw it to one side. She was naked underneath. Her full breasts sagged a little, but her belly was flat and her hips wide. He turned her around and made her bent over the back of the sofa. She pushed up her fleshy buttocks exposing her female organ. With a moan, he entered her.

He moved behind her for a long time, concentrating on her writhing body, and not paying attention to his surroundings. He became vaguely aware when the door opened behind him. The alcohol he had consumed slowed down his reflexes and made his mind dull.

When he turned his head to look at the door, he saw three burly men enter the room. They carried clubs and knives.

"What are you doing to my wife?" one of the men yelled.

Before Rhodar could react, they were upon him. With sluggish movements, he tried to defend himself, but it was useless. They hit him twice across the back. He stumbled and fell. Then things went dark.

When he regained consciousness, he hung upside down from a tree branch, his arms tied behind his back. His head still hurt. The last thing he recalled was the impact of a club against his head.

Then he grew aware of voices. Craning his head, he saw the three men who attacked him standing nearby. When they noticed that he was awake again, they came close.

One grabbed his hair. "How dare you fuck my wife?"

"I didn't know she was married," Rhodar defended his action. "She invited me into your home. I never questioned it. Besides, I was drunk."

"She told me a different story. She said you got her drunk and forced her to have sex with her."

"She's lying. That's not what happened."

"I don't believe you. My wife is a good woman. She would never cheat on me with another man, especially with a barbarian like you." He smashed his fist into Rhodar's belly.

"Let's cut his throat and end this," said one of the other two men, a brooding fellow with long, dark hair. He brandished a long knife.

"We will, but not before we make him suffer." The husband pushed the point of his knife into Rhodar's groin. "I think I'm going to cut off your organ and your bag." He moved the sharp edge of the knife forward but changed his mind. "Later. I don't want you to bleed to death —not yet."

"Let's talk this over like two honorable men," Rhodar said. "If you want money, I can get it for you."

The man laughed. "I already helped myself to that purse you carried. You have nothing else to offer."

"I'm a friend of Lord Carn."

"That's your misfortune if it's true, because it would be just another reason to kill you. Lord Carn is not popular." He kicked Rhodar in the chest.

"I'm getting tired of this. Cut his throat before somebody comes by and recognizes us," his dark haired companion said.

The man sighed. "You're right." He grabbed Rhodar's hair again and pulled back his head to expose his throat.

Before he could lay the blade against Rhodar's throat, a roar from behind him made him hesitate and turn around.

Things happened fast. A dark, hairy shape sprang at the man, throwing him to the ground. The knife fell from his hands and he let out a scream that ended in a gurgle. Blood squirted from his torn-out throat.

Rhodar recognized the animal. A treewolf.

The other two men crouched, brandishing their knives, fear in their eyes. The treewolf growled and circled them, exposing sharp, long fangs. It moved with lightning speed, attacking one of the men. Hitting his legs with full force, it felled him to the ground face down. Sinking its sharp teeth into his neck, he struggled only for a moment. Then he lay still.

In the meantime, the third man turned and ran away. The treewolf pursued him but came back to stand in front of Rhodar. It growled deep in its throat and studied him with yellow eyes. Suddenly, the outlines of its body began to blur, change shape and within moments a girl stood in front of him. A girl he recognized.

Saleen.

She picked up one of the knives and cut the cords that tied his arms together. "I can't reach that high," she said. "I'll have to climb the tree."

Fortunately, there were plenty of holds on the trunk to let her climb to the branch they had hung him from. He supported his body with his hands on the ground as she cut the rope. He landed on his feet and began rubbing his wrists.

After climbing out of the tree, she stood wide-legged in front of him with her hands on her hips. "What were you thinking having sex with another man's wife?" she demanded.

"She never said she was married. How was I supposed to know? Besides, I was drunk." He looked down at himself, realizing he was completely nude.

"If you're looking for your kilt, it's over there," Saleen said. Her gaze lingered on his manhood. "If you were this horny, there was no need for you to go to another woman. I offered myself to you. There would have been no consequences."

"I told you you're too young," he growled. "By the way, how did you find me?"

"Aarin told me about your outing with Lady Ronewa."

"It seems he isn't as discreet as he is supposed to be."

"He is my friend. We all know about Lady Ronewa's peculiar tastes. It isn't much of a secret." She watched him put on his kilt.

"What made you even suspect I might be in trouble?"

"I just had this uneasy feeling when I thought about you. Somehow it didn't feel right." She smiled. "Did you forget I'm a witch?"

"That still doesn't explain how you managed to find me here."

"You were seen leaving the tavern with a woman. It wasn't difficult to trace you steps. I confronted her and made her tell me where they took you. When I'm in my Were-form, I can follow any trail. You are fortunate I came just in time." She gave him a scolding look. "Perhaps from now on you'll be more careful when you get horny."

He laughed sheepishly. "I thought it would be Lady Ronewa who would entertain me with her favors. She made me believe she had an interest in me."

"Lady Ronewa likes to tease. Much of it is show." She made a face in apparent disgust. "What did you expect from her? After all, she is Lord Carn's sister."

"Half-sister. She assured me she wasn't like her half-brother."

Saleen's laugh mocked him. "Do you believe everything people, especially women, tell you? If you do you are a greater fool than I thought."

"Should I believe everything you tell me?"

Coming up to him, she looked him in the eyes. "You saved my life and I'm indebted to you. You and I have a special bond. I would never tell you lies or anything that might put you in harm's way." Her hand reached up to touch his cheek. "I care greatly for you, Rhodar, even though you're an uncivilized barbarian. Possibly that is the reason why. I know deep down you are not an evil person but a man with principles and respect for women. Those are qualities rare in many men, especially so-called civilized men."

"Perhaps civilization takes away those qualities," Rhodar said. "Honor and respect for everyone is very important to my people. The young respect the elderly and men respect women. Anything else would make us nothing but animals out of control." He bent and kissed her on the cheek. "I care for you too—like a brother cares for his little sister."

"Oh, you." She pummeled his chest. "I'm not your little sister, you big fool. I'm a fully developed woman with desires that have been awakened. I wish you would look at me with different eyes." She smiled suddenly. "I still believe there is a reason our destinies crossed paths. The gods move in ways we mortals cannot comprehend. You and I are not done with each other. There is still hope."

"You are a dreamer and put too much faith in gods nobody has ever seen." He walked over to one of the corpses and rummaged through the dead man's pockets. When he found the purse with his money, he pulled it out with a satisfied grunt. He also took the second purse the man carried. He'd almost died for this money which gave him the right to keep it.

"Now, tell me, how do we get home from here?"

"It is not far where Aarin is waiting for us with the carriage. We'd better hurry. It is almost time for him to pick up Lady Ronewa again. She doesn't like waiting."

She was right. It wasn't far to walk. Aarin greeted Rhodar with a happy grin. "You had me worried, big outlander. Nobody enters a tavern or even travels in that part of town without a weapon. You should have taken your big battle-axe."

Rhodar returned the stable boy's grin. "Advice that comes a little bit too late. Not taking a weapon was not my only mistake, but there is no shortage of fools and I'm one of them."

"Not keeping your satisfier under you kilt and sticking it between a married woman's spread legs was your biggest mistake," Saleen said scornfully.

'I never got a chance to get between her spread legs'. He kept that thought to himself and said, "I'm glad I have two friends I can trust, and I thank you for that and for the advice you're giving me. I made a mistake and I admit it, but let's not waste more time with that. I suggest, we pick up Lady Ronewa and return to the castle. I'm looking forward to a quiet evening and no more excitement for the rest of the time I'm staying here. I'll keep a low profile."

Saleen laughed. "I'm afraid that won't happen. Lady Gardina is planning a dinner party for tomorrow night. Those affairs are never relaxed and quiet."

"I remember her mentioning it this morning, but I was hoping to avoid it. I don't feel comfortable among a bunch of high-browed lords and nobles. I prefer the dancing and singing at the campfires under the open sky."

Rhodar closed his eyes as memories flooded back. He missed the simple life of the tribes. Had there been a choice, he would have preferred not to go on this quest, but his father urged him to go, even insisted. It was important to renew the spell that protected the big axe and it would teach him valuable lessons to prepare him for the position of one of the tribe's chief. The old chief, Rassan, was ailing and would step down soon. He had no heirs and since he was the second cousin of Rhodar's father, he requested Rhodar as his successor when his time came.

'You are like my own son, Rhodar. Since I have no heirs, I asked the gods to send me an omen. They have chosen you to take my place. I know you'll be a great and just leader. I see greatness in you not even your father is aware of, but I also see signs of recklessness. Be careful. Do not trust blindly and tread carefully. The world if full of evil; always remember that and be on constant guard'.

Rhodar smiled as he recalled with fondness the old chief's words of advice. Opening his eyes, he looked at Saleen who had been watching him silently. Not everyone was evil. There were still many good people around and he was lucky to have met at least two so far.

"Judging by your expression you must have been thinking of something pleasant. I hope it wasn't the married woman from the tavern." She tilted her head as if waiting for an answer.

He chuckled. "She's already forgotten. I remembered something someone I'm fond of told me. Today I was reminded again of his words."

When the carriage stopped, Saleen rose. "I will sit with Aarin in the front. If Lady Ronewa asks you what happened, you tell her you got lost and I found you. She knows about my talents and won't question it." She jumped out and he heard her get back onto the wagon to join Aarin.

Moments later, Lady Ronewa opened the curtain and climbed in. Taking her seat across from Rhodar, she gave him a questioning smile. "How was your day?"

He grinned. "Not as expected, as you can guess. Since you abandoned me, I was forced to look elsewhere for company. I met an exciting lady who took me home. It didn't turn out the way I planned, and I got myself lost in this wonderful city. I was lucky Saleen found me and brought me back. How was your day? Better I hope."

She stretched and yawned. "I had a wonderful day and I'm planning to take a long bath and then spending a quiet evening in my room. You can keep me company if you want."

"What a coincidence, I was also hoping to have a quiet evening. I am surprised you're inviting me into your room, since you have absolutely no interest in me or any man it seems."

She watched him with veiled eyes, like a snake watching an intended victim. "You have the wrong impression. Occasionally, I will take a man into my bed and I may even enjoy his fumbling—if I let him. You may just be that man, but tonight I want only your company." She closed her eyes. "I am exhausted and in need of rest. Don't feel you must entertain me with small talk."

"As you wish, my Lady. I won't bore you with my witty stories." He tried to hide his sarcasm.

It might be a good idea to follow her invitation. That way there was little chance for him to find himself in any trouble for at least the rest of the evening and the night. Tomorrow would be another challenge.

Chapter Eight

LIRONI REGARDED KORALLAS WITH GREEN, burning eyes.

Korallas stared at her naked body. "I won't even ask you how you got here so quickly."

She smiled wickedly. "The ability to change into a beast that runs at top speed without tiring has its advantages. Unfortunately, not everyone appreciates it. When my husband found out what I really was, I had no choice but to have him killed."

"How did he ever find out? You must have been careless."

"I admit I was not careful enough." She walked up to him and planted a kiss on his lips. "I came to thank Kastabaan for getting rid of that arrogant she-goat for me."

"It's me you have to thank, not Kastabaan. I'm the one who carried out the job."

"Then I thank you. Where is your master?"

"He is busy in the dungeons with his new creation. Besides, he is not my master. I am his apprentice and he is my teacher. Someday, I'll take his place." He chuckled evilly. "He is an old fool, believing he can control me with his spells. He doesn't know my full powers and that will be his undoing someday."

She laughed. "You're a devious man. That's what attracts me to you." She let her finger trail along his jaw. "I didn't come to waste my time talking. I need a man who can satisfy me for an afternoon. Are you that man?"

His hand shot out to grab her by the throat. "You know I am. You also know what I want."

"I know exactly what you want." The last word came out hollow and distorted when her mouth lost it shape and changed into a tooth-filled snout with long canines. Her body grew elongated and sleek. As she dropped to all fours, the shape of her arms and legs changed. She felt the long, furry tail growing from her buttocks.

Then she turned around to present her buttocks to Korallas. He stood and pushed his pants past his hips. Dropping to his knees, he moved behind her.

Looking back at him, she waited with anticipation for him to enter her inflamed sex-organ. On the outside, she might appear a wild beast, but inside she was still the same woman. Only her senses were enhanced far beyond that of a normal human. However, a necessary side-effect of assuming her beast form made her shed all her inhibitions and moral restraints. She also lost the ability to speak.

She let out a soft howl when she felt him enter and pushed back against him.

Nothing compared with the level of ecstasy she experienced when in her Wer-state. It was like a drug-addiction and her constant hunger was not easy to still. Only Korallas gave her what she craved, but she knew, eventually, she needed to find someone who shared her affliction, someone who kept her secret because he had his own secret to hide.

It was late afternoon when they finally exhausted each other and separated. Korallas gasped for breath beside her on the soft carpeted floor. Changing back into her human form, she lay beside him for a moment, her eyes closed. The feeling of joy and satisfaction would stay with her for a while, at least until she was back home. It would give her stamina and endurance to take the treacherous journey through the danger-filled forests that surrounded the castle.

"I must go," she said softly.

"I understand. Perhaps we can do this again soon?"

She smiled when she heard his weak voice. Korallas thought he was invincible and strong, but she always managed to bring him to his knees.

Rising, she slipped from the castle and into the forest, where she changed again into her Wer-form. Then she ran surefooted through the trees down the mountain, ignoring the thorny shrubs and tangle-vines that tried to ensnare her. Her clothing lay hidden in a small cave.

———

AS USUAL, Kastabaan was not happy. He wrinkled his nose in disgust and sniffed the air when he entered the room. "I can smell the stench of the Wer-beast, while the reek of your body is heavy and unpleasant in the air. At least have the decency to open a window when you decide to give up your restraints and roll in the dirt while satisfying your depraved desires. Or perhaps you should do it outside."

"Depraved is a matter of opinion." Korallas spoke with that tone of defiance he had been using lately.

Kastabaan did not remark upon it, but he filed it away for the future. He was beginning to suspect his apprentice. It seemed he was making plans that may not be in the best interest of his master and teacher. He was becoming more and more sarcastic and defiant in his remarks and actions. Kastabaan was glad he had never fully trusted Korallas since the first day he arrived at the castle and asked for permission to stay on as his apprentice. There was much the young upstart did not know about his master and he would stay ignorant of the true powers the old sorcerer controlled.

Korallas did have remarkable abilities and good control of the magic he used. He also had an affinity with animals. His mountain hawk was not tame as some might think. The hawk was a wild beast and had a taste for human flesh. It spent its nights hunting for young children, ripping them apart with its vicious beak and sharp talons. Only Korallas was able to curb its nasty disposition. Perhaps this affinity with animals also caused his depravity. That Wer-woman Lironi shared his perverted sexual tastes. They only coupled when she was in her beast-form.

It wasn't that Kastabaan's tastes were normal as far as humans were concerned, but then he wasn't exactly a normal human. Being a shapeshifter did not classify him as such. However, he did not consider himself depraved or degenerate—just different.

Korallas had been watching him with alert eyes and he wondered, not for the first time, if his apprentice could read his thoughts. He needed to create a spell to prevent such a thing from happening.

"I've been informed Lady Gardina is giving a small dinner party tomorrow night," Korallas told him. "I was thinking it would be a good idea if you and I went for an unexpected visit."

"I've changed my mind. I won't go to Falconclaw, but I want you to go. Find Saleen if she is there and bring her back with you. At the same time, you should try to get into Lady Ronewa's bed and between her legs. Then put the idea into her mind to poison her mother and her brother so she can rule over Castle Falconclaw. Once they are dead, it paves the way for you to become her advisor and perhaps her lover. Through you I will be the secret master of Falconclaw and the city of Falconview." Kastabaan smiled nastily. "It should not be difficult for you to do that. After all, you are a handsome specimen of a man with exceptional sexual prowess. Any woman will fall for that."

If Korallas was offended by it, he didn't show it. "What will you do instead?"

"The King's yearly summer festival is coming up in a few days and I shall attend. I have great plans for that bash." He chuckled gleefully. "It will be remembered for a long time. If you achieve what I hope and if I'm successful, there will be great changes coming in the Kingdom of Maridaan, and you and I will benefit greatly from it."

"It might help if you enlightened me a little?"

Kastabaan shook his head. "Discussing a plan too much and too often can easily lead to failure. In any case, I will have to improvise when I get there. I don't know what and who to expect and I will flesh out my plan as it happens. No need for you to worry about what I'm going to do. Concentrate on your job and make sure you succeed. It is important I gain control over the city of Falconview because of its strategic location and seaport."

Korallas bowed slightly. "As you wish. I will begin to make preparations. It would be best if I take only a couple of my men along. Nobody knows me in Castle Falconclaw as Korallas. If they did, I wouldn't be welcome. All they know about me is that I'm on a quest to find my lost brother. I've only been to the castle a couple of times and kept a low key."

"Excellent." Kastabaan nodded with a satisfactory smile. "I applaud your foresightedness. You never told me that about you."

"I may have a few of my own secrets tugged away," Korallas said, smiling smugly. Kastabaan raised his eyebrows. "Nothing important. Only minor things."

'I wonder what else you have not shared with me'. Kastabaan did not voice his thoughts but made another mental note to keep a closer watch on his apprentice. "I will be in my study for the rest of the evening perfecting a couple of spells I've designed. It is imperative I am undisturbed." Giving Korallas one more thoughtful look, he turned and walked toward the door. Before he walked through, he turned. "Air out this room. A person could faint in here."

Walking down the dark corridor, he pushed Korallas out of his mind. The young fool was too much taken with himself and his belief he might be a mighty sorcerer. He was becoming too confident in his abilities and so arrogant he did not see the traps that lay waiting. Magic was not to be toyed with nor treated as entertainment. It was dangerous in the hands of the fools that played with forces they did not understand. There was considerable knowledge Korallas still had to learn if he wanted to match the abilities of Kastabaan.

He was not about to teach his apprentice the most powerful spells, the ones that set him apart from the average wizard and town sorcerer. It took a different kind of mind to master those and an iron will to control them. Too many young warlocks tried to rush it and attempted to control forces they could not handle, resulting in horrendous consequences. Just as well. There was no room in the world for idiots and imbeciles.

The door to his study was locked and guarded by an Elemental. Nobody but Kastabaan could open it. Anyone unauthorized attempting to open the door would be hit with and held by a paralyzing spell until Kastabaan decided to release them. Which might be never.

The door opened automatically when he approached. "Enter, my Lord." The Elemental in the door spoke with a gravelly whisper. Its wooden pair of lips moved as it spoke.

Kastabaan walked into his room. "Encase the room with a net of protective spells," he ordered the Elemental. "Don't let anyone or anything disturb me, even you."

"It is done, my Lord."

"Good and now silence."

The Elemental was one of Kastabaan's creations. He had managed to trap a forest ghost and bind it to him with a number of complicated spells. Then he weaved it into the fabric of the door with another set of spells and made it a permanent fixture of his room.

He studied the door for a moment. "I should have given you a face instead of just lips. Perhaps someday I can remedy that omission."

The Elemental didn't comment, but he knew it was aware of what he said. It wasn't alive in the conventional sense, but it was a sentient being. Forest ghosts were pure energy and had a habit of invading living minds. That's when they were vulnerable and could be trapped by someone with the knowledge and power to do so, which meant only a powerful sorcerer was capable of such a feat. A powerful sorcerer like himself.

He cast off his robe, walked over to his desk and sank into his chair. Closing his eyes for a moment, he relaxed and cleared his mind. Here in this room he didn't have to pretend being someone he wasn't. As long as the Elemental did its job he was certain nobody would ever see him in his real body.

Holding the spell that kept his usual appearance solid was second nature to him and didn't require much energy, but there was no need to spend any energy when he was alone. Releasing his control on the spell, he relaxed completely and heaved a deep sigh. His body changed back to its original state. It felt good to be just himself.

He didn't need a mirror to see what his body looked like. Studying his bony, long-fingered hands, he flexed them slowly, watching the dark veins and blotchy skin. Time left its mark on everyone if they lived long enough. He had lived a long time. His youth lay shrouded in the far past. The memories he had felt like someone else's memories.

The surface of the oil lamp on his desk reflected his white, leathery face. It looked dead and showed no expression. The only thing alive in his face were his deep-sunken eyes. They glowed with dark and cold fire. He moved one skeletal arm to change the position of the lamp.

Nobody had ever seen him in his real form, not even Korallas. Even though his apprentice was aware of Kastabaan's shape-changing abilities, he had no idea that the man he saw was not the real Kastabaan.

He rose from his seated position and walked over to the bookcase. Removing a thick, leather-bound volume, he carried it back to his desk and opened it carefully. Most of his books were old, handed down for generations by the sorcerers in his family. Some of them held spells that should have been burned along with the books. They were dangerous in the wrong hands. Used by an unscrupulous sorcerer, they could cause chaos and destruction. Even Kastabaan shied away from some of them. He opened these books only in his study. It was protected by powerful spells that would stop anything from escaping through the walls and into an unsuspecting world.

Taking a stick of lavender-root chalk from its container, he drew a symbol on the tiled floor. Then he laid the open book in its center and began to chant from the open page. At first nothing happened, but then a faint mist rose from the page and swirled like a spiral toward the ceiling, slowly growing in size and thickening until it was a solid-looking mass.

It kept on swirling, changed from a gray coloring to a multitude of different colors until it finally settled on mainly red and yellow with a few lesser colors for accent. The mass seemed to boil and roil inside and shape itself into a humanoid body with arms and legs and a shapeless head. Finally, a face started forming, becoming more detailed until a set of large eyes, a flat nose and a pair of thick lips were clearly visible.

The eyes stared at Kastabaan and the lips opened to reveal a set of flat, large teeth. "Who dares to enter the world of my dreams?" The voice sounded rough, garbled, and clearly unhappy. While the creature spoke, the rest of its body finished forming.

Kastabaan studied the naked demonic figure. According to the description of the spell, the demon's name was Arklahahn. He was just a minor demon and not too powerful, but still powerful enough to wreak havoc should he get out of control.

"I have need of your services," Kastabaan said.

"They come with a price."

Kastabaan had done his research. "I have what you crave and am willing to pay the price."

Arklahahn regarded him silently. "What do you want done?"

"It's not what I want done. I want a spell to create a demon-horse."

The demon's laugh mocked him. "A demon-horse cannot exist in your world."

"Perhaps I should rephrase. I need a spell I can use to change an ordinary horse into one with magical powers; one that doesn't get tired and can run twice as fast as any other horse and never needs to get fed. The only thing needed is a small portion of a demon's spirit. Can you provide me with such a spell?"

The demon seemed to think it over. "I believe I can, but beware, there are always dangers attached with such a spell."

"I am aware of the dangers and prepared to deal with them. Just get me the spell."

A shiny object appeared suddenly in Arklahahn's hand. He flicked it into the air. Hovering between Kastabaan and the demon, it began to glow and then bright flames erupted from it. After a few moments, the flames died down and a vial shot out of the circle that held the demon and cluttered to the floor.

"You will find the spell inside. Now, bring me what I crave." Arklahahn's eyes glowed with a sudden fire and when he opened his mouth long canines gleamed in the light from the oil lamps.

Kastabaan rose and walked to a door in one of the walls and opened it, revealing a small closet-sized room. He reached in and pulled out a naked young child—a girl. She had her eyes closed and seemed to be in some kind of trance. When he touched her, she opened her eyes and looked at him.

Then she screamed.

He dragged her to the circle and pushed her toward the demon. Arklahahn grabbed her with clawed hands and pulled her to him. Then he disappeared with the girl clasped in his arms.

Kastabaan picked a sponge from his desk and with slow motions he wiped away the markings on the floor. Then he picked up the old book of spells, carried it to the book case, and put it back into its place. The shiny vial lay still on the floor. He took it and laid it on his desk. He would study the spell later.

Suddenly tired, he decided to call it a night. Approaching the door to his room, he said, "I am finished for the day. Lock up behind me and make sure nobody gets into the room."

The door opened and as he walked through, the Elemental spoke with its gravelly whisper. "Good night, Lord Kastabaan. I will stand guard."

Chapter Nine

LYING ON THE WIDE BED, Ronewa stretched her lithe body and turned onto her belly. She watched him with half-lidded eyes as he fastened his belt around his waist. "Did I please you last night, Barbarian?"

A couple of long strides took Rhodar back to her bed and, with a wide grin, he slapped her plump, round buttocks. "I think you mean if I pleased you. What do you care about my happiness? Especially since you don't even like men."

"I never said I don't like men. Even though I prefer women, I'm not against taking a man into my embrace and letting him enter my body." She smiled. "Especially one as well-endowed as you."

"Lucky me, then. If you must know, yes, you did please me. How can you not? You are as beautiful as a flower in spring and as wild as a thunderstorm after a hot and muggy day when you couple."

She laughed, obviously pleased at something. "You are full of surprises. Are you certain you are not a storyteller or a scribe?"

"I am neither, but telling stories is part of our tradition. They keep the memory of our ancestors alive. I hope someday they will tell stories about me and my exploits." He chuckled. "I'll make certain your name comes up. Of course, that means I'll have to share your bed a few more times just to make sure." He jumped back when she kicked at him with one foot. "It seems I've overstayed my welcome. I'd better leave."

Laughing, he walked out of the door. Even though Ronewa had not given him much opportunity to get any rest, he was not tired. He knew if he kept up these strenuous episodes, eventually it would catch up with him but not today. Since he felt ravenously hungry, he headed for the community kitchen.

The servants threw him curious looks when he took a seat at the table. He smiled at the old woman across from him and said, "I am Rhodar. I am Lord Carn's guest."

"Armina, that's my name. Welcome at our table. Shouldn't you have breakfast with Lady Gardina?"

"I was not invited this morning. Besides, I don't feel comfortable among lords and ladies." He reached for the breadbasket on the table and picked up a small loaf of bread. Breaking off a piece, he shoved it into his mouth. "Much tastier than those biscuits," he said around a mouthful.

The man beside the old woman nodded approvingly. "I've never cared much for those biscuits, either."

"You old fool. You'd be so lucky to even get a chance to taste them," Armina chided.

The man laughed, looked at Rhodar and smirked. "I'd feel even luckier if I'd get the chance to spend a night in Lady Ronewa's bed."

"Hold your tongue." Lifting her hands in an apologetic gesture, Armina looked at Rhodar. "Don't listen to him. He's not right in his head. I hope you don't mention his remark to Lady Ronewa. She doesn't like gossip, especially about her person."

"I don't even remember anymore what he said." Rhodar turned his head a little and gave the old man a wink, making certain the woman didn't see it. "Do you have anything else but dry bread to eat?"

"There is a counter over there where you can get meat and eggs." The woman pointed. "There is also a jug of Larn-milk to wash down that dry bread."

Rhodar got up and walked over to the counter. He used his knife to slice off a piece of meat from the roast. Instead of Larn-milk he filled a cup with clean water.

When he walked back to his place, a young man stopped him. "Aarin told me all about you. He said you were his friend. Is that true?"

"It's true. He's looking after my horse."

"Are you a real barbarian from the Western Plains?" The young man regarded him wide-eyed.

Rhodar chuckled. "The Western Plains are my home, but we don't call ourselves barbarians."

"But you look so...so big. I mean you are nothing but muscles. How did you get so big?"

"We start building our bodies when we are still small. We have tests of strength, we practice with weapons every day, we run and jump and push our bodies to the limit. Eventually, this is the result. I am not unique among my people. We do not sit around and let our bodies waste away and get soft." He grinned. "That is not the way of a barbarian."

"But you said you're not a barbarian." The young man seemed perplexed.

"Maybe I'm after all, but now I must finish my breakfast before I collapse of hunger and lose all my strength." Chuckling, Rhodar returned to his seat.

"There you are," said a familiar voice behind him.

Rhodar turned in his seat and looked at the girl. "Kiiri," he blurted out. "I haven't seen you since yesterday."

"You actually remember my name and didn't call me wench. I've looked for you this morning but you weren't in your room." Her tone seemed to accuse him of having made a terrible blunder.

"I was otherwise engaged," he said, feeling guilty for some unexplained reason.

"Lady Gardina wondered why you didn't have breakfast with her today. She expected you. She is giving a dinner party tonight and she commands you to attend."

"Will you be there?"

"I'll be there for a little while to serve drinks and the food. After that I have plans for tonight." She gave a little laugh. "I'm looking forward to that."

"I hope you'll have more fun than I'll be having," Rhodar said.

"I will, don't worry. I'll be entertaining Applar. His father is a guest at the castle. He is from Dragona." She giggled. "It's a secret, because Applar is not supposed to consort with commoners. Please, don't tell anyone. Oh, by the way, Saleen wants you to meet her down by the stables. She says it's important." With that she turned and rushed away on light feet.

"Pretty girl," the old man said, looking after Kiiri.

"Forget about climbing between her legs," Armina scolded. "Have you forgotten how old you are? She'd squeeze the life right out of your limp snake."

"One can dream," the old man apologized. "Besides, I'm not that old that I couldn't take on a little She-demon like her."

Armina laughed. "Dream on, Aargon, old fool. I'll remind you of that tonight when you lie beside me and moan about the pain in your bones."

"Which would go away if you would massage me a little." Aargon looked at Rhodar. "Don't ever get married, young man. In the beginning, you can't satisfy them and in later life they won't satisfy you."

"Quit complaining, old man. You wouldn't survive the night if I'd actually let you have your way. You have no idea what ferocious swamp-beast you might awaken inside me." She gave Rhodar a mischievous smile. "If I were as young as Kiiri I'd show you that beast, but now it is best we let it sleep." She rose. "We'll have to get back to our chores. Enjoy breakfast and the rest of the day, especially tonight's dinner party."

Rhodar nodded and finished his meal. He wasn't looking forward to the party. There'd probably be a number of lords and their ladies he'd have to meet and the whole evening would be boring. He'd rather spend it with simple people like Aargon and Armina.

When he finished eating, he went outside and headed for the stables. Nightwalker probably missed him already. The high-spirited animal was more than just a steed. He and his horse had been constant companions since he left the Plains and the bond between them was strong.

He looked into the brilliant sky. It would be another hot day. Possibly a good day to go on a hunt with Lord Galoor. It would give Nightwalker an opportunity to run off some of his pent-up energy and also help Rhodar. Being stuck inside these walls made him restless.

Aarin was busy rubbing down Nightwalker and the horse didn't seem to mind at all. It whinnied when Rhodar approached. Aarin looked up from his chores.

"I think he likes me," Aarin said.

"It seems that way. Nightwalker is intelligent and he knows when someone is concerned with his wellbeing." Rhodar went up to the horse and patted its neck. "Sorry, old friend. I have neglected you. I'll make it up to you soon." The horse moved its head up and down as if it understood and whinnied again.

"I'm supposed to meet Saleen here," Rhodar said.

"Not here." Aarin smiled wistfully. "That girl—she is strange and she has a secret, but I can't figure out what it is. She doesn't talk to many people. She told me once in confidence her mother was a witch and her father a Quinx. An odd combination. I figure she must be a witch too, even though I haven't seen any evidence of that. I've wondered many times what she's actually doing here, other than that Lord Carn seems to like her."

"Does she ever talk about her relationship with Lord Carn?"

"Never. Except one time she said she'd wish she could leave the castle but she can't. Lord Carn won't let her. I don't believe their relationship is sexual, if you know what I mean."

"It isn't. She told me so herself. According to Lord Carn, he feels responsible for her and regards himself as her guardian."

Aarin nodded somberly. "That would explain why she spends an awfully long time in the castle sometimes."

"So where can I find her?"

"There is a small hut hidden away in the back of the garden where young people go at night to—you know. Wait for her there. She'll find you. Follow the main path. Just before it ends, there is a narrow, almost overgrown trail on your right. Take that and it will lead you there." He smiled. "You're a barbarian. It should be no feat for you to find the place."

"I'll find it. Thank you, Aarin. By the way, thank you for picking me up last night."

"Thank Saleen. She was the one worried about you, and she knew where to find you. She likes you."

Rhodar gave Nightwalker another pat on the neck and then he headed for the garden path. It didn't take long before he discovered the hidden trail and he found the hut without great difficulties. Nestled under a couple of huge wide-spreading trees it was a perfect place to hide away from prying eyes, even though it wasn't much of a structure—four open walls and a roof. There was a wooden bench inside and a narrow cot.

Saleen wasn't there, so he sat down on the bench and waited.

His keen hearing picked up her footsteps before he could see her. She was a little out of breath when she appeared between two tall shrubs. When she saw him, she smiled and stepped inside the hut. "I've been running," she said and seated herself beside him. "I'm glad you came."

"What is the emergency?"

"No emergency. I just wanted to talk to you about what happened yesterday."

He touched her hand. "You saved my life and I am indebted to you. That's what happened."

"I only repaid a debt I owed you. Now we are even." She stared at him with her green eyes. "When I was still a virgin I could not change my body, but that all has changed. Now I'm a real Wer and today for the first time I became a Treewolf. You are the first person to see me in my beast-form. I killed two men in cold blood—ripped out their throats. How can I live with that?" She put her hands over her face. "I am not a coldblooded killer."

"Of course you're not, but you will have to face the truth eventually and accept who and what you are. From now on your life will never be the same again. You did not kill wantonly. It happened out of necessity. You did it because you rescued a friend from certain death. You had no choice."

Putting an arm around her shoulder, he pulled her close. "I have killed men out of necessity while defending myself. I don't consider myself a murderer or coldblooded killer. We live in a hostile world inhabited by evil men, ferocious beasts, and things nobody can explain."

"But why was I cursed with this affliction? I wish I were just a normal girl. I'll never be able to live a normal life, like marrying someone like Aarin."

"He is your friend, isn't he?"

She nodded. "He is, but we will never be anything else. If he knew what I am, he would fear and even shun me." She stroked his chest with her fingers. "What about you. Now that you've seen me as a beast, how do you feel about me?"

"Why should I feel any different? To me you're still the pretty girl I rescued from the clutches of the Hogee. That will never change."

"You don't find me repulsive? A horrible abomination? Someone you'd want to dispatch of with your battle-axe?"

He laughed softly. "You have nothing to fear unless you want to rip out my throat. Then I might have to smash in your skull."

"I would never attack you," she said vehemently.

"I know. That's why I don't find you abhorrent. You will always be just Saleen, a beautiful girl for whom I care."

"If you really care for me, help me escape from here," she blurted out and moved out of his embrace.

"We've been through this before. Where would you go with me? I'm a wanderer. My only quest right now to restore the magic in my battle-axe. When I'm not the guest of some lord or in bed with a willing wench, I sleep under the stars. I eat when I'm successful in my hunt, otherwise I go hungry. My food is plain and simple. You don't fit into that kind of life."

"I could be useful, like helping you with the hunt. Remember, I am part beast. I can adjust. Someday you'll go home to your people. You could take me there." She lowered her eyelids and smiled. "I would be a grateful mate to you. You said you like me."

"I do and find you most attractive. Perhaps too attractive and that is part of the problem. You are still so young." He took her small hands into his big ones and looked her in the eyes. "You'd begin to hate me because I can't provide you with the normal life you seek. I hope you understand."

"Then take me at least to Jandarin or Grahna. I could start a new life there. Even without you." Her face and eyes pleaded with him.

Letting go of her hands, he sighed. "I don't know how long I'll be staying here. Let's wait and see what happens. If there is a way I can take you with me, I promise I will."

She bent forward and gave him a quick kiss on the lips. "That's good enough for me—for now. You spent last night with Lady Ronewa. What does she have that I don't?"

"She's older."

"You realize you are nothing but a plaything for her. Everyone knows she doesn't like men."

"She could have fooled me. Besides, are there no secrets in this castle?"

"Very few. There are spies and watchers everywhere and gossip travels fast. Why do you think I wanted to meet you here, away from everyone?"

"Lady Gardina is giving a dinner-party tonight. Will you be there?"

She shook her head. "I'm merely a servant and not of noble blood. I've never been invited."

"I was under the impression you are important to Lord Carn."

"Until now I was." She shrugged. "In light of what happened to me, he may cast me aside."

"Then you'd be free of him. Isn't that what you want?"

"Lord Carn will never set me free. I'll just be another slave to be used at his pleasure. I fear what that pleasure will be."

"He can command any girl he wants into his chambers. Most of them would be more than willing," Rhodar protested. "Why would he want a girl who is not willing to share his bed?"

Her laughter sounded almost ugly. "Because he finds pleasure in hurting people. He would be pleased to violate my body and break my spirit." She rose from the bench. "I'll go now. Be careful tonight." She blew him a kiss and ran away back into the bushes.

"How can I find you if I need you?" he called after her but she was gone.

He stayed on the bench for a little while, thinking about what she told him. Then he got up and slowly walked down the trail to the main path. The sun had risen higher into the sky and it was growing hot.

"Did you find Saleen?" Aarin said when Rhodar searched him out again.

"I did and we talked. Tell me, do you consider yourself a slave? If you wanted to leave here, would you be free to do so?"

"I've never given it any thought. I live here in the castle and I look after the animals. This is my home. I have no reason to leave. Besides, where would I go? I have no family anywhere."

"What about the other servants? Do all of them live at the castle?"

"Most of them. However, many go home to their families on occasion. Nobody forces them to stay. Why do you ask?"

"Just curious." Rhodar shrugged. "Life here is so different from the Western Plains. We don't have big cities or even large castles like this one."

"Do you live in houses?"

"There are villages with permanent homes where mostly the older people live. Our homes are simple wooden structures. Many tribes are nomadic, living in dwellings that can easily be moved."

"That sounds primitive." Aarin shook himself as if to ban an uncomfortable feeling.

"It is our way of life. We follow the big herds across the prairie the way our ancestors have done as long as anyone can remember. The animals know where the water will be. Water means life."

"Why not settle near a large river or a lake?"

"That's where the permanent settlements are. When our people get too old and feeble, they stay in those settlements. Sometime even younger ones decide that being constantly on the move is not what they want and they will join the old people."

Aarin tilted his head, obviously curious. "Who looks after the old people?"

Rhodar chuckled. "Just because they are old doesn't mean they are useless. Many have skills like metalworking or pottery or weaving clothes which they still practice."

"What about the women? Don't they get tired of always moving?"

"Our women are tough not soft like those living in cities."

"It they are so tough they must be ugly."

"Our women are as beautiful as the flowers that cover the prairie in the summer. Tough does not mean ugly, my curious young friend."

Rhodar looked into the sky. Fluffy clouds were beginning to rise in the north, suddenly reminding him of younger days when he used to lie on his back in the high grass and watch the clouds, wishing he could travel with them on their journey across the sky. He missed those quiet, carefree times when he spent his summer days dreaming of adventures in foreign countries on the other side of the mountains.

The day to leave his home came when his father bequeathed him with the quest to restore the magic to his old battle-axe. "Why me, Father? Does not Singar belong to Rhardon? He is the oldest and your successor."

His father had taken him aside and put his arm around his shoulders, which he hadn't done for a long time. Not since he was a young boy. "Listen Rhodar. You may be the youngest of my sons but you are also the smartest—even though you are a dreamer. Your brother will make a great chieftain. He is strong and brave and the tribe will listen to him, but he doesn't have your imagination or your desire to travel the world—the way I did when I was your age. Only you are up to the task. You need to get those dreams and desires out of your system. When you come back you will be ready to take over the position as chief of the Riverstone tribe. I only hope Old Rassan lives that long."

His father's words haunted him sometimes at night. He had burdened him with a great responsibility, as had his uncle. He didn't know if he wanted to become a chief. It had never been one of his dreams.

"Is there one of those tough and beautiful girls waiting for you when you get back home to your people?"

Aarin's question ripped him out his deep thoughts and brought him back to reality. Shaking his head to chase away the cobwebs, he managed a small chuckle. "I'm as free as the Prairie-Eagle drifting with the currents in the morning sky. Like the giant bird of prey is searching the land below for prey to satisfy its hunger, but not knowing what exactly it is looking for, I am hoping to find my fortune and my destiny in whatever form the gods have planned for me. Like the Eagle, I don't know what I'm looking for and what I will find."

"At least you have a goal and your destiny. I don't have such a thing. I will always be taking care of the animals. I think the gods, if they exist, have forgotten about me." Aarin's voice seemed as sad as his expression.

"The gods won't even notice you unless you take your destiny into your own hands," Rhodar said. "They will not take you by the hand and lead you. You must be the one telling them what you want and expect and you must make the first move. After that, they may help you; usually, when you least expect it."

Aarin stared at Rhodar with wide eyes. "Not only are you a warrior but also a wise man. Listening to you lets me imagine those old teachers sitting at the street corners and telling their stories to anyone who wants to listen." He sighed. "Most of them are beggars."

"Wisdom has never made anyone rich." Rhodar smiled. "A real wise man doesn't talk much about things like this for fear he may be taken for a fool. Besides, those are not my words. They were told to me by one of the Elders in my tribe. I was always a good listener and I have a good memory. You see, I'm not so wise after all." He gave the young man a thoughtful look. "I'd like to take Nightwalker for a run. I could use a guide. Can you get a steed and accompany me?"

Aarin thought for a moment and then he nodded, suddenly eager. "I believe I can do that. Let's go and look for one."

Chapter Ten

GARDINA SAT in her throne-like chair and watched her guests trickle into the room. As usual, she had gone a bit overboard with the food and the decorations, but she found pleasure in impressing people.

Galoor sat beside her in a chair smaller than hers. After all, it was her castle and he only her consort. It was important to her that people knew she was the Mistress of Castle Falconclaw; not Galoor and certainly not her son Carn. She looked for Carn and found him engaged in conversation with a woman she had never seen before and she wondered who it could be. Was it possible that her son had finally found interest in a woman? She couldn't help but notice her extreme beauty.

She bent toward Galoor. "Do you know the woman talking to Carn?"

Galoor shook his head. "I've never seen her before."

"Find out. I am interested in meeting her. Something about her intrigues me."

Galoor rose from his seat and strolled toward Carn and the strange woman. Gardina watched as he reached them and talked to them. Both, Carn and the woman, turned to look at her. A moment later, Galoor came back, accompanied by the woman. Carn stayed behind.

Watching them come closer, Gardina realized the woman was quite tall. She walked easily, like a forest cat, with slightly swaying hips and her head held high. Her long blond hair fell past her bare shoulders. The silky, red dress she wore had been sewn to accent her curvy, slim figure. It was easy to see she did not come from common stock.

The woman gave her a relaxed smile, almost as if they were old friends who hadn't seen each other for a while. Her eyes flashed with green fire when she looked at Lady Gardina., "I am Lironi, my Lady," she said, inclining her head.

"Lironi," Gardina repeated. "I don't recall your name on the list of invited guests."

The woman laughed softly. "I'm afraid I wasn't on your list for tonight. You'll have to blame your son, Lord Carn, for my coming here. He gave me a standing invitation. I thought tonight would be as good as any other night."

"How do you know my son?"

"I don't really know him. We only met a few days ago. I'm a friend of Ship-builder Kaloss. I was there when your son delivered the awful news of Lady Arneena's murder. Such a terrible tragedy. Kaloss finds it difficult to accept his wife's death. He loved her very much."

"All of us were shocked by Lady Arneena's murder. She was Lord Galoor's sister. I'm sure you are aware of that. She was very dear to us. However, such are the ways of the gods. We don't question them. Tell me, why would my son invite you to the castle?" Gardina prodded.

Lironi shrugged. "I didn't ask or question. When a lord invites me to his castle, I would be foolish not to accept."

Gardina lifted one shoulder in a gesture of resignation. "My son must have his reasons for inviting you. Since you are here you might as well enjoy my hospitality." She looked away, dismissing the woman.

Lironi turned to leave, when Galoor spoke. "Did you know my sister well?"

"No, I didn't. We spoke on occasion but never on a personal basis. My business was with Kaloss."

"What kind of business, if you don't mind me asking?"

"Not at all. My late husband was a fur trader and I am keeping his business going. I asked Kaloss to fix up the old boat my husband left me so I can take it up the river to the fur trading post in Kalsatan."

"What was your husband's name?"

Lironi hesitated for a barely noticeable moment before she said,

"Mordas. His name was Mordas. He was murdered, presumably by men he cheated. To my shame, I must admit my husband was a rogue."

"I know of Mordas. I traded some rare furs with him and he gave the impression of an honorable man. I'm sorry to hear of his demise." Galoor sounded sincere, but he was always one who didn't judge hastily and was prone to give people another chance.

Gardina did not always agree with him, but fortunately it was usually her decision and not his when it came to dealing with men who were accused of a crime. "You may have been one of the lucky ones, Galoor," she said. "A wife usually knows her husband better than anyone."

"But nobody deserves to be murdered," Galoor protested.

"Of course not, no matter what the reason. Now, let Lady Lironi go and mingle. We have other guests to greet." She made no secret of the woman's unimportance to her.

"I thank you for your graciousness, my Lady," Lironi said and turned away.

Gardina waited until she was out of earshot before she spoke. "Something about that woman doesn't feel right. I hope she doesn't cause trouble."

"She's just a beautiful woman," Galoor said. "The only trouble she can cause is that she'll snare an unsuspecting male guest who should know better."

"As long as it isn't you." Gardina laughed and looked at the man who was approaching. He was short and rotund with a red face from consuming too much wine.

"Merchant Colassa," she said. "How are you enjoying Castle Falconclaw and our fair city Falconview?"

Colassa made a bow. "You've been a wonderful host and still impress me with your talent for entertaining and your exceptional taste." He chuckled. "Especially your well-stocked wine cellar with those superb wines."

"You seem to know your wines. Our region is well-known for the quality of grapes we produce and the talent of our winemakers. It is in the soil, especially around Falconview. I understand that the Kingdom of Jandarin also has favorable conditions for growing outstanding grapes near the foothills of the Crystal Mountains in the north."

"You are correct, my Lady, but you seem to have the better winemakers." Colassa smiled. "You also seem to have exceptionally beautiful women in your city. May I inquire about the lady who just spoke with you?"

"Her name is Lironi. I don't know much about her, except that she is a widow and owns a fur trading business."

"Which means she's unattached. Is she the guest of anyone?"

Gardina suppressed her disgust. The lust in the man's eyes almost screamed at her. She hoped it was just the wine and not his normal character. "My son Carn invited her, but I don't believe he has any interest in her."

"Thank you, my Lady. I feel somewhat lonely tonight. I believe I will try to make her acquaintance." He grinned sheepishly. "My wife has recently left me and I haven't enjoyed the company of a beautiful woman for some time."

She made an impatient gesture with one hand. "Then by all means try your luck with that woman, Merchant Colassa. By the way, when are you leaving for home?"

"I'm planning for the day after tomorrow. I should have my business wrapped up by then." He bowed again and retreated.

"Have a good trip home," Gardina said quietly. "I hope you'll survive until then."

"I know what you mean," Galoor chuckled beside her. "That woman is likely to kill him with her unbridled passion. Anyone can see she's a beast in the bedroom. She oozes fierceness."

"You males are all alike." She shook her head, annoyed by Galoor's remark. "Is that all you see in a woman? Her behavior between the sheets?"

"It's one of the things some men see. To them it is important, while other men look for different qualities in a woman. The way I do. Let's face it, at my age those shallow, physical attributes are not as significant anymore. Men my age have matured and look at a woman with different eyes." He gave her an innocent smile.

"You always know the right things to say, even though sometimes you do make a slip. I should not let you into my chambers tonight just to punish you."

"You'd only punish yourself, my Love." He grinned like a little boy.

She couldn't help but laugh. She had to admit, he did make her feel good and, most importantly, took away her loneliness. After losing two husbands, she considered herself fortunate to have found another man again who truly loved her. Many times, she regretted that it had not happened with Galoor until so late in her life. Lord Caran, her first husband, and Lord Raxan, her second, had been good men, but both had lacked that rare capability to make a woman feel special. Galoor had that. Even though a big and imposing man, he did possess a certain softness only a woman could see and appreciate.

"I see our friend Colassa has made contact with his target," Galoor said. "It seems she isn't opposed to his company."

"I hope they're both still alive in the morning," Gardina murmured. "I'll be glad to see him bid his farewell. I don't feel like stocking up my wine cellar so soon."

Gardina rose in her chair and rang a little bell. Her guests stopped talking and turned to look at her.

"I welcome you all to my little party and I hope you'll enjoy my hospitality. Refreshments will be served in a moment and after that we'll move into the dining room for dinner. My capable chefs have prepared meats from the mountain stag Lord Galoor has bagged only a few days ago. There'll also be different vegetables which have been grown in various regions of our fertile Kingdom of Maridaan, along with fresh juices and aged wine from my wine cellar. For those of you with a sweet tooth we'll serve delectable deserts and fresh fruit. Enjoy."

She waited for the applause to finish before she sat down, having no illusions that most of that enthusiastic clapping of hands was not sincere. They came, not because they loved her so much, but because they needed her support and good will if they wanted to trade with merchants in other Kingdoms. The majority of the lords had some kind of business and all of them had to go through her to stay in business. They paid levies to her and to King Ordar. She controlled them and they knew it.

She waved to one of the serving girls who just happened to be Kiiri. "Bring wine for Lord Galoor and me. I need to wash down some unpleasantness."

"Right away, my Lady." Kiiri rushed to bring a couple of crystal glasses filled with the red liquid. "Anything else, my Lady?"

Emptying half the glass, Gardina leaned back in her chair. "Tell

Rollas to make sure the jester comes in time, right after the food has been served. Last time he came much too early. Go, tell him that."

Kiiri rushed away again and out the door. "I wish I had her energy." Gardina sighed. "To be so young again."

———

"NOW YOU BEHAVE YOURSELF TONIGHT, KIIRI." Latalia gave her daughter a stern look. "Some of those lords can be quite lewd with their remarks after they've been drinking too much wine and may invite you to accompany them to their quarters. Keeps those legs of yours closed. Am I clear?"

"Yes, mother." Kiiri looked demurely to the floor. "I shall behave my best tonight." She didn't tell her mother that she had already been invited, but not by one of the lords, unless one regarded Applar a lord. After all, his father was Lord Randahr and someday Applar would inherit his estate.

For a small dinner party, there were quite a large number of guests. But Lady Gardina never did anything really small. She knew most of the lords, but a few were strangers, especially the ones from other cities or from other Kingdoms. One of the guests was a Captain Karras from Rolandia. She had seen him a couple of times already at the castle. He was a dark-haired, handsome man with magnetizing eyes and not easy to forget, but he never looked at her. It seemed he had set his interest higher than just a servant girl. He had eyes only for Lady Ronewa.

Most people underestimated Kiiri. They saw only a simple servant girl, and the men considered her a pretty girl with a pair of slim thighs ready to spread when asked. Possibly they were correct in that respect, but she was not stupid. She had a good memory for faces and names and possessed a talent for observing and seeing things others did not.

She did not miss the short, rotund man's clumsy attempt to get the attention of one of the most beautiful women in the room. She didn't know her, but she knew the man. His name was Colassa. He was a merchant from Jandarin. It seemed he had desperately been trying to empty singlehandedly every bottle in Lady Gardina's wine cellar. She had seen him stumbling around the castle grounds on more than just one occasion. To her surprise, it appeared as if the woman was actually showing an interest in the man.

Her attention was drawn away by somebody else, somebody much more impressive than Colassa.

The Barbarian Rhodar.

He still wore his kilt, but now he also wore a shirt to cover his upper body. It seemed a bit ill-fitting. He probably borrowed it from Lord Galoor, who was as large as Rhodar, but somehow more massive with more fat than muscle and a small paunch; a sign of his age.

She smiled when she remembered feeling Rhodar's muscular, hard body lying between her spread thighs and his large pole inside her. It had been almost too easy to seduce him. It proved again that even the strongest male was too weak to resist the lures of a pretty, willing woman. His interest in her had been short-lived and she didn't blame him. She was not ignorant of the fact that he had coupled with Lady Ronewa. Everyone in the castle knew. Things like that spread quickly, especially since everyone knew that Lady Ronewa usually preferred women to men. She had used the big barbarian and then cast him aside.

Kiiri had seen Rhodar with Saleen and wondered about their relationship. Saleen was a strange one. She kept to herself most of the time. Some people were afraid of her. There were rumors that she was a powerful witch; which had not been proven by anyone. She was under Lord Carn's special protection and people speculated about that.

She got a large mug and filled it with wine. Then she searched out Rhodar and offered it to him. "You seem thirsty and without company at the moment."

The barbarian smiled. "Are you offering your company?"

"I wish I could, but I have to work. You are not the only one who's suffering from a thirsty throat." She chuckled.

"Didn't you tell me you had other plans for tonight?"

"I have but not until later. Let me ask you a question. Do you know that beautiful woman with that short, red-faced man?"

"I don't know her personally, but I know she is an acquaintance of Kalo's father. I'm sure you heard about the little boy we rescued."

"I know about Kalo. He's the boy in Arina's care. Everyone knows about Lord Galoor's sister Arneena, Kalo's mother. That was a terrible tragedy." She studied the woman. "Why would a woman like that be acquainted with Kalo's father, a shipbuilder?"

"Strange question, Kiiri. Are only certain types of men allowed to know beautiful women?" Rhodar took a swig from his jug. "Good wine," he said and wiped his mouth with the back of his hand. "By the way, I remember her saying her name was Lironi."

"Lironi. Hm. I'm also wondering why an attractive woman like her is even remotely interested in a short fat man like Colassa."

"He must have something she likes." Rhodar shook his head, obviously puzzled by Kiiri's remark.

"He is a drunk," Kiiri said. "My mother always told me to stay away from men who like their wine too much. They are nothing but trouble."

"Probably good advice. You should listen to your mother." Rhodar emptied his jug and held it out toward her. "Be a good girl and fill this up again. I'm thirsty. It seems this wine is the only thing keeping me company tonight, since you are busy."

"Any other night I'd gladly spend it with you but not tonight. Remember, I told you I had plans?"

"I remember. Don't let me hold you up. I don't want Lady Gardina getting mad at you if you're neglecting other guests. I'll find something to keep me busy." He winked. "Enjoy whatever you're planning."

She favored him with a teasing smile, took his empty jug, and left him standing there. "I'll be back."

After bringing him another full jug, she headed toward Colassa and the woman she now knew was called Lironi, carrying a second mug. "I thought you might like more wine," she said to Colassa but looked at Lironi. The woman was even more beautiful from close. She had gorgeous, long blond hair and bright green eyes.

"I'll have some more, but I think my friend here will have to go easy on the wine." Lironi looked at Colassa from lowered lids. "I don't want you falling asleep later one. I have plans," she said with a throaty voice.

Kiiri was almost ready to throw up. That woman couldn't be more obvious about what she planned. As Lironi turned to hold up her empty cup for Kiiri to refill, Colassa put a pudgy hand on her buttock and laughed. "I guess you'll have your work cut out to keep me awake," he said, his words coming out in a slur.

"I've never had a problem keeping a man awake," Lironi said, laughing softly and pinching his cheek.

Kiiri walked away, disgusted by their open display of lust. Pictures of the woman lying naked on a blanket, her legs spread and the fat man between them rose up in her imagination and didn't help her mood. She forced herself to think about Applar whom she was going to meet later. She was glad he had a nice-looking body. Nothing like Rhodar, but the barbarian was an exceptional specimen of a male.

Not paying attention, she bumped into another person and stumbled. "I'm sorry," she stammered, trying to regain her balance by holding on to the man. It was the handsome Captain Karras.

"No need to apologize," he said, laughing. "A beautiful girl like you can bump into me anytime."

She blushed and let go of him. "I wasn't paying attention where I was going."

"Where are you going?" His black eyes studied her curiously.

"I was going to get more wine." She felt mesmerized by those eyes. They seemed to see right into her soul.

His white teeth flashed in a playful smile. "A girl your age shouldn't be consuming any wine yet. You'll never know where that can lead."

"Oh no, the wine is not for me. I'm just a serving girl." She let out a silly laugh. At least it sounded silly in her ears. She gave him a coquette smile. "Perhaps I should drink a cup of wine. Sometimes to find out where it leads is the adventure."

He lifted a finger and waggled it like a lecturer. "You may be treading dangerous grounds here, pretty girl. A man may take of advantage of your curiosity."

"Do you mean a man like you, Captain Karras?" she said feeling a little reckless.

"It seems you know my name? I'm surprised."

"I have a good memory for faces and names, and I make it a point of remembering Lady Gardina's guests."

"I'm afraid I don't know your name."

"I'm Kiiri."

"I hope Lady Gardina knows what an exceptional jewel she has in you, Kiiri. I certainly will remember you and your name. Perhaps you and

I should get better acquainted, but right now I have to attend to business with Lady Ronewa."

The touch of his hand sent tingles along her arm and she shivered. There was some strange power emanating from him and it made her knees weak. She knew she'd be a willing puppet in his hands should he decide to give her his complete attention.

"Then you better not let her wait." She turned and rushed away.

Standing in the kitchen, she stood for a moment and tried to calm herself. Why would his touch have such an effect on her? Thinking about this mysterious Captain Karras awakened a powerful desire in her.

"Kiiri, don't stand there doing nothing. Help us put the food on the table." It was her mother who called and she hurried to her side to grab a bowl with steaming meats.

The rest of the evening passed in a daze, and she couldn't wait for the time to finally go and meet Applar.

He waited for her in the garden. "You're late," he said.

"I know but I didn't have any choice. They needed my help in the kitchen." She smiled and gave him a quick kiss on the lips. "I'm here now and I'll make it up to you. I even brought wine."

She offered him the small jug and he drank from it. Then he held it to her lips and made her drink some. "I'd better not drink too much," she said. "You'll never know what it makes me do."

Laughing, he grabbed her hand. "Lead the way to that secret place," he said, his breath suddenly coming fast. "I can't wait."

They almost ran toward the hut hidden away in one corner of the garden.

When they got close, Kiiri stopped and lifted a finger to her lips.

"What is it?" Applar said.

"There is somebody already in the hut."

"Didn't you say not many know about this little hideaway?"

She shrugged. "It's true, but it is not completely unknown. I only wonder who it could be."

They advanced slowly, trying to move as silently as possible. They could hear the chuckling of a man and the giggling of a woman. Hiding behind one of the tall shrubs, Kiiri could see the shadows of two people in the flickering oil lamp they had lit, but it was too dark to make out any details.

"We'll have to get closer," she said. "We'll need to be quiet, though. If they can't hear us, they won't see us."

They crept closer and found a hiding place behind a clump of shorter shrubs. From there they had a good view of the two people inside the hut.

When Kiiri saw the short, rotund man she wasn't surprised. "That's Colassa," she whispered.

"Who is the woman?" Applar whispered back.

"Probably Lironi. I saw him coming on to her. I recognize her blond hair and red dress."

As they watched, they saw the woman slip her dress over her head to expose her naked body. Kiiri heard Applar inhale his breath beside her. "What a body," he said louder then he should have.

"Hush," she hissed and put a hand over his mouth.

The woman pushed Colassa onto his back and straddled him. Her soft sigh was loud enough for Kiiri to hear and she didn't have to guess why the woman sighed. She had seen the man's large stiff pole for an instant. The woman began moving her pelvis back and forth in Colassa's lap with ever increasing speed. After a while, she let out a little cry and quivered on top of the man.

She lifted off and got onto her knees, pushing her plump buttocks high. "Take me from the back," she told Colassa.

The rotund man moved behind her and obeyed her wish. This time he let out a loud moan as he entered her. He moved behind her with slow motion, his pudgy hands clamped around her curvy hips.

Watching them, Kiiri felt that familiar itch between her legs and knew she needed to feel Applar's man-pole inside her. Pulling her dress up past her hips, she lay down on her back with open legs, letting Applar know what she expected.

He didn't need any encouragement. With a suppressed moan, he pushed down his pants and moved between her legs. She had to stifle a cry of joy when she felt him slide into her. Never before had she felt such strong desire. Her whole body shook when he slammed repeatedly into her and she kissed him with great passion.

It was over much too soon and she felt a moment of regret and loss when Applar rolled away from her. "I'm sorry," he whispered. "I've never been so turned on. It was too much."

Kiiri turned onto her belly to look at the two people inside the hut and she sat up in surprise, stuffing a hand into her mouth to keep from screaming. Colassa was still on his knees, pushing his male-pole back and forth between the two buttocks in front of him, except it was not a woman he coupled with but a beast with a fur-covered body. From its snout came a low growling sound.

Applar saw it also. "What in the name of the seven demons is that?" He almost shouted it.

"That woman is a Wer," Kiiri said, fear coloring her voice.

As they watched, the Wer-beast pulled forward, turned and stood in front of Colassa, staring at him. The man froze, still on his knees. With a rumbling roar the beast sprang and threw him onto his back.

This time Kiiri couldn't help but scream when she saw the beast's open jaws close on the man's throat. She wanted to get up and run but her knees didn't obey her. Sitting petrified, she watched the beast leave Colassa. Turning its head, it looked in her direction and she knew they had been discovered.

A ripple went through the beast's body and it changed. In moments, a naked woman rose from her kneeling position and stretched her lithe body. She bent and picked up her dress. Slipping into it, she smoothed it out with her hands. Then she turned, brushed her long blond hair out of her face and looked in Kiiri's direction.

The bright light from Rumos, one of the night suns illuminated her face and Kiiri held her breath in surprise. She had never seen this woman before. It certainly wasn't Lironi as she had assumed.

"Don't run away," the woman called. "I know you are there." She laughed softly. "I hope you enjoyed what you witnessed. I certainly did." She walked toward them on naked feet. Standing in front of them, she smiled when she saw Applar still with his pants pooled around his ankles. "I see you haven't been just idle watchers."

"We didn't see anything," Applar stammered while pulling up his pants. "We've been...you know..." He grinned crookedly.

"Have you been drinking wine?" she said.

"Just a little," Applar said.

"I don't know what you believe you saw. Drinking wine, the light from an oil lamp and your imagination, coupled with strong bodily desires, can sometimes create strange visions in your mind, making you see things that aren't really there. What do you think you saw?"

"We saw Colassa coupling with a beast that ripped out his throat," Kiiri blurted out, feeling brave.

The woman laughed. "Come and take a look at the man with his ripped-out throat."

Reluctantly, Kiiri and Applar entered the hut, fearing the worst. Colassa lay on his back with his eyes closed. Kiiri looked at his throat but didn't see any blood, as she had expected. As she looked at him, he opened his eyes and sat up.

Seeing three people staring at him, he looked down at his exposed genitals and covered them with his hands. "Who are you young people? Have you never seen a naked man before? What are you doing here?"

"I'm sorry," Kiiri said. "We didn't know you were here. Not many people know about this place."

"I'm sure glad about that, otherwise we may have a huge audience." He sat up and rubbed his neck. He looked at the woman. "Did I fall asleep after all?"

She chuckled. "Only after we were done. You didn't disappoint me."

"I had a strange dream." He rubbed his neck again. "It was probably the wine. I have a tendency to drink more than I should."

"Yes, the wine can play tricks with your imagination. These two found that out. Now, let's get back to the party before we're missed." She turned to Kiiri and Applar. "You two run along, also. If I were you, I wouldn't mention this incident. We don't want people spreading rumors about me or Colassa."

"Who are you, anyway?" Kiiri said. "I don't remember seeing you at dinner."

"Then you're not very observant, girl. I am Lady Shanta."

"I thought you were a woman by the name of Lironi. It seems I made a mistake. She wore the same dress as you."

"I'm fully aware of that woman. Obviously, I am not she. I have to talk to my dressmaker about this dress. No woman likes to see another one wearing the same dress." She made shooing motions. "Now, go. Give my friend here some privacy so he can get dressed. I wouldn't mind cleaning up a little, too." Her laugh was almost apologetic. "I must look a bit disheveled, especially my hair. I tend to go somewhat crazy when I'm with a virile man, and Colassa is a virile man."

Kiiri and Applar breathed easier once they were out of earshot. "Did you believe what she told us?" she said to Applar.

"I don't know what to believe. I would suggest we don't talk about this to anyone."

"I agree."

Chapter Eleven

RONEWA WAS NOT ALWAYS FOND of her mother's dinner parties. They tended to become boring. Listening to those uninteresting lords and their wives and watching them trying to impress her mother, her, and her brother Carn, became tedious after a while.

The only man in the room who might lift her boredom was the barbarian, Rhodar, but she wasn't sure if she should make a play for him again. She had spent one passionate night in his embrace, and he had certainly not disappointed her with his savage prowess, but she tended to get bored very quickly. Her preference would be to find a couple of women who shared her tastes and were willing to play her games.

Even though she preferred women, a virile man would be just as acceptable. It didn't matter to her.

Scrutinizing the guests, her interest peaked when she saw a handsome dark-haired man standing by himself. She had never talked to him, but she had seen him on at least one occasion at the castle. She didn't remember his name, though. He seemed to keep to himself, at least until now. As she was watching, Kiiri bumped into him, which did not surprise her. That girl apparently had no compulsion to seduce any man who'd be willing. They only talked for a short time, and then Kiiri rushed away to disappear in the kitchen.

As if sensing Ronewa's watching eyes, the man turned his head and looked in her direction. She held his gaze for a moment and then she looked away. It was not polite for a woman to stare at a stranger. When she let her gaze return in his direction, she saw him walking toward her.

Her curiosity aroused, she didn't look away and watched him come closer.

The man smiled when he reached her and made a slight bow. "Lady Ronewa. Why is it that the most beautiful woman in this room is sitting by herself?"

She laughed and looked into his black eyes. It was like looking into a deep well that drew one into its mysterious depth. "Why does the most handsome man in the room appear so lonely?" she countered. "There must be a few unattached women in this room looking for company."

"Because I've been interested in only you, my Lady," he said, his even teeth flashing white in his tanned face.

He emanated a strange force that attracted her. "Why me?"

"I've wanted to make your acquaintance since the first time I saw you. I'm Captain Karras from the tiny Kingdom of Rolandia."

"How interesting. We don't get many visitors from Rolandia. How is Queen Givanna?"

"She's dead. Her son Aran is King now."

She chuckled. "I knew that. I was only testing you. You wouldn't believe how many charlatans we get."

"I have no interest in scamming anyone. My only quest in life right now is to find my lost brother." His face seemed to go dark for a moment but then he smiled. "However, I'm not against spending a few hours in the company of a beautiful woman to lift my mood."

"It so happens that I've got nothing planned and I wouldn't mind the company of a handsome man. Come, sit with me and tell me about yourself."

"There really isn't much to tell. I live a boring life. My brother and I inherited a small estate from our late father. Our mother passed away a few years ago. Last year, my brother decided to pursue his dream and travel across the ocean and go north to Agastan to visits a cousin. Our mother is originally from Agastan. I was worried about him and traced him to Falconview, but there is no record of him ever boarding a ship."

"You believe something happened to him here in Falconview?"

He shrugged. "It's only an assumption. The trail I followed ends here." He lifted his cup and looked into her eyes. "Don't let me bore you with my uninteresting life. I came here to forget about it for a while and what better way than in the arms of a passionate woman."

She couldn't stop looking into his dark eyes. "How do you know I'm a passionate woman?" she murmured.

He held the rim of his cup against her lips. "I can tell by the shape of your lips and the arch of your eyebrows, by the way you walk and by the way you look at me. I can sense the fire smoldering inside your sensuous body, waiting to be fanned into a roaring flame. Let me be that fan."

"Then I suggest we leave here and look for a more private place... like my room."

"Great idea."

She grabbed his hand and pulled him with her. The sudden desire to feel his naked body against hers was overpowering and could not be denied. They fairly ran down the corridor to her room. Once inside, she slipped out of her dress and helped him to get undressed in feverish haste. Naked, she clung to him and kissed him hungrily. He pushed her down onto the carpet. Her legs flew open and pulled him between them. When he entered her, she screamed with the pleasure that surged through her.

Afterwards she didn't remember much. They lay in each other's arms, exhausted and satisfied.

"Tell me," he said in his soothing voice, "wouldn't you like to be the mistress of Castle Falconclaw?"

"Of course," she said, dreamily, still lost in the rapturous feeling of their lovemaking.

"I could help you achieve that," he said.

She looked at him with veiled eyes. "How could you help me? I will never be the mistress. When my mother dies, it will be my brother who inherits the position of Master."

"What if your mother and brother were to die suddenly?" His voice sounded monotonous yet insistent.

"That won't ever happen. Not naturally, anyway." She stretched and rubbed her breasts against his hard chest. Running her foot along his leg, she purred. "I'm ready again."

He chuckled and rolled her onto her belly. Putting his hands onto her hips, he pulled up her lower body. Then he moved behind her.

She moaned deeply when she felt his hardness.

"There are ways to make it happen," he whispered into her ear. "I have potions you can mix into their morning brew Nobody will ever suspect it."

She cried out and pumped her pelvis.

"Let me help you," his voice persisted. "Nobody will ever know."

"Yes," she cried out. "Yess...yesss!"

He slammed into her buttocks. "You will do it." his voice droned. "You will do it because you want to do it. It is your utmost desire."

"It is my utmost desire," she repeated; feeling it and believing it.

She must have fallen asleep. When she woke, she lay in her bed, naked but covered with a thin sheet. She felt exhausted and yet, there was this wonderful sense of being completely satisfied. Looking around for Captain Karras, she didn't see him anywhere and disappointment took hold. When she saw the vial on her dresser with a note attached to it, she slipped from the bed and picked up the note.

Thank you for letting me enjoy your body. I hope I brought you as much pleasure as you brought me. As my token of appreciation, I'm leaving you a gift. Put a couple of drops from the vial into your mother's and brother's morning drink. The potion is tasteless and they will not suspect. Death will not be instantly. It may take a while. So be patient. Please, destroy this note after you read it.'

"THANK YOU," she whispered. "Finally, I will be free of them."

———————

KORALLAS WAS HAPPY. He had achieved one of the things he came to do. Ronewa would poison her brother and her mother. There was no way she could resist the spell he cast on her. Unfortunately, he had seen no sign of the girl Saleen. Kastabaan would just have to wait to get her in his clutches.

He had actually enjoyed seducing and ravaging Ronewa. She was a beautiful woman and passionate beyond compare. Putting her under a spell had, of course, played an important role in the way she behaved, but much of it had been of her own choice. She had held nothing back and given herself to him completely. In a way, he almost felt sorry she had not been aware most of the time what she was doing and what he did to her. She would have no memory of anything that happened, but Captain Karras would always have a special place in her heart.

Once her mother and brother were dead, he would visit her to console her as her advisor first and then her lover. He had all the confidence in the world that the plan would succeed.

He had seen Lironi there. He had also seen her disappear with a stubby man for a little while. He came back, disheveled and exhausted looking, but she never returned. That the man came back at all, surprised him a little. He knew her hunger and what she sometimes needed. Not all her victims survived coupling with her. Something must have gone wrong.

"I still have some business to finish," he told his two men. "You go back to the castle."

Without saying anything, they rode off. They were always silent because they had no tongues. None of Kastabaan's and his men had tongues. Kastabaan removed them with a spell when they became his minions.

Karras rode to the poor area of Falconview searching for a suitable subject. When he spotted a young man sitting alone on a fence, he stopped his horse and told him to follow him. The young man got up and walked beside him, not realizing what he was doing.

Lironi was surprised to see him when she opened the door to her home. When she saw the young man, she smiled. "How did you know what I needed?"

"I always know what you need."

Lironi walked up to the young man and touched his neck with one hand. "Strong pulse," she said and began undoing the thongs that held his shirt together. Exposing his chest, she ran her hand across it. "Good muscle tone. Now—take off your pants. I want to see what you've got."

The young man complied.

When he was completely nude, Lironi manipulated his manhood until he was rigid. Then she slipped out of her dress, pushed him onto his back and straddled him.

Korallas made himself comfortable in one of the chairs and watched. It was obvious, Lironi enjoyed coupling with the young man immensely, and she played with him for a long time. Korallas waited for the moment when she would morph into her beast form. When it happened, she let out a joyous cry; the outlines of her body rippled, changed from human to beast. With a growl, she closed her jaws over the young man's throat and began to drink from his blood.

Korallas rose from his seat, pushed down his pants and moved behind Lironi. He took her with a satisfied grunt. She pushed her buttocks against him but never ceased feeding. When he spilled his seed into her, she lifted her head and roared her satisfaction. She morphed back into her human form while they were still locked together.

Turning her head, she looked back at him and smiled. "You always know what I need," she said, her voice still thick and barely intelligible.

He left her then and laughed. "And you know and anticipate my needs. That's why we get along so well." He looked at the blood on the young man's throat as he lay unmoving on the floor. "I hope you didn't suck him dry."

She licked her lips. "You know better than even suggesting that. The last thing I need is to leave a trail of corpses behind. Now, if you can use one of your spells and make him forget what happened here before we let him go, everything will be perfect."

"I was under the impression that your victims never remember their encounter with you."

"They don't remember me, but they remember they had sex. I want you to make sure he forgets about being here in my home."

"I can do that. He may wonder why he feels so tired but content."

"I just gave him the best fuck he ever got in his life. Perhaps you should let him remember his sexual encounter with me—without any details, of course."

"If that's what you want and if it will satisfy your ego, I can do that, too." He studied her as she stood naked in front of him. "One wonders why you have such a perfect human body since you're not really human. Probably because you use it to lure males into your potentially deadly embrace."

"I've only killed twice," she said. "It is not a smart thing to do and I didn't feel happy about it."

"I've never had such compunctions. Sometimes it's best not to leave any witnesses." He chuckled. "You may not feel happy about it, but you had no problem having your husband murdered and Lady Arneena, your lover's wife, eliminated. Your conscience isn't exactly without guilt."

"I suppose you're right." She stepped closer and pressed her nude body against him.

Feeling her soft breasts on his chest and her nearness caused his body to react. He knew it was her natural talent to attract males. Her body and her mannerisms were designed to attract males and he was not immune to her magnetism.

She laughed softly when she felt his reaction. "Even you cannot resist me," she whispered and kissed him on the lips. "I'd ask you to stay the night, but it would be best if you took this young man away from here. If he should leave by himself, someone might see him and wonder what he was doing here."

Stepping away from her, he smiled. "If I stayed, we might both kill each other. I may be virile, but even I have my limits. Lady Ronewa demanded much of my energy as did the spell I used on her. I understand you also had a strenuous night at the castle. I could use magic to keep us both going but somewhere down the road we'd have to pay our dues. Everything comes with a price, especially magic."

"A good thing then I'm not a magician."

Korallas looked past her at the young man who was beginning to stir. He opened his eyes and looked around. His gaze fastened on Lironi. "Where am I? Who are you? Why are you naked?" he croaked. Then he realized his own nudity. "What happened to my clothes?"

She laughed and poked him with a naked toe. "I like my men nude when I couple with them. It is so much more enjoyable."

He sat up. "Did you and I couple? I don't even know you." Then he groaned. "I remember now. We did and it was incredible. I've never felt like that before. I also remember something that cannot be—a beast on top of me and teeth on my throat." His eyes widened suddenly and he took a step backward. "You!" He pointed an accusing finger at Lironi. "You must be a Wer. I've heard stories."

"I don't know what you heard, but those are only stories. I'm not a Wer." She touched his manhood with a foot. "I'm just exceptionally talented and your fantasy ran wild while we copulated. Consider yourself a fortunate young man that I chose you. By the way, what is your name?"

"I'm Rakall." He stared at her exposed golden fluffy triangle so close above him.

"Rakall. It was wonderful to get to know you so intimately. Now get dressed and run along with my friend here. He will take you home."

Rakall got up and put on his clothes. Then he looked at Korallas. "What role did you play in this?"

"My role? I'm here to take you home safely." He touched Rakall's shoulder and looked him in the eyes. "Once we leave here you will remember your experience but nothing else. You won't remember the woman's face. You won't remember me and neither will you remember this house. Now let's go."

Outside, he mounted his horse and told Rakall to take his place behind him. When they were near where he picked up the young man, Korallas sent him on his way. He only did that to please Lironi. If it would have been his choice, he would have killed him and left him lying by the side of the road.

———

RONEWA SAT in front of her mirror rubbing cream into her skin. Humming a little tune, she studied her features. Soon she'd be mistress of Castle Falconclaw, free to do as she pleased, without waiting for approval from her mother or even Carn. All she had to do was find a way to add the drops Korallas had left with her to their morning cup of tirka-brew without raising suspicion.

She could ask Kiiri to do it. The girl would be the logical choice since she was her mother's handmaiden and responsible for serving the brew, but could she take that chance? If she told her the drops were extracts of different spices she got from a friend and they would add taste and other benefits to the drink Kiiri would not question it. She was not too bright, most of time too occupied with chasing anything with a male organ willing to climb between her spread legs, and there was no shortage of those men around. That girl's brain was between her legs and not in her head.

She'd talk to Kiiri within the next few days. She'd just have to make it clear to her not to mention it to anyone, especially Carn and her mother, because the elixir was rare and she wouldn't be able to replenish the vial once it was gone. Lady Gardina may not believe it and hold Kiiri responsible for getting more, which would not be possible. It would be in Kiiri's best interest to keep quiet. Yes, that would work.

Standing up, she looked at her nude body, pleased with what she saw. Her breasts were firm, her figure trim and her buttocks full and round. She was young, in her prime, and should have no problem finding a man she could control, someone who would not object to her pursuing her peculiar tastes. In fact, she could have a male and a female consort at the same time living with her and satisfying her cravings. Nobody would be able to deny her that once she ruled Castle Falconclaw.

Her thoughts wandered to Captain Karras. Something about that man kept her enthralled. She'd never met a man who gave her such satisfaction. Her body still tingled when she thought about his virility and stamina and the level of pleasure she experienced with him. He knew where to touch her and how to stimulate her to sexual highs she didn't know existed.

The vial with the poison was his gift to her and she was grateful. Finally, she had the means to fulfill her secret dream—to get rid of her brother and mother.

Chapter Twelve

"KING ORDAR WILL BE CELEBRATING the yearly summer festival in a few days. We've been invited as usual." Lady Gardina smiled smugly. "No surprise there. After all, I'm his sister." She waited for Rhodar to comment, but he kept silent. Her revelation about being the King's sister was not new to him. "I want you to come with us to meet my brother."

"I would be honored to meet King Ordar," Rhodar said. "I heard of him from my father who knew him when both of them were young. He told many stories about him."

"Strange that I never met your father," Lady Gardina mused. "Especially since your father and Lord Galoor were good friends. But then I was the younger sister and not allowed to play with the young men. It wouldn't have been proper. Our father, King Ordarin, was strict and worried about my chastity." She laughed. "He had no idea I wasn't as innocent as he thought, but that is something else entirely and in the past." Her eyes glazed over for a short moment. "Things were different in those days. Much simpler somehow."

"I wouldn't know about life in Maridaan so long ago, my Lady," Rhodar said. "Life in the Western Plains is not as complicated and difficult as on this side of the mountains. I don't believe it could be much simpler."

She regarded him silently for a moment. "I envy you, Rhodar. You live a carefree life without many responsibilities. Sometimes I wish I were a man so I could just pack a few belongings and explore the world beyond this kingdom. There is so much to see out there. As a woman, that world is closed to me." She sighed. "Of course, now that I'm getting old, it doesn't matter anyway."

Rhodar chuckled. "Traveling through the countryside isn't as glamorous as it may sound, my Lady. Sleeping under the stars in nasty weather isn't a wonderful experience and having nothing to eat for days can make you miserable. Not to mention the bandits and cutthroats one meets along the way, the ones who would kill you for your meager belongings without blinking an eye. That is the carefree life of a wanderer—always on guard and sleeping with one eye open." He smiled. "I'm grateful to you and Lord Carn for allowing me to stay here at the castle as your guest where I feel safe and among friends. Even if it is only for a short time. It is a rare treat."

"By saving Saleen and little Kalo's life you have earned the right to stay here. We gladly offer you our hospitality as will King Ordar. He will be most interested in meeting the son of a man he knew in his youth. We'll be leaving tomorrow morning."

"I'll be ready. How long will the journey take?"

"If we leave early enough we will get there before nightfall. I do not like traveling after sundown. Too many dangers lurking in the mantle of darkness. And it is not only animals I'm talking about. There have been reports lately about bands of Larkis attacking and murdering lone travelers and even small caravans."

"Larkis?" Rhodar asked, surprised. "They are usually quite peaceful and hardly venture far from their region deep in the forests."

"As you said—usually. Not these. Apparently, there rose among them a seer who claims to have descended from a god. He calls himself Mardaas and he is building an army of warriors who are fierce and not afraid to die. According to what we hear, the followers of Mardaas believe they will join the gods at their table if they die in battle and become like gods themselves."

"Sometimes it takes only one man to change many in their behavior with promises that are not always true," Rhodar observed. "I remember a man who called himself a speaker for the gods. It was during a period of long droughts when water was scarce. He proclaimed the gods spoke to him, and they told him to go forth among the primitive tribes and gather men and women and build a following of worshippers. He also said the gods demanded children as sacrifices for the gift of rain. He stated he was invincible because the gods protected him from harm."

"What happened to him?"

Rhodar chuckled. "He was killed by one of his followers when he claimed the man's woman for his own."

"It proves again the gods are no match for a jealous lover," Lady Gardina laughed.

"Will you be accompanied by a few guards to protect you should we be attacked?"

"I will be traveling in a carriage. Kiiri and Saleen will be my hand-maidens. Aside from Lord Galoor, Carn, and you there will be a number of my most trusted warriors for my protection." She smiled. "Don't forget your enchanted battle-axe. Yes, Carn told me about that weapon. I find it intriguing, so does my son. He is a collector of weapons and would have liked nothing better than to add yours to his collection."

"He would never be able to wield it," Rhodar said. "Only its rightful owner can. Unfortunately, the magic is fading and I must soon move on to find the sorcerer Arguss who put the spell on the axe."

"Do you know where to find this sorcerer?"

"According to what my father told me, Arguss lives deep in the forests of Agastan."

"Agastan?" Lady Gardina wrinkled her forehead. "There was a Captain Karras from Rolandia at my dinner party who claimed to have a cousin in Agastan. He might know about this sorcerer."

"Too bad I didn't get a chance to talk to him."

"I saw my daughter talking to him. She may know where to find him."

"I'll ask her when we come back. Any little bit of information may help." Rhodar smiled apologetically. "If my Lady permits, I will go and get my horse ready."

"Good idea. Tell young Aarin he will accompany us on this trip. I want him to drive the carriage."

"I'm happy to hear that. He's good with animals. My horse seems to like him." Rhodar bowed and walked away. He was looking forward to a change in scenery, but not much to spending another evening in the company of highbrowed Lords and Ladies at the King's court. He would have preferred to go on a hunt with Lord Galoor.

It pleased him to hear that Kiiri and Saleen would also be coming along. To see two familiar faces among strangers would make it more enjoyable. He remembered Kiiri's forwardness that first morning and her fierce passion. He had enjoyed their coupling and wondered about his reluctance to become intimate with Saleen, who had offered herself to him several times. Saleen was about Kiiri's age and more than ready for a man's attention. He was attracted to Saleen and she to him. Could it be he was afraid to get too deeply involved with a woman? Deep down he knew this was the wrong time for that to happen. He had to finish the quest bestowed upon him by his father. After that, his duty was to travel home and become chief of the Riverstone tribe, a position he didn't really want, but he could not fight the will of the gods. They had made their wishes known through old Rassan, who was of Rhodar's blood.

He shrugged. There was no need to fret over it. The gods in their infinite wisdom would guide him. If his and Saleen's destinies were to merge somehow, as she had stated, it left him with no choice but to accept it.

They left shortly after daybreak. Rhodar rode behind Lord Carn and Lord Galoor. Being of different breeds, horses and Sekua didn't get along well. Four warriors armed with bows and swords followed Rhodar. The carriage, carrying Lady Gardina, Kiiri, Saleen, and Latalia, Kiiri's mother, was pulled by two Sekua that didn't seem happy in their role as draft animals. Aarin had to stay vigilant to keep them under control.

An additional four warriors riding behind the carriage made up the escort.

Rhodar inhaled the crisp morning air, happy to leave the city behind, if only for a short time. He barely felt the weight of the battle-axe on his back, but he knew there would come a time when the weapon would lose the spell and be nothing but a normal axe. He needed to find Arguss before that happened. He traveled with his meager belongings stuffed into the two saddlebags hanging across the broad back of Nightwalker, not sure if he'd come back to Falconclaw and the city Falconview.

For part of the morning they followed a well-traveled road along the river, but then they took a road that led toward the mountain and traveled through lush meadows and fields. The majority of the wagons they met belonged to farmers working in their fields. Around noon, they stopped beside a lake to water the animals and to give them a rest. From the debris that littered the grounds and the fire pits with the charred partially burnt logs it was obvious this was a popular resting place.

Aarin climbed down from his driver's seat and joined Rhodar as he watched Nightwalker quench his thirst. He carried two buckets which he filled with water for the two Sekua pulling the carriage.

"I wish I could be riding instead of sitting on a hard bench," he complained to Rhodar. "My buttocks are already sore. I won't be able to sit when we finally get to the King's palace. I've never been on a long journey like this one."

"Riding all day isn't for everyone, either," Rhodar commented, amused by the young man's lamentation. "You have to get used to that."

"I've heard rumors about Larkis attacking travelers." Worry colored Aarin's voice.

"I wouldn't be concerned," Rhodar tried to calm his fears. "We have eight capable warriors protecting us, plus Lord Carn and Lord Galoor."

"And you, Rhodar." Aarin grinned. "You're probably the strongest warrior among them. Knowing you are here makes me feel safer already."

"I'm honored you think so highly of me." Rhodar looked at the carriage and watched Kiiri and Saleen climbing out. Saleen looked in his direction and gave him a little smile. Then she headed for him.

Aarin nodded to her and left, carrying his two buckets with water.

"I'm glad you're here," Saleen said to Rhodar.

"I'm not sure if I can say the same thing about you," he replied.

She seemed surprised to hear him say that. "Why not? I thought you'd be happy to see me."

"Or course, I'm always happy to see you, but this is a dangerous journey and I worry about you. Lady Gardina told me there are rumors of malicious Larkis roaming the forest."

"Why should I be concerned about that? I have you as my protector." She gave him one of her innocent smiles.

"Don't try to manipulate me, little wench." He looked her with a stern expression. "You know why I worry? It's what you may do when you get cornered. Are you sure you can control it?"

Her faced turned serious. "I don't know that, Rhodar. It's all new to me. I admit I'm scared, but I cannot hide myself away in some dark corner." She came close to him. "That you worry about me tells me you care for me and that makes me happy. I'm yours whenever you want me." Her green eyes were bright as she searched his face. "I will not give myself to another man. I will wait for you." She turned and rushed back to the carriage. "And don't call me wench" she called. "You know my name."

Rhodar watched her climb into the carriage, his mind in turmoil. She was right, he cared for her and he wanted nothing more than take her into his arms and crush her slim body to his, kiss her sweet lips and listen to her moans of pleasure as they satisfied their sexual hunger for each other. Then he smiled. She had fire, too, just like Kiiri, who had also objected to being called a wench.

"She desires you," the voice of Aarin said beside him. "I wish I had a beautiful girl like her want me." He sighed. "I'm nothing but a stable boy and no girl even looks at me."

"I'm positive they are. You just don't notice them. Perhaps you should make the first move and not wait until a girl approaches you." Rhodar bent and splashed water into his face and onto his neck.

The temperature had been rising and it was getting hot. He was used to riding with his upper body bare, but Lady Gardina had made it clear she wanted him to wear a shirt. Lord Galoor had been kind enough to lend him one of his. He didn't really feel comfortable in it, because it didn't fit properly.

They broke camp after all the animals had been watered and fed. Rhodar ate a couple of the dry biscuits he picked up at breakfast and drank water from a narrow stream that emptied itself into the river. It looked clean enough and didn't have a foul taste.

The landscape changed slowly and soon the fields and meadows were replaced by a forest of tall old trees. The road they followed seemed narrower and the thick canopy of branches above the road didn't let in much light, which meant the forest interior was in perpetual semi-darkness.

Rhodar's senses were at heightened alert, listening for every sound the forest produced. The clammy air seemed to create a heavy pressure inside his head, dulling his thinking. He had never been fond of the forest and he longed to see the open sky above.

He didn't know how long they had traveled, because he couldn't judge the time by the sun's movement in the sky, when he heard the sound of hoofs coming toward them. It wasn't long before two men on horseback appeared around the bend in the road ahead. They reigned in their horses when they were near. Both men were covered in blood, either someone else's or from wounds they had received.

Sliding off their steeds, they sank to their knees and sat in the dirt, obviously totally exhausted.

Lord Galoor slid off his Sekua and walked up to the men. "What happened?"

"Larkis," one of them said, his voice rough and tired.

"They overran our settlement and killed everyone. We were the only ones to escape," the other one said. He rubbed his bloodstained face with the torn sleeve of his tattered shirt. "Don't travel any farther. They outnumber you and they are ruthless and bloodthirsty. They will show you no mercy."

"We are on our way to Mountainsong to visit King Ordar," Lord Galoor said.

"You will all be killed if you follow this road. Take the next side road. It will add half a day to your journey, but it should be safe. There is a small settlement where you can spend the night. You'll be able to reach it before dark."

"What about you? Where will you go?" Lord Carn asked.

"We will go to Falconview. I have a brother there," the first one said.

"We come from Falconview," Lord Carn told them. "You will be safe there. Go to Castle Falconclaw and ask for Lady Ronewa. Tell her Lord Carn offered you the hospitality of the Castle. Lady Ronewa is my sister and will honor my request. Have our healer tend to your wounds."

"Thank you, my Lord," the man said. "You have my eternal gratitude. I will not forget this."

"Before you move on could you spare some water?" his companion begged.

Lord Galoor unclipped his water bladder and threw it to the man. "Keep it. You will need it for the rest of your journey."

The man caught it and gave Lord Galoor a grateful look. "You are most gracious, my Lord. May the Gods of Travel be with you."

"Be safe," Lord Galoor said and turned to Lord Carn. "With your permission, we will take the new road?"

Lord Carn nodded. "I don't make the decisions, my mother does. I will confer with her." He slid off his steed and walked stiff-legged to the carriage, but before he got there, the curtain parted and Lady Gardina stepped down.

"I heard," she said. "Let's not waste any more time and move on. I want to get to that settlement before it's too dark to recognize any potential threat lurking in the forest."

"You heard Lady Gardina," Lord Carn told the warriors. He jumped back onto his steed and clucked his tongue. "Go, Desert-runner," he said in a low voice. "It won't be long until you can rest."

Darkness descended quickly within the tunnel under the trees. Fortunately it was still bright enough for them to see the road. They finally heard the sounds of people and before long the road grew wider and finally spilled into a brighter area that had been cleared of the tall trees. The sky above was already darkening, so it was a welcome sight.

Rhodar saw a number of houses built from logs on either side of the road. They were fairly close together surrounded by small yards. A few small children played in front of one of the houses. When they saw the group of riders, they stopped their shouting and huddled close together. One of them ran into the house. Moments later, a man in a dark shirt and dark pants appeared in the doorway, carrying a longbow.

Lord Galoor, who was in the front, lifted one hand. "I am Lord Galoor from Castle Falconclaw. This is Lord Carn. We are on our way to Mountainsong to celebrate the summer festival with King Ordar. We ask your permission to spend the night in your settlement. We won't cause you any inconvenience."

"Why didn't you take the main road that leads to Mountainsong?" The man's left hand gripped his bow tightly. "You'd already be there."

Rhodar recognized the man was uneasy, but he nevertheless put on a brave front. He wouldn't even get an arrow nocked should they decide to take him out.

"We were planning to, but the settlement Woodrop has been destroyed by a band of Larkis, and traveling the main road is not safe." Lord Galoor explained.

"Larkis?" The man sounded suspicious. "They are not hostile, not to the point of raiding and plundering the settlements of humans."

"These are. We have not seen it, but we were warned by the only two survivors. Apparently, all the residents of Woodrop have been murdered."

"We don't have enough room to let all of you into our houses." The man lowered his bow and seemed to relax, but his eyes moved nervously as he watched the warriors dismount.

"That is not a problem. We prefer to sleep outside with our animals," Lord Galoor said. "We ask you, though, to provide shelter for Lady Gardina and her entourage. I'm certain you can find room for four women?"

"Did you say Lady Gardina?" A woman's voice came from behind the man.

"That's what I said." Lord Galoor smiled. "She is in the carriage. Do you know her?"

The woman stepped past the man and came outside. She was old, dressed in a long gown, her head covered with a shawl. "I used to be a midwife. I delivered her son. I wondered whatever happened to him."

"I am her son," Lord Carn said and dismounted. He walked toward the old woman who seemed to watch him with narrow eyes.

When he stood close to her, she lifted her hands and touched his face with her fingers. "I'm nearly blind," she said with an apologizing voice as she ran her fingers across his face. "Let me get an image of you with my fingers." She laughed softly. "You've grown into a handsome man. When you were born, you were a skinny, squirming little bundle. I carried you in my arms for a long time."

"You are Megarin," Lord Carn said with a gentle voice. "I owe you my life."

She nodded. "We almost lost you many times. It wasn't your time yet. You left your mother's womb much too early, but you had a strong will to live and, with the help of my herbs, you survived."

"And with the love and care you gave me," Lord Carn added.

"All the sleepless nights you caused me how could I not love you? I wish I could have been a part of your life, to watch you grow, and be there for you. My failing eyes left me no choice but to leave Castle Falconclaw and move in with my son so he could take care of me." She turned around to speak to the man. "This is Lord Carn. He is welcome in our home."

The man relaxed completely. "I trust my mother's judgment. Make yourself at home and tell the women to come into our humble house.

Chapter Thirteen

THE VILLAGERS SEEMED to welcome the break in their daily life. They hung lanterns from poles to light up one of the open areas and lit a few fire pits. The Elders sat around one of the fire pits and drank wine from clay cups, laughing and exchanging stories they had probably told many times before, while a number of younger men broiled meat and fish on long sticks.

Besides Megarin, there were a number of women of her age and a few younger ones preparing vegetables in one of the houses. Rhodar also saw a surprising high number of young girls coming out of different houses and disappearing inside one of the houses. It seemed they were not allowed to join the festivities outside. He didn't see young boys, unless they were hiding inside one of the other houses.

Only four younger women, about the same age as Kiiri and Saleen, served wine to the warriors.

Rhodar also noticed all the females wore gray robes that covered them from their neck to their ankles and wore thin scarves on their heads.

One of the young women stopped beside Rhodar and gave him a shy smile. "Would you like some more wine?"

"Why not." He held out his empty cup and let her refill it from a large jug she carried.

While she filled it, she gave him a sidelong glance. "I am Janissa. Is there anything else you would like me to provide for you?"

He looked at her and smiled, understanding full well her meaning. "Any other time and place, perhaps, but I don't think your parents would approve. My name is Rhodar."

As if by accident, her hand touched his shoulder. "You are different from the others. Where are you from, Rhodar?"

"The Western Plains beyond the mountains are my home."

She giggled. "I knew it. You are a barbarian. I could tell by your huge muscles. Do you mind if I sit with you for a while?"

He patted the ground beside him. "Not at all. How can I refuse a beautiful girl like you?"

"You think I'm beautiful?" She folded her legs under her to get comfortable.

"I'm sure you've been told before."

"Not often enough. The young men in our village are too busy going hunting and fishing. They have no time for girls. We don't have much contact with other people. Many shun us because of what we are. We have few opportunities to meet men from other villages."

"You live in a remote area. What do your people do to survive?"

"We hunt animals in the forest for meat. There is a lake nearby where we catch fish and collect seeds from the reeds growing in the water. The reeds have many uses. We use them to weave baskets and other things we need. They are strong enough to fashion arrows. The ground around the lake is very fertile and we plant grains and vegetables. We also plant vegetables behind our houses."

"Do you get your water from the lake? It must be difficult to bring it to the village."

She shook her head. "It would be. We have a community well. The water is always fresh and cold."

"It sounds like you are self-sufficient. Do you trade with other villages?"

"Not much." She bent close to him and whispered into his ear, "I can meet you after midnight behind the woodpiles. I'll do anything you like."

Before he could reply, she rose and was gone. He saw her filling the cup of one of the warriors. While he watched her, she looked back at Rhodar with her large, expressive eyes and smiled, touching her lips. She then went to serve another warrior.

She was no ugly hag and her offer was tempting. She moved gracefully with her head held high. Her breasts strained against the thin material of her robe and it was plain to see that her body was slim and well-formed.

Someone cleared his throat beside him and he turned to see who it was. "Lord Galoor," he said. "I didn't see you standing there."

Galoor lowered his bulk onto the ground. Crossing his legs, he took a swig from his cup. "Surprisingly good wine," he observed.

"It is," Rhodar agreed. "Tell me, I can't help but notice all the women wear long, gray robes and cover their heads. The men wear the same dark pants and shirts."

"They worship Kalana, the Wood Goddess. They don't believe in exposing their bodies to the eyes of strangers. Of course, that doesn't mean they don't copulate. You may also have noticed the large number of young people." He took another swig of wine. "She's a beautiful girl," he said.

"Who?"

"The one who's making eyes at you. She's most likely still a virgin and looking for a man to change her status. You may be held responsible for her if you are that man. You seem to know little about these people. If I were you, I'd keep that snake of mine hidden under my kilt. Just a friendly word of advice."

"I appreciate your advice, but I have no intentions to follow her invitation. I've enough problems already. No need to add more." He thought of Saleen and in a way also of Kiiri, who might believe she had a claim on him because she spent one passionate morning in his arms.

"I wish the villagers wouldn't have gone to all the trouble to feed and entertain us. This sort of puts an obligation on us. They may expect some kind of payment for their hospitality. Besides, I want the warriors fresh and well rested in the morning in case we run into any problems. Eating and drinking too much and little rest makes them weak and vulnerable."

"I would think they are disciplined enough to resist temptation and know their limits," Rhodar said.

"Too much wine can bring the strongest man to his knees and make him do unreasonable things. Believe me, I know." Lord Galoor rose to his feet. "I have to go and spend some time with Lady Gardina before she gets angry at me," he said with an apologizing grin.

"I understand." Rhodar stared into the fire, watching the dancing flames swaying to some kind of rhythm only they knew. The crackling wood and the smell of smoke brought back memories of the Great Plains, making him wish he were sitting in front of a fire with his childhood friends around him. He could almost hear them telling the stories of their adventures and their conquests, some real and some imagined. He missed the loud boasting and the bantering. Would his travels ever lead him home again?

The touch of a soft hand on his neck startled him and his hand moved to the knife on his belt, but he relaxed when he heard Saleen's voice. "I saw you talking to one of the girls. What did she want from you?"

"She asked me where I came from, that's all."

Saleen squatted beside him. "I noticed how she batted her big eyes at you. She's beautiful and despite all your big muscles when it comes to women, you are weak."

"What does that mean?"

"Kiiri told me about what happened between her and you." Her voice faltered when she said that. "I feel betrayed and hurt. Why would you couple with Kiiri and not with me? I thought you cared for me."

He turned and reached for her hands. "That's precisely the reason I don't want to get intimate with you. I care for you too much. I don't want to hurt you. You and I can never be lovers. I will be moving on and won't be able to take you with me. It wouldn't be fair to you or me. There is too much difference between the two of us. I am a barbarian and I live in a tribe. My people are on the move most of the time. You are civilized and used to living in one place, inside a solid building. Life on the Plains is too primitive for you. You would hate it after a while. You would end up despising me."

Her eyes were large in the dim light of the fire as she looked at him. "I would never despise you, Rhodar, because I love you too much. Every day that goes by I realize it more and more. There is only one man I ever want and that is you." She bent forward and kissed him on the lips.

At first, he didn't respond, but the wine he consumed made him relax his control over his emotions and he began kissing her back. She tasted so sweet and her lips were so soft. He wanted to crush her to him and cover her whole body with his kisses, but then he regained his senses again and gently pushed her away.

She smiled and touched his cheek. "You do love me. I know you do. You cannot escape your destiny. I want to sleep in your arms tonight."

"Out here?" Her naivety perplexed him. "How much wine did you consume? We are not alone, not here. Besides, it is much too dangerous outside. I cannot be distracted. There are vicious animals lurking in the woods. We must be on guard in case the Larkis decide to pay this settlement a visit. You sleep inside the safety of the house and don't get any crazier ideas, wench."

She pulled her lips into a pout. "There you go again calling me a wench. Don't do that." She rose and stomped away.

Rhodar looked after her, shaking his head. That was another reason he didn't want to get too close to a woman. He'd rather have her spent her passion lying in his arms instead of using it to get angry at him. Sometimes he wondered if women were of the same species as men. They seemed to be ruled by their emotions instead of their brains; shouting in anger and stomping their feet when things didn't go their way or crying for no apparent reason, like little children. How could a man ever understand them?

He looked up when he heard the soft footsteps of someone approaching him. It was one of the women. She carried a wooden plate with food. "Would you like something to eat?"

"I wouldn't mind," he said and accepted the plate she handed him. "It smells good."

She laughed happily. "Fresh vegetables from the garden, boiled tubers, and grilled Gastor-meat. It's a little bit charred because our men don't usually turn it fast enough. That white chunk is boiled Grar, caught this morning in one of the nets we always keep in the lake. They're not easy to catch. Enjoy." She walked away, humming to herself.

These people seemed to be living a happy life. It would be a shame if something happened to them. He bit into the piece of meat, found it a little tough but otherwise tasty. It reminded him of the Lopers that roam the Great Plains.

"More wine?" A voice asked.

He looked up from his plate, recognizing Janissa. "I've probably had too much already," he said, "but how can I refuse you?" Holding out his cup, he watched her refill it. "You ran away before I could give you an answer."

"I wanted to give you time to think about my offer." Her dark eyes seemed to study him. "You would not be disappointed," she said with a voice full of promise.

"It would not be a good idea," he countered. "There are many dangerous animals prowling the woods in the dark of night."

"I'm not afraid of the darkness and the creatures it hides. They need to be afraid of me." She sounded ominous. Then she laughed. "Perhaps you should be afraid of me. I might just consume you with my great hunger. It's been much too long." She spoke barely loud enough for him to hear. "I'm suffocating in this village. I need to get away from here. I was hoping you'd take me with you."

"Is that the only reason you are offering me your body?" He was almost disappointed.

Her hand was on his cheek. "Oh no. I would never do that. There is something about you that attracts me to you, some beastly ferocity that is asking to be set free, to be allowed to still its nearly insatiable craving. I could give you what your subconscious desires, because that is something I also desire." The reflection of the flickering flames lent her large eyes a yellow color and for an insane moment he saw the image of a feral beast staring at him. It was gone in an instant but left him wondering.

"As appealing your offer is, I cannot accept it," he said, looking across the fire at Saleen who seemed to be watching him from her place beside the fire-pit not far away. "There is someone else who I would hurt deeply should I accept your invitation."

She followed his gaze. "I didn't know. I saw you kissing her, but I assumed she was just another one of your conquests. What claim does she have on you?"

"No claim," he said. "We are not lovers if that's what you imply. I saved her life, and I care for her."

"Then I don't understand. If you are not lovers what harm would it do if you and I spent a night of animalistic passion to satisfy our yearning?" Her gaze was almost hypnotic when she stared into his eyes. "This great hunger is burning inside me begging to be released. I would put no claim on you if that's what you fear." She surprised him by pressing her hot lips against his and forcing her tongue into his mouth.

He could feel himself react physically to her demands but forced himself to push her away. "Please, don't do this. It's much more complicated than I can explain. I admit, right now I want you more than anything else, but I cannot."

Her hand reached under his kilt and her fingers curled around his erection. "Your body speaks to me," she whispered, her voice throaty. "I don't understand your problem. Why do you deny your own body?"

He groaned, shocked by her boldness and the sudden pleasure surging through his body when she moved her hand up and down. "Don't!" he almost shouted. It took all his willpower to rip away her hand.

Rising, he turned away from the fire and walked into the darkness, hoping nobody had noticed his physical condition. He cursed himself for being so principled. It didn't take much imagination to envision the exhilarating pleasure waiting for him in the arms of Janissa. Here was a young woman almost throwing herself at him and he rejected her. What a fool he must be in the eyes of every man who would hear about it.

Approaching footstep caused him to turn around. It wasn't Janissa as he half expected but Saleen. "What's wrong?" she asked with a concerned voice.

"Everything," he said fiercely. Trying to hide his erection, he turned away from her and faced the dark forest. She put her arms around him from the back and held him tight. "That girl was sitting with you again and I watched her. I also saw you get up so abruptly and walk away. What did she say or do that made you act so strangely?"

He gave her a strangled laugh. "What do you think? She's offered herself to me in no uncertain words and deeds."

"Did she touch you?" Her hand moved down and found him under his kilt. "Like this?"

It surprised him that her action didn't anger him. "She did," he said, "but I told her the same thing I'm telling you, don't."

She took away her hand and moved around to face him. "You've made me very happy by your action, Rhodar, and I love you for that." She stood on her tiptoes, put her arms around his neck and kissed him gently. "I'll wait for you," she said softly. "Whenever you're ready I'll be there for you." He couldn't see her clearly in the dark, but he sensed that she was smiling. "But don't let me wait too long." She grabbed his hand. "Come and sit with me by the fire."

"I never finished my meal," he said.

She pulled him to the fire pit. "I'm sure nobody ate it."

Janissa was gone but his plate rested on the ground. The vegetables were cold as was the meat. He was still hungry so he ate everything, washing it down with a cup of wine.

Saleen watched him quietly. When he was finished, she moved closer and snuggled up against him. The fires were slowly burning down, but the embers glowed strongly. One of the men had brought a musical instrument and was strumming the strings while accompanied by the voices of two women. Rhodar sat silent, listening to the haunting melody and enjoying Saleen's nearness.

"I sense something strange about these people," Saleen said. "I can't put my finger on it... yet."

"They pray to the Wood Goddess Kalana."

"She's a Dark Goddess. I don't know much about her, but I heard they practice bizarre rituals. They involve bloodletting and sexual ceremonies. No wonder that girl came onto you the way she did. What did she tell you?"

"She said a great hunger is burning inside her waiting to be released. That and other things."

Saleen chuckled. "She's not the only one with a great hunger." Then she became serious. "Don't let your guard down. I don't trust them. They act friendly and hospitable, but are they? What are their motives for feeding us all this good food and offering us so much wine?"

"Perhaps we're a welcome diversion in their daily routine. You have to admit they are happy people. They have music and sing songs. What's so evil and odd about that?"

"I don't know. It's just a feeling I have."

"That old woman used to live in Falconclaw as a midwife. She helped deliver Lord Carn into this world," he reminded her.

"Not necessarily a good thing," Saleen joked. She stretched out beside him, laid her head into his lap and looked up at him with sleepy eyes. "I'm getting tired. I wouldn't mind going to bed soon."

Rhodar looked up into the sky. The two night suns, Seal and Rumos, rose above the treetops, bathing the village with their pale light. "It's getting late and I agree it's time to get some rest." He looked into Saleen's relaxed face, admiring her natural beauty. She had her eyes closed and seemed to be asleep. Gently moving her head out of his lap while trying not to wake her, he rose and looked for Lord Galoor. He found him sitting beside Lady Gardina. She was leaning against him with her eyes closed.

"Lord Galoor," he said. "I believe we should stop celebrating and find a place to sleep. We need to be fresh tomorrow."

Lord Galoor looked at Lady Gardina. "I suppose you are right. All our women are already sleeping. I'd hate to wake them." He chuckled. "I'd rather wake a sleeping forest-beast than a sleeping woman." He rose and searched for Lord Carn.

Lord Carn was engaged talking with the son of the former midwife. "Lord Carn," he called. "Your mother is asleep. We should end this day."

Like Rhodar had done, Lord Carn looked into the sky. "You are correct. It has been a long day." He raised his voice. "We'll be bedding down. All warriors rise. Find a place to sleep. Two of you will take the first watch. Change every couple of Cellas." Then he spoke to the man with him, but Rhodar didn't hear what he said.

The village women gathered all the dishes and carried them to one of the houses, while the men collected the wine-cups.

Rhodar went to pick up Saleen. He carried her in his arms toward the first house. "Where can she sleep?" he asked the woman who greeted him at the door.

"Just follow me," the woman said and led him to a room. "We cleaned it out for the Ladies," she explained. They had covered the floor with thick furs and brought blankets. Rhodar laid Saleen down and covered her up. She smiled in her sleep when he gave her a quick kiss on the cheek.

"She'll be fine," the woman said, smiling at him. Rhodar didn't sense anything evil about her and was confident Saleen was safe. Safer than outside.

As he walked outside, Lord Galoor came to the house, carrying Lady Gardina. Behind him walked Kiiri and her mother. They rubbed the sleep out of their eyes, stumbling as they walked. Rhodar stopped to help the older woman up the steps into the house, wondering why all of them were so tired.

He went to find his horse where he had tied it to a tree and patted its neck. "Time to rest," he said. Taking his battle-axe out of its sheath, he laid it onto the ground. Then he removed the rolled-up blanket from Nightwalker's back and spread it.

Feeling suddenly tired, he lay down and closed his eyes.

He turned onto his side and felt a body beside him. Groping with his hand, it closed over a naked breast and he wondered why a nude woman would lie beside him. His mind seemed to be in a foggy state while his body was on fire. When soft fingers curled around his swollen manhood, he groaned loudly.

"Hush," said a female voice beside him. "Everything is alright. Let me still your terrible hunger."

He didn't protest when a warm, naked body slid on top of him. The soft pressure of a pair of breasts on his chest increased his desire for relief. She kissed him with unrestrained fire; then she sat up. Sitting in his lap, she guided his aching member with one hand. He let out a loud moan when he slid with ease into soft, hot flesh and pushed up against her.

He couldn't form a coherent thought and wondered if this was a dream. His body had been in a high erotic state all evening and screamed for release of the built-up tension. Clamping his hands on the thrusting hips, he dug his fingers into their soft flesh, overwhelmed by the pleasure the woman gave him.

Her face was in darkness, but he could see the silhouette of her sinuous body swaying above him against the starlit sky. There was a moment when her body became rigid and she turned her head to look at the sky when he saw her face.

It was not Janissa's face as he had suspected but the image of a beast and the howling sound coming from her open jaws was not human.

It didn't matter, because this couldn't be real. He swam in a sea of incredible pleasure that was only possible in a dream.

She stretched out and pressed her slick, twisting body against his. He felt a stinging sensation in his throat, which only intensified the pleasure. Putting his arms around her body, he held her in a tight embrace, his mind and body lost in a world of nearly inconceivable joy.

How long they stayed in that position he didn't know. Only when she said, "You can let me go now," he relaxed his arms.

He felled tired and sluggish, drained of energy.

"Don't move for a while," she said, gliding to one side to lie beside him. "Let your body recover."

He recognized Janissa's voice. "It seems you managed to couple with me after all," he said, slurring his words a little. "Or am I dreaming?"

She laughed softly. "This is no dream. Unless I'm the one dreaming."

"I saw you change into a beast."

"An illusion," she said. "The wine makes you imagine things."

"I remember a sting in my neck," he insisted, touching his throat with one hand.

Her long hair caressed his face as she bent over him. She pressed her lips on his and kissed him. Then she whispered, "Do my lips feel like the lips of a beast?"

"Perhaps I'm still dreaming," he murmured, closing his eyes. "It doesn't matter. It is a beautiful dream."

While he lay beside her, he heard the loud moaning sounds of a man and the growling of a beast coming from Lord Galoor's direction, but he was too tired to give it much thought.

When he woke again, it was to the sound of men shouting. Sitting up, the first thing he became aware of was that it must be close to dawn. The sky was painted with reddish color. Rising to his feet, he felt a wave of dizziness but it passed quickly. As his eyes adjusted, he saw men locked in battle with creatures he recognized.

Larkis.

There was no mistaking their ugly shapes. Short, squat bodies with large heads and huge hands and feet, they looked ungainly, but they moved with an agility that belied their appearance. There was a horde of them running around between the houses.

He picked up his battle-axe just in time to defend himself against one of the invaders. With one mighty strike, he buried the sharp double-blade in the creature's neck, nearly severing the head from its body.

As the first attacker fell, another one took its place. He barely managed to ward off the studded heavy club the Larkis swung at his head. He kicked the ugly brute in the chest with one foot and swung his axe again, splitting the huge skull. After that he kept swinging the enchanted weapon, smashing one skull after another. There seemed to be no end to the attackers. Beside him, he heard the snorting of Night-walker as he kicked with his hoofs, knocking out at least one of the vile creatures.

When he finally got a moment to breathe, he realized that the fight was nearly over. The dusty street was littered with corpses. A few Larkis still stood among their dead kind, but then he watched them fall, their bodies pierced by arrows. When he looked toward the houses, he saw men with longbows standing in the doorways.

"Well done, my barbarian friend," said a voice from nearby.

Lord Galoor stood bent over, his bloody sword still in his hand, while he pressed the other hand against his side. Rhodar saw blood seeping from between his fingers.

"You are injured," he said, climbing over the corpses around him to get to the man.

"One of them got me." Lord Galoor grimaced. "Those clubs with their studs are dangerous weapons. They can do a lot of damage if they hit you right."

"You'll need to get that looked after. That's a nasty wound. You're losing blood."

"I'll live. It seems a couple of my warriors weren't so lucky." Lord Galoor called to the warriors who were still standing. "Report to me. If anyone is injured let the women check you out."

Rhodar turned around when he heard a woman's voice calling his name. Saleen came running toward him and put her arms around him. "You're alive," she sobbed.

He laughed and stroked her hair. "It takes more than a bunch of Larkis to kill me."

"I was worried about you. What happened last night? I remember sitting beside you and suddenly I couldn't keep my eyes open. When I woke up this morning I was in the house. How did I get there?"

"I carried you. You must have been really tired, because you never woke up. Did you sleep well?"

"Never slept better," she said. "I feel rested this morning." Her eyes were shiny when she looked at him with a happy smile. "You do care for me. It makes me happy." She lifted up to give him a quick kiss. "I must speak to Lord Carn. Lady Gardina wants me to find out if he has been injured or not."

More women came out of the houses now. Even a few of the men came closer. They still carried their bows. "It seems we were fortunate you stopped by our village," one of them said. "With your help, we defeated them." He looked over the carnage. "We probably wiped out a whole tribe of them."

"Not enough," Lord Galoor growled.

Lord Carn joined them. He seemed without any injuries. He wiped the blood from his sword on a piece of fur he had taken off one of the dead bodies. "I must congratulate your people on your excellent marksmanship with your bows."

The man chuckled. "We are not very skillful with a sword, so we concentrated on developing our proficiency with the bow and arrow. The woods are full of dangerous creatures. They also serve us well when we need to fill our need for meat."

"Perhaps you can still help us to get rid of these bodies before you travel on?" one of the villagers said to Lord Galoor.

Some of the men brought a few wagons drawn by docile draft animals. Rhodar and the warriors helped load the corpses onto the wagons.

"What will you do with them?" Rhodar inquired.

"We'll take them deep into the woods for the carrion eaters," the man explained.

Rhodar looked for Saleen, but instead of her, he saw Janissa among the women. Dressed in her long gray robe and her head covered with a shawl, she looked demure and almost uninteresting. When she noticed him looking at her, she smiled and walked toward him.

"You are covered in blood. Are you injured?"

"Not my blood," he assured her. "I'm fine except for a few bruises." He regarded her with a solemn look. "How did you sleep last night? Did you dream?"

She tilted her head and smiled. Then she reached up and touched his neck. "Did you?"

"I think you know what I'm talking about."

"Forget whatever you believe you saw last night. As I told you it was the wine."

"What are you people?"

"We are just simple worshippers of Kalana. She protects us, but she exacts a high price for her protection. A price that can only be paid in blood." She came close to him and whispered, "Your seed will grow inside me and if our child is a boy he may be chosen as a sacrifice to the Wood Goddess. If it's a girl, there is a good chance she'll become a High Priestess. I will remember you in my dreams." With that she turned and rushed away.

Chapter Fourteen

CARADIN SQUINTED against the morning sun as it climbed above the spires of Castle Dragonwings. The city of Dragona was coming to life as its citizens rose from their sleep to go about their daily chores. Dragona was the capital of Jandarin and the largest of all the cities, even larger than Mountainsong, the capital city of the neighboring Kingdom Maridaan.

Ilita watched her husband as he seemed to silently reflect upon his journey.

"I don't know why you want to travel to Maridaan to celebrate the summer festival," she broke into his contemplation, "King Ordar does not like you. He's never acknowledged you as his brother and never will. You are the bastard son of King Ordarin with no claim to the throne."

"My brother may not even recognize me with my beard and short hair." Caradin laughed and shrugged. "Even if he does, my dear wife, he won't dare harm me. I'll be representing Queen Kharana of Jandarin. After all, I'm her son-in-law and General of the Jandarin Army. Causing me bodily harm would cause friction between our two countries and possibly start a war. He will not chance that."

"You don't know. You told me yourself he's not rational. What if he challenges you to a duel?"

"First of all, he is much older than I and probably out of shape.

Ordar was never a good swordsman. While I've practiced my combat skills, he practiced other skills. I think he spent half his time in the bed of every female who was willing and there was never a shortage of them."

She pouted. "You had your share of willing females as you bragged, especially Lady Gwenlin, who is now King Ordar's wife and the Queen. Your brother may remember that she preferred you to him and that may start the rivalry again between you two. I'm not pleased to see you go. She's the reason you were exiled in the first place. If I weren't with child I'd come with you just to keep you from harm, but the Royal Physician warned me against traveling the long and difficult road to Mountainsong."

He bent to kiss her. "You have nothing to worry about. I only love you, and Gwenlin means nothing to me anymore. It happened so long ago, anyway. You're carrying our child and that is the most important thing for me. I won't let anything happen to jeopardize that."

"So I hope." She put the silver chain with the amulet she'd been clutching in her hand around his neck. "This will protect you against evil magic. Arawan made it especially for you."

He tucked the small pendant into his shirt and chuckled. "If Arawan made it, then I feel safe. He is a sorcerer, even if not a very good one."

"You just don't like him. He knows many spells. If it hadn't been for him, I might have been killed when I was attacked by a wild Drago. Arawan's spell made it drop dead from the sky before it reached me."

"It was a well-aimed arrow from Thorga's bow that pierced the Drago's heart." Caradin smiled. "It doesn't matter. If you believe in Arawan's powers I won't argue about it. Now I must leave if I want to reach Argassa today. I would feel safer there than setting up camp somewhere in the forest."

He gave her one last hug and kiss and then he mounted his Sekua. The animal had been getting restless and seemed as eager to leave as Caradin.

———

ILITA WATCHED HIM RIDE AWAY, accompanied by three of his most trusted soldiers.

"That was a touching scene," said a voice behind Ilita.

She turned to look at Queen Kharana who seemed to study her with an amused smile on her lips. "Mother, I didn't know you were there. Why would you say that?"

Kharana laughed, obviously enjoying herself. "You may fool him but not me. What if the child you carry doesn't have his red hair? What if its eyes are purple? How will you explain that to your loving husband?"

"I don't know what you're talking about, Mother?" A cold shiver ran down Ilita's back. She had never given that possibility any thought.

"You know quite well what I'm talking about. How can you be so stupid, daughter? I can almost forgive you that you took a lover and couldn't keep your legs closed but to get yourself pregnant by another man is unforgivable." Kharana spoke sharply and her eyes flashed.

"You have no proof of that," Ilita said with a sinking feeling in her stomach.

"I'm afraid the proof will come when your child is born." Kharana's anger was clearly displayed in her lined face. "It will ruin everything I've been planning for so many seasons now. With Caradin's help, I've built up my army. My soldiers are ready to strike when the opportunity arises. Caradin isn't going to Maridaan to enjoy the summer festival. His mission is to judge the strength of King Ordar's army and his defenses. From what I hear Ordar has become complacent and neglected to keep his army in shape. His soldiers are not trained like mine. Maridaan is ripe for a takeover. I wanted you to sit beside Caradin on the throne as Queen of Maridaan. That won't happen if you bear him a bastard child."

Ilia swallowed. "The child could always be stillborn. Caradin will never see it."

Kharana pointed an accusing finger at her. "Even if the child is not his, it will still be my grandchild and I will hold you responsible for its life."

"You misunderstood, Mother. I didn't mean what it sounded like. I meant to say it is possible the child may not be born alive. It happens. Besides, what makes you assume the child is not Caradin's?"

"I'm not blind. I see what goes on in the palace and I have eyes and ears everywhere. There are no secrets that I don't know about, and I know about you and Arawan, as do many of the servants. You have a lot to learn, daughter."

Pulling herself erect, Ilita looked her mother in the eyes. "If you must know, I never loved Caradin. You forced me to marry him. Don't forget that."

"Like I said, you have a lot to learn. Only peasants are allowed to marry for love. We aren't. My parents arranged my marriage to your father. I came to love him, and I hoped you would learn to love Caradin in time. At one time, you did love him. I don't know what happened to you. I know Caradin loves you. He's a handsome man and ambitious. He will make a good king someday and you would be wise to stay by his side. Of course, you may have already jeopardized that with your stupidity. Don't tell me you love Arawan. He's a sorcerer and a nobody. His position as Royal Sorcerer is precarious. I can have him removed any time I feel like it." Kharana turned on her heels and stalked away. Even her walk conveyed her anger.

Ilia waited until her mother disappeared through the door into the palace and then she headed for another wing of the massive building. Looking around if any of the servants were about, she turned into a side corridor and stopped in front of a narrow door. She knocked four times. When the door opened, she hurried through it.

"Caradin is finally on his way." She laughed and rushed up to Arawan who had been waiting for her in his room.

He took her into his arms and kissed her. "Did you give him the amulet?"

She nodded. "The fool will believe it protects him from magic even if he pretends he doesn't. If we're lucky, an accident will befall him and he will never return." Her expression turned serious. "My mother knows about us and she suspects that the child I carry is yours."

"Which, of course, is true. I wouldn't worry about it. I put a spell on the amulet that will practically guarantee that we've seen the last of your husband." An unpleasant smile crossed Arawan's narrow face. "By the time our child is born, we may have taken care of your mother as well, and you will be Queen Ilita of Jandarin."

"We must be careful, Arawan. My mother has spies everywhere and if she ever suspects anything, she will not hesitate to banish me forever or worse throw me into the deepest dungeon she can find. You, my love, you will lose your head to the executioner's axe."

He chuckled. "Did you forget I'm a sorcerer? I can cloud your mother's mind so she will only see things I want her to see." He held her face in his hands and kissed her gently. "Nothing can stop us," he whispered into her ear. "Nothing." He put his hand under her blouse to touch her naked breast.

Shuddering, she inhaled sharply and sighed. "You always know what to do and how to heat up my body. Caradin barely touches me anymore and when he does, it leaves me cold." She opened his robe and let her hand travel down his belly. "Let's not waste time talking with our mouths. I want your body to speak to me."

They tumbled onto his cot and lay in each other's arms, inflamed by their desire for each other. When their bodies became one, she cried out and moved against him with fiery passion.

———

ILIA LEFT Arawan's room feeling happy and satisfied. She touched her slightly swollen belly and smiled, hoping the child she carried would be a boy.

She decided to go to the bathing pond in the garden to wash her body. Arawan's vitality always demanded her full attention and usually left her exhausted and her body in need of a bath.

There wasn't anyone in the pond, which was nothing unusual. The servants were only allowed in the pond by invitation, either by her, by Caradin, or her mother when either of them wanted a massage or help with the washing.

Even guests never bathed in this pond. There was a larger pond somewhere else in the garden for the guests and the servants.

She stripped off her clothes and dipped her toes into the water. Then she slowly immersed her whole body with only her head showing. The water was cool and refreshing. Closing her eyes, she listened to the gurgling of the small waterfall in the creek that delivered the fresh water. The creek eventually poured into the larger pond, but it wasn't deep enough to swim to the other pond.

After a while, she was getting chilly and moved her legs and arms to get warm again but still kept her eyes closed to shut out the world around her. Sometimes she needed to get away from everyone and be by herself. She daydreamed of the time when she was a little girl and her father, King Zandorin, was still alive. He had been a powerful man, kind and loving, unlike her mother, who never liked her, blaming her for the death of Zandor.

Zandor, her older brother.

How can a toddler be responsible for someone's death? Was it her fault when her mother left her unsupervised and she wandered into the swamp between the river and the palace grounds? She had been too small to realize the swamp was a dangerous place and not a playground. The curiosity of a small child made her crawl into the swamp.

Zandor, who was only four seasons older than she, found her in time and jumped into the swamp to save her. He threw her onto dry land and rescued her from being sucked into the quack mire but could not save himself. He had not been strong enough to free himself and sank below the dark surface of the swamp where he suffocated and died. The servants came too late for him.

If anyone was at fault, it was her mother for leaving her alone, but nobody would ever dare to accuse the Queen of being negligent.

Sometimes in her mind she played out little scenes how it would have been had her brother lived.

"You're carrying a child in your belly, little sister, but it is not your husband's. You are playing a dangerous game. Aren't you afraid Caradin will be suspicious when the child doesn't resemble him?"

"You worry too much, big brother." She laughed. "I'm hoping he won't come back."

"Do you hate him that much?"

"I don't hate him but I don't love him, either. Never have."

"But you slept in his bed."

"I was a dutiful wife." She laughed again. "I admit I did enjoy the coupling with him. No sense to waste my energy without getting any benefits. I used him."

"Do you love this Arawan?" As usual, his face was concealed behind a foggy veil. She wished she could see his face, but it was forever hidden from her.

"When we copulate every fiber in my body is on fire and the pleasure is so great I sometimes think I'm going to explode."

"But do you love him, Ilita?"

"Is it really necessary to love him? Won't what we have be enough?"

"The physical attraction will fade with time but true affection and love will always bond you to each other, remember that."

"The son we'll have together will bond us."

"He will, but he'll grow up and leave you."

She sighed. "Oh, Zandor, you always argue with me."

Even though his face was veiled, she knew he was smiling. "That's what siblings do, little sister. They argue but they love each other. I will always love you."

She wanted to answer him, but he disappeared and no matter how hard she tried, he didn't come back. Opening her eyes, she saw a man standing beside the pond. He was young, handsome, and tall. When she looked into his colorless eyes, they seemed to draw her spirit from her body.

"Who are you?"

A smile lit his handsome face. "Does it matter who I am?"

She shook her head but kept silent.

He beckoned to her. "Come," he said, and she moved toward him.

She didn't cover her nakedness as she rose from the water. He watched her and grabbed her hand to help her climb on land. When he took her into his arms, he was as naked as she. She had not seen him undress. His body was hard and muscled, reminding her of Caradin.

His lips were soft and warm on hers, and she responded to his kiss. They sank to the ground and he put her onto her back into the soft grass. She opened her thighs willingly and let out a satisfied cry when he entered her.

Their lovemaking was slow and gentle. She floated on a soft cloud of pure pleasure, losing all sense of time. He was a stranger and yet familiar. She felt his love for her and she loved him back.

"Don't leave," she called out when she felt him slipping away. The air was suddenly cool on her naked body and she sat up to look around. She was alone. Shivering, she rose to her feet and searched for her clothes. They lay not far away and she dressed.

What just happened? Closing her eyes, she could still feel the stranger's kiss, still felt his muscular body on hers and his hard manhood moving inside her and yet—there was no evidence of a man having been here.

Had it all been in her imagination, a wishful dream, or had she been visited by some magical being, some invisible entity that had the ability to create a physical body? Or had it been a sorcerer with the power to transport his mind into hers and make her believe what she experienced was real?

Something had happened and it left her confused and questioning the direction her life was taking.

Was having an affair with Arawan a mistake? Had it been her idea to let him impregnate her? She couldn't remember. He could have planted it in her mind, making her believe that's what she desired. He was a sorcerer. He could influence people's minds and make them do anything he wanted.

A horrified thought entered her mind. 'What if my memory has been manipulated? My mother said that I loved Caradin at one time, but I don't remember that. I remember always loathing him. Is my memory false?'

Suddenly, she felt alone and helpless with nobody to turn to or rely on. Nobody she could trust.

"Princess Ilita."

She turned and looked at the old woman standing beneath one of the fruit trees. She held a basket in her hand which she'd been filling with small berries she picked from the tree.

"I saw you by the bathing pond," the old woman said and put down her basket. "Come and talk to me for a while."

No servant would ever dare ask that of Ilita, but Salana was more than a servant. She was a teacher and had taught Ilita when she was old enough to learn about the world. She taught her how to be a Lady, how to walk and how to talk. Ilita had loved and respected her more than her mother.

She felt guilty for having forgotten about the old woman who had tried so patiently to teach a stubborn child reluctant to learn, but she never gave up and Ilita was grateful for that now.

Salana had grown old. Her face was thin and deeply lined and her hands marked by age-spots, but her eyes were still clear and alert. "You have become a beautiful woman." Then she smiled. "And you're aglow with the joy carrying a child in your belly brings."

"I'm hoping it will be a boy."

"Your husband must be as anxious as you. Every man wants a son to carry on his name."

"Yes, he is quite anxious." Ilita felt uncomfortable with the topic and tried to change it. "He left for Maridaan today to celebrate the yearly Summer Festival."

"I hear your husband is half-brother to King Ordar of Maridaan."

"Yes, but he is also the bastard son of King Ordarin, which means he has no claim to the throne." She smiled. "Even though he believes he has."

Salana's face became serious. "I know it's not my place anymore to give you advice, but there are ugly rumors about you and the palace sorcerer. Arawan is a dangerous man with ambitious plans that may not be in your best interest."

"What kind of plans?"

"It's gossip and I don't want to be part of it. My only advice to you is be careful." She picked up her basket. "The chellies are sweet this year, and the crop is excellent. I'm going to make nectar from these. If you want, I can have some sent to you when I'm done."

"That would be wonderful. I remember you always made great tasting chellie-nectar." Ilita didn't know what else to say and realized she lost that special connection with the old teacher. She didn't know why it would affect her so much, but she felt a great sense of loss. It only added to her gloomy mood.

"It was nice talking with you again, Salana, but now I must hurry. I have a few things to do."

Salana reached out and touched Ilita's hair, the way she used to do. "You take care of yourself now, child, and may the gods smile favorably upon you and your unborn child."

Ilia took the old woman's hand into hers and put it to her lips. "I haven't forgotten the things you taught me. For that I will always be grateful. I wish you would have been my mother."

"Then I would either be the queen or you would be just a peasant girl." Salana laughed. "I don't know which would be the preferred situation."

"Maybe being a peasant girl wouldn't be so bad. There are times when I hate being what I am. I feel trapped. Always to be proper, never be able to do the things I would like to do. Everyone seems to watch me, judge me, hoping I do something stupid." Ilita felt tears rolling down her cheeks. "You were the only one who didn't put on a false face. You scolded me when I did something wrong and when I didn't pay attention. To you I was not a princess who needed to be treated with soft gloves but just another student to be taught and you did that with dedication and love. I know that now." She swallowed. "I'm sorry if sometimes I gave you the impression I did not care about you and what you taught me."

Salana smiled. "I loved you like my own daughter. You could do nothing wrong," she said gently. "You acted no different from any girl your age. No need to be sorry." She looked at the basket in her hand. "Now I must go. These berries are best right after they've been picked."

Ilia watched the old teacher walking away. She walked slowly, her frail body bent forward a little as if carrying a burden, which she was. The burden of old age. She carried the many years she had lived; she carried her memories—the good and the bad ones, and she carried the things she had done and the ones that needed to be done but didn't do.

"I love you, Old Teacher," she whispered, but there was nobody there to hear her, except for the wind that suddenly sprang up and rustled the leaves of the chellie-tree.

Chapter Fifteen

RHODAR, sighed, still exhausted from the fighting and from his stint with Janissa. Even a man with his constitution and endurance had a limited reserve of energy. He looked forward to sleeping safely and unmolested in a palace bed for some needed rest.

The royal party didn't leave the village until noon. It took that long to wash their blood-covered bodies and some of their garments, though not all the bloodstains could be eliminated. However, Lady Gardina would not arrive in the King's palace with an entourage grimy-looking and dressed in filthy clothing.

At least the weather stayed pleasant and it looked like it was going to stay like that for the next few days. The tall trees shut out most of the light and the air in the forest felt damp, but it was warm. Rhodar had removed his borrowed shirt because of its wet condition and felt more comfortable without it. He knew he'd probably have to wear it again once they arrived at the palace.

Lord Galoor slowed his steed and waited for Rhodar to ride beside him.

"You fought well," Lord Galoor said, smiling. "Of course, I didn't expect any less from the son of an old friend. I see a lot of him in you."

"Was my father an honorable man?"

"Why would you even ask that? Of course he was. I trusted him with my life. Men like your father are a rare breed. I hope you will always do him honor." He stayed silent for a while as he seemed to think about something. "What do you remember about last night?" His question came a bit as a surprise.

Rhodar chuckled. "I remember drinking too much wine." He turned his head slightly to give Lord Galoor a sidelong glance. "I don't know what was in that wine, but my sleep was filled with strange visions."

"About that." Lord Galoor cleared his throat. "We both know they probably were not visions. Whatever you saw and seem to remember has to stay between us. It would be best not to tell anyone about it, especially the women. You have nothing to lose, but Lady Gardina may not look favorable upon me if she knew about last night. I hope you understand."

"I understand. You don't have to worry. I have no desire to discuss what happened with anyone. It would make me look weak. It was the wine and possibly a touch of magic that made us act the way we did. I'm not even sure if what I believe happened was real and not just my imagination."

He lifted his hand to his neck. There was no pain, not anymore, but the memory of a sharp sting and the unbelievable pleasure that followed haunted him. He seemed to remember holding Janissa's naked body in his arms and the euphoric feeling of her soft lips on his. How could a woman cause such pleasure in a man's body and leave him weak and exhausted? It had never happened to him before.

"Good. I'm glad you're sensible."

"It is in my best interest. I'm curious, Lord Galoor. The old, blind woman who claimed to have delivered Lord Carn, did anyone know that she was a Wer, possibly even a shapeshifter?"

Lord Galoor gave him a sharp look. "Is that what you think these people are?"

"Aren't they?"

Lord Galoor stayed silent for a moment. "I suppose in a way they could be called Wers, but they are different from the real Wers, the ones where their whole body becomes a beast. These people do not change completely, only their heads change. Their bodies keep the human shape. Instead of becoming vile creatures, they keep their humanity and gentle nature. That's the difference. They're quite civilized."

"But they sacrifice living children to the Wood Goddess Kalana. That does not sound civilized to me," Rhodar objected.

"Where did you hear that?"

"Janissa told me." He didn't tell Galoor she was going to sacrifice his son to Kalana, should the child she would bear be a boy.

"The young woman that was all over you last night?" Lord Galoor chuckled. "How could I miss that? Didn't I warn you about keeping your snake under your kilt?"

"You did." Rhodar grinned lopsidedly. "She was more than persistent. The wine didn't help."

Lord Galoor's expression turned serious. "She told you the truth. Not only do they sacrifice children, they also sacrifice adults. It is an honor to be chosen."

"How do you know so much about them?"

"My mother was one of them."

Rhodar turned his head to stare at Lord Galoor. "That means you are one of them."

Lord Galoor shook his head. "The ability to change transfers only from mother to daughter. The men are not affected. My sister, Lady Arneena, was one."

"Perhaps that was the reason she was murdered."

"Perhaps. We may never know." Galoor looked at Nightwalker showing signs of agitation. "I don't believe your horse and my steed get along that well. I think I'll join Lord Carn again." He clucked his tongue to signal his mount to a faster pace.

Rhodar watched the big man catch up with Lord Carn, somewhat surprised by the revelation. It could be the reason Lord Galoor never took a mate and had children of his own. His thoughts drifted to Saleen. She was a witch and a Wer; not a true shapeshifter, either. She could only change into a specific beast, while a shapeshifter had the ability to take on many different forms. What would her children be like?

He thought about the previous night and the girl Janissa. Just because she seduced him and drank his blood didn't make her a vile creature. It was in her nature to do so. She gave him incredible pleasure and a night of passion he would remember for a long time. There was nothing gained in telling anyone about it, especially Saleen. Whatever happened was a private thing between him and Janissa and it would stay buried in his memories.

Lord Galoor need not worry his secret would be revealed to anyone. Of course, there were the warriors. He didn't know if a few or even all of them had been involved with any of the females. There was a good chance at least one of them would be liable to brag about it, but it was up to Lord Galoor or Lord Carn to keep them silent.

They left the forest behind and traveled again on a road that had fields on either side. A cool breeze blew from the north. He could almost smell the salty ocean air, but he knew that to be an illusion, because the ocean was many days' ride away. The city of Mountainsong was located beside a river that eventually spilled its waters into the ocean.

They passed a number of small settlements populated mostly by farmers and their workers. Children playing in the street stopped their games and watched in silence as the riders and the carriage rolled down the dusty street. Rhodar observed the poor state of their clothes and wondered about that. Most houses were small but in good shape. He saw the odd house that was bigger with a larger yard; obviously, those houses belonged to the farmers.

Rhodar received his share of curious stares, but none of the children approached them, as if they were afraid of doing something wrong.

Soon they arrived at the outskirts of Mountainsong. The city was larger than Falconview, which meant there was also a larger slum area. Had they traveled the main road they would have missed that part of the city. The houses they passed looked shabby and in need of repair. It was evident their owners didn't have the means to repair them or the desire. The people sitting in front of their homes or the ones walking on the street gave them hostile looks. Rhodar had no doubt had it not been for the armed guards some would have thrown stones at them. These people did not appear happy. He remembered the same frosty air in Falconview.

No river divided the city and gradually the homes appeared bigger and nicer looking and the attitude of the people they met also changed.

When they finally arrived at the King's palace, Rhodar had to admit it was imposing and full of splendor. Tall spires rose from the many towers and the rooftops of the buildings sported beautiful statues. Two giant stone statues, one of a female and one of a male warrior guarded the gate to the palace grounds. Six armed warriors barred the way with naked swords in their hands.

Lord Carn lifted his hand in greeting. "Lady Gardina, the sister of King Ordar, to celebrate the summer festival. I'm her son Lord Carn, the King's nephew. Let us pass."

"You've been expected, Lord Carn," one of the warriors said. "I beg forgiveness, but we must look into the carriage." He walked stiff-legged to the carriage and pulled aside the curtain. Stepping back a moment later, he gave his companions the order to move aside and let the carriage pass.

While the road through the city had been paved with cobblestones the road beyond the gate was smooth and well-kept. If Rhodar had been impressed with the grounds at Castle Falconclaw, it was nothing compared to the landscaping he saw in the courtyard of the King's palace. Larger and on a much grander scale, it showed the King's wealth. Smooth graveled paths wound their way through the grass-covered grounds were dotted with flowers, shrubs, and tall, massive trees.

A number of people stood or walked on the manicured lawns. The ladies sat on benches under umbrellas, protected from the burning rays of the sun, while the men strutted around in front of them with sticks in their hands, playing some kind of game unknown to Rhodar.

When they reached the entrance to the palace, servants met them and put down stools to make it easier for Lord Carn and Lord Galoor to dismount. They ignored Rhodar and the six warriors.

Rhodar jumped from his horse, but when one of the stable boys tried to lead the horse away, Nightwalker snorted a warning and the stable boy backed off.

"I'm afraid Aarin is the only one who can touch my horse," Rhodar explained. He turned to search for Aarin and saw him climbing down from the carriage. When he called his name, the young man came running.

"I had a feeling you might need me," Aarin said and grinned. He turned to give the stable boy a triumphant look. "Just show me the way and I'll follow you with the horse."

Before he left, he spoke to Rhodar in a low voice. "You might want to put on your shirt."

"Probably good advice," Rhodar said and pulled the shirt out of the saddlebag. It looked wrinkled and still felt damp, but he put it on anyway.

Lord Galoor asked one of the servants to show his warriors where they should take their Sekua and then to the place where they would stay. Then he gave Rhodar a nod. "You are our guest and welcome to accompany us to meet the King."

Lady Gardina stepped down from the carriage. She looked tired and walked slowly, supported by Latalia. Kiiri and Saleen walked behind her, seemingly fresh and rested.

"I'm getting too old for these long trips," Lady Gardina said. "Swallowing the dust from that awful road did not make it any more pleasant."

Lord Galoor, who obviously heard her complaining, waited for her. "You'll be able to wash the dust away with a glass of your brother's finest wine," he said with a little smile. "Besides, if you believe you are old I should be feeling ancient, which I don't. I'm still a young man and you are the radiant beauty I worship and desire. Admittedly, I'm a little tired and feeling a bit weak right now otherwise I would carry you through those doors."

Lady Gardina touched his face with her gloved hand and chuckled. "Even if you weren't tired you would never make it up those steps carrying me without collapsing. You're a dreamer, a charmer, and a big liar. Just for that I shouldn't let you into my chambers tonight. Now, let's not waste any more time. I want to get out of this heat and into a tub filled with water."

"If I recall correctly, there is a large bathing pond behind the palace. Perhaps all of us should make use of it," Lord Galoor suggested.

"You just want to look at all those young nude girls," Lady Gardina chided him, but then she smiled and glanced at Rhodar. "On second thought, it may be a much better idea than mine. You can ogle those young girls while I enjoy the sights of rippling muscles and other interesting parts of the younger men."

Lord Carn, who had been listening to their bantering impatiently, spoke. "The King is waiting. I suggest we get moving."

"Nobody is stopping you," Lady Gardina spoke somewhat sharply. Then she headed for the stairs without the aid of Latalia, who hurried to catch up with her.

Lord Carn didn't comment, but he couldn't hide his suppressed seething anger when he stared at his mother's back.

"I guess we'd better follow," Lord Galoor said to Rhodar. "I for one do not want to awaken her wrath. Fortunately for us, she's not a shapeshifter. She'd tear all of us apart in her beast-form." He hurried after her.

Rhodar couldn't help but smile. Sometimes he had difficulties understanding how strong men would let a woman intimidate and control them. As her son, Lord Carn should respect and love his mother, but Rhodar hadn't seen any love or even respect in Lord Carn's eyes, only resentment. It was a different situation with Lord Galoor. He obviously respected and even loved Lady Gardina, but his attraction for her was also sexual and she used that as a tool to control him.

'I'm never going to let a woman control me that way,' he thought and wondered fleetingly if that was another reason he didn't want to get close to Saleen, even though he had to admit to himself his feelings for her were strong and he was drawn to her, and it wasn't strictly a sexual attraction. There was more to it than that.

He sensed somebody walking beside him and looked to discover it was Saleen. She gave him a smile and said in a low voice, "King Ordar is also given to angry outbursts, which is nothing unusual; after all, he is Lady Gardina's brother. Tread carefully. Just a little bit of advice to an uncouth barbarian."

"You've been in the palace before?"

She nodded. "A few times. I'm familiar with the palace and even some of the gossip and intrigue among the lords and ladies, and also the servants. Watch your tongue and who you confide in and especially who you visit during the night."

"Who would I visit?"

Her laugh teased. "You're a stranger, a barbarian from the Western Plains. The women will be attracted to you because you're a novelty. To be bedded by you would be a welcome change from their usual boredom. You'd be considered a trophy, nothing else." She touched his arm. "Not every woman cares about you the way I do, remember that."

"How can I forget? You remind me of that constantly." He chuckled and laid an arm around her shoulder. "I am fond of you, but you know that."

"How about me? Does anyone care about me, if only just a little?"

Rhodar turned his head to look at Kiiri, who had come up to his other side. "I care about you, also." He laughed. "Just a little."

"Kiiri pouted. "I was hoping for more. What does Saleen have that I don't?"

He shrugged. "I saved her life and she saved mine. It created a strong bond between us, one that can never be broken. Besides, she's constantly trying to seduce me."

"I can do that," Kiiri said, batting her eyes.

Saleen slapped him on the arm. "Oh, you uncivilized barbarian. Always making fun of me. I think I hate you." She removed his arm from her shoulder and stalked ahead of him.

"She has a temper," Kiiri observed. "I would never treat you like that."

"Sure you would. Females are all the same." He gave her a slap on one round buttock.

She jumped, surprised by his action. "All males are the same," she said, pouting. "You let them bed you only once and they think they own you." She pretended to be angry but smiled at him over her shoulder as she walked away.

He watched both of the girls climbing the stairs, enjoying the movement of their plump buttocks under their short skirts. One he had coupled with and one wanted to couple with him. He'd better watch himself, because he was entering dangerous territory.

Hurrying to catch up with the others, he took three steps at once. Two servants held open the doors. He stepped into a large vestibule. Oil lamps attached to the smooth stonewalls illuminated it with their flickering flames. More servants greeted the newcomers. He also saw armed guards standing by the walls.

One of them came toward Rhodar. "No weapons allowed inside the palace. I will take your axe and knives."

With a grin, Rhodar handed him his axe. The guard took it, but when Rhodar let go of the handle, the weapon dropped to the floor with a loud thud. The guard tried in vain to lift it off the floor.

He looked at Rhodar. "Why can't I lift this axe?"

"Because it's an enchanted weapon," Rhodar explained. "Only I can lift it. Just tell me where you want me to put it and I'll carry it there." He bent and picked up the battle-axe with ease. In his hands, it weighed almost nothing.

"Are you a sorcerer?" The guard took a step away from Rhodar, fear in his eyes.

"I'm no sorcerer. Just a simple warrior. My name is Rhodar."

"You're an outlander."

"My homeland lies beyond the mountains," Rhodar confirmed the guard's guess.

"The Western Plains." The guard nodded. "I've heard of them. What is your business with King Ordar?"

"I was invited by Lady Gardina to join her at the King's summer festival."

"Lady Gardina is your friend?"

"I'm Lord Carn's guest. I performed a service for him." Rhodar smiled. "It's a long story."

"Come, I'll show you where you can leave your weapons." The Guard chuckled. "At least you don't have to worry about someone stealing your axe."

Rhodar walked with the guard who took him to a small room. It looked like an armory. He put his axe and knives onto a shelf. When he came back into the vestibule, the others were gone, but then he saw Saleen standing near one of the doors and went to her.

"I've waited for you. Come now. We'll have to hurry. What took you so long?"

He shrugged. "I had to give up my weapons. Why am I the only one?"

"Lord Carn and Lord Galoor are allowed to keep theirs, but they carried only knives. Why didn't you leave your axe with your horse?"

"I like to have it near in case I have need for it. I'm a stranger here and I don't trust anyone."

"Perhaps you should. Nobody is going to murder you in your sleep. We are civilized," she said, not hiding her contempt.

"Why are you angry with me?"

"Because you're so stubborn and blind, that's why. Now, let's go."

They walked down wide corridors, passing many people, mostly servants going about their business. Finally, they entered a large room with a high ceiling. The walls were decorated with pictures and statues on pedestals and inside small recesses. The ceiling displayed pictures of muscular warriors battling each other or giant beasts. Men and women in fancy clothes rested on loungers or stood beside small tables, sipping from delicate cups or nibbling on fruit and cakes.

"That's King Ordar," Saleen whispered and pointed at a gaudily dressed corpulent man sitting in a huge chair decorated with elaborate carvings. The woman sitting in a smaller chair beside him looked much younger than the King. Obviously, she was the Queen. She was talking to Lord Galoor, who, Rhodar remembered, was her cousin. Even from the distance he could tell that she was slim and beautiful.

In front of the King, stood Lord Carn and Lady Gardina.

Saleen tugged on his kilt. "Don't stand here like this. Go and meet the King."

"Aren't you coming?"

"No. I'm only a simple servant. Servants don't approach the King openly like this. Go."

Rhodar headed for the King, not knowing what he was going to say, but he needn't have worried. He hadn't even reached the King, when he looked in Rhodar's direction.

"You must be the outlander my sister told me about," the King boomed.

Rhodar waited until he was closer before he answered. "I hope she put in a favorable word for me," he said with a smile and bowed. "Forgive me if I commit a few blunders, your Majesty. I'm not used to being in the presence of royalty."

King Ordar laughed. "Just relax and you'll be fine. Lord Galoor tells me you are the son of Rhor, a barbarian warrior I met a long time ago. You look a lot like him and the way you carry yourself you could be him. How is your father?"

"Getting old which he won't admit. He is High Chief of the Serpent Clan."

"He was an honorable man. Lord Galoor and I spent many hours going on hunts with him. Whatever happened to that enchanted battle-axe he carried?"

"He gave it to me. That's why I'm in your kingdom, your Majesty. I'm on a quest to have the spell renewed."

"I'd like to spend some time with you after the festival. You can tell me everything about your father and that quest of yours." The King gave him a friendly smile. "For now, go and find yourself a female and enjoy yourself."

Rhodar knew when he was being dismissed and wasn't at all sorry.

"Your Majesty," he said and bowed. Then he looked at the queen and made another bow. "I look forward to seeing more of you, Lady Gwenlin," he said.

She laughed and crossed her legs which were visible through the slit in her long skirt. "I have a feeling that was your first blunder, outlander. What was your name again?"

"I am Rhodar. Forgive me if I offended you, my Lady."

"Oh no. I don't feel offended. I'm amused that a young man wants to see more of me, but I don't think my husband, the King, would be pleased if I showed you more." She bent forward and spoke in a loud whisper, "Of course, what he doesn't know..." Her teasing laughter sounded loud in the room. "By the way, I'm usually addressed as Queen Gwenlin."

Lord Galoor chuckled. "You are embarrassing him, Gwenlin." He turned to Rhodar. "Why don't you follow the King's suggestion and go before my cousin makes a fool of you. She has a strange sense of humor."

"Thank you, my Lord." Rhodar turned and walked away, vowing he'd stay away from the queen as far as possible. Even the King had disappointed him. Somehow, he had expected a friendlier welcome.

As he walked across the room, he noticed the smirks on the men's faces, but he also saw the open desire in the eyes of the females. He didn't know where he should go so he just headed for the exit, not feeling welcome at all. It proved again, this was not his kind of environment. He didn't fit in with these highborn lords and ladies.

Before he reached the exit door, someone rushed up to him and touched him on the shoulder.

"Don't leave," said a woman's voice.

He stopped walking and turned to look at her. Seeing a young, pretty woman with a beautiful, friendly smile, dressed in a thin, short dress that revealed more of her body than it hid lifted his spirits. Her face was framed by short, black hair. She had a pretty face, but it still had that immature look of a young girl; her fully developed body said otherwise. Maybe this day wouldn't be a complete loss.

"Come and sit with me." She grabbed his hand and dragged him to a lounger away from the crowd. She sat down, crossed her slim, bare legs and patted the seat beside her. "Keep me company for a little while. I'm feeling lonely."

He followed her invitation. "I'm surprised a beautiful girl like you is not surrounded by a horde of suitors."

"There usually are plenty of them but not today. My parents wanted me to spend some time thinking about my future without being pestered by a group of young men in heat who have nothing in their head but trying to get me into their bed." Her laughter was fresh and honest when she noticed his surprised expression. "Did I shock you? I know I'm supposed to be this innocent, proper little girl. I used to be, but now I'm a grown woman with my own thoughts and desires."

"Perhaps your parents wouldn't be happy if they saw you talking to me," he said with a crooked grin. "Are your parents here?"

"Oh, yes, they are, but they are not watching, because they don't know I'm here. I'm not supposed to be, but I was getting bored and lonely. They should be more concerned with my younger sister. She is the wild one not me." Her eyes searched his face. "Tell me about the place where you come from. Is it far away?"

"It is beyond the mountains. I have lost count of the many days it took to get here."

"What is it like in your home country?"

"Things are different. My people don't live in large cities. I'm more comfortable on the back of a horse during the day and sleeping under the stars at night than spending my time inside a dwelling, especially one as big as this palace." He looked around the room. "We don't have lords and ladies lounging around all day doing nothing but eat and drink. In my world, everyone has a job to do, contributing to the survival of the clan. There are no parasites that live off the hard work of others." His last words came out more bitter than intended.

"You don't approve of royalty?"

"This is a different country with different people and customs. It is not my place to judge. Our way of life would probably not even be possible here. My world is the open grassland where wild horses roam and shaggy Lopers travel in herds so huge you cannot see the end. Where the Giant Stone Serpent can swallow an unwary man with one bite and enormous winged reptiles attack small groups of travelers from the sky."

"That doesn't sound like a place I'd want to live." She shook herself. "There must be some things that are attractive and pleasant."

He chuckled softly. "Our rivers and lakes are teeming with fish that almost jump into your nets. Wild berries are growing in abundance and fruit trees are laden with fruit so heavy the branches break. The sky is high and blue and at night the stars are rarely covered with dark clouds. The air is fresh and clean."

He didn't tell her about the wildfires with smoke so thick it was impossible to breathe without a wet cloth over your mouth and the storms and the torrential rains, because they didn't matter. The Western Plains were his home and he longed to be back there. Especially at this moment.

"Maybe it isn't as bad as I thought." She sighed. "You are lucky to have seen so much already. To be able to travel carefree must be exciting. I've never been anywhere but in Mountainsong."

"It is lonely to travel," he said. "My only companion is my horse."

She smiled impishly and touched his hand in a casual gesture. "There must be occasions when you are not lonely. I mean, a rugged, handsome warrior like you will have no problem bedding any girl he wants."

He felt suddenly uncomfortable. There was no doubt in his mind what she hinted at. Had she been a peasant girl, he would have had no qualms, but she seemed to be the daughter of some influential lord and he didn't want any trouble.

She must have sensed his discomfort and withdrew her hand. "I'd better leave before my parents see me," she said and rose. Before she left, she bent and kissed him on the cheek. "I hope I'll see you again. I'd like to get to know you much more intimately." She turned and rushed out of the door.

He looked after her, wondering who she was. Scanning the room and seeing all the laughing and happy men and women, he felt out of place. He didn't belong here. Nobody even seemed to pay any attention to him. The novelty of his appearance in front of the King had already worn off. Perhaps that was a good thing.

One of the servants headed his way. "You look lonely," she said with a little smile. "Would you like a piece of cake and a cup of tirka-brew?"

"How about a tankard of ale instead?"

She laughed. "I don't blame you. The cake isn't very good and the tirka-brew…" She made a face. "It's easy to see you feel out of place with all these highbrows. Come with me. I'll take you out of here. I'll introduce you to my brother and you can share a tankard of ale with him."

She took him down the main corridors and then turned into another one. They didn't walk far before she stopped in front of a door. Opening it, she called, "Jador, I'm bringing someone you might want to meet." She entered the room and invited Rhodar to follow.

There was only one oil lamp burning in the room and it took his eyes a moment to adjust to the dim light.

"I'm in here," a male voice came from another room.

The next room was just as dark with only one lamp burning, but the woman went and lit another lamp on the opposite wall. From the shadows in one corner a figure rose and came forward. When the light illuminated his face, Rhodar saw a man with a short beard. He also saw that the man was dragging one foot behind him.

The beard made him look older, but as he came nearer, Rhodar noticed he was still a young man.

"I never did get your name," the woman said.

"I'm Rhodar."

"Rhodar, meet my brother Jador. He used to be one of the King's personal guards until a fall from a Sekua made him a cripple. Now he's one of the cooks." She chuckled. "Not a very good one, but he's learning."

Jador scrutinized Rhodar with a critical eye. Then he grinned. "You're an outlander and not comfortable among all those noblemen. Don't deny it. Why else would my sister bring you here to spend some boring time with a cripple?"

"She told me you'd be offering me a tankard of ale."

"That I can do, but it'll cost you."

"How much do you want?"

Jador chuckled. "I don't want your kaales. You can entertain me with some of your adventures. That will be payment enough."

"I have to go," the woman said. "I'll be back later."

A short time after she left, somebody knocked on the door. Jador opened it to let in a woman carrying a tray. The young boy with her carried two large mugs.

"Tasia told me to bring you some food and ale for you and your guest, my Lord," the woman said.

"I told you not to call me that. You know my name. It's Jador, in case you forgot."

The woman laughed and walked out, followed by the boy.

Chapter Sixteen

"TIME TO GET UP," said a familiar woman's voice.

Rhodar opened his eyes and blinked against the bright light streaming through the open window. Sitting up, he rubbed his forehead, trying to still the throbbing in his head. Too much ale last night. He hadn't sensed somebody else in the room. The soft life of sleeping inside an apparently safe environment made him careless. Apparent safety was a dangerous illusion when in strange surroundings.

"I trust you slept well?" The woman didn't hide her curiosity as she looked over his naked body.

"Where am I?" He looked at the rumpled bed and then back at her.

She laughed merrily. "You're in my apartment and in my bed. No, we didn't share the bed. I slept alone in the other room. You were too drunk to be of any use anyway, had I been so inclined."

He scanned the room. "Quite a fancy apartment for a servant."

"What makes you believe I'm a servant?"

"You offered me cake and tirka-brew last night."

"I did, because that's what I was doing, serving food and drinks to the lords and their ladies."

"Then you are a servant," he said.

She threw him his shirt and kilt. "Put these on before I get ideas. To answer your question, I'm in charge of some of the activities in the summer festival."

"That still doesn't explain this apartment." He underlined his statement by making a circular motion around the room with his outstretched arm.

"Don't you think the daughter of King Ordar deserves something like this?"

He stared at her. "You are the King's daughter?"

"His illegitimate daughter. My mother is the King's mistress."

"That makes your brother the King's son. The heir to the throne."

She shook her head. "Not the heir. King Ordar has a son with Lady Gwenlin, his wife. My brother is considered the bastard son of King Ordar. The King and my mother were never married."

"I'm surprised Lady Gwenlin lets you stay here in the palace, or doesn't she know about you?"

"Oh, she does and she isn't happy about it, but the King leaves her no choice. You see, my brother and I were born before King Ordar married Lady Gwenlin. By the way, Jador and I are twins."

"You're prettier than him," Rhodar said with a little smile. "Does your mother live in the palace, too?"

"No. She lives in the city."

Rhodar pulled his shirt over his head and slipped into his kilt. "What should I call you, my Lady?"

"Just call me Tasia." She came up to him and straightened his collar. "The shirt doesn't fit you well."

He chuckled. "It's not mine. I borrowed it from Lord Galoor."

"The Queen's second cousin. Their grandfather was the infamous Lord Galasan. Lord Galoor is a good man who can be trusted." Her face became serious. "Unlike the Queen. Don't trust her. Better yet, don't trust anyone."

"Can I trust you?"

"That's up to you. Trust your heart." She stepped away from him. "What are your plans for today?"

He shrugged. "I have none. Actually, I feel somewhat lost."

"If you want, you can spend the day with me. I have a little spare time between chores. I'll take you around the palace grounds, but come now.

I'll show you were you can wash up and do whatever you must do in the morning. If you want to eat breakfast I'll show you that."

———

THERE WAS INDEED a large pond behind the palace, just as Lord Galoor had said. There were also shrubs and tall trees for shade. Many of the people frolicking in the water were nude. All of them were young with trim bodies.

"Care to go for a swim?" Tasia gave him a hopeful smile. At least, Rhodar thought it was hopeful.

"Only if you also go," he said, anxious to see what she looked like under her wide dress and loose blouse.

Instead of giving him an answer, she unbuttoned her blouse and shrugged out of it, exposing a pair of well-shaped breasts. Then she pushed her dress past her hips and let it pool on the ground.

Rhodar didn't want to stare, but he couldn't help but notice her slim thighs and flat belly. She had trimmed her pubic hair into the shape of a heart. He felt suddenly attracted to her.

"Your turn," she said and smiled. "Remember, I've seen you naked before." She came closer and tugged on his shirt. He let her take it off, but when she began to open his belt, he growled, "I can do that myself," to hide his sudden embarrassment when he felt himself reacting to her nearness.

She looked down at his kilt and laughed. "Don't get any ideas now." Her sultry voice didn't help his condition. "Does looking at my naked body do that to you?"

"Don't tease," he said, his words coming out rougher than intended.

"I'm not teasing." She turned away. "I'll race you to the water. It'll cool you off." With that, she ran toward the pond.

Looking at her wiggling round buttocks did nothing to calm him down. He ran after her, still wearing his kilt. Just before he reached the water, he quickly removed his kilt, threw it onto shore and dove into the water. It was cool at first but only for a moment.

Surfacing and rubbing the water from his eyes, he looked for her. She stood not far away, with only her breasts showing above the surface, an amused smile on her face. When she saw him, she swam toward him.

"It was not my intention to turn you on like that," she said. "Especially not in public. Does seeing a naked woman always cause such a strong reaction?"

"Not always," he admitted.

"Why me?"

"Perhaps you remind me of someone or perhaps it's your sensuous body and the way you conduct yourself." He shrugged. "I don't know."

"Then I should feel flattered. Too bad I'm not interested in men."

"You're the second woman I've met now who isn't interested in men." His disappointment must have shown in his face.

"You sound surprised. Are there no women like me where you come from?"

"If there are, they keep it a secret. I've never heard of it before."

"How about men? Many men prefer men to women. You don't have them, either, I suppose?"

He grunted, feeling uncomfortable with what she implied. "They would be shunned and forced to leave the tribe, because it is not natural. It is a man's duty to father children with a woman. Were it not so, people would soon disappear. A man cannot father a child with another man."

"For me it's normal to sexually desire another woman. I can only ever be a good friend to a man, but that's all. To think that a man would put his organ into my body repulses me." She looked into his eyes and lifted a hand to stroke his cheek. "I'm sorry, but that's how it is. I cannot change that. That doesn't mean I have no feelings for you. I am attracted to you, but in a different way. I hope you understand."

"How can I understand such a thing? To desire a woman and wanting to hold her, to kiss her and become one with her, to feel her respond with uncontrolled passion is something every healthy man dreams of. Not being able to do that is pure torture, unthinkable, and not a natural condition."

"Are you saying you are repulsed by me now?"

He looked at her beautiful face, feeling a sudden sadness and loss inside him. "You don't repulse me, but it makes me sad that I will never hold your naked body in my arms, never hear your passionate breathing in my ear, and never feel your body shudder when you are gripped by the greatest joy a man and a woman can experience together."

"I can have that joy with another woman," she said and smiled.

"Yes, with another woman but not with me."

"Does that mean we can't be friends?" She sounded sad and disappointed.

On impulse, he took her into his arms and held her for a moment. "We can be friends. I need a good friend here in the palace." He chuckled. "So you're a woman. What does it really matter?"

"I'm glad you feel that way." She laughed happily and splashed him with a spray of water, and then she ducked under the surface and shot away like a huge fish.

He watched her pale form disappear and sighed. He had obviously misread her signals. He wondered how many other men she had disappointed.

When he perused the pond, he noticed that there were no children in the water or on dry land. Even the youngest woman was old enough to be sexually active. He saw proof of that not far away from him where an older man swung a young woman back and forth in front of him while he cupped her buttocks with both hands and she had her thighs wrapped around his lower torso.

Sighing again, he looked away, feeling even more disappointment. This day was not going the way he had hoped. When someone splashed him from the back, he turned to find Tasia rising out of the water. She pressed her naked, wet body against him and grabbed his head to plant a kiss on his lips. Her breasts felt soft and warm on his chest.

Taken by surprise by her strange behavior, he stood rigid, not knowing how to react. Laughing into his mouth, she stopped kissing him and moved away again, looking at him with what seemed like a mocking smile.

"What was that all about?" He felt his body react again.

"I'm just so happy you accept me the way I am. Not many men do. Some get angry at me when they find out I'm not interested in them sexually."

"Perhaps it's the way you come on to a man. You're giving the right signals but you're not prepared to follow through. Like right now."

"I don't understand." The gaze of her eyes moved down his body. When she saw his erection under water, she blinked. "Oh, why would you react that way? I thought now that you know how I feel you wouldn't..." She didn't finish the sentence but gave him a questioning look.

He grimaced. "I may know, but my snake doesn't. You see, any healthy, viral man gets turned on when he sees a naked woman. It's a natural reaction and a good thing. It doesn't make any difference if the woman he looks at is interested in him or not."

"You mean all males are like that?"

"I don't know about all males, but the ones I know are."

"I don't mind if a male admires my body. I take good care of it and am proud of it, but my intention is not to get him all worked up when he looks at my naked body."

"You may not intend that to happen, but you're a tease, unknowingly perhaps. You may find yourself in a predicament you do not desire."

"Are you suggesting I should never take off my clothes in front of a male?"

Rhodar nodded grimly. "That would not be a bad idea and a good start."

"I guess going swimming with you in the nude was not one of my better ideas. I'm sorry." Her dark eyes searched his face. "Can you forgive me?"

He laughed and reached for her. "Only if you never offer me cake and tirka-brew again."

"I promise I never will." Her hand lingered on his cheek. "Friend." Then she disengaged herself from his embrace. "I have things to do. You can stay, if you like."

"I've had enough. I think I'll take a stroll around the palace grounds."

Heading for shore, squinting against the sun, he thought he saw the familiar figure of a woman. Getting closer, he recognized Saleen. She was standing not far from the water's edge watching him with a thoughtful expression.

He climbed back on land. "Have you been searching for me?"

She nodded and looked at Tasia. "Do you have plans for Rhodar, my Lady?"

Tasia gave her a curious look. "I remember seeing you before, but it's been awhile. You're the silent, strange girl with Lord Carn."

"I'm Saleen, my Lady." Her eyes seemed to challenge Tasia.

"Yes, now I remember your name. No, I don't have any plans for him. Actually, I never had any. I was just trying to make him feel welcome and keep him company. He looked so lonely. Now I must go. My duties are calling me." She quickly got dressed and walked away.

Saleen turned to Rhodar and looked at his naked body. He could see the interest in her face. "You don't look lonely to me," she said. "In fact, you seem to do just fine. What happened to you last night?"

"I spent an interesting evening with Tasia's brother, Jador."

"He's the King's son and Tasia is the King's daughter. Were you aware of that?"

"I am. Tasia told me so. Why, what's the problem?"

"I'd like to know where you slept last night." Her eyes were large and shiny in her face.

He shrugged. "I spent it in Tasia's bed."

Her lips quivered slightly when she spoke. "You disappoint me, Rhodar. I've offered myself to you freely, because my feelings for you are genuine, and yet you reject me. I don't understand why you bed every woman who throws herself at you but refuse me."

When he saw the sudden tears staining her cheeks, he stepped up to her and reached for her, but she eluded him. "Don't touch me."

Exasperated, he stepped back.. "Nothing happened between me and Tasia," he said almost sharply. "The King dismissed me and there wasn't anyone there to welcome me. Tasia did. She introduced me to her brother and we had a wonderful evening. I got drunk and had no place to sleep it off. She took me into her room and put me into her bed. That's all."

"But you went swimming with her—naked. I saw you holding her in your arms," she said with a tearful voice. "How do you explain that if nothing happened?"

He shook his head, trying to find the right words. "We declared our friendship. There will never be anything else between her and me. Men don't attract her sexually. She prefers women, just like Lady Ronewa."

Saleen's eyes were still wet and shiny, but there was a glimmer of hope in them. "I didn't know that. I'm sorry I accused you of something that didn't happen." Her face lit up with a big smile. "You want to swim naked with me?"

He lifted his hands. "I've had enough of that for one day. Why don't we go and sit in the shade? If you have the time."

She came into his arms then and covered his face with kisses. He laughed and held her away from him. "Take it easy, wench. I'm naked and may not be able to control myself."

"What would be so bad about that?" She smiled wickedly and wiped her cheeks dry. "I'd be the last one to complain." Then she pouted. "Why do you always call me wench? Don't you like my name?"

"I love your name and I can't explain why I call you wench. It just slips out that way." He retrieved his clothes from the ground and put them on while she watched him with her strange, bright-green eyes.

When she grabbed his hand and pulled him toward a clump of trees, she seemed happy. Reaching the shade, she lowered herself to the grass-covered ground and sat on her legs. "Lord Galoor wondered what had happened to you. He and the King went on a hunt this morning and he wanted you to come along."

He joined her on the ground and sat cross-legged beside her. "I would have gladly accompanied them, but I'm not used to being on standby. I'm a guest, not a servant, and deserve better treatment. King Ordar and Queen Gwenlin did not make me feel welcome. I felt like an unwanted guest as I stood there among all those lords and ladies, alone and forgotten. Even now I don't have a place to spend the night," he said bitterly. "I might end up sleeping right here under this tree." He chuckled. "It may not even be such a bad idea."

She touched his hand. "You're not an unwelcome guest. There was a mix-up. You do have a room and I will take you to it later." She snuggled up to him and leaned her head against his shoulder. "Before we go let me enjoy your company for a while. You said you felt alone? I don't have any friends here either, and I'm alone. We need each other, Rhodar. With you I feel safe and happy."

Feeling awkward, he sat silent for lack of knowing what to say. Yes, he was lonesome sometimes, but he was used to traveling alone. She might need him but did he need her? It felt good to have her near and he enjoyed her company. He didn't know what it was about her that attracted him. She was pretty with a bubbly personality. Tasia had called her the silent, strange girl, something he could not call her. She had never been silent with him, sometimes even talking too much. On top of that, she had a temper and he must never forget she was a Wer.

He suddenly thought of something. "Tell me, how did you know where to find me?"

She laughed. "Did you forget I'm a witch? I can find you anywhere."

"How?"

"I picture you in my mind and I see where you are."

"Just like that?"

"It's not quite that easy, because it involves magic, but it's not difficult either; especially with you."

"Why would that be?" He turned his head to look at her, curious about her answer.

She shrugged. "Because you and I have a special bond. It will be even easier once we copulate. Then I can mark you."

"Could that possibly be the reason why you are so anxious to have sex with me? So you can control me?" It was something he suddenly wondered about.

"Oh no. Don't ever think that. I want to join my body with yours because we are fond of each other, because we love each other. I would never want to control you."

"No man likes to be controlled, especially not by a female."

She smiled. "No female likes to be controlled by a man."

"Does Lord Carn control you?"

Her face clouded over. "I'm no more than a slave to him. That's why I asked you to take me with you when you leave. Now more so than ever."

"You move around quite freely. What does he make you do that you don't want to do?" For some reason, he questioned her claim. He hadn't seen any evidence she was mistreated, kept on a leash, or in some kind of bondage.

"He doesn't make me do anything, but I'm not free to leave the castle. He wants me around in case he needs me. He told me many times I belong to him." She spoke vehemently. "I belong to no-one and I want to be free like you."

He put his hand on her head and stroked her hair. "You seem like a beautiful bird kept in a cage and not allowed to spread its wings. Its only purpose is to sing for its master's pleasure."

"Then you understand what I'm saying, Rhodar. Why are you so reluctant to get close to me?" She almost pleaded with him.

"Perhaps because I don't want to put you in a cage and I don't want you to cage me." He shrugged. "I don't know myself."

"When will you know?" Her expression was hopeful. Then she put both arms around him and held him tight.

"I don't want to discuss that right now. Let's enjoy being close for the little time we have."

Chapter Seventeen

"HOW DO you know Caradin will come this way?" Lironi gave Kastabaan an inquiring look. "The other question is how long will I have to sit here in this tent waiting for him?"

"Not long. According to the message Arawan sent with one of the ravens, Caradin left three days ago. If things went smoothly for him, he should be here either tonight or the latest tomorrow by noon."

"Why is it so important to intercept him? Couldn't you search him out once we are in the palace?"

"I could, but I want to bond with him, get to know him in detail."

She sighed. "The things I do for you. I hope you'll reward me well after this is over."

"How would you like to be a real lady instead of pretending to be this fictitious Lady Shanta? Someone with real power, an estate, and servants? Would that be reward enough?" He wasn't certain if he would keep his promise. She was getting to be a nuisance with her whining, but it wouldn't hurt to assure her that her efforts would not go unrewarded. Right now, he would promise her anything to keep her happy and in line. "Don't forget we don't know who he is. I don't want him to get suspicious."

"You don't have to worry about me. I'm good at keeping secrets," she assured him. "How about making a fire? There is a sudden chill in the air."

Kastabaan looked at the driver of the coach. "Gather some wood and make a fire. While you're at it boil a pot of water and make us some tirka-brew."

The driver nodded. "Yes, my Lord."

It was nearly evening, when Kastabaan heard the screaming of a Sekua and it wasn't long before four riders came around the bend. They stopped beside the camp.

"Ho, weary travelers," Kastabaan greeted them. "Where are you headed?"

"We're on the way to King Ordar's palace to celebrate the summer festival," the bearded rider said.

"So are we," Kastabaan said. He made a motion with his hand. "It is getting dark soon and traveling through this forest can be dangerous at night. Why not join us for the night and tomorrow morning we can travel together?" He smiled. "We've got enough tirka-brew for everyone and we can also offer you some grilled Gastor-meat. You look like you've been traveling a long distance and must be tired. This way you'll be fresh and rested in the morning."

"It sounds tempting." The bearded man seemed to hesitate, his eyes searching the surroundings, as if looking for something. "We wouldn't want to impose."

"Nonsense. You would not impose. There are only three of us in our group, myself, my driver, and my companion, Lady Shanta. She's taking a nap in the tent."

At that moment Lironi came out of the tent, rubbing her eyes. "I heard voices," she said and then, as if realizing they had company, she brushed a strand of blond hair out of her face, looking at the bearded man. "I wasn't aware we had guests. Will you be joining us for supper?"

The bearded man laughed and slid of his steed. "How can I refuse the invitation of a beautiful woman? We've been on the road since early this morning and we're dead tired. This seems like a safe place to spend the night." He turned to his companions. "We'll stay here until tomorrow morning."

"Yes, my Lord," one of them said and dismounted. The other two did the same. Stalking over to the treed area with their Sekua in tow, they roped the animals to the trees.

"May I ask where you come from?" Kastabaan asked the bearded man. "Besides, I didn't catch your name."

"I'm General Caradin of the Jandarin Army," the bearded man informed him with a little smile.

"General Caradin? Are you saying you've traveled all the way from Jandarin just to celebrate the summer festival with King Ordar? Don't you celebrate your own festival?" Kastabaan acted surprised.

Caradin chuckled. "We do, but there is a good reason I'm coming here. I want to see my brother again. I haven't seen him in a long time." He grinned. "Ever since he exiled me to Jandarin."

"I don't understand."

"King Ordar is my half-brother. I'm King Ordarin's bastard son."

"I'd say that is welcoming news. It may help us gain entry into the palace. We're fortunate to have you as our guest, Prince Caradin." Kastabaan bowed toward Caradin.

"Perhaps not so fortunate for you but fortunate for me. Remember I'm living in exile. I think it's best if nobody knows who I am and you'll declare me and my men as your escort." Caradin looked thoughtful. "Yes, that would work. I'd be grateful to you."

Kastabaan nodded, pretending to be mulling it over. Then he held out a hand. "I'd be honored, Prince Caradin."

When Caradin took the offered hand, Kastabaan opened his senses to let Caradin's memories and personality flood his system. His mind absorbed everything he needed to know to be able to step into the persona of Caradin. He would become Caradin when the time was right.

Caradin's eyes widened for a moment and then they went blank. Letting go of Kastabaan's hand, he shook his head and looked at the sorcerer. "It seems this journey took much from me and a good night's rest before we enter the palace will be of great benefit." He smiled. "A chunk of grilled Gastor-meat and a cup of tirka-brew will lift my spirits."

———

KASTABAAN GLARED at the warrior guarding the entrance to the palace. "Of course I'm not on the list of invited guests, you imbecile. It was a last-minute decision to come here. Send word to King Ordar that Lord Garrin from Spanaria and his Lady-companion have arrived to celebrate the summer festival with him. I've come a long way and I have no intention to turn around again without seeing King Ordar."

"I have strict orders not leave my post," the warrior said.

"There are still five warriors standing guard. You won't be missed." Kastabaan spoke with an annoyed voice. "I suggest you go now without delay. We are tired from the journey. Lady Shanta is in need of rest and food."

He slid from his black stallion and stalked stiff-legged to the carriage. Climbing into the carriage he sat down across from Lironi who gave him a questioning look.

"Don't worry," he said in a low voice. "There will be no problem. I put a spell on the guard. He will run his legs off to get word to King Ordar to announce us." He smiled. "By the way, you look ravaging as Lady Shanta."

She waved it off. "You don't have to humor me, Kastabaan. I suffered on this long journey just to please you and you are not wrong when you told the guard I'm in need of rest. A glass of wine and a relaxing bath would be nice now." Her smile seemed tired. "Since we are complimenting each other I must admit that you look splendid as Lord Garrin. Sitting on your horse, you present an imposing figure. How many other forms can you assume?"

He chuckled. "I can be anyone I want to be."

"You're a man to be feared, Kastabaan. I'm glad I'm your friend."

"If anyone else but me knew about your shape-changing abilities they'd be afraid of you, too, Lironi."

She gave him a sharp look. "How do you know what I can do?"

"Are you forgetting what I am?" His smile was patronizing. "The first time you came to my castle I recognized you for what you are. You may have fooled Korallas making him believe the only form you can assume is the beast he couples with, but you cannot deceive me. In many ways, you are like me, except you lack the ability to practice magic. As a sorceress you'd be a dangerous adversary."

She shook her long blond hair out of her face and looked him squarely in the eyes. He noticed for the first time she had changed the color of hers from green to violet. "I rely on your digression to keep this between us. What I mean is don't tell Korallas."

"Korallas is an arrogant fool with great ambitions, but he doesn't know I can see through him. I'm not in the habit of volunteering any information to him. Your secret is safe with me, Lironi."

"Call me Lady Shanta." She gave him a haughty smile. "After all, am I not supposed to be your Lady-companion?"

"Only for the duration of this trip. From now on we'll be Lord Garrin and Lady Shanta. Now I'd better go back outside and sit on my horse to look more intimidating." He laughed softly.

"That's quite a horse that black stallion of yours. I could have sworn I saw it breathe fire."

"Perhaps your eyes didn't deceive you. That's not an ordinary horse. It's possessed by a demon."

"A demon? Sounds menacing. Should I be worried?"

"I control it and you have nothing to fear. My spell binds the demon to the horse and it has no powers in our world."

He closed the curtain and addressed one of the soldiers. "Any word?"

The warrior shook his head. "Not yet, my Lord."

Kastabaan walked back to his horse and swung himself onto its back. The stallion snorted and shook its head. Kastabaan saw the faint smoke coming out of the horse's nostrils. He patted the muscular neck. "Calm down," he said under his breath. "I don't want to have to punish you."

A few moments later the warrior returned, accompanied by a servant dressed in brightly colored clothes. Approaching Kastabaan, the servant spoke. "King Ordar says you're welcome to join in on the festivities, but he wants to meet you tonight at dinner."

"It will be an honor for me and Lady Shanta. I was hoping the King would want to see me," Kastabaan replied.

The brightly dressed servant bowed to Kastabaan. "If you would be so kind and follow me, my Lord, I'd gladly guide you to your quarters."

Kastabaan moved his hand in a gracious gesture. "Then let's get on with it. We've already lost precious time." His horse began moving before Kastabaan could give the order. He heard the rumbling of the wheels as the carriage followed him.

Prince Caradin and his men rode behind the carriage.

Kastabaan had never been inside the King's palace, but he knew much of the layout from interrogating Cordaras, the former knight who was now suffering as a winged beast in the dungeon below Kastabaan's castle.

Kastabaan chuckled to himself as he thought of Cordaras. The fool wanted to bed King Ordar's oldest daughter. Perhaps he would get the chance to climb between the royal legs of the Princess, only it would not be Cordaras in the flesh but Kastabaan in the guise of the handsome knight.

The palace grounds were immaculate and Kastabaan admired the space and the landscaping. If his plans worked out, he would be walking among the flowers and sitting under the majestic trees once he was ruler of Maridaan. He checked himself. One step at a time. He was in no hurry to put his plans into action. He couldn't afford any mistakes just because he was impatient.

The servant took them to a smaller section of the palace. A number of stable boys were already waiting to take care of the carriage and the animals. Kastabaan jumped from his horse and whispered into its ear, "Behave yourself and act like any normal horse or there will be consequences."

The horse moved its head up and down and displayed its teeth, snorting as it did so, but it stood still when one of the stable boys approached.

"May I take the reins of your horse?" the boy said.

Kastabaan handed them to him. "Take good care of it. I will hold you personally responsible for its wellbeing."

"Not to worry, my Lord. Your horse will be in good hands with me. I'm already looking after the horse of another guest. His name is Rhodar and he's a barbarian warrior from the Western Plains. He trusts me completely with his horse." He pushed out his chest proudly. "He's my friend, you know."

"A barbarian warrior from the Plains? Interesting." Kastabaan put a few coins into the boy's hand. "What's your name, boy?"

"Aarin. It's Aarin, my Lord."

"Give it a good rubbing down, Aarin, and don't forget to water it." He looked into the horse's eyes and noticed the glint. "Never use a rod on it; only talk to it, you understand?"

"Completely, my Lord. I will treat your horse as if it were my own."

"You do that and there may be a reward in it for you." Kastabaan gave the young stable boy a friendly smile and looked at the boy who had replaced his driver on the carriage. "Same goes for you," he told him. "Don't forget to wash the carriage—inside and outside. It has become dusty from the long journey."

"I will look after it," the other boy said eagerly. "The carriage will be so shiny it will blind your eyes."

Kastabaan chuckled. "No need for that. Just make sure it's clean." He turned to Lironi and reminded himself he must think of her as Lady Shanta. "Are you ready to go, my Lady?"

"I've been ready since we got here," she said, almost indignantly.

"Then let's not waste time." He turned to the servant. "You heard. Show us our quarters."

"Don't forget my luggage," Lironi reminded him.

The servant reached into the carriage and picked up the two leather bags. Pulling them out of the carriage, he looked at Kastabaan. "There is a trunk in there, my Lord. I apologize because I can't carry that."

"You can have someone pick it up later," Kastabaan told him. "Make certain to also take care of my warriors and their steeds."

"They will be looked after," the servant assured him.

Prince Caradin didn't give Kastabaan a second look when he and his men followed the stable boys. It seemed he wanted to go unnoticed for now.

They entered the building through a wide entryway and walked down a long corridor. The servant stopped and used a key to open one of the doors. "Here we are, my Lord and Lady."

"Are we both staying in one room?" Lironi said as she stepped across the threshold into the room.

"There are two rooms for your convenience," the servant explained and put down the luggage.

"It will do," Kastabaan said. "We'll probably use only one room and one bed."

The servant kept a straight face. "I didn't mean any insult, my Lord."

Kastabaan smiled. "None taken. Here, take these." He gave the servant a handful of coins. "If you hear any noises coming from our room, ignore them and be discreet about it. Never enter the room without knocking first. Understand?"

The servant nodded. "Fully. Thank you, my Lord. Before I leave, I have to ask you to give me your sword. No weapons allowed inside the Palace."

Kastabaan removed his sword belt and handed it to the servant. "I trust it won't get lost somewhere."

"You don't have to worry about that. It will be stored in a safe place. Now, if you allow, I will leave."

"You are free to go. Remember what I said."

After the door closed, Lironi spoke, "I'm not sharing a bed with you. I'll be sleeping in my own bed in the other room."

"I won't stop you. I only said that for his benefit." Kastabaan chuckled. "We want to make certain everyone thinks we are a couple involved with each other. It won't arouse any suspicions."

"Why should it? What are you planning?"

"It doesn't really concern you. I won't ask about your plans, either. You are free to do whatever you feel like doing. Fuck anyone who's willing. I'm sure you won't have any problems finding more than one young, horny male. Just don't bring anyone into this room." His eyes bored into hers. "Whatever you do, don't get carried away or caught and control your animal urges."

She laughed and put one hand behind his neck. "Too bad you don't have Korallas' appetite. I feel some of those animal urges right now."

He removed her hand. "I'm not Korallas. My needs are different than his."

She pouted. "Too bad. We could have had such a good time."

"You, perhaps, but not me," Kastabaan growled. He almost regretted taking her along and hoped she wouldn't make a nuisance of herself. "Why don't you go and find a place where you can take a bath and relax for a while," he suggested. "Perhaps you can find someone who will relieve your itch."

She moved away from him and shrugged. "Maybe I will, but I'll have to change into something more comfortable. These boots are killing me." With that she pulled off her boots and began to undress. Naked, she threw her clothing onto the bed and rummaged in one of her bags. Pulling out a short kilt, she slipped into it. It showed off her long legs nicely and when she bent down, it revealed her plumb, naked buttocks. He had to admit she had an attractive body. Had he been so inclined, he would have taken her up on her offer. While he still watched, she covered her breasts with leather cups and tied the thin straps behind her back.

"I hope you don't plan to wear that tonight when we meet the King," he said.

"Why not?" She gave him a haughty, challenging look. "You never know. I might just arouse his interest me."

"Don't get your hopes up. King Ordar is getting on in years and, from what I hear, Lady Gwenlin is keeping an eye on him. I also hear that she doesn't look kindly upon women who are trying to seduce him. Apparently, some have met with nasty accidents. I suggest you set your sights on safer targets."

"I'll take it into consideration." Laughing, she walked out of the door.

He looked at the closed door and shook his head. That woman was going to get herself into a lot of trouble and could become a liability.

There was a full-length mirror against one wall and he went over to it and studied the image of the tall wide-shouldered man with the long, curly hair looking back at him out of dark, haunting eyes.

He smiled at his reflection. He presented a striking figure, Lord Garrin from Spanaria. He might just persuade Queen Gwenlin to give him a private audience in her bedroom. It should be easy with his good looks and the help of a minor spell.

———

LIRONI HAD no problem finding a young male servant to show her where she could immerse her nude body into a tub filled with warm water. He offered to wash her back and she told him she'd be delighted and grateful if he would perform that service for her.

Sliding into the scented warm water, she sighed. "Take your time. I'm in no hurry."

He used a container to scoop water from the tub and pour it onto her back, washing it at the same time with his hand. After a time, she turned around and lay back. "Now, do my front," she told him. "And don't leave any part of my body unwashed. I mean any part, you understand?"

"Yes, my Lady. I'll do a thorough job." He began with her shoulders and slowly moved his hands down her body. He spent a long time rubbing and kneading her breasts.

She closed her eyes and enjoyed his hands as they traveled down to her belly and finally to her feminine part. She moaned deeply when his fingers massaged her swollen mound and when he stroked her cleft with one finger. It was enough to arouse her to a point where she needed release.

Opening her eyes, she looked at the young man and noticed the bulge in his loose pants. "Is there a chance somebody might come in here?" Her whole body quivered in anticipation.

"We are quite alone, my Lady," he said with a hoarse voice. "Nobody comes in when the door is closed."

"Good." She stood up and stepped out of the water onto the stone floor. "I want you to take off your clothes," she commanded him.

"As you wish, my Lady." Without hesitation, he fairly ripped off his shirt and pants. Standing naked in front of her, displaying a huge erection, he waited. She noticed the slight tremor in his body, but he didn't say anything.

"Lie down."

He obeyed and lay on his back, looking up at her with great anticipation. Straddling him, she rode him for a long time with her eyes closed. When she couldn't control the urge any longer, she morphed into her beast-form and sank her teeth into his jugular, drinking deeply from his blood, but not enough to drain him. She had enough control left to realize a corpse would cause many questions and an investigation.

Shuddering in the throes of her orgasm, she lay on top of him until she came down from the peak of her ecstatic release. Kneeling beside him, she looked into his eyes. They were clouded over but he had a happy smile on his face. His chest rose and fell with his heavy breathing. She kissed him on the lips and wiped the traces of blood from his neck. He wouldn't remember much when he woke up, except an incredible sexual experience. He would not remember her at all.

She smiled. He'd be in need of a good night's rest, while she felt refreshed and full of zest. Picking up one of the towels she found on a shelf, she rubbed down her body. Then she dressed and left the room. There was nobody around to see her come out of the room and she decided to go back to the rooms she shared with Kastabaan. It was time to get ready for the audience with King Ordar.

Kastabaan gave her a disapproving look when she entered. "Even though you look glowing right now, I hope you didn't leave a corpse behind."

"Give me some credit," she said, annoyed at his comment. Sinking into one of the chairs, she scrutinized him. "You don't look so bad yourself. I notice you're wearing a uniform."

"That's because I'm an officer in the Spanarian army," he told her.

"Where exactly is Spanaria? I've never heard of it."

"I'm not surprised. It's a small Kingdom south of Grahna. Not well known. I chose it because there is little chance I'll ever meet another nobleman from that Kingdom who could betray me."

"Why didn't you make yourself a king or prince already?"

"I could have, but I didn't want to push my luck." He gave her an inquiring look. "Are you going to change into some descent clothes?"

In answer to his question, she got up and removed her breast cups and then she pushed her kilt past her hips and stepped out of them.

"What do you suggest is proper to wear in the King's presence?"

"Obviously not what you're wearing right now or, more precisely, what you're not wearing," he said, his voice dripping sarcasm. He waved a hand. "Just cover up and try not to wear anything provocative. Remember, the Queen will be there. If you want to make friends in the court, you have to gain her confidence and approval."

"I'm not interested in women, only men." She laughed and walked to the bed to retrieve her bags, swinging her hips suggestively trying to get a rise out of him, even though she knew it was useless. She decided to wear her long, red dress; the one she wore at Castle Falconclaw in her Lironi persona. It would show off her figure nicely without being too offensive. The dress was not a unique design and therefore there wouldn't be much of a chance somebody might connect her with Lironi.

She wiggled into the dress and then she tied her long, blond hair behind her head with a ribbon. A pair of silver earrings finished her attire. Slipping into her knee-high boots, she walked over to the mirror to look at herself. "I just love myself in this dress. It shows off my figure nicely."

"Perhaps too nicely," Kastabaan commented. "It doesn't leave much to the imagination. You might as well go naked."

"I would, but it wouldn't be appropriate. Some people might be offended by that." She gave him a mischievous smile. "Are you ready to go?"

"I've been ready for quite a while, but we'll have to wait for a servant to take us to the throne room. And behave."

It wasn't long before she heard a knock on the door.

"It's open. Come in," Kastabaan called.

A servant in red and yellow livery walked into the room. "I'm to escort you to the King."

They followed him down the maze of corridors until they arrived in a lavishly decorated large room. The King and the Queen sat on a settee covered with furs. They weren't alone in the room. On another sofa sat two young women and, kneeling on a pillow on the floor, a boy. He was playing with a small furry animal, a Lurrex. It would grow into a ferocious beast. Already it was displaying its nasty temperament.

King Ordar was dressed in a gaudy-looking flowing outfit that couldn't hide his rotund body. As Lironi came closer, she saw the lines in the King's face and she wondered about the young boy. Could he really be King Ordar's son? Even the girls seemed to be a bit too young. She smiled inwardly. 'It seems the old lizard is still quite capable'.

Queen Gwenlin was slim and much younger looking than the King. She watched Lironi with great interest. Her face didn't show it, but it was easy to see in her eyes that she disapproved of Lironi's provocative way of dressing.

Amused, she smiled at the Queen. "It was a last moment decision for me to come along. I didn't have much time to go through my wardrobe. I let one of my servants pick for me." She gave a little chuckle. "I had my seamstress sew this dress for me, but I never got a chance to wear it. It seems she made it a bit too tight for my figure."

"You don't have to worry about that," King Ordar said. "We are not that critical here." He laughed. "I for one don't think it's too tight. Nothing wrong with a woman showing off her figure, especially one like yours."

Queen Gwenlin gave him an annoyed look. "I'm not surprised you would say that. If that was some kind of compliment for her, then you are way off the mark, my dear husband." She looked at Lironi. "If you're not happy with the dress, perhaps we can find you something that suits you more."

"That's very kind of you, your Highness, but not necessary. I don't want to cause any trouble."

"It'll probably cause less trouble than that dress might cause," Queen Gwenlin said with a sweet smile.

Lironi didn't miss the sarcasm in her voice. The claws were coming out. She'd better be careful.

Kastabaan cleared his throat beside her. "You must forgive Lady Shanta. I've told her many times not to leave all the decisions to the servants, but she is usually too busy playing dongo with the other ladies."

"Some things you have to do yourself," the Queen responded.

"Are you ladies quite finished?" The King didn't wait for an answer. "I'm told you are from Spanaria, Lord Garrin. We don't get many visitors from your Kingdom. In fact, I can't remember when we had any." He laughed. "Does it actually exist?"

Kastabaan smiled. "I'm living proof that it does. We even have a well-trained army. I'm an officer in that army and we take pride in serving our King and Kingdom as small as it may be."

King Ordar lifted his hands. "I didn't mean to offend you or your Kingdom, Lord Garrin. Let me welcome you to Maridaan and I hope you enjoy the festivities and our hospitality."

Kastabaan made a deep bow. "Thank you, your Majesty. Perhaps someday I can repay your kindness. It takes only four days to travel to Spanaria."

"That may be so, but one has to travel through Grahna and we don't have a great relationship with that Kingdom, especially with Queen Dalina. She's a nasty She-beast with long, sharp teeth." The king gave a booming laugh. "Everywhere."

"I've heard rumors," Kastabaan said carefully with a little smile. "That's why we took the back roads through Grahna. It takes a little longer but is much safer."

Lironi had to admire Kastabaan for his glibness. Either he had been to Spanaria or he made up everything on the spot. He sounded quite convincing.

"Perhaps you can join us for a game of dongo one afternoon," Queen Gwenlin said, addressing Lironi.

"That would be wonderful, but I'm wondering if you play by the same rules."

"There's only one way to find out. Play a game with us." The Queen chuckled. "I'll give you one hint—no old males allowed."

The King snorted. "No self-respecting man would play that game with a bunch of snickering females anyway. It's boring."

"How do you know, dear husband. You've never played it."

"And I never will." He moved his bulky body into a different position. "All this talk is making me thirsty. I need some more wine." He picked up a goblet from the small table beside him and looked into it.

One of the servants came rushing with a decanter and filled the goblet with wine. The King took a long sip, wiped his mouth with a pudgy hand, and sighed loudly. "Lord Garrin, did you know that Maridaan is famous for its superb wines?"

Lironi kept half her attention on following the conversation between the king and Kastaban.

"I'm familiar with the wines of Maridaan," Kastabaan said. "Unfortunately, in our Kingdom they are difficult to come by and, when one does, prohibitively expensive."

"It seems some of our merchants are familiar with Spanara, since they deal with merchants in your Kingdom."

"Spanaria, your Majesty. It's Spanaria not Spanara. We might be small, but we have a large ego."

King Ordar dismissed Kastabaan's remark with a wave of his hand. "Spanaria—Spanara, it makes no difference to me." He leaned forward. "I don't like to be corrected in front of my children, remember that, Lord Garrin."

Kastabaan made a little bow. "I apologize. It won't happen again. Speaking of your children, they seem well-behaved. Your two daughters are lovely and your son is very handsome. I can see the resemblance in his face. Playing with a Lurrex demands bravery. He'll be a great warrior someday."

"He'll be more than a warrior; you're looking at the future King of Maridaan. Arleen, our oldest daughter, is betrothed to Prince Sordan of Agastan. Even though it lies on the other side of the ocean, it will be a positive alliance. Ireleen, our youngest daughter?" He shrugged and smiled. "Perhaps we can marry her off to Prince Randoll. It may change our relationship with Queen Dalina."

"Father, I've told you before I'm not marrying Prince Randoll. He's an overweight sniveling coward and I'm not moving to Grahna. And that's final," one of the two young women said loudly.

"I've told you that you don't have a say in it, Ireleen," King Ordar thundered. "You'll do as you're told, just like your sister and that's final."

"I won't," Ireleen said with a tearful voice. "You tell him, Mother."

"Your father and I will discuss that but not now," the Queen said. "Now and here is not the time and place."

Lironi felt sorry for the girl. She looked much too young to be married off, especially to someone she didn't even like. The older sister didn't seem to have much choice in the matter either. To be the daughter of a tyrant like King Ordar was equal to being a slave.

"I'd like to thank you for inviting us into your palace," she broke into the sudden and uncomfortable silence.

"Yes," Kastabaan said beside her. "We are looking forward to the celebration."

"As long as you're happy with the accommodations. I must apologize for the location, but you've come unexpectedly and all the quarters in the guest section are filled with invited guests. You're welcome to join the other guests for breakfast tomorrow morning in one of the dining rooms. I'm afraid you're too late for supper. If you're hungry, just ask one of the servants to bring you something to eat." The King changed his position on the settee. "I'm getting restless and it is getting late anyway. It's been a long day for me. Perhaps I'll see you again at the festival." He made shooing motions with one hand. "That will be all for today."

Lironi saw Kastabaan make a bow beside her so she bowed toward the King and then to the Queen and turned to follow Kastabaan out of the room.

Back in the corridor, she let out a deep breath. "That went quite well," she said.

"I don't think the Queen likes you," Kastabaan observed.

"King Ordar wasn't greatly impressed by you," Lironi countered.

"He's as pompous as a male Krall-bird with the brain to match," Kastabaan snorted contemptuously. "The feeling is mutual, because I don't like him, either, which make what I'm planning so much easier."

"What are you planning?"

His evil laugh sent a chill down her back. "The less you know the better it will be, but I will need your assistance."

"Doing what?"

"Don't worry about it. You'll enjoy it."

Chapter Eighteen

THE FESTIVITIES HAD BEGUN. The palace grounds teemed not only with highborn lords and ladies but also with a carefully picked group of men and women from the lower classes. Most of them wore some kind of mask or disguise and nobody asked questions. It was a time when many lords searched out young peasant women and the ladies gave themselves to some young buck without knowing his identity or giving away theirs.

There were jugglers and other performers to entertain the revelers. Wine flowed freely and food was abundant.

The only disguise Rhodar chose was to go without his shirt. His tall, muscular physique would have made him standout even had he completely covered his body, except if perhaps he wore some loose cape or gown.

He wasn't the only one walking around bare-chested, though. There were others but none with his superb build. Some wore masks, but some wore only skullcaps that left the face uncovered.

It seemed everyone recognized him for what he was.

"Hey, Outlander, how about a test of strength and skills?"

Rhodar stopped to look at the man who stood inside the entrance to a tent. He was big and bulky, his arms and upper body displaying corded muscles. His skullcap had slits for his eyes but left his mouth uncovered.

"What do you have in mind?"

"Come inside and you'll see." The man smiled. "Unless you're afraid."

Amused by the man's taunting, Rhodar chuckled. "Since you seem to know where I come from you should know that a warrior from the Western Plains is afraid of nothing."

"Then come and prove it."

Shrugging, Rhodar followed the man into the tent. It seemed larger inside than it had appeared from the outside. There was a roped off area in the center. Two men inside that open space were fighting each other with bare fists. Both had blood-spattered faces and bodies. Spectators sat in the grass or on small benches watching the spectacle and cheering them. Off to one side stood a small group of men, most of them with bare upper torsos, displaying their muscles. A few were small and wiry looking, their bodies hidden inside robes. He even spotted one female. Her head was covered with a hood that left only her eyes visible, but her upper body was bare. Her breasts, even as small as they were, betrayed her gender. Her muscles could put many males to shame.

She held a mace in her right hand and a small, round shield in her left.

"I'm not fighting her," Rhodar said, pointing at the female.

The man chuckled. "I'm surprised to hear you say that. Most will want to fight her, believing she'd be easy to defeat. Of course, they are wrong most of the time. Marlia is as strong as any man, but what sets her apart are her fighting skills. She's fast and agile. Rumor has it she killed seven men in a fair fight."

"I don't fight females," Rhodar growled. Then he grinned. "Only when they're lying naked on a bed of furs."

"Perhaps you should fight her then. I hear a male who defeats her gets to bed her. Of course, I don't know anyone who ever managed to do that. You might be the first. It could be worth trying." The man glanced slyly at Rhodar. "Besides bedding her you might even win a lot of kales, because she's everyone's first choice. The odds are in your favor."

"That may be so, but it's against my principles. I could kill her with one good blow against her head or in her face."

"I doubt you'd ever get that close to her, my Outlander friend. Should you manage to evade her kicks to your head and somehow get near her, she'll knock you unconscious with her mace and then rip off your snake and both of your globes just out of malice." He smirked. "Of course, I could be wrong. You might end up making her scream with pleasure when she lets that snake of yours enter into her den, but she might just bite off its head when you're done." His laughter was not malicious.

Rhodar had been watching the two fighters in the ring. One was down while the other one was still pounding him with his fists. The watching crowd was on its feet. Some of the spectators cheered loudly while others whistled their displeasure.

"It seems their champion is losing," Rhodar's companion commented. "They don't like that."

"Isn't anyone going to stop the fight? Once a competitor is down the fight is over and the winner should be declared," Rhodar shook his head in disapproval.

"Sometimes they get up again."

"I doubt this one will get up again—ever. Look at the angle of his head. His neck has been broken."

His companion shrugged. "It happens. Why would you care?"

"To kill an opponent in a competition fight is not honorable. It's barbaric," Rhodar said, not hiding his scorn.

"I'm surprised to hear you talk like that. I mean a barbarian from the Western Plains is squeamish about the death of a commoner?"

"A commoner? Is that what that man is to you and his death means nothing? I take it you must be some kind of highborn then."

The man laughed. "If you must know my father is an important lord and one of the King's trusted advisors."

"Is that why you aren't in that ring fighting?"

"Nobody dares to fight me. They know I always win."

Rhodar snorted. "I think you're afraid to fight."

The man pushed out his chest. "I'm afraid of no-one, but I don't feel like getting down into the mud."

"You think it's beneath you to fight a commoner. You're afraid he might just beat you," Rhodar taunted him.

"I told you I'm not afraid, you dimwitted Outlander." He spoke sharply. "You have no idea who I am. I expect some respect from a lowly commoner like you."

"I'm not a commoner," Rhodar said proudly. "My father is a chief and I'll be a chief when I return home."

The man laughed. "A chief of what? A tribe of uncivilized, stupid barbarians."

"Now you're insulting my father and my people. I don't take kindly to that." Rhodar's hands curled into fists as he tried to suppress his anger.

"I don't take kindly to that," the man mocked him. He took a step toward Rhodar and gave him a shove with his flat hand. "I'll say it again. All the people living in the Plains are nothing but a bunch of stupid savages with a brain as small as that of a Krall-bird. What are you going to do about that, you dimwit?"

"This." Rhodar growled, pulled back his fist and smashed it into the man's belly. As he bent forward with a surprised grunt, Rhodar lifted his leg and hit the man in the face with his knee. Then he pushed him into the tent where he went sprawling into the dirt.

Getting to his knees, he held his belly and stared at Rhodar, his lips pulled back to display his teeth. Blood dripped from his nose, streaking his chin and chest red. With a snarl, he ran at Rhodar, but Rhodar moved to the side at the last moment and the big man crashed into one of the bystanders, toppling him over.

Cursing, the other man pushed the big man away from him and kicked him in the face, which made him attack that man. Swinging both fists, the big man hit the new opponent in the face and in the chest until the man went down. Then he used his booted feet to kick him in the head.

Rhodar moved in, grabbed the big man by the shoulder, and pulled him away from the man on the ground. Roaring like a wild Lurrex, he turned and swung his fists at Rhodar. He was angry and out of control and Rhodar knew he could do nothing but fight the man. He also knew this would not be a clean fight.

He took a few steps backward toward the center of the tent while the big man followed him, his face contorted into a demon's face.

"I'll kill you, you insolent, stupid Outlander!" His words were slurred and his voice abrasive.

Rhodar fell into a crouch, his muscles tensing, his senses alert, ready for a fight for his life. He had no doubts his opponent meant what he said. There was no escaping this moment and he regretted having lost his temper. He was a stranger here and the odds were not in his favor. If he killed the man, he would suffer the consequences. Of course, his opponent was not exactly a weakling. He was as large and muscular as Rhodar, possibly even more massive and there was a good chance Rhodar would not walk away from this fight.

Somebody threw a long staff between them and the other man picked it up and attacked, swinging it expertly, aiming for Rhodar's head. The fight could have been over right then and there if Rhodar hadn't avoided the deadly thrust by diving forward. He hit his attacker's legs and they both rolled on the ground. Rhodar was on top of the other man and tried to wrestle the staff away from him.

Both ended up on their feet again. Rhodar lost the grip on the staff and his opponent kicked him in the belly with one food sending him backward. He regained his balance and was ready to ward off another strike at his head when someone rushed up and thrust a staff into his hands. He brought it up in time to ward off the descending staff.

The other man laughed madly and sneered, "I'm the champion with this weapon. Nobody has ever beaten me."

"Then I'll be the first," Rhodar said, feeling confident again with a weapon in his hands.

They danced around each other, thrusting and hitting. Silence filled the tent. The only noise came from the cracking sound as the two staffs met. Rhodar possessed an incredible level of stamina but after what seemed like many cellas he felt the strength lessening in his arms and legs. His opponent seemed tireless, attacking him ferociously and without mercy.

Rivulets of perspiration mixed with dust streaked the man's body and Rhodar knew his own body didn't look any different. He ached from hits he had suffered against his chest, side, and legs and he knew he was bleeding from at least a couple of wounds.

Suddenly, his opponent stumbled and tripped over his own staff. He fell to the ground and lay face down for a moment. It was enough time for Rhodar to move in and push his opponent's face into the dirt while he kept him down with one knee pressing into his back, using his full weight.

The man struggled, but his movements were feeble and then he lay still.

Rhodar got up and turned him around so he lay on his back, hoping he hadn't killed him, but the man was still breathing, even though his breathing was labored and noisy. His face looked terrible, covered with blood and dirt. It looked like his nose was broken and the skin on his cheek was split by a long cut that would leave an ugly scar if not treated correctly. He had lost his mask during the fight and his long hair was matted with dirt.

Rising, Rhodar threw down his staff with an angry gesture. This fight had been so senseless. He felt tired and wanted nothing more than just leave and ride away, but he had to face the consequences of this brawl.

When he heard the watching crowd cheering, he looked up, surprised. A couple of men came rushing up to him and clapped him on the shoulder. "He deserved everything you gave him," one of them said.

"The best fight we've seen in a long time," the other one said. "They'll be telling stories about this for a long time."

"You should have killed him," said a third man. "He wouldn't have let you live."

"I don't kill unless I must and never as entertainment," Rhodar growled. He turned around when someone pulled on his arm and looked into the green eyes of Saleen.

"Leave this place now," she said urgently.

He let her pull him outside and then away from the tent. She didn't stop until they were standing in a crowd of people. "What were you thinking?" Her eyebrows pulled together as she stared at him.

"Thinking?" He shrugged. "One never thinks before a brawl. They just happen."

"Why is it they only happen to males?" She didn't wait for a comment. "Do you know who you almost killed?"

"He said his father was some kind of advisor to the King." He winced from the sudden pain in his shoulder as he tried to move it. When he touched it with his hand it came away bloody.

"His name is Zangarian and he is the son of Lord Zagaar, the King's top advisor." Her expression changed to one of concern. "You are bleeding from a number of wounds. Your face looks a mess and by tomorrow your muscles will be stiff and your whole body will show all kinds of colors, but mainly blue. Come, we'll go to my room and I'll clean you up and treat your wounds."

He didn't argue when she pulled him along. As they walked through the crowd, some people stopped and pointed.

"By tomorrow the news will be all over the city that a barbarian from the Plains fought and almost killed Lord Zagaar's only son. This was not a wise thing to do."

"I got the impression he wasn't very popular," Rhodar said in defense of his action. "I might have made many friends." He grinned lopsidedly.

"Friends among the peasants mean nothing. You need to have the goodwill of the Lords… and the King."

"I have a friend in Lord Galoor, and Lady Ronewa seems to be fond of me. Possibly even Lady Gardina."

"The only one I'd trust is Lord Galoor. As for the Lady Ronewa and Lady Gardina, I wouldn't trust either of them. Lord Carn doesn't like you. He's made that clear." Saleen shook her head. "You don't have many friends here." She squeezed his hand. "There's only one who cares for you without reservation and that is me, but I'm nobody. My friendship means nothing."

"It means a lot to me."

They entered the palace through one of the side doors and walked down a narrow corridor. After a maze of corridors, they stopped in front of a plain door. "I'm not staying in the fancy part of the palace. My room is small." Saleen explained. "This is where the servants live, but I'm fine with that."

She opened the door and ushered Rhodar through the door. Looking around, he had to admit, the room was not large. The room he slept in was not fancy, either, but it was much larger.

"Sit down on that chair over there and relax," she told him. "I'll get water and a few bandages, and perhaps some ointment to take away the pain and speed up the healing." With that she left the room.

Rhodar relaxed as she suggested and realized the fight had taken much out of him. He looked at the narrow bed and decided to lie down. Taking off his boots, he lay down on the bed and closed his eyes.

He awoke and opened his eyes when someone shook him. Saleen was bending over him, a concerned look on her pretty face. "I thought you were dead," she said. "You wouldn't wake."

"It takes more than just a simple fight to kill me," he said, his voice brittle. "I need some water. My throat is dry." Then he saw an older woman standing behind Saleen.

"I'm Laana," the woman said when she saw him looking at her. She carried a large basin filled with water and a washcloth.

"She's a healer," Saleen explained. "I'll get you some clean water to drink."

Laana studied Rhodar. "That's quite some beating you took."

"It looks worse than it is." Rhodar sat up and tried to get off the bed, but a sudden hammering inside his head made him lie back. "I hope you have medicine to take away the pain in my head."

"I have but first we'll have to examine you. That's a nasty wound above your ear." Her fingers touched him gently on the side of his head, making him wince. "Saleen tells me you and Zangarian were going at each other with a couple of staffs. They are dangerous weapons in skilled hands. You might have been killed with one single blow in the right place. This one came close."

Saleen came back with a small pitcher of water. "Here, drink this," she said. He took the pitcher, but before he could drink from it, Laana handed him a couple of yellow berries. "To ease your pain," she told him. "They are strong and might leave you a bit lightheaded."

He swallowed the berries and then emptied nearly half of the pitcher. "Water never tasted so good," he said, wiping his mouth.

"First thing we'll do is clean off that grime. Can you stand?"

His head didn't hurt so much anymore and he managed to stand.

"Take off your kilt," Laana said. "I'll have to wash your whole body. Besides, you may have injuries beneath that kilt." She seemed to suppress a smile as she said that.

He did as told. When he stood naked, he didn't miss the older woman's brows go up a little, but all she said was, "Everything looks fine." She began rubbing him with a wet cloth. It stung but Rhodar didn't complain. Then Saleen dried him off with a towel.

"Feeling better already," he joked. "There is nothing better than being pampered by two beautiful females."

"This is not pampering, you big dimwit," Saleen scolded him. "We're trying to take away your pain and clean you."

"The last person who called me a dimwit lies unconscious in the tent," he growled.

"Don't try to start a fight with me," Saleen warned, her eyes sparkling with green fire. "You don't stand a chance against me."

"I wouldn't dream of it." He grinned. "There is a ferocious beast hiding inside that lovely body of yours that I don't want to tangle with."

She gave him a warning look. "If you weren't in such sad shape I'd show you what this ferocious beast can do." She turned to Laana. "I've been trying to seduce him ever since we met, but he resists my attempts."

Laana laughed softly. "He's a fool if you ask me. Not many men would turn down such an invitation. Do you want me to leave the room? Cleaned up, he looks almost presentable. Perhaps a night of passion will cure him completely." Then she became serious. "I'm only jesting. He needs rest. So don't get any ideas. He's feeling better because of the painkillers I gave him. Those deep cuts need stitches or he'll have ugly scars and take too long to heal." She produced a needle and thread and looked at Rhodar. "I'll put healing balm on the wounds to take away most of the pain, but it will sting."

"I've endured pain before," he assured her. "Go ahead."

It did sting, and he clamped his jaws together. It seemed to take forever until Laana finished, but the pain was not as severe anymore. She stepped back and examined her handiwork and nodded, apparently satisfied. "You're as good as new. Now, forget any ideas you might have, because you're probably feeling much better by now. Remember, it's the berries and the ointment. By tomorrow most of the pain should be gone, but give those wounds time to heal." She smiled. "Your skin will most certainly show many different colors for a while, but that is the price you pay for fighting." She looked at Saleen. "Let him stay with you tonight so you can keep an eye on him and don't let him walk around. The yill-berries sometimes cause hallucinations."

"He's not going anywhere even if it means I have to tie him to the bed," Saleen said grimly.

"I don't think that'll be necessary. There's a good chance he'll be sleepy and tired." The older woman gave Rhodar one more look-over and then, with a little sigh, she left.

Saleen chuckled. "I believe she wishes she were younger and you were in better shape."

"Why would you think that?"

"Those berries must really diminish your observation powers. Anyone with eyes in their head could not miss the desire in her eyes when she looked at your... you know."

"Do you have the same desire when you look at my... you know?"

She came close and touched him. "My desire for you goes deeper than that. I ache for not just one part of your body but for all of it. I want to lie in your arms and feel your skin on mine. I want to kiss your lips and let your breath caress my face, and I want to hear your heart pounding in your chest as you carry my mind and body to heights I've never experienced before."

He held her close. "If I weren't so tired I might just give in," he murmured into her ear. "I desire you, but we can't let that happen. I don't know if I could deal with the consequences."

She stroked his cheek. He could see the moisture in her eyes and kissed her gently. "Just know that I love you. Let that be enough for now."

Letting him go, she nodded. "I love you, too. Now you'd better lie down on the bed and rest so you can heal."

He looked at the bed. "It is narrow."

She smiled. "Big enough for you. I'll sleep on the floor."

He wanted to argue, but he felt suddenly very tired and stumbled onto the bed.

"Sleep, my Love," she whispered and covered him with a blanket.

Chapter Nineteen

KASTABAAN WAS curious when he heard about the fight that took place the day before between the son of one of the King's advisors and a big barbarian warrior from the Western Plains. It was all over the palace that the barbarian had nearly killed the son of Lord Zagaar, who was King Ordar's top advisor. Obviously, they were talking about Rhodar, the barbarian the stable boy had mentioned. Either that or there was another barbarian here; and that seemed highly unlikely.

Apparently, King Ordar was not happy about the fight and was holding a special inquiry into the case, because that's what Lord Zagaar demanded. Kastabaan decided to attend. It was important to be informed about anything that happened in the palace and on the palace grounds.

"To be there might be in your best interest," he told Lironi. "Information is crucial and can be used to your advantage in whatever you're planning."

When they arrived in the courtroom, most seats were already taken, but they managed to find a couple empty ones adjacent to each other. The King wasn't in the room yet, so the throne was empty, but one of the seats behind a massive desk was occupied by a corpulent man dressed in fancy clothes. Obviously, Lord Zagaar. The young man beside him was big and massive. Even under his clothes his rippling muscles were evident. It didn't take much to guess that he was Lord Zagaar's son, especially since his face looked swollen and was covered with red streaks.

In a separate chair to the right of the desk sat another large man. His face didn't look much better than that of the other man, but he emanated an animal magnetism the other man didn't possess. He had tied his long hair behind his head with a piece of rope. A large tooth fastened to a golden chain hanging from his broad neck spoke stories to anyone familiar with the ways of the Clans. It was the tooth of a Stone Serpent, one of the giant snakes that lived in the Western Plains. No question about it. This was the barbarian who was on trial. He wasn't surprised. If anyone was stupid enough to get into a brawl with one of the Lords, it could only be an ignorant savage.

Everyone stood when the King finally arrived. He sank into his throne and heaved a loud sigh. "I'm not in a pleasant mood this morning," he announced. "I have better things to do than waste my time with trivial things like a brawl between two grown men. Normally I wouldn't bother with this, but it involves my personal advisor, Lord Zagaar, and he requested I look into the matter."

His eyes focused on the big barbarian. "Rhodar, you are a guest here and I'm disappointed in your behavior. I have a good mind to ban you from the palace, but I can't ignore the advice of someone who has taken a liking to you. I'm talking about Lord Galoor. Why he likes you is beyond my understanding, but he is the Queen's cousin and the escort of my sister, Lady Gardina. I value his opinion… to a point."

He shifted his attention from Rhodar to Lord Zagaar's son. "As for you, Zangarian, you have a reputation for getting into trouble." He held up a hand when the young man seemed about to speak. "You'll have your say when I'm done, but I'm warning you, both of you, not to give me stupid excuses for your behavior. There are witnesses who were present and anything you say will be verified. You may speak now, Zangarian."

The young man stood. "I won't make excuses for what happened, but the Outlander attacked me without provocation. I only defended myself."

"From what I hear you called him a dimwit."

Zangarian chuckled. "I've called many of my friends dimwits. It means nothing. That's just the way we talk among each other."

"Obviously, it meant something to Rhodar. Remember, he's a stranger and not familiar with our ways. You should have used restraint." He looked at Rhodar. "What's your excuse?"

"He insulted me, my father, and my people by calling us uncivilized, stupid barbarians. I know that is no excuse and I shouldn't have lost my temper." He smiled crookedly. "But what can you expect from a barbarian?"

The King shook his head and sighed again. "Both of you are impulsive and seem to have a problem controlling your temper. I urge you to make an effort and practice restraint before either one of you gets maimed or killed because of a stupid argument. In the spirit of the summer festival I will overlook this incident this time, but next time I won't be so generous."

"Don't you think the Barbarian should be punished for nearly beating my son to death, your Highness?" Lord Zagaar protested.

"From what I hear your son was not exactly an innocent bystander, Lord Zagaar," the King said, not hiding his irritation. "I've made my decision and that's finished." He rose from his chair and walked away.

Kastabaan turned to Lironi and smiled. "I've had an inspiration, but I'll need your help. Don't worry, it won't be anything unpleasant. I think you will like it. If you'll excuse me, I want to talk to this Rhodar."

"I'll come with you. He won't recognize me, but I've met him before in my Lironi persona. He was with Lord Carn when they brought Kaloss the news about his wife's death. I never talked to him, but I'm as intrigued by him as you are."

He chuckled. "Then you won't be disappointed when I'll tell you what I'd like you to do. Let's go before he leaves the room." He didn't wait for an answer and got up from his seat. The big barbarian was still sitting in his chair as if waiting for someone. He gave the impression of someone who wished he were somewhere else. Kastabaan couldn't blame him. He never felt comfortable in a crowded room, either.

Rhodar was about to rise, when Kastabaan reached him. The big barbarian gave him a questioning look, his eyes narrow and his stance alert, like a serpent ready to strike.

"I'm Lord Garrin from Spanaria," Kastabaan introduced himself. "I'm intrigued with that amulet you wear around your neck. Am I wrong to assume it is the tooth of a Stone Serpent?"

"You are not wrong," Rhodar said.

"It's been a long time since I visited the Great Plains, but I still remember that killing a Stone Serpent is no easy feat. Not many warriors who try survive the encounter with one of those giant snakes."

Rhodar smiled thinly. "That is true. I was lucky."

Kastabaan chuckled, as if amused by Rhodar's remark. "I don't believe it was luck. You shouldn't be so modest. A little bit of bragging might be helpful to gain the favors of the ladies." He made a movement with his head toward Lironi. "Just ask Lady Shanta."

Lironi gave a little laugh. "I must admit I do have a soft spot for strapping, young warriors. They can be so virile. You must have bedded your share of willing, beautiful ladies, Rhodar."

"Don't embarrass him," Kastabaan chided her.

"Oh, I'm sorry. I didn't mean to." Lironi reached up to touch Rhodar's cheek, making him flinch. "That looks like a nasty wound. Fortunately, whoever stitched it up did a marvelous job. It should leave only a faint scar. I do have some knowledge about treating wounds and injuries; that's why I'm interested."

"It was done by a healer. She lives in the palace. I suppose I was fortunate she was here." Rhodar seemed to study Lironi. "You look familiar. Have we met before?"

"I don't believe we have." She laughed. "I would remember you. What makes you say I look familiar?"

"I can't rightly say. Your stance, the way you tilt your head, and the way you speak." He smiled. "In my world, it is important to remember those things."

"I don't even notice things like that, never mind remembering them," Lironi said with a smile. "I have enough trouble remembering a name or a face."

Rhodar looked at Kastabaan. "You said you are from Spanaria. That's a long way from here."

"It is and not an easy trip," Kastabaan agreed. "But not as perilous as your journey from your homeland must have been. At least we didn't have to cross any mountains the way you did. May I ask what your purpose is for taking such a long voyage?"

"My journey is far from over. I'm looking for Arguss, the sorcerer, so he can renew the spell he cast many seasons ago on my father's battle-axe."

"Where does this sorcerer live?"

Rhodar shrugged. "I'm told he lives in Agastan. I haven't met anyone yet who knows him and I'm afraid my quest may be hopeless."

"Does it have to be this Arguss? Couldn't another sorcerer help you?"

Rhodar shook his head. "According to my father, it has to be Arguss."

"Where is this battle-axe?"

"In the King's armory. There are no weapons allowed in the palace or on palace grounds, but you must be aware of that."

"Of course I am. Aren't you afraid someone might steal it?"

"They might try, but only I can lift it." Rhodar didn't appear to be worried.

"A powerful, evil sorcerer might be able to neutralize the spell and use the axe for his own purpose," Kastabaan suggested.

"It has a strong protective spell against evil sorcery. Anyone trying to break the spell will suffer terrible consequences. The axe can never be used for anything evil." The barbarian sounded convinced and Kastabaan had no reason to doubt him.

"On your travels have you ever been to Spanaria?" Kastabaan wasn't too concerned about it, but in case the barbarian had been there, he needed to be careful with what he said about that small country. It would be easy to cause suspicion, since much time had passed since his last visit. Things have a habit of changing.

"I've never had the opportunity," Rhodar said. "I crossed the mountains into Grahna and from there I traveled north." He chuckled. "I hear Spanaria is famous for its beautiful and passionate women." His gaze moved to Lironi.

She gave him a mocking smile. "What makes you think I'm from Spanaria?"

"Judging by your beauty there can be no other place."

"Are all men from the Great Plains so charming?" She laughed. "And they call you savages."

"I believe we've taken up enough of Rhodar's time. We should leave." Kastabaan reached for Lironi's arm and accidentally brushed against Rhodar's. "Perhaps we'll run into each other again," he said and smiled. "Take care of those wounds and good luck with your quest."

"Have a pleasant and uneventful trip home to Spanaria." Rhodar touched his forehead. "I think I'll rest up this afternoon. I feel a sudden discomfort in my head."

Kastabaan turned and walked away, pulling Lironi with him. "Did you mark him?" he asked Lironi in a low voice.

"I did. He'll be as pliable as clay," she murmured. "How about you?"

"I put a spell on him. Everything should run smoothly and as planned."

———

RHODAR SPENT the afternoon in his room. Had anyone asked him why he did that he couldn't have given them a reasonable answer. He just knew it had to be done. The only time he left his room was to get something to eat in the common hall with all the servants. He sat by himself and didn't talk to anyone.

His head still felt strange when he went to bed. When he heard a knock on his door, he got up without bothering to get dressed and opened the door, not wondering who it could be at this late hour.

Staring at the woman who stood in the doorway, he didn't know what to say; only when she walked into the room he stammered, "Queen Gwenlin."

She laughed throatily. "Close the door before someone sees me."

He followed her order and turned around. She came into his arms and kissed him hungrily. Surprised by her action, he nevertheless returned her kiss. When they parted, she gasped, "I hope that kiss fulfills what it promises." With that she stepped back and undid the belt that kept her gown closed. Opening it, she let it slip to the ground. Naked, she stood in front of him, letting him look at her.

Even though his mind still seemed foggy, he was fully aware of what was happening. Looking at her voluptuous form, he moaned deeply. "You are beautiful, my Queen." Boldly taking a step forward, he took her into his arms and pulled her to him. Her nude, warm body pressing against his caused him to react almost immediately.

She laughed softly and curled her fingers around his manhood. "Let's not waste any time standing here. We are both ready. Carry me to your bed and put this thing into me."

He gathered her into his arms, carried her to his bed and laid her on top of the blanket. Even though he was driven by a terrible desire that nearly seemed to consume him, he was plagued by sudden doubts. He looked down at her exposed body.

"Are you sure this is what you want?"

"Why else would I come to you? I need to feel a real and viral man in my arms and between my legs. The King is getting old and of little use in bed. Don't make me wait. I'm dying with desire. Come into my embrace."

He couldn't control his actions. Something inside him forced him to comply and he lay down beside her on the narrow bed. Moving on top of her, he slipped between her spread thighs. She gave a little cry of joy when their bodies joined and moved against him with unrestrained passion. She was like a wild animal and he swam in a sea of pure pleasure, losing all concept of time. When she finally left his bed and his room, he felt exhausted, not only physically but also mentally.

He lay on his bed, contemplating what just happened. His mind seemed suddenly much clearer and he wondered if he really coupled with the Queen or if it had it been only a wishful dream? He wasn't certain and almost hoped he had been hallucinating. The yill-berries might have caused it. To be sexually intimate with the Queen could prove fatal for him.

What possessed him he couldn't understand, but what was he supposed to do? She came to his room. To deny her would have been an insult and there was nothing more dangerous than a scorned woman, especially if she happened to be the Queen. He had no choice but to yield to her advances.

He tried to console himself with those thoughts, but there were other thoughts. Why did he feel so guilty? From what he remembered, or seemed to remember, it was one of the best couplings he'd ever had. He had no doubt she enjoyed it as much as he did. He didn't rape her, and she wasn't exactly passive. He'd never met a female with such a lusty appetite for sex. He didn't believe she would tell anyone about it. It would be their secret as long as nobody saw her.

He kept drifting in and out of sleep and must have finally fallen fully asleep, because when he opened his eyes, light fell through the tiny window high above. Getting out of bed, he stretched and was surprised to not feel any pain, just some discomfort in his arms and legs. Remembering the previous day and night, he expected to be tired but wasn't. He didn't know how long he slept, but from the amount of light outside, it wasn't early morning anymore.

With the memories also came thoughts of remorse, but then he shrugged. There was nothing he could do about it now. It had happened or maybe not. He would have to watch the Queen's behavior toward him when he saw her next. Of one thing he was certain, he would not be the one to speak.

Feeling hungry, he dressed and went to the common hall. Only a few servants sat at the tables. It seems he missed the rush early morning brings. Nodding to a couple of them, he took one of the crude clay plates and went to the food pots. There wasn't much left, but he scraped out enough from the thick stew to satisfy his appetite. Then he broke off a few pieces of dry bread and filled a jug with larn-milk. Not exactly a feast for noblemen, but he was used to simple fare. Sometimes he didn't even eat this well during his travels.

"You are the outlander who beat Zangarian yesterday," a voice said behind him.

He turned to look at the servant girl standing behind him. She gave him a shy smile and he nodded.

"It isn't a secret," he growled. "I don't feel like talking about it. It seems I displeased the King."

"The King may be displeased," she said, "but you also created many admirers. Zangarian is not very popular."

"I gathered that much. I'm honored to please so many, but for me it is most important I please the King, the Queen, and the noblemen in the palace."

She chuckled. "There are many noblemen and ladies who you pleased. They just won't say it. I have a message for you from one such admirer. She wants to meet you. Go to the spot where the jugglers perform and you will find her there."

"Who is she?"

She shrugged. "I can't tell you that, but does it really matter?" She smiled. "Go to her. You won't be sorry. Remember, this is the summer festival and is meant for celebration. To deny a woman when she summons you is a bad omen and it will anger the gods."

Before he could answer, she rushed away.

He finished his breakfast and went outside, wondering who this strange woman would be. The sun was already high in the sky and it was nearly noon. He couldn't remember the last time he had slept this long if ever. He didn't know how much longer he would be able to live among these people who considered themselves civilized. He was getting soft and complacent and losing his animals instincts. Sleeping so long without being on guard could prove dangerous.

The grounds were already bustling with people and the sound of laughter and other noises that occur when many people crowd together filled the air. He walked through the crowd, looking for the jugglers. He finally spotted one of them and headed for him. Before he could reach him, someone touched his arm. He swung around, eyes and senses alert. Judging by the slim curvy body and the swell of breasts he knew it was a woman. It was difficult to judge her age, because she wore a skull cap that also covered part of her face. Her eyes glittered blue behind small slits, but he couldn't tell the color or length of her hair. Even though the mask did not cover her mouth, it was concealed behind a small veil.

She wore a short skirt that showed off her long legs. Judging by their shape and muscle tone, she was probably quite young. Slippers made from soft cloth covered her feet.

"Are you the one I was supposed to meet here?"

She nodded, grabbed his hand, and pulled him with her.

"Where are we going?"

She put a finger against her lips.

"Are you planning to stay silent?"

Her nod confirmed what he suspected. Not expecting an answer, he spoke anyway. "Because you are unable to talk?"

She nodded again but also shook her head, confusing him.

"How are we going to communicate? Never mind, don't answer that." He chuckled. "It seems this is going to be a one-sided conversation."

She laughed at that and squeezed his hand.

"It appears you can make some sounds. That's comforting."

They walked on in silence. He was leery about her, wondering where she was leading him. Staying alert, he watched the people around him, searching for any signs of danger. Nobody paid them any attention, except for the usual stares from men and women. His physique made him stand out in any crowd and his lion-wolf kilt proclaimed him as an outlander. It was a hot day and he had chosen not to wear the shirt he borrowed from Lord Galoor. It was too tight for him, anyway.

Many stared at the serpent tooth. Either they wondered what animal it came from or, if they knew, admired his courage to fight and survive the encounter with a Stone Serpent. He knew the giant snakes were not unique to the Western Plains. They could also be found in the mountains. Sometimes they came down into the valleys to terrorize people. Even though of different species, they were as dangerous as the Stone Serpents.

The crowd began thinning and then they finally left the people behind. He realized they were heading for a small building hidden inside a grove of tall trees. Arriving at the building, she steered him toward a door. Opening it, she made a motion for him to enter. Being cautious and not trusting her, he shook his head and indicated she should go in first.

She laughed softly and slipped through the door. He followed her slowly. The room they entered lay in semi-darkness and it took his eyes a moment to adjust. He saw a small window, but a curtain drawn across it shut out the light from outside. He also saw a table and a couple of chairs. Thick furs lay on the floor against the wall in the back of the room.

The woman closed the door and walked farther into the room. She turned to face him and, with a little chuckle, she removed her top to expose a pair of small breasts. Hooking her fingers into the top of her skirt, she slowly pushed it past her hips. It slid down her slim legs and pooled around her feet. Naked, except for a satiny small piece of cloth that covered her pubis, she came toward him. When she was close, she lifted the veil hiding her mouth and kissed him. Her lips were soft and warm on his.

Stunned by what had happened so unexpectedly, he stood rigid, not sure how he should react. This was the second time in two days a woman offered herself to him. One had succeeded in seducing him, and he still had misgivings about that because it was the Queen.

Who was this woman? Certainly not a servant, but it didn't matter; he didn't feel comfortable letting it happen a second time.

She let go of him and on silent feet she patted over to the table. The sight of her round buttocks and curve of her slim hips caused a gentle flutter in his loins. He watched her pour red liquid from a jug into two clay cups. Coming back, she carried the full cups and offered one to him.

She lifted one cup to her lips and drank from it, indicating for him to do the same.

He decided to trust she wasn't going to poison him and took a small sip. As he had guessed, it was wine and tasted sweet. Shrugging, he emptied the cup. The wine went down easy and left a warm feeling in his belly. Deciding he needed something to calm his nerves, he held out the empty cup. She emptied hers and took his cup from his fingers. Filling the cups again, she brought his back but left hers on the table. The second cup went down even easier than the first and he was beginning to feel much better.

She took the empty cup from him and put it onto the floor. Standing in front of him, she began to undo his belt. Then she tugged on his kilt and pulled it down, exposing his manhood. She chuckled behind her mask when she saw it come to life and touched him. With a loud groan, he stepped out of his kilt and crushed her to him. She didn't struggle. Molding her slim body against his, she kissed him with great passion.

He decided there was no reason for him to turn down her offer. She wanted him, and he wasn't going to waste the opportunity to copulate with her. Scooping her up, he carried her to the furs. They tumbled onto them. Rhodar landed on his back with the woman on top. When he wanted to turn with her, she pushed on his chest to keep him down and straddled him.

"I prefer to be on top," he growled.

She laughed. "So do I."

Her sudden ability to talk startled him. "You can talk, so why the charade?"

"I didn't want you to recognize me." Her lips formed a mocking smile.

"Your voice sounds familiar. Take off that mask."

She grabbed the skullcap and pulled it off. Shaking her short, black hair to fluff it, she laughed at his expression.

"You're the bored, lonely girl I talked to at my meeting with the King when everyone else ignored me, the one who wasn't supposed to be there."

"I told you I'd see you again." She wiggled her bottom. "Here we are locked together like two sex-starved lovers."

He groaned. "Are you even old enough to do this?"

"I'm no innocent young girl, and I'm older than I look. I've always had a young-looking face."

"I don't want any trouble with your parents. They seem to be keeping close watch over you."

"Nobody knows I'm here. You have nothing to worry about."

After that they stayed silent for a long time, except for his grunts and her soft cries of joy.

Chapter Twenty

KASTABAAN STUDIED his image in the mirror and nodded with satisfaction. He turned and looked at Lironi. "What do you think? Will I pass inspection?"

"You would pass mine, but will you be able to fool the Queen?"

"According to Caradin, they haven't seen each other for years. I have the bulk of Caradin's memories and I should be able to answer all her questions without any problems." He grinned, feeling elated about what he planned. "I won't give her much opportunity to talk when I fuck her. She'll be too busy screaming with the pleasure I'll give her and unable to form any coherent thoughts."

"Lironi chuckled. "I can't comment on that. You and I have never had sex with each other, so I cannot judge how competent a lover you are."

"There is no reason you and I should become intimate. Your peculiar tastes do nothing for me. Not to mention that I don't couple with beasts. I leave that up to Korallas."

She gave him a hurt look. "Is that what you think of me? A beast?"

"Aren't you? Isn't that what you become when you copulate?"

"Not always. Only when I want to feed, and even then I'm still me. My outside appearance changes, but not my mind. As I've already proved to you, I can become anyone I want to be, but inside I will always be the same."

"Be that as it may, I feel no desire to climb between your legs, no matter how attractive you look or how passionate you are. I have no doubt there is no shortage of males who would like nothing better than to do that. For tonight, I want you to seek out Caradin and keep him busy in his room. Become the Queen and let your imagination go wild. Give him the best night he ever had. Can you do that?"

"Of course I can." She smiled. "I hope the real Queen will give you the same pleasure I will give him, but I doubt that. Because of what I am, I've been blessed with special abilities. Any male who gets my attention is lucky indeed. No human woman can give him the joy he finds in my arms."

He snorted. "Don't let that be your downfall," he warned. "Never lose control of any situation and be aware of your surroundings. Above all, avoid witnesses."

"You don't have to worry about me," she assured him, but he detected some hesitation before she answered and he wondered about that. She could become a liability.

With another look into the mirror, he turned and headed for the door. "Tomorrow will be an important day. Things will be put into motion that will change the future in this corner of our world. If you play it right, you will be part of it in a big way. Do anything you want with Caradin. Drain every last drop of his blood if that's your pleasure. Make sure he's dead in the morning and get rid of his body."

She gave him an astonished look. "You mean that?"

"I wouldn't say it if I didn't." With that he left.

Making his way into the section of the palace where most other dignitaries were staying in their assigned quarters, he headed for the kitchen area and stopped one of the servant women.

"I need to send an urgent message to the Queen. Would you be so kind and find me one of her personal maids?"

The woman looked at him and he made a motion with his hand while looking into her eyes. "Just take me to her."

"As you wish, my Lord. Please, follow me." The woman turned around and walked away.

Kastabaan smiled smugly. Magic was such a wonderful thing.

He paid close attention to the corridors they used and memorized them. He should have no trouble finding his way back again. The corridors became wider and they walked past rooms without doors. Once they encountered one of the armed guards who barred the way.

"I need to find one of the Queen's personal maids," the servant said

"Why?" The guard eyed her suspiciously.

"Urgent message for the Queen," Kastabaan said and looked into the guard's eyes.

His eyes glazed over and he pointed to one of the rooms with no doors. "In there."

"Thank you," Kastabaan said. "Remember my face. I may be back tonight and I want you to give me no trouble."

"There will be no trouble," the guard said in a monotonous tone.

Kastabaan made sure he was seen by the servants who were busy in the room. They looked at him with obvious curiosity. One of them came to meet them at the entrance.

"You're not supposed to be here," she told them.

"I have a message for the Queen. Tell her an old friend from Jandarin wants to meet her under the old Barkla-Tree after sundown. I will wait for her answer."

The girl nodded and rushed away through one of the doors in the back of the room. It didn't take long before she came back again. "The Queen wants you to come to her quarters after sundown," she told Kastabaan. He had not expected a different answer; at least he hoped that wouldn't happen. He was fairly certain the Queen would not take the chance to be seen in public with a strange man.

"Tell her I accept her invitation. Will you be here so you can take me to her?"

"I will make sure I'm here." She looked at him with questions in her eyes. "May I inquire who you are?"

He gave her a little smile. "I'll tell you, but only because you are so beautiful. I am General Caradin. The Queen and I are old acquaintances. I hope you can keep a secret."

She inclined her head. "My Lord, your secret is safe with me."

'I'm confident it is. By tomorrow everyone will know about this.' He chuckled and walked away, not waiting for the servant who had brought him. With just one word he could have prevented the girl from talking, but that would have defeated part of his plan.

Now, if Lironi did her job, everything would fall into place.

He went to one of the many small dining halls and had a leisurely meal. He wasn't in any hurry now. If he was seen and if people remembered him, it would serve his purpose. Darkness came and he was on his way again.

Queen Gwenlin stood by the window and looked at the darkened sky when he entered her quarters. She turned and stared at him with large eyes. Then she rushed into his arms.

"Why have you come, Caradin? Your life is not safe here."

He kissed her gently. "I needed to see you, my Love. We've been apart for too long."

"If Ordar sees you, he will have you arrested. He has never forgotten what we did."

"Neither have I. My nights have been filled with your memories. How is our daughter?"

"Arleen has grown into a beautiful young woman." She searched his face. "She must never know Ordar isn't her real father. Promise me you won't tell."

Holding her face between his hands, he smiled. "Only you and I will ever know. However, I want to see her."

"How long are you staying?"

"Just long enough to do what I came to do."

"What would that be?" He felt her heart beating against his chest and saw her lips tremble.

"To feel your naked body against mine, to touch your satiny skin, to kiss your warm, soft lips, and to experience your passion as you lie in my arms," he whispered. "My life has been empty all these years. I was forced to marry Queen Kharana's daughter Ilita, but she is cold and does not love me. I am a lonely man, my Love."

She covered his face with kisses. "Destiny has not been kind to us," she whispered through tears. "Ordar and I haven't been intimate for a long time. I have suffered through many nights, aching for love and fulfillment of my desires. One night cannot make up for the time we've lost."

"Then let us not waste more time," he said and cupped her breast.

She sighed deeply and pressed her body against his. Then she stepped back and opened her gown, exposing her naked body. Again, he stepped into her embrace and, grabbing her full buttocks, he pulled her near.

"You're as beautiful as I remember."

She laughed. "My body has grown older, my breasts are sagging, and my skin has lost its elasticity, but my sexual appetite has not diminished and everything still works. Come, take off your clothes and join me on my bed. We have all night to catch up. I hope you're up for it."

———

LIRONI WATCHED KASTABAAN LEAVE. She had to admit, he looked handsome in the persona of Caradin and nobody would doubt his identity, not even his guards. According to what Kastabaan told her, Caradin and the Queen had been lovers before King Ordar married her. Caradin was also the King's half-brother, born of an affair between their father, King Ordarin, and a common woman. No wonder, King Ordar hated Caradin. He could be a potential threat to Ordar's throne.

She didn't know what Kastabaan planned, but she suspected something big and momentous was going to happen, especially since he told her to kill Caradin.

Suddenly anxious to keep her rendezvous with Caradin, she morphed into the persona of the Queen. Unlike Kastabaan, she did not have to touch the person she wanted to become. Actually, she could only take on the form of a female, never a male, but it was enough to see her, watch her and listen to her voice. She did not know if Kastabaan had such limitations.

Satisfied with her ability to become the Queen, at least on the outside, she changed back into being Lady Shanta. Then she went to search out Caradin. She knew he was living in the servant's quarters and that's where she began her search. She asked a couple of servants if they had seen a man with his description, but she couldn't get any information. She remembered Kastabaan telling her that Caradin and the Queen used to meet under an old Barkla-Tree. Following an intuitive feeling, she went looking for that old tree. After asking a few people, she managed to find it.

It was a tall, wide-reaching tree on the shore of a pond. The pond was overgrown and the shrubs that surrounded the pond gave the impression that this part of the King's palace grounds was not used much.

As she came closer, she saw a man sitting in the grass and leaning against the thick trunk of the tree, staring at the still water of the pond. She recognized Caradin. He was alone, as she had hoped. Checking her surroundings, she slipped behind a group of thick shrubs and transformed her body into that of Queen Gwenlin. Then she walked slowly toward the man by the tree.

Caradin looked up when her shadow fell across him. His eyes widened when he recognized her. "Gwenlin," he gasped. "How did you know I'd be here?"

"I didn't, but I come here often to dream about us. Something told me to come here today." She squatted down and touched his face. "Is it really you or am I dreaming?"

"I should be asking that question. How did you recognize me with this beard and my short hair?"

She gave a little chuckle. "When I saw you sitting beside the tree, there was no doubt in my mind it could only be you. Nobody comes here but me. Why are you here?"

He took her hands into his and, rising from his sitting position, he pulled her upright. Then he pulled her into his arms. "I came to celebrate the summer festival and I was hoping I could make peace with Ordar. Too many years have gone by. After all, he is my brother. And you…" he paused. "I was hoping to at least get a glimpse of you. I've missed you, my Love."

"I've missed you, too," she said and kissed him. "We are all alone here," she whispered. "We have plenty of time. Nobody is going to miss me. Ordar and I are strangers. He's getting old and of little use when it comes to performing his duties as a husband."

She knew he was already under her spell. She did not control magic, but nature had endowed her with other abilities. All she needed to do was touch a man and he would react to her sexually. Caradin wanted her and his desire for her was not something he could control.

It didn't take long before they both lay naked under the tree, locked together like two Lurrex in heat. She had no intention to hurry this. She would prolong their copulating for as long as his strength lasted and enjoy every moment until he was ready to collapse, then she would change into her animal form. He would not be aware when she sank her teeth into his jugular and begin feeding. His mind and body would be lost in an ocean of ecstasy until the moment he died. There would be no pain, only extreme pleasure.

THE LIGHT of dawn fell through the window. Rhodar turned to look at the young woman lying by his side. She had her eyes closed and seemed relaxed and happy. He studied her features and found her beautiful. He still didn't know her name or who she was; obviously, the daughter of one of the influential families, some Lord close to the King. He hoped it wouldn't turn out to be the brother of Zangarian, the man he almost killed in that fight. In a way, it didn't matter. If she was, she must be aware of that fight and it seemed she didn't care.

As he watched, she opened her eyes. "Have you been watching me?" she said with a sleepy smile.

He nodded. "I have and enjoyed what I saw. Even after a night of furious passion, you still manage to look beautiful. Not many women can do that."

"How can you say I'm beautiful? My hair must look all matted." She ran her fingers through her hair. She studied his face. "I hope I didn't let myself go too much last night, but you awoke a beast inside me. No man ever made me feel like that." She laughed softly. "But why am I surprised? You are a barbarian—a ferocious beast from the Plains."

His thoughts suddenly shifted to Saleen and he wondered what would happen if he coupled with her. Would she turn into a beast when her moment came and would she be able to control her beast-side? Was that one of the reasons he rejected her because he was afraid of what might happen?

"You seem far away," the woman broke into his thoughts. "Are you already bored with me?"

He bent to kiss her. "I don't think you could ever bore a man. You're much too wild for that."

"Like you?" Her hand snaked down his belly. Laughing, she touched him. "Perhaps I should tame this wild beast."

He rolled on top of her. "Perhaps you should."

They spent most of the morning coupling, until they both were satisfied and in need of recuperation.

Rhodar gave her one last kiss and rose. "I feel grubby. Is there a creek or pond nearby where I can wash my body?"

"No creek but a small pond. Very private." Naked, she walked to the door in the wall beside the bed and opened it. It led into a short corridor. There were a couple of doors along the wall, but they headed for the door at the end.

Bright light flooded in when she opened it. Rhodar saw a small pond hidden among tall shrubs. "Nobody will find us here," she said and pulled him toward the water. Letting go of his hand, she dove headfirst into the pond.

There was no reason for him to hesitate and he followed her. The water was pleasantly warm. Spitting water, she rose up in front of him. "I'll do your back if you do mine."

He closed his eyes and enjoyed the feeling of her soft hands on his back. He felt happy but knew it would be only for a short time. Reality would soon come back to his life.

After their bath, they went back into the building. He was surprised to see the table covered with food. He saw the two girls standing beside the table. "I thought this was a private affair."

The young woman laughed. "It still is. Lorni and Simmi are my personal maids. They are sworn to secrecy about what I do. If they talk, they'll lose their tongues."

Rhodar recognized one of the girls. She was the one who had brought him the message. She smiled at Rhodar and nodded. "That's true. Nobody will know about you being here." She couldn't hide her interest as the gaze of her eyes traveled up and down his naked body.

"Perhaps I should get dressed before we sit down to eat," he said.

After they finished eating, the young woman donned her skullcap again to hide her hair and face. Before they walked out of the door, she spoke to the two girls, "We'll be back later in the afternoon. Make sure everything is cleaned and come back in the evening with food and some wine." She looked at Rhodar. "You don't know my name and I won't tell you. Nobody must know you and I spent this time together."

"I have no reason to tell anyone. You can count on my silence."

She smiled. "Oh, believe me, I know I can." She gave one of the girls a sign. "Lorni, you know what to do."

Lorni came forward and touched Rhodar. He felt a slight tingle running through his body. "You will remember what happened here but you won't be able to tell anyone any details about her or us." Moving her hands, she created an intricate pattern in the air.

"You're a witch," he said.

She nodded with a little smile. "Not a very good one but good enough to prevent you from talking. This spell should hold you." She shrugged. "At least as long as you stay here at the King's palace."

The veiled young woman chuckled softly. "You must forgive me, Rhodar, but I cannot take any chances. You will remember me and I will remember you. Let that be enough." She grabbed his hand. "Come and enjoy this day with me."

It promised to stay warm and sunny for the afternoon and Rhodar looked forward to spending the rest of the day and another passionate night in the company of his beautiful nameless female companion, but it wasn't going to happen.

When they joined the crowd on the festival grounds, the people seemed strangely silent. There was no laughter and no celebrating, but before Rhodar and the girl could ask what had happened, they were stopped by a troop of six of the King's guards.

"Are you the Plainsman Rhodar?" their leader asked.

"Yes," he acknowledged.

Two of the guards grabbed his arms while the others aimed their swords at him.

"You are under arrest," the leader told him harshly.

"On what charge?"

"The murder of King Ordar."

Before he could ask more questions, one guard kicked him in the belly and then they dragged him away. Rhodar looked for the veiled woman but she had disappeared.

"You're making a big mistake," he growled.

"Shut up." The guard kicked him again, this time hitting his ribcage.

Wincing from the sudden pain, Rhodar felt like hitting back but constrained his urge. He was innocent and he would be able to prove it, so he let them take him away without struggling.

They threw him into a dark, damp cell underneath the palace and he hoped they wouldn't forget about him.

———

THE COURTROOM WAS PACKED with people. At a long table in the front sat the King's advisors, with Lord Zagaar sitting in the chair King Ordar had occupied only days before. He glared at Rhodar and it was clear he had no intentions to even listen to any testimony. This would not be a fair trial. Lord Zagaar would never forgive Rhodar for what he did to his son and he would see to it that Rhodar was found guilty and punished for a crime he hadn't committed.

At another table sat Lord Galoor and Lord Carn. Neither of them looked happy. Beside Lord Zagaar sat Queen Gwenlin and Lady Gardina, and between them a young boy.

Rhodar was surprised when he saw the two young women sitting beside the Queen. The older one with the short hair was the young woman from the cabin. She stared at Rhodar without expression. She and her two maids knew he was innocent, and with a few words she could set him free, but he realized he couldn't count on her help. She'd stay silent to protect her private life and her good name.

The realization hit him that she was the King's daughter.

"Plainsman Rhodar, you have been accused of King Ordar's murder. How do you plead?" Lord Zagaar's voice rang across the courtroom.

Rhodar stood up and said, "I am innocent of the crime, my Lord."

"Do not arouse the anger of this court, Barbarian," Lord Zagaar thundered. "The only way you can expect fair treatment is to confess freely to this atrocious deed. We have a witness who was with our King when you committed this cowardly act by stabbing him in the belly with your sword. After that you raped her over and over to satisfy your animal urges like the beast you are. Do not deny it."

Rhodar stood erect and pushed out his chest. "I am Rhodar, Son of Rhor, High Chief of the Serpent Clan. Someday I will be Chief of the Riverstone Tribe. I do not commit coldblooded murder. I state again I did not murder King Ordar. What reason would I have to commit such a crime?"

"Reason? You are a savage with a taste for violence. You nearly beat my son to death. What other reason did you have for that but to still your craving for blood?"

"Your son provoked me, my Lord. I defended my honor and the honor of my people. Had I not beaten your son, he surely would have killed me. I saw it in his eyes."

Lord Zagaar laughed. "You saw it in his eyes. Since you're so apt in reading in people's eyes what they think, tell me what I'm thinking right now."

"I never claimed I can read anyone's thoughts. I cannot read yours but I know you already have found me guilty and you want me punished. You will ask for me to be executed."

"If he doesn't, I will," the high voice of a juvenile proclaimed shrilly. "You murdered my father and you will be punished for that."

Rhodar looked at the boy. "You must be Prince Rowarin, my Lord. If you ever want to be a just king, you will not condemn me to death without finding out all the facts. Your father would want you to do that."

"You don't know what my father would have wanted," Prince Rowarin cried out. "You heard what Lord Zagaar said. There is a witness and there is no doubt in my mind that you are guilty. I want you dead." He put his face between his hands and sobbed. "I loved my father."

"Who is this witness?" Rhodar looked at Lord Zagaar. "Let her confront me and tell me to my face what she says I did."

Lord Zagaar glared at him. "You do not make any demands, Barbarian, but I will honor your request." He turned to one of the guards. "Bring in the woman."

Moments later, the guard brought in an older woman. She seemed subdued, but when she saw Rhodar, she lifted her arm, pointed at him and spoke with a sobbing voice, "That's him. I will never forget the expression on his face when he stabbed the King and how he laughed when he..." she faltered but caught herself. "When he ripped off my gown and forced himself on me—again and again. I thought he'd never stop. He was like a wild animal."

"When was this supposed to have happened?" Rhodar demanded with a raised voice.

The woman looked at Lord Zagaar but stayed silent.

"Tell us," Lord Zagaar said in a surprisingly gentle tone.

"Yesterday morning, my Lord." Her voice was weak and barely audible.

Rhodar glanced at the young woman beside the Queen, remembering his promise not to tell anyone about what happened between them. He was with her when King Ordar was murdered. She could prove his innocence if she'd speak. "I was with a woman yesterday," he said.

"What's her name?" Lord Zagaar spoke with a bored voice, obviously not interested in what Rhodar had to say.

"I don't know her name. Even if I did, I wouldn't be able to tell you. I promised."

"Not even to save your life?" Lord Zagaar gave him a cynical grin.

"I never break my word."

"Very convenient. You want us to take your word for it that you were in the company of an unnamed woman when the murder took place?" Shaking his head, Lord Zagaar scanned the room. "Does anyone believe the Outlander?"

"He's lying—"

"Execute him—"

"You can't believe a savage—"

"He's guilty—"

"Cut him open with his own sword—"

Lord Zagaar held up one hand. "I've heard enough and I'm convinced." He turned to look at the other advisors who had been silent. "Do any of you doubt his guilt, my Lords?"

"I would like to advise caution." A deep, familiar voice spoke. "We don't want to execute an innocent man."

"Lord Galoor." Lord Zagaar gave him a questioning look. "I realize Rhodar is your guest, but what valid reason can you give for advising caution? He is accused of the King's murder; a horrendous crime that cannot go unpunished. Remember, we have a reliable witness putting this man at the scene."

"It seems that way, but somehow my gut feeling tells me not to rush into something that cannot be undone."

"Your gut feeling?" Lord Zagaar's laugh didn't hide his contempt. "Since when do we trust a gut feeling when we have facts that scream us in the face? My gut feeling says he's guilty."

"You contradict yourself, my Lord," Lord Galoor said. "It seems to me you do follow your gut feeling after all."

Rhodar was listening to the arguments with a sinking sensation. He knew Lord Zagaar would not budge. His mind was made up and he wasn't going to listen to reason. Looking around the courtroom, he didn't see any friendly faces. Their King had been murdered and, as far as everyone was concerned, the murderer had been caught. When he saw one of the servants approaching the table of Lord Zagaar, he wondered what she was going to say. Probably one more statement that would determine his guilt.

"May I speak, my Lord?" The woman looked from Lord Zagaar to the Queen as if seeking encouragement from her, but Queen Gwenlin stayed silent. It almost seemed to Rhodar as if she wasn't interested in the proceedings.

Lord Zagaar waved an impatient hand. "Speak up, woman."

"My name is Lita. I am one of the Queen's maids. I saw the Barbarian leaving the Queen's quarters early yesterday morning after the Queen's Lord-Visitor left. I don't know if that is important information." She lowered her head. "My apologies for not coming forward earlier."

"No need to apologize." Lord Zagaar looked at the Queen. "Can you vouch for the truth of what this servant just told us, your Majesty?"

Queen Gwenlin stayed silent for a long time before she spoke. "She speaks the truth." Her voice sounded resigned.

The silence in the courtroom was suddenly interrupted by loud voices. Rhodar stared at the Queen with surprise.

"Are you saying the Outlander spent the night in your chambers?"

The Queen looked straight at Rhodar and spoke in an accusing tone. "Not the whole night, only part of it, but long enough to rape me."

Lord Zagaar banged his fist against the table top. "Silence!" he roared trying to be heard over the clamor in the courtroom. "Let the Queen speak."

"What else is there to say? He came into my bedroom and forced himself on me. Isn't that enough?"

It took Rhodar a moment to digest what he just heard. Why would the maid make up such a story and why would the Queen lie? Before anyone could stop him, he took a few steps forward and confronted the Queen.

"Your Majesty, what you said is not the truth. I was never in your room and I never raped you. Why would I rape you when you visited me in my room the night before?"

"What?" Queen Gwenlin stared at him with large eyes.

"You came to me willingly and shared my bed," he said. "I speak the truth."

"That is a blatant lie, Barbarian!" She almost screamed. "I am the Queen and would never willingly let a savage barbarian touch me. You took my body by force and after that you murdered my husband, the King. That is the truth."

Rhodar violently shook away the strong hands that grabbed his arms. "I am innocent of either charge, your Majesty," he said in a low voice.

He didn't struggle when the two guards dragged him back, away from the Queen.

"Queen Gwenlin, who was the Lord-Visitor the Maid mentioned?" Lord Zagaar seemed genuinely interested.

The Queen hesitated for a moment before she replied, "He was an old friend. We spent the night together talking about old times."

"Does this old friend have a name?"

"Yes, he has." It wasn't the Queen who answered but a male voice from the back.

Everyone turned, including Rhodar, to see who had spoken. He saw a bearded man with short, black hair, wearing a uniform, walking toward the tables. He stopped in front of Lord Zagaar. "I am General Caradin of the Jandarin army. I am also King Ordar's brother." He smiled. "Actually, only his half-brother. Since my brother is dead, I claim his throne." He looked around the courtroom. "Hail your new King."

Chapter Twenty-One

HE DIDN'T FEEL any pain, only a sensation of being tired, when he opened his eyes and tried to sit up. His hand went to his throat, but when he pulled his hand away and looked at it the expected blood wasn't there. Why he had expected blood he didn't know.

"He's awake," someone called.

He turned his head to see a young boy sitting beside him. He also noticed that he lay in a bed.

"Where am I?" His voice came out in a croak. He managed to sit up and take a look around him, finding himself in a small room. "How did I get here?"

Hearing footsteps, he looked at the door and watched an older woman walk into the room. She smiled when she saw him. "So you finally decided to wake."

"Where am I and who are you?"

"I guess you're getting better. Two questions at once. That's good. For a while I thought we might lose you. You've been unconscious for three nights. To answer your first question—you are in my home. I am Quirma. Now you can tell me who you are." She gave him an inquiring look.

"I'm Caradin."

"Caradin. Hm." Her eyes studied his face. "I remember a Caradin who lived in the palace a long time ago. He was King Ordar's half-brother. One day he left never to return."

He nodded. "Not by choice, I can assure you, but I've come back to make peace with my brother."

Her eyes widened. "If that's your reason for coming then you've come too late. King Ordar is dead."

"Dead? How?"

"He was murdered by a barbarian from the Western Plains. That's all I know."

"When did this happen?"

"A few days ago." She eyed him with suspicion. "Can you prove that you are this Caradin?"

"Prove? Of course I can." He rubbed his hand over his beard. "Perhaps if I cut off my beard you may recognize me, even though I've aged." He chuckled. "I'm certain Queen Gwenlin will vouch for me." He stopped himself as he remembered. "Queen Gwenlin… is she alright?"

"She is. Why wouldn't she be?"

"Because I was with her under the old Barkla-Tree by the pond, but that's all I remember." He wiped his forehead with a shaky hand, trying to bring back his memory.

"That's where my daughter and her husband found you, but they didn't see Queen Gwenlin, only a…" she hesitated.

"Only a what?"

"A beast crouching over your naked body. The beast ran away before either my daughter or her husband could get a closer look. They didn't see anyone else."

"A beast? I don't recall the presence of a beast. Queen Gwenlin and I met by the pond and we…" He hesitated, not sure if he should say more. "We shared a moment of intimacy." The memory of the incredible pleasure she had given him was strong, but he remembered nothing else. "Is it possible this beast killed Queen Gwenlin?"

"No. Queen Gwenlin is alive."

"I can't explain what your daughter saw." Caradin suddenly became aware he was naked under the thin blanket. "Where are my clothes?"

"I washed them and put them onto the small table on the other side of your bed. I also washed your body." She gave a little laugh. "You needn't be embarrassed. I've seen plenty of naked men in my life." She turned solemn. "You were barely conscious when my daughter found you. It seems that beast sucked much of your blood from your body and would have sucked you dry had it not been interrupted. As it was I wasn't sure you'd survive, but I fed you sap of the sequa-plant, lots of it, and I'm glad it worked. How are you feeling?"

"Weak but otherwise fine. I'm in your debt for saving my life."

"My daughter and her husband are the ones you should thank. Only their quick thinking and determination saved you. They could have left you lying there and not get involved." She smiled. "I raised my children to have compassion for others and not to look the other way when someone is in trouble."

Her face became serious again. "I'm not saying I don't believe you about being Caradin, but there is something I need to tell you. You see, the day of the accused killer's trial a man appeared in the courtroom claiming to be King Ordar's half-brother. He said his name was Caradin."

"Impossible!" Caradin gaped at the woman. "I know I'm Caradin, which means that man is an imposter and a liar." He pushed back the blanket and swung his legs off the bed, forgetting for a moment that he was naked. "I'll have to get into my room to get my uniform so I can expose this imposter. Whoever he is, he will have to answer for this. I am General Caradin of the Jandarin Army. My aids will testify to that."

"You're not going anywhere," the old woman said sternly. "You're still far too weak. The first thing you'll do is eat something so you can gain your strength back and then you will rest. It will take time before you are strong enough to leave here." She looked at the boy. "Go and fetch a bowl of the stew I've got standing on the stove and don't forget the spoon."

The boy nodded and got up from his chair. Before he left the room, he turned around, looked at Caradin and giggled. "You'd better cover up before my sister comes. If she sees you naked and conscious, she will ravage you and you'll die of exhaustion."

"Don't talk such rubbish, Quindor," the old woman said harshly, shaking her head.

Quindor laughed and disappeared into the next room.

"He's at the age now where he's beginning to look at girls. He thinks he's a man already and can make manly jokes." She chuckled. "I don't believe he's even seen a naked girl yet."

Caradin got back onto the bed and pulled the blanket over his legs

217

and lap. The sudden movement had made him dizzy. "I suppose you are right. I'm feeling a bit faint and a bowl of stew may help to get me onto my feet again."

"I'll go and bring you a wet cloth so you can wipe your hands and face. It might refresh you."

Quindor came back into the room, carrying a wooden bowl filled with steaming food. He handed it to Caradin with a wide grin. "I heard my mother. She's wrong, I've seen a naked girl already," he whispered. "More than one. I climbed on top of the wall and watched the bathers in the pond. I even watched a couple as they… you know… in the bushes. I'm not as innocent as my mother believes."

Something occurred to Caradin. "Why would you have to climb the wall to look into the palace grounds?"

"Because we're outside the wall. Didn't you know?"

"No, I didn't. How will I get back in again?"

Quindor shrugged. "I don't know, but my mother will figure something out."

"What will Mother figure out?" said a voice from the door.

Caradin watched a young woman walking into the room. She carried a small bowl, a towel, and a cloth.

"How to get him back into the palace." Quindor turned to Caradin. "That's my sister. The one I told you about." He grinned again.

"What nasty things did you say about me?"

"Nothing nasty," Caradin assured her with a smile. "Just man-to-man talk."

She gave her brother an annoyed glance. "I can just imagine what he said. He's got a dirty mind. By the way, I'm Mirnani. My mother told me to bring you water and a cloth so you can clean up."

"I appreciate that. I want to thank you for saving my life."

"Oh no, don't thank me. That was my older sister Marshia." She approached and removed his bowl of stew to place it on the table beside the bed. "Let me wash your back. It'll cool you down and refresh you." Without waiting for an answer, she began scrubbing his back with the wet cloth. Then she dried him.

Caradin had to admit it felt good and closed his eyes. "It's been a while since a woman washed my back," he murmured.

She laughed softly. "If you had been awake you would know it wasn't that long ago."

"What do you mean?"

"I've done your back twice already, including your front. Lie back so I can wash your chest."

He lay back and looked up at her as she hovered over him. "As long as you know when to stop," he said with a crooked smile.

"I will today." Chuckling merrily, she used the cloth to scrub his chest. When she was done, she gave him back the bowl with stew and took a seat on the chair Quindor had sat on before. "Tell me, where are you from?"

"I've lived in Jandarin for many years, but I was born here in Mountainsong."

"What made you move to Jandarin?"

He grimaced. "King Ordar exiled me."

"Why? What did you do?"

"It was my misfortune to have the same father as he but not the same mother. He never forgave me for that."

She inhaled noisily. "Are you saying you are King Ordar's brother?"

"Half-brother. Remember, a different mother."

"Did my mother tell you that King Ordar is dead? He was murdered. It happened the day after my sister and her husband brought you here."

"She told me. She also told me something unpleasant and unexplainable."

She eyed him curiously. "That a man named Caradin is claiming the throne after announcing he is King Ordar's brother? Everyone talks about that. How many of you are there?"

"There is only one. Me. I am the real Caradin."

"If that is true, then you are a prince."

He chortled. "They used to call me that, but it's been a long time."

"Is there anyone here who can testify to what you claim? Anyone from your youth?"

"If anyone could recognize me, it would be Queen Gwenlin and, of course, my mother."

"Your mother lives in Mountainsong?"

"She did. I don't even know if she's still alive. If she is, then she is quite old. I haven't seen or heard from her since I left." He sighed. "King

Ordar threatened to have me arrested and executed if I ever showed my face again. It was a deterrent to keep me from visiting."

"What's your mother's name?"

"Laeema. She was just a peasant woman, but she was beautiful and caught the interest of King Ordarin. What girl would reject the attention of her King?" He smiled, trying to remember his mother's face. "She didn't and that's how I was born."

"Perhaps we can find your mother? Where did she live?"

"In the northern part of the city. Near the flour mills."

"That part of the city is considered a slum area. It's not safe to go there."

He nodded. "My grandparents were simple and poor people. The only thing my mother had going for her was her beauty. She had nothing else to offer."

"Obviously enough to catch King Ordarin's eye." She smiled. "Are you married?"

"I am, to a princess. She's the daughter of Queen Kharana."

Her eyes widened. "The queen of Jandarin? That makes you a prince."

"My title is General. I prefer that."

"Is your wife here, too?"

He shook his head. "No. I came alone. My wife and I are not close. She pretends she loves me, but I know she's pretending it. She thinks I don't know that she has an affair with the castle sorcerer."

"I'm sorry to hear that."

"Don't be sorry." He gave her a rueful smile. "Ours was an arranged marriage. Queen Kharana has ambitious plans and I play a part in them, only I have my own agenda."

"Which is?"

He laughed. "You really want to know?"

"I do." She seemed genuinely interested.

"I came here to make peace with my brother, but now that he is dead everything changes. Now I want to take my rightful place on the throne. I want to be king of Maridaan."

"Oh…" She put her hand over her mouth.

"Why does that surprise you? Isn't that what the imposter wants?"

"If he is indeed an imposter. You still have to prove that you are the real Prince Caradin. Even then your claim will be challenged."

"Who will challenge me?"

"Didn't you know that King Ordar has two daughters and one son?"

"I didn't know about the son, but that changes nothing. By law, I'm the rightful heir to the throne."

"You'll still have to prove your identity," she said, stubbornly, expressing her doubts.

"I will. Don't worry about that. My first act as the king will be to punish the imposter." He looked toward the doorway when he heard footsteps. It was the older woman.

"Has my daughter washed your back?"

"She has and I feel so much better." He chuckled. "Not only does she have gentle hands, she's also inquisitive and smart."

"That she is." She sighed. "Unfortunately, her keen mind won't do her any good. She'll spend her life working her fingers raw in the palace kitchen, preparing food and scrubbing floors."

"Don't be so sure. I won't forget what you've done for me. I'll make you a solemn promise. When I'm king, she won't have to toil in the kitchen any longer. She'll be wearing fine clothes and eating food prepared by someone else. She'll mingle with the other Ladies of the Court, and so will you."

Quirma gave him a sad smile. "If you become king, you will quickly forget about us. I believe you have good intentions, but once you'll get pulled into the life of intrigue and backstabbing that exists in the palace, you won't have time to worry about people like us. I have no such illusions."

"Why would you say that?"

"My husband was one of King Ordar's personal guards. He died defending his king when the Royal Coach was ambushed by a band of rogues. The King didn't even bother to visit me in person to tell me he was sorry about my loss. He sent me flowers and a basket full of stale bread." She made no effort to hide her bitterness and resentment.

"I'm not Ordar. My father may have been a king, but my mother was not one of the highborn. I will never forget my roots." Caradin spoke gently, meaning every word he said.

"We'll see." Quirma looked at her daughter. "You'd better get going.

The palace guests will be unhappy if they don't get fed and their chamber pots emptied."

"Maybe they should go hungry and empty their own pots," Mirnani said with a mischievous laugh.

"Go if you want to keep your precious job in the palace," her mother chided her.

"You won't have to do that much longer, I promise," Caradin said, "but perhaps you should listen to your mother and go. There is another reason I want you to go. I'd like you to keep an ear open for the gossip and keep me informed about what's happening in the palace. Will you do that for me?"

"I will."

Caradin watched her leave. "I'm feeling a bit tired. Do you mind if I close my eyes and rest for a while?"

———

"I'VE HAD my doubts about Rhodar from the beginning." Carn spoke angrily. "What can you expect from a barbarian other than treachery?"

"I still refuse to believe it," Lord Galoor said in defense of Rhodar.

"How can you still have doubts?" Carn shook his head. "He was seen coming out of the Queen's bedroom after he raped her. She attested to that and I don't question her words. She's my aunt and your cousin. She would not lie about something like that. But the most convincing evidence is the rape of King Ordar's servant after he killed the king. She watched the murder happen. How much more evidence do you need?"

Lord Galoor stroked his chin. "I admit that everything points to his guilt, but at the same time I can't believe he is so stupid as to leave so much evidence behind. Why didn't he kill the servant after raping her? Why did he walk so brazenly out of Lady Gwenlin's bedroom and again out of the King's chambers? It seems he wanted to be seen. Yes, Rhodar is a barbarian, a savage, but that also means he is cunning with strong survival instincts. He would never commit a crime like that and leave so many witnesses behind. Another thing that puzzles me. Why did he use a sword and not his axe to kill King Ordar? By his own admission, he is not proficient with a sword."

"His axe is in storage. He probably found it easier to obtain a sword.

Anyone can stab somebody with a sword. How much skill does that take?" Carn didn't understand why Lord Galoor refused to see the truth. "If you can't accept that Rhodar committed this horrible crime then tell me who do you think did it? Does he have a twin-brother?"

Lord Galoor shrugged. "We would know if there is another one like him around," he said with a little smile. "A man of his stature and mode of dress will find it difficult to hide anywhere."

"Unless…" Something occurred to Carn, but he wasn't keen in voicing his suspicion. It would only serve to seed more doubts about the barbarian's guilt.

"Unless what?" Lord Galoor's keen mind picked up on those things. One had to be careful around him starting a sentence without finishing it.

"It's just a thought." Carn tried to shrug it off but knew Lord Galoor would not give up.

"Let's hear it."

"Is it possible there is magic involved here?" Carn speculated. "Even a minor magician can cloud people's mind by making them believe they see something that isn't there."

"That thought has occurred to me. I'm surprised you would mention it since you're so convinced Rhodar is guilty. As far as we know, there is no real magician in the palace. The only one with magic powers great enough to do it is Saleen. However, she is infatuated with Rhodar and would never frame him for such a crime." Lord Galoor looked thoughtful. "Something has been nagging me. Rhodar said that Gwenlin visited him in his room and she vehemently denied it. I'm inclined to believe her, so why would Rhodar claim such a thing?"

"He's a savage. His mind works different from ours. Perhaps he dreamed it. To think that Lady Gwenlin would copulate with an uncouth barbarian is unthinkable. Besides, he's more than half her age. She would never stoop that low." Carn shook himself when a vision of his aunt having sex with Rhodar popped unbidden into his mind. "That never happened," he declared with a loud voice.

"Rhodar also claims he was with another woman during the time King Ordar was murdered," Lord Galoor mused.

Carn made a snorting sound. "So he says, but he won't give us this mysterious woman's name. Very convenient."

Their conversation was interrupted by the arrival of Rowarin, King Ordar's son. "I am not happy," he announced.

Carn gave the boy an inquiring look. He noticed Lord Galoor's eyebrows moving up for a moment. Either he was annoyed by the boy bursting in like that or surprised.

"Nobody is happy at the moment," Carn said. "Your father's murder is resting heavy on everyone's shoulders. We will avenge him, but before we do we have to make sure we have the right man who did it."

"That's not it," Rowarin said. "I don't like him."

"You mean Rhodar?"

"No, not him. I don't like the man who claims to be my father's brother. He has no right to the crown. I am the rightful King of Maridaan."

"The Grand Council will determine that," Lord Galoor said.

Rowarin looked at Carn. "You have to do something, Carn. You are my favorite cousin and the oldest. I've always looked up to you. The crown is mine."

Before Carn could make another comment, a young woman rushed into the room. It was Kiiri, one of his mother's maids. She looked from Lord Galoor to Carn. "I need to talk to you about something I witnessed. It has been troubling me."

"What is it, girl?"

She fidgeted before she answered. "I know I should have come forward earlier, but I was afraid. Even now, I'm not certain if I should talk about it. I don't want to spread stories, but what I saw is true. It's about the Queen, but not really about the Queen."

"You make no sense, Kiiri," Carn said, getting impatient.

"Two nights before King Ordar's murder I saw Queen Gwenlin visit Rhodar in his room."

"You saw what?" Lord Galoor spoke harshly. "Why were you there? Where you watching Rhodar?"

She squirmed and hung her head for a moment. "I wanted to spend the night with him. When I saw the Queen going through that door, I was jealous and waited outside, hoping she'd come out again, but she was in his room for a long time."

"Are you sure it was Queen Gwenlin?"

"I saw her enter. I also saw her come out again. When she went in the wrong direction, I followed her, wondering where she was going next. She stopped in front of Lord Garrin's door, but before she entered, she changed."

"Changed?" Lord Galoor lifted an eyebrow. "What did she change?"

"Her body. Suddenly she wasn't the Queen anymore but a woman I recognized from the dinner party at Castle Falconclaw. A friend and I watched her copulating with one of the guests, Lord Colassa. As we watched, she turned into a beast. At first, I thought it was Lady Lironi, but when she changed back and turned her head to look at me it was someone else. She told us her name was Lady Shanta. It was the same woman that was with Rhodar pretending to be Queen Gwenlin."

"That's quite some story," Carn said. "Did you have something to drink that night?"

"Just a little wine, but not much, my Lord. Lady Shanta or whoever she was claimed we had been imagining things. She suggested we forget what we thought we saw."

"You admit you have been drinking." Lord Galoor gave her a sharp look.

"Not two nights ago. I stand by what I saw," she said with a defiant expression.

"You said there was a friend with you who could confirm your story," Carn said. "Who was this friend."

Kiiri blushed. "Just a boy."

"What's his name?"

"His name was Applar. He's the son of Lord Randahr."

"I know of him. Can't say I'm surprised. You do get around." Lord Galoor's face clearly showed his disapproval. He looked at Carn. "I remember this Colassa. He's a fat merchant from Jandarin. Loves his wine. I also remember that woman Lironi and how she tried to seduce Colassa. It was obvious to anyone who saw her with him. If Kiiri's story is correct we may be dealing with a shapeshifter here. That would explain some things. Lady Gwenlin denied visiting Rhodar in his room and I believe her."

"Lironi," Carn mused. "She was with Kaloss when I delivered the news of his wife's murder." He glanced at Lord Galoor. "I neglected to mention that to you. You had enough grief already hearing about your sister's murder. Finding out about your brother-in-law's involvement with another woman would have served no purpose."

"Are you certain he was involved with her?"

Carn shrugged. "I have no proof, of course, but it almost seemed obvious to me. They seemed to celebrate something with a bottle of wine."

"How did that woman get invited to the King's summer festival? Besides, I don't remember seeing her anywhere in the palace or on the grounds."

"We wouldn't have if she's a shapeshifter. She may have come wearing the persona Lady Shanta." Carn bent forward. "My question is who brought her and why?"

"She went into the room of a Lord Garrin. He may be the one who brought her." Lord Galoor rose. "I suggest we go to the King's court now and bring this new evidence to the attention of the Council. We don't want an innocent man punished for a crime he didn't commit."

Carn agreed. "You accompany us to the court," he told Kiiri. "We may need your testimony."

She wasn't happy about that, but he gave her no choice.

Caradin sat on the King's throne. The members of the King's Council were seated on either side of the isle that led to the throne.

Caradin looked up when he saw Carn and Lord Galoor coming into the council chambers. "Lord Carn, Lord Galoor, you are not members of the Council and therefore have no business in these chambers." His eyes glinted momentarily, showing his annoyance.

"Forgive our intrusion," Carn said, "but new evidence has come to light that may prove the barbarian's innocence. We thought it was important."

Caradin stared at him coldly. "His guilt has been established without a doubt. There are witnesses who saw him coming out of the Queen's chambers after he brutally raped her. The servant who was present when he cold bloodedly shoved his sword into King Ordar's belly, delivering the fatal blow, and then raping her as well has identified him as the man who committed that horrible deed." He took a short pause while his eyes seemed to stare into emptiness. "The murder of my brother will be avenged," he said with a trembling voice. "The barbarian will be executed tomorrow. That is my final decision and it isn't open for discussion any longer. Now I ask you to leave the Council Chambers"

Carn was ready to retort with an angry comment when Lord Galoor spoke. "I might remind you that your position as the King of Maridaan has not yet been established. There is a certain protocol that has to be followed. For one thing, the King's Council has to proclaim you as the new King and then you need to take the oath. Until that has been done, you have no powers and no right to make any decisions. Then, there is the question of who really is the heir to the throne. Prince Rowarin, the son of King Ordar and Queen Gwenlin, has put in a legitimate claim and it needs to be taken into consideration by the Council."

"You are wrong, Lord Galoor. I am the son of King Ordarin and therefore I have the first right to the throne of Maridaan." Caradin's chuckle was not friendly. "Aside from that, I have taken control of the Council and I will not be challenged. Most importantly, Queen Gwenlin has accepted me as the King. Now leave before I have you forcefully removed." He made a movement with one hand.

When Carn turned his head, he saw a number of armed soldiers coming into the room, naked swords in their hands. Lord Galoor reached out to touch his arm. "Let it be," he said with a low voice.

With an angry glance at Caradin, he turned around and followed Lord Galoor out of the room. "This isn't over," he muttered under his breath.

Chapter Twenty-Two

BLINKING against the sudden light falling through the opening door, Rhodar rose from his sitting position when he saw the armed guards walking into his cell. From their grim expressions, he knew they weren't coming for a friendly visit.

Two guards stood with drawn swords while one of them bound his arms behind his back. Then the same guard removed the chain that kept him bound to the wall from his manacles.

"Move," he told Rhodar.

Shuffling as fast as his manacled feet would allow between the guards, he steeled himself to what he feared was going to happen, yet, somehow, he refused to believe that his quest would end here in Maridaan.

The courtyard was already packed with spectators when he appeared in the open, flanked by his guards. Angry shouts rose from the crowd as the guards marched him across the cobblestones toward a black-painted dais in the middle of the courtyard. They tied him with strong ropes against a pole.

He looked at the archers who stood in a row not far from him, waiting for the command to pierce his body with their arrows. Then he lifted his head to stare into the cloudless sky.

"Great Serpent," he said in a loud voice, "if it is your will that I join my ancestors then give me a swift and painless death, but if it is your will that I should live, then rescue me."

Closing his eyes, he tried to recall his mother's face, using her gentle nature to give him calm and acceptance. When he heard surprised cries and screams, he opened his eyes and watched as dark, thick fog began to form over the watching spectators, and within moments he couldn't see them anymore. The fog was all around him. Then he noticed that the ropes that bound him to the pole had fallen off and his shackles were open.

Rubbing his wrists, he stepped away from the pole and was ready to jump from the dais, when a dark shadow came out of the fog. He recognized Nightwalker, his horse. On its back sat a woman. She slid off the horse and came toward him. In her hands, she carried a battle-axe.

"Saleen," he growled. "Is this your doing?"

She smiled grimly and handed him his axe. "Here, I thought you might need this."

He took the enchanted axe from her hands and hefted it easily. "How can you carry this weapon?" he wondered. "Nobody but me can lift it."

She chuckled. "Did you forget I'm a witch? That spell means nothing to me. I even strengthened it to make it lighter for you to swing." She came up to him and pulled his head down to kiss him on the mouth. "Get on your horse and ride away."

He looked at the swirling, dark clouds around them. "How can I find my way through this fog? Even if I managed to get away from here, where would I go? The King's soldiers would hunt me down. I'm a stranger in your country and everyone will know who I am. There is nowhere for me to hide. I must stay and prove my innocence."

She looked at him with angry eyes. "Somehow I expected that from you. You're a thickheaded barbarian and determined to get yourself killed. I will surround you with a spell that will protect you from the arrows, but the spell will last only for a short time. If you can't establish your innocence within that time, I cannot help you. Perhaps, you should use your enchanted battle-axe to kill as many soldiers as you can and make them believe you're a god who cannot be killed. You might get away then."

He smiled at her. "I'm not a cold-blooded killer. These soldiers are not my enemies."

"So be it then," she said. "I will help you to convince them that you are either a god or a powerful sorcerer. Get onto your horse." The outlines of her body began to shimmer and change and then he looked at a ferocious Treewolf.

The animal stared at him with green, blazing eyes. He nodded and jumped onto Nightwalker's broad back.

The fog began to lift as sudden and swift as it had appeared, except for a few narrow bands swirling around him. He sat immobile on his horse with his battle-axe in one hand and a snarling beast beside him. He knew the sight had to be intimidating and daunting to the watching crowd, especially after he had been shackled and bound to a pole, helpless and ready to be pierced by the arrows of the King's archers. Now he sat on a horse that had not been there a few moments ago, free of his bonds and as fierce-looking as an angry god of war. There would be no doubt in anyone's mind that magic had been involved.

The tendrils of fog spinning above his head added to the mystique. He lifted the axe over his head and spoke in a loud voice. "I am Rhodar. You have condemned me to die for a crime I did not commit. As you just witnessed, I cannot be bound or kept prisoner. I could have slain your soldiers and escaped had I chosen to do so, but I will stay to prove my innocence."

As he spoke, a rain of arrows arched toward him, but they clattered harmlessly to the ground before they reached him.

Rhodar chuckled grimly and rode slowly toward the archers. "Your arrows cannot touch me and you are at the mercy of my battle-axe, but I have no quarrel with you and bear you no ill will. Lay down your bows and accept surrender." He lifted his axe menacingly. "I will split anyone's skull should I be forced to do so."

His gaze wandered across the crowd, looking for the new King. He found him standing on one of the balconies. Forcing his horse through the parting crowd, he rode toward Caradin. Saleen in the disguise of a Tree-wolf followed him closely. Rhodar was aware that it was her presence that made the people fear for their safety more than his appearance. He saw it clearly in their eyes.

The King watched him with an amused expression on his face. There was something about him that didn't seem right to Rhodar, but he didn't know what it could be.

Caradin waited until Rhodar stopped his horse in front him before he spoke. "It appears I made a mistake when I condemned you to death. Obviously, I also underestimated you and the powers you command. You play the role of a barbarian but it seems that is a charade. What just happened was clearly magic. Tell me, who are you? Are you a sorcerer?" His eyes rested on the Treewolf beside Rhodar. "Your beast is not an animal but a Wer. Who is she?"

Rhodar laughed. "You are correct with your assumption in part. I am not a sorcerer but I am protected by magic. The Great Serpent God of my people is my protector and more powerful than any sorcerer. I also command the beast beside me. Even as high up as you are, you are not safe. One word spoken by me and it would rip out your throat. Your guards would not be able to stop it. They are helpless against the magic that surrounds me. I will meet you in the courtroom and we will discuss what happens next." With that he rode to the entrance that led into the castle. Jumping from his horse, he strode through the wide doors, his battle-axe casually in his hand.

Before he entered the castle, he was aware that Saleen bounded away. It didn't matter. He was confident that the spell she had cast would protect him.

Walking down the long corridor, he found the courtroom and entered. It was empty, but he knew soon it would fill with people. He walked over to the chair reserved for the criminals on trial and sat in it, laying his axe across his knees.

It wasn't long before people began to pile into the room. The seats were soon filled and many spectators stood against the walls, eager to follow the proceedings. The members of the King's Council took their places and then Caradin walked in, accompanied by Queen Gwenlin and her two daughters. Rhodar noticed the absence of Prince Rowarin. He also noticed the presence of Lord Galoor and Lord Carn in the front row that was reserved for noblemen. He also saw the maid Kiiri with them. She stood with her eyes downcast, looking frightened and worried.

Lord Galoor gave him an acknowledging nod when Rhodar looked at him. Even Lord Carn's expression was not filled with hatred, giving him hope both men might be on his side.

The courtroom was silent when Caradin rose. He looked at Rhodar. "You claim to be innocent of King Ordar's murder, but the evidence is still against you. Can you enlighten us why we should believe you to be innocent?"

"I cannot except for what I've already claimed. I was with another woman the morning King Ordar was murdered."

"I know all about that," Caradin sneered. "The woman without a name. Unless you can suddenly remember it."

"She never told me her name. I didn't know it then, but I know it now." As he said those words, he suddenly realized he didn't feel compelled anymore not to talk about her or the two maids with her; one of them had been a witch. He remembered it clearly now. Saleen's spell must have neutralized the spell she put on him.

"Strange. How can you suddenly know her name? When did she reveal her name to you?"

"She didn't, but she is here in this room."

"Then tell us her name," Caradin said.

"I promised to keep it our secret," Rhodar said, throwing a quick glance at Arleen. "I may be a barbarian, but I am a man of my word."

"How noble of you." Caradin shook his head in apparent disbelief. "You would rather die than disclose the name of a woman who could confirm what you claim?"

"I will not stain her reputation," Rhodar said, stubbornly. "It is up to her to come forward."

"I do not believe you, Rhodar," Caradin said. "I think you are lying about that nameless woman, just as you lied about the Queen visiting you in your room."

"That is not a lie." Rhodar spoke sharply, trying to suppress his anger and annoyance at Caradin's sneering attitude.

"Are you saying Queen Gwenlin lied when she denied what you claim happened?"

Rhodar looked at the Queen. "I will not call the Queen a liar, neither will I change what I said. Perhaps she was under some kind of spell and doesn't remember."

"May I address the King's Council?"

Rhodar turned when he heard Lord Galoor's voice, wondering what he had to say.

Caradin seemed annoyed at the interruption, but he had no choice but to answer. "Whatever you have to say, Lord Galoor, make it quick. I'm getting tired of this charade. We've been through all of this before, but go ahead and speak."

"When a man's life is at stake, we don't want to rush it, Lord Caradin. As I've said already at the last meeting of the Council, we have discovered new information, disturbing information. We have come to the conclusion that neither Rhodar nor Queen Gwenlin are lying. Rhodar believes the Queen shared his bed, because the woman who came to his room that night, appeared to be Queen Gwenlin." He lifted a hand to silence the sudden loud voices erupting among the spectators. "I say appeared, because she looked like her. However, it wasn't the Queen who was in his room but an imposter."

"Preposterous," fumed Caradin. "Where did you get such an absurd idea?"

"From a reliable source." Lord Galoor turned to Kiiri. "Tell the Court what you witnessed that night."

Kiiri rose from her chair. She appeared scared and Rhodar noticed her shaking hands. When she spoke, her voice trembled. "I saw a woman appearing to be the Queen going into Rhodar's room. I also saw her coming out of the room. I followed her to Lord Garrin's room. Before she went into his room, her body changed. She didn't look like the Queen anymore but like a woman I saw at Lady Gardina's dinner party." Her voice faltered. She looked at Lord Galoor.

"Go on, tell us what else you saw," Lord Galoor encouraged her.

"I watched her change into a beast while she coupled with one of the guests."

A sound like a sudden wind gust went through the room as the spectators reacted, holding their breath and expelling it again.

"You are certain of what you saw?"

Kiiri nodded. "Quite certain."

Lord Galoor looked around the room. "You all heard her testimony. I'd say what Kiiri saw was a shapeshifter."

"And I say she has a fertile imagination," Caradin said with a snort "She's an uneducated servant. Who knows what she imagined she saw that night. You have no proof."

"Oh, I believe I do." Lord Galoor turned his attention back to Kiiri. "Is that woman here in the courtroom?"

"Yes."

"Can you point her out to us?"

Kiiri turned and pointed at a woman in the second row. "That's her. That's the woman I saw."

Rhodar recognized her as the woman he had seen with Lord Garrin from the tiny Kingdom of Spanaria. He even remembered her name.

Lady Shanta.

His hand went up to his face in an involuntary gesture, dimly remembering how she had touched him at that brief meeting and how her touch had sent a faint shiver through his body.

If what Kiiri claimed she saw was true, this was the woman who had copulated with him, pretending to be Queen Gwenlin. It seems, it had all been a ruse to frame him for a murder. Yet that still left the question— who was the murderer?

He wondered about the whereabouts of her companion Lord Garrin. He did not see him in the courtroom.

"She's lying," Lady Shanta said in a calm voice. "I am no more a shapeshifter than any of you."

"It seems to me it's the word of a highborn woman against that of a lowborn servant girl." Caradin chuckled merrily. "I'm inclined to believe Lady Shanta."

Rhodar turned in surprise when he heard the voice of someone who had been silent until now. Looking at the young woman who he now knew was the King's oldest daughter; he hoped she would tell everyone that he had been with her when her father was murdered. However, she didn't, but from what she did say, he realized she was trying to help him without revealing her involvement with him.

"There is a way we can establish if Lady Shanta is a shapeshifter or not. One of my personal maids does have minor powers. She will be able to detect if Lady Shanta is what she says."

The girl who had been hiding in the shadows behind Arleen stepped into the light. She hesitated, but then she came around and walked toward Lady Shanta. "I need to touch her," she said.

"I won't be touched by an unwashed servant girl," Lady Shanta said with an indignant voice.

"I may be a servant girl, but I'm not unwashed," the girl protested, her voice equally indignant.

"Stand up and let Lorni touch you," Arleen said. "If you're not what you've been accused of, you have nothing to fear."

Lady Shanta looked at Caradin for help. "You are the King. Only you can tell anyone what to do."

"He is not the King!" Lord Galoor thundered. "Princess Arleen is King Ordar's daughter. She has given you an order."

Caradin shrugged. "Let her touch you. I trust there will be no problem."

With obvious reluctance, Lady Shanta stood up and bent forward. Rhodar watched as Lorni reached toward Lady Shanta to touch her on the shoulder. He didn't miss the sudden stiffness in Lorni's posture. She pulled back her hand as if she had been burned. Her face was almost ashen when she looked at Arleen. Then she declared with a shaky voice, "She's not just a shapeshifter. She's also a Wer and this is not her natural form."

A moaning sound went through the spectators again and Caradin lifted a hand to silence everyone. "It appears I was wrong." He looked at the four guards standing beside the throne. "Seize her and throw her into the deepest dungeon!"

Lady Shanta pointed an accusing finger at Caradin. "You promised to protect me."

Caradin's eyes were cold when he stared at her. "I don't know what you're talking about. You deceived me and everyone in this castle, including Queen Gwenlin."

"I never liked that woman from the moment I saw her," Queen Gwenlin said. "I knew there was something about her. Perhaps she also killed the King."

"No, she didn't, your Majesty," Lorni said. "She cannot change into a man."

The Queen's eyes searched out Rhodar. "Your innocence has still not been established, Barbarian."

"But there is doubt," said Lord Galoor. "Do you notice that Rhodar possesses a battle-axe? Yet, King Ordar was killed with a sword."

"But I remember the Barbarian brutally raping me. Perhaps that was also an imposter, but who? Another shapeshifter?"

"It was Kastabaan," Lady Shanta cried out shrilly, struggling in the grip of the two guards as they began to drag her away. "He forced me to impersonate the Queen. He killed the King."

"Stop!" Lord Galoor called with a commanding voice. "Let her speak."

Lady Shanta drew herself erect and faced the crowd. "The only crime I'm guilty of is having sex with the Barbarian as Queen Gwenlin. There was no harm in that." She looked at Rhodar and smiled. "I believe I gave him a good time, because I enjoyed our coupling, but I had nothing to do with the murder of King Ordar. That was all Kastabaan's doing." Her eyes searched out Queen Gwenlin. "He also suggested I meet Lord Caradin down by the pond pretending to be you, my Queen. He told me to kill Lord Caradin."

"Obviously, you didn't succeed, since Lord Caradin is sitting here in King Ordar's throne claiming to be King of Maridaan." Lord Galoor said.

"That is not Lord Caradin," Lady Shanta said. "He's an imposter."

"Enough of this nonsense," Caradin roared. "I remember the pond she's referring to. I'm alive because I was never there. That woman is insane, inventing outrageous stories to save her life. I have in mind to have her executed immediately before she causes irreparable damage to my or the Queen's reputation. Take her away—now."

"Not so fast." Lord Galoor stopped the guards. "I'm intrigued by this woman's claim, but there is another matter I'd like to clear up. Lorni claimed that the woman you are showing us is not your true self. Who are you?"

She shrugged. "I guess it doesn't matter anymore." The outline of her body began to shimmer and glow with a gentle fire. She began to change and within moments a different woman stood looking defiantly at Lord Galoor.

Rhodar recognized her as the woman he had seen in the shipbuilder's office.

"I am Lironi," she said with a little smile. "Remember me, Lord Galoor?"

"You are the woman who came uninvited to Lady Gardina's dinner party, claiming Lord Carn invited you to the castle. How can I forget you?"

"Lord Carn invited me," she said. She turned her attention to Lord Carn. "Or did I misunderstand you?"

"You didn't misunderstand, and you did come," Lord Carn acknowledged her, "but it seems you took advantage of one of our guests, a merchant by the name of Colassa. Kiiri watched and witnessed as you changed into a beast, except, when you realized you were observed you morphed into your Lady Shanta persona to keep from being discovered. Do I have that right?"

"I'm afraid I can't say you're not right. That's what happened, but in my defense, no harm was done to anyone. I believe I gave Colassa what he craved." She smiled disarmingly.

"I will not listen to this any longer," Caradin fairly shouted. "Nobody is interested in her affairs. I want her gone."

"Why are you in such a hurry? What about her claim that you are not the real Caradin but an imposter?" Lord Carn gave Caradin a sharp look.

"You surely don't believe that nonsense she's sprouting, Lord Carn. Who would I be?" He glanced at the Queen. "Queen Gwenlin will testify that I am Caradin. She and I were close at one time and how would an imposter know about any of that?"

Lord Carn shrugged. "Anything is possible when magic is involved." He turned to Lorni, who still stood near Lironi. "Can you detect any magic around Lord Caradin?"

Lorni took a few cautious steps toward Caradin, looking at him with wide eyes. She shook her head. "I detect nothing."

"I told you so," Caradin said with a triumphant chuckle. "Are you satisfied now, Lord Carn?"

A sudden murmur went through the crowd. Many turned their heads to look at the entrance to the room. Rhodar looked and watched a man walking slowly down the walkway. The man looked tired. He wore peasant clothes, but there was no mistaking the resemblance to Caradin. He could have been his twin.

When he saw all eyes on him, he stopped walking. There was a sudden silence in the room as everyone waited for him to speak.

"I am Caradin," he said into the silence. He pointed at the man on the throne. "That man is a fraud."

"This farce has gone far enough," Caradin shouted, rising from his sitting position. "I don't know where you come from and who you are, but you are not me." He addressed his two remaining guards. "Remove this impersonator from my courtroom immediately and execute him. I won't stand any longer for these feeble attempts to undermine my authority as King and I am getting tired of listening to these lies."

"You are not the King; neither is your name Caradin," the newcomer said. "I've been listening for a while. That woman shapeshifter came here as the companion of a Lord Garrin. I also entered the palace with Lord Garrin. I find it curious that he isn't here. What happened to him?"

"How should I know? Besides, it was I who accompanied Lord Garrin, not you." He made a contemptuous sound. "You claim to be me. How is it that you are dressed in peasant clothing? You should be wearing the uniform of a general, because that's what I am. A general in the Jandarin army."

"I would have worn it had it not been stolen from my room," the newcomer said loudly. "Stolen by you."

Caradin laughed, almost as if he were amused. "You can accuse me as much as you want. It doesn't change the fact that you are nothing but a common criminal who happens to look like me." He banged his fist against the armrest of the throne. "Enough of this! Get him out of here—now."

"I don't believe that is going to happen," the newcomer said. He drew a sword from the sheath hanging from his belt. "I will cut down your guards. I am an excellent swordsman. They won't stand a chance against me." He looked at Lironi. "Now that I know you're a shapeshifter and a Wer I know it was you who came to me down by the pond. You almost sucked all the blood from my body. I survived your attempt to kill me because you were interrupted by the people who rescued me. I heard you mention the name Kastabaan. Did you mean the sorcerer? If you did, then everything makes sense. Where is he?"

She pointed at the man who claimed to be the King. "That's him. That's Kastabaan." Her eyes were suddenly large and she looked frightened. "He has great powers and will kill us all."

"Not if I can help it," said a voice from behind the newcomer.

Rhodar moaned as he recognized Saleen. She had proven to him that she was a strong witch, but she'd never be able to go against a powerful sorcerer. If this man was really Kastabaan, he'd crush her without giving it another thought.

Saleen made a movement with her hand. A small ball of white fire left her hand and flew across the room toward the man in front of the throne. Before it reached him, he lifted his hand. The ball of fire bounced off his hand and disappeared with a bright flash.

"I know who you are," he said. "You are Saleen and I know about your powers. Don't waste your efforts and energy fighting me. You cannot win. I might as well admit to it now; I am Kastabaan and I possess powers other sorcerers can only imagine. I've been trying to capture you for a long time now, but you've always managed to elude me. Join me in my castle and become my bride. You and I will conquer the world together. Nobody will be able to stand against us."

Saleen's laugh mocked him. "I don't trust you, Kastabaan. You are evil, and I am not like you. The last thing I would ever want is to become your bride. You feel secure and trust in your abilities, but you underestimate me because I'm still young. I also command great powers, possibly greater than yours. I will give you two choices. If you're smart, you will leave without fighting me. I may be untested, but I have confidence in my capability to beat you. Should you want to fight me, I promise I will show no mercy. I will kill you."

"For a little girl, you speak big words. I would prefer not to kill you. It would be a shame to waste your abilities. You have an unusual gift and that should be nurtured. Forget this foolishness about fighting me and join me at my castle."

"Never, Kastabaan. That will never happen."

"Perhaps if I change into a different person? Would you find me more desirable?" His body began to glow for a moment and then Rhodar looked at the image of Lord Garrin.

"Don't waste your efforts. I know that is not your real body, but it won't matter, anyway. Now that you revealed yourself to everyone here, I suggest you leave the palace while you still can." Saleen spoke with a soft voice, but there was no mistaking the underlying threat.

The chill in her voice sent a cold shiver down Rhodar's back. This was not the gentle girl he knew, but a mature woman confident in her powers.

Kastabaan laughed coldly. "I gave you a chance, little girl. Now you will feel my wrath." With that, he performed an intricate pattern with his hands. A bright bundle of light left his hands and shot toward Saleen, but she lifted both hands and the light died before it reached her.

She responded to his attack with a lightning bolt of her own. A sound like a clap of thunder echoed through the courtroom. The bright bolt of raw energy hit the floor in front of Kastabaan. It had come close. The acrid odor of charcoaled wood hung heavy in the air.

The battle lasted for a long time. Neither of the opponents was willing to yield. The spectators sat petrified and scared as the courtroom filled with blinding light and as rolling thunder deafened their ears.

There came a sudden break, when one of Saleen's bolts seemed to have hit Kastabaan. He swayed and hesitated just for a moment when Saleen took advantage. Another of her bolts got through his defenses and hit the sorcerer in the chest. He sank to his knees, apparently helpless, but he managed to fend off another ball of light.

Rising with great effort, he let out an eerie call that seemed to reverberate from the walls. Rhodar's keen hearing picked up the sound of hoofs that came closer rapidly and then a black horse with glowing eyes galloped into the room. It stopped in front of Kastabaan.

He swung himself onto the animal's back and headed for the exit. Tongues of fire escaped from the horse's nostrils as it snorted loudly. It reared up on its hind legs and roared like a beast of the swamps as Kastabaan pulled on its reigns. He turned his head to look back at Saleen. The face Rhodar saw was not the face of a man but that of a demon-creature.

The sunken eyes in the skull-like head glowed red as Kastabaan shouted in a hollow voice. "You think you beat me, little girl. Believe what you will, but be on guard from now on, be on guard." Digging his heels into the horse's flanks, he galloped out of the room.

It seemed nobody noticed the beast bounding after him. When Rhodar searched for Lironi, she was gone. The only thing he saw lying on the floor was a shredded red dress. Shrugging, he turned his attention back to Saleen.

Saleen stood silent, then she staggered and collapsed onto the floor.

Rhodar reached her with a few long strides. He picked her up and cradled her in his arms. She opened her eyes and gave him a weak smile. "Rhodar," she whispered. "Take me out of here."

Epilogue

THE SKY DIDN'T SEEM as dark as it had been, but it was still raining and the wind blew cold air into the room. Rhodar pulled the heavy curtain across the window to keep out the wind. Then he walked back to the bed.

Looking down at Saleen, he studied her features and took pleasure in her exceptional beauty. She looked so peaceful and innocent in her sleep, like a little girl. It was difficult to imagine that she had defeated the most feared and most powerful sorcerer known.

Her eyes fluttered open and, yawning, she sat up. The cover slipped down to expose her naked breasts and it was clear she wasn't a little girl but a fully-grown woman. She smiled up at him. "How long have you been standing there gawking at me?"

He chuckled. "Long enough. I felt a draft and pulled the curtain. The weather is nasty out there."

She lay back and lifted her arms. "Then come back to bed and make love to me." She giggled. "I can see you're ready."

"A man sometimes wakes up like that." He grinned. "But you're right. No need to waste it."

He joined her under the covers and pulled her close. "You're warm," he murmured into her hair.

She snuggled against him. "I don't want to get up—ever. I feel safe in your arms and under these covers." She kissed him gently. "I love you and

I'm so happy you finally gave in. This is what I've wanted all along—to lie in your arms, to feel your body on mine, and to give myself to you." Moving on top of him, she moaned deeply. "Like this…yes…that's it…"

They stayed silent for a long time, only their bodies talked. He held her tight when his final moment came. She clung to him, whimpering softly, like a wounded fawn, and he felt her shudder in his embrace. "You make me feel like I've never felt before in my life. I didn't know being with a man was so pleasurable." She sighed and slid off him.

He turned to look at her. Her face was flushed and her hair disheveled, but it did nothing to blemish her beauty. "You are so beautiful," he said gently. "I'm a lucky man."

Her hand touched his face. "No, I'm the lucky one. Even though you are a rough barbarian, you treat a woman with respect and tenderness. Not many men do. You've made me so happy. I only wish you would not leave me."

Her eyes were moist and he felt guilty for what he must do. "I wish the same thing, but I cannot abandon my quest. It is important I find the sorcerer Arguss so he can renew the fading spell he put on the battle-axe my father gave me. Then I must return to my homeland to assume the role as Chief of the Riverstone tribe. It is not something I desire, but the old traditions demand it of me. I cannot change that. It is the path the gods have chosen for me."

"How do you know that?" she asked in a tearful voice. "Is it not possible you could be wrong? Perhaps the gods have chosen you to stay with me—to protect me from harm and to love me. What about what the gods have planned for me? Am I not important?"

"You are more important than you can imagine. You have been given great powers and great responsibilities. That cannot be denied."

"I never wanted such powers. I would prefer to be just a normal girl. Perhaps then you would take me with you. I would be a good mate to you and I would make you happy until we are both old and ready to meet the gods."

He smiled and stroked her hair. "It is a dream I also share, little one, but only a dream. It cannot be. Without you, the sky over Maridaan would be dark. You are the only one who can defend Maridaan against the evil that is Kastabaan. That is your destiny."

She nodded as tears rolled down her cheeks. "Deep down I cannot deny what you say is the truth. I owe Lord Carn and Lady Gardina my life and I cannot abandon them, but I still wish things were different. Perhaps someday you will come looking for me and I'll be here, waiting for you." She kissed him, her tears making his face wet.

He held her tight, wishing it could always be so.

THE END

Glossary of Characters

Rhodar – of the Serpent Clan, Barbarian from the Western Plains.

Arguss – Sorcerer (good).

Kastabaan – Evil sorcerer. A Shapeshifter. Alternate ego: Lord Garrin from the Kingdom of Spanaria.

Korallas - Kastabaan's apprentice. Has a tame hawk. Alternate ego: Captain Karras from the tiny Kingdom of Rolandia. Dark hair. Black, mesmerizing eyes.

Saleen – Girl with special powers as long as she is a virgin (according to folklore). A were. She can change into a Treewolf. She has green eyes.

Larso – (A Quinx) Saleen's father.

Salina + (a witch) Saleen's mother.

Kalo – a little boy. Son of Lady Arneena and Kaloss (A merchant – ship builder).

Lord Galoor – Kalo's uncle. Brother to Lady Arneena. Son of Lord Galas. Cousin of Lady Gwenlin. Known as Nandarin in his younger days.

Lord Galas – Father of Galoor and Lady Arneena. Husband of Mirlini. Grandfather of Kalo. Brother of Lady Gwenny.

Mirlini – former slave. Wife of Lord Galas. Mother of Galoor and Arneena. Grandmother of Kalo.

Lady Ronewa – Lord Carn's half-sister. Daughter of Lady Gardina and Lord Raxon. Violet eyes.

Lord Carn – Son of Lady Gardina and Lord Caran.

Lady Gardina – Ronewa and Carn's Mother. Sister to King Ordar. Wife of Lord Caran and wife of second husband Lord Raxon.

Lord Caran + Father to Lord Carn. First husband of Lady Gardina.

Lord Raxon + Father to Lady Ronewa. Second husband of Lady Gardina.

King Ordar – Brother to Lady Gardina. Uncle to Carn and Ronewa. Father of Arleen, Ireleen, and Rowarin.

Lady Gwenlin – wife of King Ordar. Aunt to Carn and Ronewa through marriage. Mother of Arleen, Ireleen, and Rowarin. Cousin of Lord Galoor and Lady Arneena.

Princess Arleen – oldest daughter of King Ordar and Lady Gwenlin.

Princess Ireleen – daughter of King Ordar and Lady Gwenlin.

Prince Rowarin – son of King Ordar and Lady Gwenlin.

Lady Galeena – Mother of King Ordar and Lady Gardina. Grandmother of Arleen, Ireleen, Rowarin, Lord Carn.

King Ordarin + Father of King Ordar and Lady Gardina. Grandfather of Lord Carn, and Lady Ronewa and Arleen, Ireleen, Rowarin.

Lady Arneena + − Mother of Kalo. Daughter of Lord Galas and Mirlini (a former slave).

Brother of Lord Galoor and cousin of Lady Gwenlin. Also of Tasia and Jadar (King Odar's illegitimate children with Celani (a common woman).

Kaloss − (A ship builder) Father of Kalo. Husband of Lady Arneena.

Arna − Kalo's sister. Daughter of Lady Arneena and Kaloss. She is missing.

Lord Galasan + Father of Lord Galas and Lady Gwenny. Husband to Lady Mirni, Great-grandfather of Kalo. Grandfather of Gwenlin, Galoor, Arneena.

Lady Mirni + Wife of Galasan. Mother of Galas and Gwenny.

Lord Rastar − Husband of Lady Gwenny. Father of Lady Gwenlin. Grandfather of Arleen, Ireleen, and Rowarin.

Lady Gwenny − Wife of Lord Rastar. Daughter of Galasan and Mirni. Sister of Lord Galas. Mother of Lady Gwenlin, Grandmother of Arleen, Ireleen, Rowarin.

Celani − A common woman (Lover of King Ordar) Mother of twins Tasia and Jadar.

Tasia − (Twin of Jador) Daughter of Celani and bastard daughter of King Ordar.

Jador − (Twin of Tasia) Son of Celani and bastard son of King Ordar. Jador and Tasia are half-brother and half-sister of Arleen, Ireleen, and Rowarin.

Laeema – King Ordarin's mistress. Mother of Ordarin's bastard son Caradin.

Caradin – King Ordarin's bastard son. He lives in exile in the neighbouring country, Jandarin. He is a General in the Jandarin Army. He is King Ordar's half-brother. Husband to Princess Ilita.

Queen Kharana – Queen of Jandarin.

Princess Ilita – Daughter of Queen Kharana. Wife of Caradin. Lover of Arawan.

Arawan – A minor sorcerer in Castle Dragonwings in Jandarin. Lover of Princess Ilita.

Cordaras – Former Knight in the court of King Ordar, now a winged beast. Desired the King's oldest daughter Arleen.

Mordas + a Fur trader. Bludgeoned to death by hunters he (apparently) cheated. His death was planned by his wife Lironi.

Lironi – widow of Mordas. Lover of Kaloss. Green eyes. She is a Shapeshifter. Can change into a Beast. She can take on any form she wants. (Lady Shanta is one of her alternate identities). Blond long hair as Lironi and Lady Shanta.

Colassa – a rich merchant from Jandarin. Short and rotund. Red face. Loves wine.

Palani – a maid at the King's Palace.

Applar – Son of Lord Randahr. He has sex with Kiiri. They witness Lironi (as Lady Shanta) having sex with Colassa. She convinces them she is Lady Shanta.

Lord Randahr – a guest at Lady Gardina's dinner party

King Sandaran – King of Grahna.

Sordan - Son of the King of Grahna (a Prince) Supposed to marry Princess Arleen.

Aarin – a stable boy in castle Falconclaw.

Kiiri – maid in Falconclaw, Lady Gardina's maid. Has sex with Rhodar and also with Applar.

Latalia – Kiiri's mother. She is the seamstress for Lady Gardina.

Jaran – Kiiri's father. One of the cooks.

Rhor – Rhodar's father. He is Chief of Rhodar's tribe. High Chief of the Serpent Clan.

Rhardon – Rhodar's oldest brother of two.

Regani – Woman in tavern. Rhodar has sex with her.

Rassan – Chief of the Riverstone tribe. Rhor's second cousin. He is old and ailing.

Rhodar has been chosen to replace him.

Arina – older woman at the Castle Falconclaw. Chosen to look after Kalo temporarily.

Arklahahn – a minor demon.

Armina – old woman at breakfast in Falconclaw. Wife of Aargon.

Aargon – old man at breakfast in Falconclaw. Husband of Armina.

Shanta (Lady) – Alter ego of Lironi

Givanna + Queen of Rolandia.

Aran (King) – Son of Givanna

Rakall – young man who has sex with Lironi.

Mardaas – A Larkis. A seer. Claims he descended from the gods. Has many followers. They are violent. Mardaas teaches when they die in battle they will join the god at their table and become like gods themselves.

Megarin – old woman. Former midwife. Helped deliver Lord Carn.

Janissa – young woman in village. A type of Wer. Has sex with Rhodar

Kalana – The Wood Goddess. A dark Goddess.
Zandaar – a young man.

Thorgo – killed a Drago with his arrow when it attacked Ilia.

Zandorin, King + Ilia's Father.

Zandor + Ilia's brother.

Salana – old woman (teacher) in Castle Dragonwings in Dragona in Jandarin.

Queen Dalina – Queen of Grahna.

Prince Randoll – Son of Queen Dalina (an overweight sniveling coward).

Marlia – a female fighter at the King's palace.

Lord Zaagar – Advisor to the King.

Zangarian – Son of Lord Zaagar.

Laana – a healer woman at the King's palace.

Quirma – an old healer woman. Nourishes Cardiff back to health.

Quindor – Quirma's teenage son.

Marshia – Quirma's oldest daughter. Married.

Mirnani – Quirma's second daughter.

Lorni – Personal maid of Arleen. A minor witch.

Simmi – Personal maid of Arleen.

Note: + This symbol behind a name indicates this person is deceased.

Special Information:

Singar – Rhodar's enchanted Battle-axe. Rhodar also carries 2 knives.
   Sorcerers
   Giants
   Quinx (Elves)
   Dwarfs.
   Hogee. Troll. Fat and ugly. Trunk for a nose. Large, floppy ears on narrow head.
   Protruding, yellow eyes. 2 long teeth growing from protruding jaw. Huge, clawed hands and
   Feet. Not too smart. Vicious.
   Sekua. Riding animals. Reptilian.
   Stone Serpent – Giant Snake living in the Western Plains
   Serpent Clan – over 100 tribes
   Nightwalker – Rhodar's horse. Black coat.
   Desertrunner – Lord Carn's steed. A Sekua.

Money: kaales

Gras – a fish. Not easy to catch

Gastor – Game animal.

Lopers – Game animals in the Great Plains

Krall bird – 'as pompous as a Krall bird'

Lurrex – a ferocious wolf-like predator

Drago – a giant winged reptile

Cella – equivalent to one hour

Woodrop – a village on the road to Mountainsong when traveling from Falconview.

Grahna – a country south of Maridaan

Jandarin – a Kingdom east of Maridaan

Spanaria – a tiny Kingdom south of Grahna (by the ocean)

Rolandia – a tiny Kingdom and north of Jandarin by the ocean

Dragona – capital city of Jandarin

Crystal Mountains – in the northern part of Jandarin –good soil for grapes-

Argassa – a village in Jandarin on the road to Mountainsong in Maridaan.

Agastan – a country in the North across the ocean, reachable only by ship

Kalsatan – A small settlement with a fur-trading post up river.

Dongo – a game of chance

Barkeater – treedweller (makes droning sounds)

Swamp-tiger – A large cat-like animal living in the swamps

Yill-berries – pain killers. They can cause hallucinations.

Larn-milk – mild from a Larn, a domestic animal

Lion-wolf – a ferocious wolf-like animal living in the Western Plains.

Sequa plant – It has healing sap.

Larkis – Ferocious Dwarf warriors. Usually not aggressive.

THANK YOU FOR READING

Did you enjoy this book?

We invite you to leave a review at the website of your choice, such as Goodreads, Amazon, Barnes & Noble, etc.

DID YOU KNOW THAT LEAVING A REVIEW...

- Helps other readers find books they may enjoy.
- Gives you a chance to let your voice be heard.
- Gives authors recognition for their hard work.
- Doesn't have to be long. A sentence or two about why you liked the book will do.

———

Don't miss out on your next favorite book!

———

Join the Melange Books mailing list at
www.melange-books.com/mail.html

Subscriber Perks Include:

- First peeks at upcoming releases.
- Exclusive giveaways.
- News of book sales and freebies right in your inbox.
- And more!

About the Author

Herbert Grosshans was born in Germany. Even as a young boy he was already a voracious reader. He read every book in the small school library at least three times. His teacher even gave him a few books from his own private collection. His favorite books were stories about heroes and gods. He loved the old legends.

At age fourteen, a friend gave him a Science Fiction book and he fell in love with that genre, saving his allowance to buy every SF book he could find, but he also loved Westerns and Mysteries. Later he became a member of the Science Fiction Club Deutschland (Germany) and began writing his own stories.

One of his short stories was made into a play and broadcast via radio to schools in Germany. In his early twenties, he immigrated to Canada. He began reading books written in English and studied to become proficient in this new language. There is no better way to learn than through writing.

Writing became his passion and he enjoyed making his fertile imagination come alive in his stories. During his lunch hour, he wrote into a scribbler and at home he pounded away on his manual typewriter whenever time allowed. The majority of his stories were Science Fiction.

With the arrival of computers and the internet, it suddenly became much easier to write, and, most importantly, to get published.

His first full length novel Daughter of the Dark, Book One of his The Xandra series, was published in 2006 by Midnight Showcase. Then followed Book Two Mother of Light and Book Three Goddess of Life. The series has since grown to eight volumes.

To date, Herbert has published more than 30 books in different genres. Most of Herbert's stories contain erotica and are for adult readers. His books are available from his publisher Melange Books, LLC, but also from Amazon and other outlets. To find out more about Herbert's books, please, visit his website and his blog.

Website: www.fictitioustales.weebly.com
Blog: www.hegro.blogspot.com
www.hergros.blogspot.com

Also by Herbert Grosshans

WITH MELANGE BOOKS

Lizard World

Epsilon

Epsilon City

Raptor's Tooth

Operation Stargate

Codename Salamander

Web of Conspiracy Series

Death of a Hero

Traitors and Patriots

Tarnished Valor

Rhodar

Clouds over Maridaan

Mysteries

Bullet of Revenge

Mark of the Cobra

Novels

Orola

Orion

Anthologies

Dual Visions

Time Flares